Outstanding praise for the ~~Jackson Square~~

"Fast-moving and entertaining, evoking the gay scene in a sweet, funny, steamy and action-packed"
—*The New Orleans Times-Picayune*

"Herren does a fine job of moving the story along, deftly juggling the murder investigation and the intricate relationships while maintaining several running subplots."—*Echo Magazine*

"An entertaining read."—*OutSmart*

"A pleasant addition to your beach bag."—*Bay Windows*

And praise for *Bourbon Street Blues*

"This enjoyable book takes its pleasures in fantastic coincidences and the outrageous behavior of its larger-than-life characters. Herren offers a paean to New Orleans, and his fondness for the streets, the sights and smells are lovingly rendered on every page . . . an entertaining, Big Easy read."—*Philadelphia Gay News*

"Upbeat prose compounded of humor, caustic observations of Bourbon Street tourists and far-reaching subplots recommend this first novel."—*Library Journal*

"Crackling with all the steamy heat and erotic adventure of New Orleans, this is a sexy gay noir for the twenty-first century. I couldn't put it down!"—William J. Mann, author of *Where the Boys Are*

"Herren's characters, setting and dialogue make the book seem absolutely real."—*The Houston Voice*

"Herren's sassy, amusing mix of sex and sleuthing marks the debut of what promises to be a titillating series."
—Richard Labonte, "Book Marks," *Q Syndicate*

"*Bourbon Street Blues* shines as the first installment in a delightful new suspense series. You're bound to enjoy it. And then you'll want more."
—Michael Craft, author of the Mark Manning and Claire Gray mystery series

"Greg Herren gives readers a tantalizing glimpse of New Orleans."
—*The Midwest Book Review*

BOOKS BY GREG HERREN

Bourbon Street Blues

Jackson Square Jazz

Published by Kensington Publishing Corp.

JACKSON SQUARE

JAZZ

Greg Herren

KENSINGTON BOOKS
www.kensingtonbooks.com

This book is dedicated to
The New Orleans Fire Department,
who risk their lives to preserve
New Orleans' heritage
and history

KENSINGTON BOOKS are published by

Kensington Publishing Corp.
850 Third Avenue
New York, NY 10022

All Kensington titles, imprints, and distributed lines are available at special quantity discounts for bulk purchases for sales promotions, premiums, fund-raising, educational,
or institutional use.

Special book excerpts or customized printings can also be created to fit specific needs. For details write or phone the office of the Kensington special sales manager: Kensington Publishing Corp., 850 Third Avenue, New York, NY 10022, attn: Special Sales Department; phone 1-800-221-2647.

Kensington and the K logo are reg. U.S. Pat. & TM Off.

ISBN 0-7582-0215-6

First Hardcover printing: April 2004
First Trade Paperback Printing: March 2005

10 9 8 7 6 5 4 3 2 1

Printed in the United States of America

ACKNOWLEDGMENTS

Anyone who has the ability and knowledge to write a book without the help of a single person is a hero to me, because there is certainly no way I could have written this book without the support of a large group of people.

Lee Pryor and Julie Smith are two of the kindest and most gracious people in the world—and a lot of fun. Thank you, again, for letting me write yet another book in the magical, inspirational world of Casa Mysterioso.

My editor, John Scognamiglio, who takes my calls and answers my e-mails; for a neurotic like me, that helps.

Jim Sefcik, the Director of the Louisiana State Museum, for sharing his knowledge of the Cabildo; the fire as well as the history and lore of the building. There's definitely another novel in the Cabildo. Any faults and errors that appear in the manuscript are entirely my invention.

My partner, Paul Willis, who willingly came along for the rollercoaster ride and still holds his arms up in the air to enjoy the downs.

And to all the other people who keep me sane and my life full: Marika Christian, Mark Richards, Evelyn Rodos, Heidi Haltiner, Eddie Coleman, Josh Solomon, Dawn Lobaugh, Darren Brewer, Felice Picano, Michael Craft, David McConnell, Michael Kooiman, Jeffrey Jasper, Ken Thistlewaite, Tom Hellenthal, William J. Mann, Jess Wells, J. M. Redmann, Kelly Smith, Patricia Nell Warren and everyone at Wildcat Press, Jay Quinn, especially Victoria A. (my God, my phone bill!) Brownworth, everyone at the LGC-CNO, and many, many others. Thank you all for inspiring me and helping me enjoy life.

A good-looking boy like you is always wanted.
—from *Orpheus Descending* by Tennessee Williams

PROLOGUE

Danger is my middle name.

Okay, so that's not strictly the truth. My middle name is Scott. But when your first name is Milton and your last name is Bradley, you've got to do something. Yes, that's right, my name is Milton Bradley, and no, I'm not an heir to the toy empire. My parents, you see, are counterculturists who own a combination tobacco/ coffee shop in the French Quarter. They both come from old-line New Orleans society families; my mom was a Diderot, of the Garden District Diderots. Mom and Dad fell in love when they were very young and began rebelling against the strict social stratum they were born into. The Bradleys blame it all on my mom. The Diderots blame my dad. My name came about because my older brother and sister were given what both families considered to be inappropriate names: Storm and Rain. According to my older brother, Mom and Dad had planned on naming me River Delta Bradley. Both families sat my parents down in a council of war and demanded that I not be named after either a geological feature or a force of nature. After hours of arguing and fighting, Mom finally agreed to give me a family name.

Unfortunately, they weren't specific. So she named me Milton after her father and Scott, which was her mother's maiden name. Hence, Milton Scott Bradley.

My older brother, Storm, started calling me Scotty when I was a kid because other kids were making fun of my name. Kids really are monsters, you know. Being named Storm, he understood. My sister Rain started calling herself Rhonda when she was in high school. Our immediate family still calls her Rain, which drives her crazy. But then, that's the kind of family we are.

So, yeah, danger really isn't my middle name, but it might as well be. Before Labor Day weekend when I was twenty-nine, my life was pretty tame. I'm an ex-go-go boy; I used to tour with a group called Southern Knights. I retired from the troupe when I was twenty-five, and became a personal trainer/aerobics instructor. The hours were great, the pay was okay for the most part, and I really liked spending a lot of time in the gym. Every once in a while I would fill in dancing on the bar at the Pub, a gay bar on Bourbon Street, when one of their scheduled performers canceled—if I needed the money. That Labor Day weekend, which was Southern Decadence here in New Orleans, I was looking forward to meeting some hot guys and picking up the rent money dancing on the bar. I certainly wasn't expecting to be almost killed a couple of times or to have my apartment burn to the ground. I also didn't expect to wind up as an undercover stripper for the FBI.

It's a *really* long story.

The one good thing that came out of that weekend was I met a guy: Frank Sobieski, this mound of masculine, hard muscle with a scar on his cheek, who also happened to be a Fed. They don't come any butcher than Frank. We hit it off pretty well, and he decided that once his twenty years with the FBI were up, he'd retire and move to New Orleans. I've always been a free agent. It's not that I didn't want to have a boyfriend, I just never thought I would find one. I enjoyed being single. I mean, young, single, and gay in New Orleans is a lot of fun. It doesn't hurt that people find me attractive, either. I'm about five nine, with wavy blondish hair that's darker underneath. I wrestled in high school, mainly because the other kids were bullying me because they sensed I was gay. I've been working out ever since. Anyone who tells you being in shape doesn't make a difference in your life is lying. It does.

Anyway, I digress from the point. Frank suggested I become a private eye. I was getting kind of bored with the training gig, so I decided to look into it. It turned out to be a lot easier than I thought. All you had to do was take a forty-hour course, pay a registration fee, and find a licensed agent to be your "sponsor" until you've worked enough hours to qualify for your license. I took the class, which turned out to be a lot more fun than I thought it would be, and was all set. All I needed was to find a sponsor, which wasn't as easy. Some of them were apparently not too thrilled by my background as an ex-go-go boy. Storm put some feelers out for me, and I went on interviews, but nothing had panned out so far. It was very frustrating. It's kind of like what I call the credit cycle of stupidity—you can't get credit unless you already have credit, so how are you supposed to get credit?

So, I was still training some clients to pay the bills (credit card companies don't seem to care very much that you're homeless). Storm, who is a partner in a very large and successful law firm, promised to start throwing some work my way if I could ever break through the brick wall and get my license once and for all. So there I was, Scotty Bradley, not quite private eye, but oh so close. . . .

And I was living with my parents.

Sounds pathetic, doesn't it? I only had about two hundred dollars in the bank when my apartment burned down, taking everything I owned with it, and I had nowhere else to go. My two landladies, Velma Simpson and Millie Breen, a lesbian couple in their late fifties, were insured, but insurance companies don't move very quickly when they have to pay out, no matter what their ads say. So I moved back into my old room in my parents' apartment over their shop, the Devil's Weed. Cool as my parents are, it didn't take long for this arrangement to start pushing me over the edge.

I'm a bit of a slut. I am the first to admit it. I like having sex with hot guys. Sue me. Frank and I were taking things slow, and we didn't commit to monogamy. (Actually, this is a good thing. With us living about a thousand miles apart, I'd have been cheating on him pretty quick. I'm nothing if not honest.) Do you have any idea what it's like to pick up a hot guy, find out you can't go back to his place, so you have to bring him home to Mom and Dad's at three in the morning? It wouldn't be quite so bad if we had to sneak in and be quiet, you know, kind of like some high school adventure (a humiliating thought in and of itself), but my parents are night owls. They disdain the morning, thinking no one civilized should truly be out of bed before noon. They stay up till four or five in the morning, smoking pot, watching old movies, discussing politics, writing strongly worded letters to the editors of newspapers and newsmagazines. They are thrilled and delighted having a gay son. They hang a rainbow flag outside of their shop. They march in gay pride parades with P-FLAG wearing T-shirts that say I LOVE MY GAY SON or whatever the P-FLAG catchphrase of the year is. They write letters to congressmen and judges. They donate money left and right to gay causes.

Don't get me wrong. It's *great* to have supportive parents. I know lots of gays and lesbians who come out to their families and are thrown out. Others suffer emotional abuse. Some parents *never* accept it, which is horribly painful for their kids, like it's not hard enough to be gay as it is in a homophobic society—

Great. Now I'm starting to sound like my parents!

So, it's Mom and Dad's mission in life to make sure that I am a well-balanced, emotionally nurtured gay man in every respect. And by that, I am including my sex life. As long as I use condoms, Mom and Dad are all for my having a healthy sex life. "Sex," as my mom says, "and especially good sex is important, not only for the body but for the mind. The body needs it, and when people aren't having good sex it seriously affects their thinking and their attitudes and the rest of their life." Her theory is that all the tight-assed people out there who try to force their own twisted sense of morality on everyone else just need a good fuck now and then.

Which also tells me more about their own sex life than I care to know.

So, imagine yourself in this position: You've met a guy in a bar you desperately want to sleep with. You can't go back to your place for whatever reason, so you ask if you can go to his place instead. He sighs a little and says, "Yes, but I live with my parents, but they're cool with it. I just wanted you to know what you were getting into." At first you think he's kidding, and as you walk up the street and he continues to explain you begin to realize he isn't kidding, he *does* live with his parents, but still, you're horny and you find him attractive, so you keep going along with him. He explains about how it's only temporary because his place burned down. You get to his place. It's ablaze with light. His parents are sitting in the living room arguing about the latest crisis in the Middle East and what should be done about it. The room is filled with marijuana smoke. They greet you warmly, introduce themselves, offer you marijuana and wine, tell you if you need anything just call. Then he is dragging you down the hall and into a bedroom with high school wrestling trophies on bookcases and Marky Mark posters on the wall. Could you have sex under those conditions? It was bad enough for me (I have a tendency to be rather loud), but for a total stranger? Sheesh.

Most guys never made it past the "I live with my mom and dad."

Sigh.

Then I got lucky. My workout partner/best friend, David, owns a double shotgun in the Marigny District, which is just across Esplanade Street from the Quarter. He bought it for next to nothing and renovated it himself. He lives in the bigger half, but the other half was empty. One Saturday morning in late September we were having lunch at La Peniche, and I was explaining to him how I'd met this porn star–caliber hot guy the night before. At three in the morning we decided to leave Oz and go get it on, but he was sharing a hotel room with someone else, so we had to go to my place. I took a deep breath and started explaining the situation to him on the corner outside the bar. He smiled at me, said, "Nice talking to you," and went back inside.

"I don't know how much longer I can take it, David," I said, dumping Sweet'N Low into my iced tea. "I mean, I don't mind going to the bathhouse to get laid, but I kind of miss meeting guys in the bars, you know? I mean, the bathhouse is fun and all—but I don't want it to be my only option."

"Why don't you move into my place?" he asked. David is a high school marching-band director, about ten years older than me. He's about my height, and about twenty pounds lighter. He's one of those people whose bodies don't store fat. This might seem a blessing to some, but it's a double-edged sword. Not only does he have no body fat, at the same time it's hard for him to gain muscle weight. "It's just sitting there empty."

"Well, I can't really afford to right now."

He shrugged. "I don't need the rent money. The house is paid for, and besides, it's just temporary, until Millie and Velma finish rebuilding."

"If you are just yanking my chain—"

"Seriously." He winked at me. "Besides, it'll be kind of fun having you next door."

Famous last words, I thought, but didn't say anything. I really wanted to get out of Mom and Dad's.

The next problem was furniture, but my family came to the rescue. When I dropped out of college, Papa Bradley and Papa Diderot both washed their hands of me financially. Since they control my trust funds, I was on my own. So, my old apartment had been a mismatched hodgepodge of thrift store furniture, which gave the place the kind of funky Bohemian atmosphere I liked. Besides, all you had to do with a scarred and stained old table was drape some fabric over it. I guess the fire, added to the fact that I had almost been killed, softened the hearts of the Papas. They didn't come across with any money, but both sets of grandparents had tons of furniture in their Uptown manses they were more than happy to let me have. The apartment had three big rooms opening into each other (hence the term "shotgun"— supposedly, if you fired a shotgun through the front door the bullet would pass through the entire house without hitting a wall). I made the first room the living room, the next the bedroom, then the kitchen. There was a front porch and a nice little backyard. David and I rented a U-Haul, collected furniture from various grandparents (Storm and Rain contributed some pieces as well), and got me all set up. I was officially back on my own by October 1.

Storm also bought me a present. A computer. "You'll need this to be a private eye," he said. He was right. He started sending me some work, which he billed as "research assistance," so I wouldn't get in trouble with the state licensing board. Most of the work he sent my way basically consisted of doing background checks on people, all of which could be done on the Internet, billed at fifty dollars per hour.

Okay, I was probably the last person on the face of the planet to get a computer. I'm a bit of a Luddite. My cell phone is almost always turned off, and I always misplace it. I had played on David's computer a few times, but really had no idea what I was getting myself into. David's computer was really amazing. He had a digital camera, one of those webcam things, a scanner—you name it. "If you really want to use the Internet to its fullest advantage," he said, "we need to take some hot pictures of you." So, one afternoon we went into the backyard and I stripped down to my underwear and started posing. I posed in a thong, in a jock, in loose fitting jeans, as well as completely buck naked. I mean, it's not like I'm ever going to run for public office or anything, right? David showed me how to access chat rooms, post a picture of myself on various Web sites, and suddenly I was being deluged with e-mails from guys. It was like dancing on the bar wearing a thong again—only this time they weren't offering me money, just sex. Before long, I had folders full of pictures of total strangers in various stages of undress. It opened up an entire new world of getting laid. David referred to it as "ordering in."

Frank also had a computer, and so we started chatting on-line or sending e-mails rather than running up long-distance charges.

Everything was going great. I was working again, money was coming in, and when I had nothing to do, well, there was always the Internet to play on. All I had to do was convince some licensed private eye to sponsor me and I was on my way.

Okay, so the work was really kind of boring. When Frank first suggested being a private eye to me, I thought it was going to be exciting. I saw myself in a fedora and a trench coat, following mysterious individuals around in the fog, not sitting at a computer tracking down information and getting eyestrain. And while the Internet is a fun, exciting, and interesting place, there are also a lot of drawbacks to it as well. They never talk about things like computer freezes and crashes, getting knocked off-line three or four times per hour, and dealing with their No-Help lines. These oh-so-helpful people blame everything on your computer or your modem, because *they* certainly couldn't be at fault. It's enough to make you want to reach through the phone line and kill someone—especially after you had to wait thirty minutes to get through to a real person.

Ah, well, it was a living, and I could do it at home in my underwear, or naked if I wanted to. And did.

So, everything was going well for the most part. The contractors kept promising Millie and Velma that we'd be able to move back in by Christmas. It was kind of fun living next door to David. Halloween was coming up, and we came up with the greatest costume idea, ever. The only problem was I really missed

Frank. One Saturday morning, after another enormously disappointing Friday night in the bars (I kept comparing everyone I thought hot with Frank), I got up and wrote a really sappy e-mail to him about how much I missed him. I really got on a roll, talking about what I wanted to do to him the next time I saw him.

Apparently, I could have a future as a porn writer.

Frank got so aroused by my email that he went on-line and bought me a plane ticket to come up to DC and visit him. What a great surprise! I was really excited about it. I'd never been to DC before, and the thought of seeing Frank again . . . I really did miss him. I was going for a week. I didn't even consult my tarot cards before going—which is unusual. I have a bit of a psychic gift, and reading the tarot helps me to focus it and get answers. I just didn't see the need. I was going to see Frank, and we were going to have a week together, just the two of us, no distractions. If we wanted to stay in his apartment the entire time, we could . . . and I was pretty sure we were going to spend a lot of time together naked.

Frank is really hot, did I mention that?

I was nervous, excited—all that good stuff. The weekend Frank and I met he'd been working on a case, so we really hadn't gotten to spend a whole lot of time together. This was going to be different—romantic and impetuous. Frank said we wouldn't plan anything. We'd just see what we felt like doing every morning when we woke up, and go from there. I was planning on getting to know every square inch of his body intimately, and I was also excited about seeing the museums, the Civil War battlegrounds. It was going to be a great opportunity to spend time with Frank, get to know him better, see what his life was like and how I fit into it. I boarded that airplane with almost every hair on my body tingling from excitement. As Washington drew nearer and nearer, I was tapping my feet with impatience. I wanted the damned thing to land. I wanted to see Frank.

If I'd only known, I never would have gotten on that damned plane.

CHAPTER ONE

Page of Wands

a young man with blond hair

I woke up with what was easily the worst hangover of my life.

It was horrible. My teeth felt like they'd grown hair while I slept. My eyelids felt like they were glued shut. My head was pounding, like the seven dwarves were in there, thinking my head was a diamond mine and cheerfully digging their pickaxes into the sides. My stomach was churning. My skin felt hot. I was sweating under the blankets. My tongue had somehow managed to swell up to twice its usual size, and sometime during the night it had apparently become as absorbent as cotton. I was so dehydrated it felt like I'd been wandering in the desert for several days. I fought to get my eyes open. After what seemed like an eternity, the left came open, then the right. The light streaming through the bedroom window blinds pierced my corneas like a laser, cutting right through into my brain. I quickly threw one of my arms across my eyes to block it, but the movement made the sulfuric acid eating through my stomach lining splash around. My head swam; my vision briefly blurred. My stomach clenched, and I fought down the urge to throw up. It's one of my rules to never throw up anywhere other than the toilet. Throwing up is unpleasant enough in and of itself, but then to have to clean up the rancid mess on top of that? Just the thought brought the nausea back in a swelling wave. Yuck.

I closed my eyes and opened them again. I swallowed and took several deep, cleansing breaths. There, that was better. What the hell had I been drinking the night before? Oh yeah, tequila shots. Never a smart thing to do. The ever-popular mentality of "oh gee, I'm not getting drunk fast enough, so I'll do some shots. Yeah, that's the thing to do." Ugh.

Jose Cuervo, you are *not* a friend of mine.

That's when I became aware of the arm around my waist.

Oh, boy. I thought for a minute. Okay, who the hell is this? But I still felt like someone had lobbed a hand grenade into my head. Nothing was clear. The memory banks had been neatly erased by the alcohol. He wasn't lying next to me—his arm was just kind of loosely thrown over my waist. His skin felt deliciously cool, but I needed to get out of the bed. I wasn't in the right frame of mind to deal with him just yet, so I gently lifted the arm up and slid out from under it. Just as gently I set it back down and slid slowly out of the bed, not wanting the bed to bounce and wake him up. Mission accomplished, I realized with a start that I was completely naked. Well, that really shouldn't have come as a surprise. Had we had sex?

I stared down at his face. He had sandy reddish blond hair, and a sprinkle of freckles across his face. The hair was standing out in all directions from his head. His mouth was open and he was breathing through it. He looked completely at peace with the world. Damn, he was a little cutie, I thought as I stared at him. He also looked really young. Who the hell was he? And where had I found him?

I padded into the kitchen and started coffee. I popped a couple of aspirin and washed them down with water. My stomach was still churning, so I got out a couple of pieces of bread. The bread just dried my mouth out again. My tongue felt like it was sticking to the roof of my mouth, which had apparently grown some fur during the night. I washed the bread down with water. Maybe that would help absorb the alcohol in my stomach and stop the churning, keep the nausea down. What I really needed was a greasy bacon cheeseburger, fat grams be damned. I walked back into the bedroom. The bread was helping a little bit. Each step didn't make me think my head was going to fall off.

He hadn't moved. I stared at him for a few minutes, but still nothing came to mind.

Okay, what did I do last night? I asked myself as I walked into the bathroom and scraped the fur out of my mouth with my toothbrush. Even after brushing, my teeth felt weird to my tongue. I started the shower. I got back from Washington around five and David picked me up at the airport.

Oh, yeah, the fucking trip. I gulped down several handfuls of cold water from the tap while the shower got hot. I was starting to come out of it.

The trip had been a disaster, almost completely. I'd flown into Reagan Airport the previous Saturday. (Mom and Dad would have thought the name of the airport was a bad omen.) Frank was waiting for me at the security checkpoint. He looked so damned good I wanted to jump his bones right there. He was wearing a black turtleneck sweater and a pair of tightly pressed khaki pants, with a black leather jacket. The outfit showed off his heavily muscled body to perfection. Of course, we couldn't hug or kiss or anything like that at the airport. Some of Frank's coworkers or someone else who knew him might see him. Ah, the joys of being a homo working for the Federal government. I could tell, even though we didn't do anything more than shake hands, that he was glad to see me. All I had to do was look at the bulge in the zipper area.

We got my suitcases and headed back into the city to his apartment. He drove me past monuments and statues, showed me the FBI Building where he worked, all the normal tourist crap. I was in a pretty good mood. It was a beautiful autumn day, though a little chilly. The streets were packed with cars, the sidewalks jammed with pedestrians. The city fairly hummed with life.

The whole time he drove my hand was in his crotch. Yeah, he was definitely glad to see me all right. Every once in a while he would look over at me and smile, or just put his hand on my inner thigh.

His apartment was in the city's gay ghetto, DuPont Circle, which I thought was odd for a closeted Fed. There were a lot of pretty boys walking along the sidewalks as he headed up Sixteenth Street. Some were walking dogs, others were holding hands, others were obviously just with friends. Occasionally, I spotted some straight people too, pushing baby carriages, carrying bags or briefcases, or walking alone jabbering away on cell phones. They were all dressed extremely well, in nice slacks and overcoats. I tried to imagine what it would be like in the summer when everyone would be in shorts and tank tops.

It would be a gay man's candy store was what it would be, I thought as Frank found a place to park his little blue Miata on S Street. We got my bags out of the trunk and started walking up to Seventeenth Street. His apartment was on Seventeenth, between S and T Streets. Someone put a lot of thought into naming the streets here, I thought. Okay, I'm a little spoiled, coming from New Orleans, with our great street names. The area kind of reminded me a little of the Quarter—the number of people walking around, the old-looking houses and buildings, and the trees. I smiled at a hot-looking guy as we passed each other and our eyes met. He immediately looked away.

Huh? Did I suddenly grow two heads? I looked back after him. He was walking even faster than he had been before. Definitely strange.

Frank's place was in an extremely sterile-looking yellow brick apartment building on the corner of Seventeenth and New Hampshire. He let us in through the glass door with his key. A couple of people were waiting for the elevator. One of them was wearing a sweaty white T-shirt and black bike shorts with blue stripes up the sides. He was holding a bicycle and breathing a little hard. I took in his smooth legs and noted a little razor cut just below his muscular calf. Definitely family, I thought, as he pointedly watched the lighted numbers above the elevator door change. The other person was a woman in a gray overcoat. She was holding a plastic bag of groceries. She was wearing sunglasses, and her graying black hair was pulled back into a severe bun at the nape of her neck. I glanced into her bag. Fettucini, a jar of spaghetti sauce, a loaf of garlic bread. The elevator door slid silently open and we all got inside, various people hitting numbered buttons, which lit up. I kept looking back and forth at the strangers. No one spoke as the elevator moved up. No one said hello; no greetings, no smiles of recognition. I looked at Frank and he winked at me, but didn't say anything. The elevator smelled vaguely of body odor—like a pair of sweat socks I'd taught aerobics in and then left in my gym bag for a few days.

The guy with the bike got out on three. The woman with the bag got off on four. Again, total silence.

It was creepy.

We got off on five and I breathed a sigh of relief. I'd been getting claustrophobic in that stale air. Frank led me along a dingy hallway with the drabbest brown carpet I'd ever seen. He stopped at a door with the numbers 522 on the frame. The door was forest green. He pushed the door open and held it for me.

"Welcome." He smiled at me.

I walked into the smallest apartment I had ever seen an adult out of college living in. It couldn't have been more than four hundred square feet, tops. The whole place would have fit into my living room with some square footage left over. There was a tiny kitchen directly to my right, complete with a refrigerator, sink, and stove that looked about the same size as the ones in Barbie's dream house. There was also a walk-in closet right beside the kitchen, and I could see the bathroom opened off of it. There was a simple table with a computer and a printer sitting on it. There was another small table with a television sitting on it, with a VCR on top of that. The clock on the VCR was flashing 12:00. There was a double bed pushed up against the wall with the lone window. The window had yellowed blinds but no curtains. There was nothing on the beige walls: no posters, no artwork, nothing. Everything was neatly put away. There was no dust anywhere. Everything gleamed and looked brand new.

There was a small wooden bookcase with three shelves sitting in the corner by the computer desk. I set my bag down and said, "Wow." Not exactly dialogue by Noël Coward, but I didn't know what else to say. I wandered over to the bookcase and looked at the names on the spines. The books were all hardcover, and apparently each was a nonfiction study of a specific serial killer. I swallowed.

How romantic.

Frank took off his jacket and held out his hands for mine. I shrugged it off and handed it to him, watching him as he walked into the closet to hang them up. He switched on the closet light, and I glimpsed clothes hanging, sorted by style and color. Everything in its place, a place for everything.

He walked out of the closet with a big grin on his face, and took me into his arms, kissing my neck. "God, how I've missed you."

Finally, I was being greeted the way I wanted to be.

The rest of the week was spent going to movies, and museums, and drives in the country. There isn't a battlefield in Northern Virginia I didn't see. We ate every meal out. Frank's kitchen was much too small to cook in. Besides, if I wasn't sleeping or having sex I wanted out of that horribly sterile little apartment. I didn't meet any of Frank's friends or coworkers. His phone never rang. Frank had told me he was pretty much married to his job, but I thought he was exaggerating. It's just a phrase, right? But the week I spent up there, despite the fact that I had a great time and we got along great, had me doubting if Frank and I had a future.

How can we ever have a relationship if Frank has no friends?

I like people. I like being around people. Frank didn't want to go dancing or go to any of the bars. Maybe it was an in-the-closet-at-work thing, but I wasn't about to give up going out. I like dancing. I like seeing people I know at bars, and chatting and gossiping about nothing. Okay, maybe it was just a Washington thing for him, and he'd be different in New Orleans, but Goddess help me! I couldn't be the only person in his life. There were even times during the trip I felt claustrophobic with him. Maybe it was the tiny apartment. Maybe it was that dreadful elevator and all those people who wouldn't even nod, let alone smile at me.

I brooded on the plane all the way back to New Orleans. Frank had dropped me off at the passenger drop-off place, and as I climbed out of the car he smiled at me. "I'll be down for Mardi Gras," he said, before I shut the car door, "if not sooner."

Mardi Gras?

The first thing I did when the drink cart came around was beg for a Bloody Mary. I envisioned spending the rest of my life with Frank, 24/7, never escaping from him, having no privacy, no private time for myself, not being able to talk to people because Frank was always around. I was no saint, and Frank seemed not to care, but maybe that was because he'd never been with me in a bar in New Orleans, surrounded by lots of guys I'd had sex with. Frank was a Fed. If he came down for Mardi Gras I certainly wouldn't feel comfortable doing Ecstasy and going out dancing with him in tow. He might even arrest me on the spot!

By the time I saw David's silver Accord drive up at passenger pickup in New Orleans, I had worked myself into a fine state.

"How was the trip?" he asked as I threw my bags into his backseat.

"I need to get drunk."

"That bad?" He shook his head as we drove out of the airport. David's a great guy, one of the best friends I've ever had. We'd been friends for three years, and workout partners for the last year or so. He had grayish eyes and graying reddish blond hair he kept cut very short, and a reddish mustache with some stray white hairs starting to creep into it. He doesn't tan very easily. I often teased him about being the "whitest queen this side of Elizabeth II." He glanced at his watch as we headed up the on-ramp to I-10. "Kinda early, isn't it?"

"Yeah, well."

He opened the ashtray and pulled out a freshly rolled joint. "Here."

I took it from him and hesitated. I was already feeling really paranoid about this whole thing with Frank; this might make it worse. Then I thought, "Fuck it," and lit it.

By the time we reached Causeway Boulevard ten minutes later, I was pleasantly stoned. Everything would work out with Frank if it was meant to, and if it didn't, oh well. It wasn't my idea for him to move to New Orleans in the first place. David and I agreed to meet a little later for dinner before we went out, and I headed into my apartment to unpack.

I was still feeling a little shaky, but at least I was able to re-member yesterday. I stepped into the hot spray of shower water. Okay, good. I held my head under the spray. As I massaged sham-poo into my hair, I remembered unpacking, showering, and get-ting dressed. I met David at La Peniche, on Royal Street in the Marigny. After we ate, we went back over to his place. We smoked another joint and had a couple of drinks. We made it down to the corner of Bourbon and St. Ann around eleven o'clock, prime party time. We had a couple of shots the minute we walked into the Pub, and then . . .

Blank. Completely blank.

I finished rinsing the soap off my body and climbed out of the shower. I toweled dry my hair, vigorously rubbing the water off my body. I looked at myself in the fogged mirror. I still didn't feel great, but it was better. I walked into the kitchen and poured myself a cup of coffee before wandering back into the bedroom. I put on underwear and cutoff sweatpants and stood there staring at the kid. Who the hell are you? Where did I meet you?

His eyes opened. They were liquid brown, but slightly blood-shot. He smiled at me. "Morning." He yawned and stretched as he sat up in bed.

"Morning." His chest was completely hairless. His entire torso was free of hair, and free of body fat. He was fair skinned, and there were freckles spreading across the top of his chest and shoulders.

He smiled at me. "Scotty, right?"

Okay, so he was one up on me. "Yeah."

"Bryce." He kept smiling. "You kept calling me Brian last night."

I sat down on the edge of the bed. "Sorry about that."

" 'S okay." He yawned again. "You were pretty drunk."

"Yeah, I was. You want some coffee?"

He shook his head. "Don't drink it. Do you have any green tea?"

My parents being who they are, of course I did. "I'll make you some. Do you want to shower?"

He nodded at me sleepily. He climbed out from under the covers. He was also naked. But where the muscles of his upper body were wiry and lean, his legs were thickly and heavily mus-cled, completely and perfectly defined. There was reddish blond hair on his calves, but very little above the knee. And his butt was round and hard and looked solid as a rock.

It was very impressive.

He picked up his underwear and walked into the bathroom. "Towels are under the sink," I called after him. Who the hell were you, Brian? Where did I meet you?

I sat the green tea down on the coffee table in the living room. I heard the water stop running, and I quickly shuffled my tarot cards and spread them out in a reading. I have a gift for reading tarot cards—I'm a little psychic. I can't predict lottery numbers or earthquakes, but I was pretty good at the cards. Not many people know about it—it's not something you make public knowledge. Not even David knows.

He's a troubled soul, the cards told me, *in need of guidance. Be careful of what you do or say. He's vulnerable.*

Terrific.

He came into the living room with one of my green towels wrapped around his waist. His wet hair hung into his face. He grinned at me. Damn, but he was a cutie. He sat down and he sipped his tea. "You read the cards?"

"A little." I shrugged. "It's a hobby." I smiled at him. "Want me to read them for you?"

He shuddered and looked away. "No thanks. I don't want to know what the future is."

Hmmm. Interesting. I picked up the cards and started shuffling them. "Brian, I was pretty drunk last night . . ."

"Oh, don't worry," he said quickly. "I'm not looking for a boyfriend or anything, and as soon as I finish my tea I'll be on my way."

His face was so earnest I had to laugh. "That's not what I meant. I mean, I don't remember meeting you, or even where we met."

"You were pretty bombed." He laughed with me. "We met at the Brass Rail at about three in the morning."

It came back to me in a flash. I had been pretty drunk. At two thirty I'd staggered out of the Pub determined to go home. I'd flirted with a couple of cute guys but changed my mind at the last minute. I'd walked home down St. Philip Street, weaving, actually, and stopped in at the Brass Rail to get a bottled water. He'd been sitting there on a barstool, completely out of place amongst the older men. The Brass Rail was more of a tavern than a bar, and they had a strip show every Friday and Saturday night. Their stage even had a pole on it. I'd never danced there, although in my drunken stupor I thought swinging on that pole in a thong might be fun. I walked up to the bar and ordered my water right next to where he was sitting. He said hello, and half an hour later we were heading back to my place.

"You remember now, don't you?"

"Yeah." I smiled at him. "Did you have a good time?"

He grinned back at me. "The best." He set his teacup down. "I'd better get dressed. They'll be wondering where I am." His face clouded for a moment, and he scowled. "Good."

"They?"

"Never mind." He got up and walked back to the bedroom. I stared after him, then reshuffled the cards. Before I even had the chance to lay out another reading, he came back out fully dressed. He kissed my cheek. "Thanks, Scotty. That was great."

I walked him to the door. "Sure, man."

He waved as he walked down the stairs.

I shut the door and walked back into the living room. I picked up the cards and started shuffling them again. I laid them out. This time there was no questioning their meaning.

He needed help.

I debated going after him, but I still felt woozy from the hangover. And by the time I could throw on some clothes and go after him, he'd be long gone. I didn't even know his last name. Great going, Scotty. Ah, well, I thought, picking up the phone to order a bacon cheeseburger from Verdi Marte, it's not like I'll ever see him again.

Boy, was I wrong. So much for being psychic.

CHAPTER TWO

Seven of Cups

*an imagination that has been
working overtime*

David came over while I was eating what was, without a doubt, undeniably the best bacon cheeseburger ever cooked in the world. He was wearing a pair of paint-spattered jeans and no shirt, the green serpent tattoo on his left pectoral standing out against the whiteness of his skin.

"I would ask what happened to you last night," he said, sitting down in a wingback chair and lighting the joint in his hand, "but I saw the boy leave a little while ago. Did you check his ID?" He grinned.

I just gave him a look. I couldn't talk, because my mouth was full of food and ketchup was dribbling down my chin. I chewed for a few more moments, than swallowed. "No, I didn't check his ID, but I met him in a bar." I took a swig out of my Pepsi and stifled a belch.

"Like that means anything here." He had a point. All the bars in the French Quarter have signs posted saying No Minors Allowed—Gaming Devices Inside. I've always thought that was kind of funny. Minors shouldn't be in bars anyway, right? The implication was that if it weren't for the video-poker machines, minors would be more than welcome. But then again, I started going to the bars when I was seventeen and no one ever carded me. In fact, I was having *sex* with men I met in the bars when I was seventeen. Imagine, if you will, what my life was like at seventeen. I was out to my parents, my hormones were rampaging out of control, and I lived a block away from a gay bar. Four others were just up the street, within easy walking distance. Mom and Dad didn't believe in curfews (as Dad said, "I will not buy into the fascism so prevalent and inherent in parenting"), so I could stay out as late as I wanted. No one ever carded me, or even really paid much attention to my teenaged self as I ordered drinks and scanned the crowds for that night's trick du jour.

Ah, the French Quarter. How can you *not* love it?

David blew out smoke and passed me the joint. He laughed. "You should see your face, Scotty."

I inhaled and held the smoke. It was good grass. My parents always get the best, and David buys it from my dad at cost. Dad doesn't believe in marking it up. Mom and Dad are hemp activists and unrepentant pot smokers. Dad's theory is that if he sells it at cost, he can't legally be considered a dealer, since he isn't making any money. He and my lawyer brother Storm have gone round and round on this point umpteen times. "Well, it's not like I want to go to jail or anything. What is the age of consent in Louisiana, anyway?"

He shrugged. "Don't know. Seventeen? Eighteen? He had a nice ass, though, one of the best I've ever seen, and he was polite." He whistled. "Was it fun?"

I groaned. "I don't really remember. So, you talked to him?"

"I was painting one of the new shutters outside when he came out." One of the things I missed about my old apartment was the way Millie and Velma didn't really care about the guys I brought home. Sometimes they wanted details, which always struck me as odd, but they didn't come over and start talking about it whenever they saw someone leaving. Not that I usually minded talking about my sex life with David, but I wasn't in the mood at the moment, and I kind of wanted to be left alone until I felt like a human being again. The cheeseburger was taking away that nau-seated feeling, but my head still hurt. The pot, though, was help-ing a bit. Maybe I should take some more aspirin. "He looked kind of familiar."

"Don't tell me he's another one of your former students." I had long ago stopped counting how many of David's former stu-dents we ran into at bars, all grown up and seeming to be happy, well-adjusted, young gay men. They always called him "Mr. Andrews" at first, until he finally convinced them to address him as "David." It never failed to crack me up. My favorites, though, were the parents of former students we ran into sometimes at Mardi Gras. There David would be, in assless leather chaps and nothing but a black leather jock underneath, leather arm bands around his biceps, and handcuffs attached to his belt, chatting away with some nice, middle-aged, middle-class parents. It never seemed to put them off, but then again, Mardi Gras is pretty much an anything goes–type event.

Still, I often marveled he didn't lose his job.

He shook his head. "No, but he looked really familiar. I'd swear I've seen him somewhere before." He shrugged and passed the joint back to me. "I guess I've just seen him out before, but you'd think I'd remember a cutie like that."

"It's the pot," I said seriously, and we both laughed. "I met him at the Brass Rail on my way home." My memory was still fuzzy and vague. "I was pretty drunk."

"Yeah, you were." He took the joint from me, inhaling with his eyes closed. "One minute you were there on the dance floor getting groped by that guy with the goatee, the next minute you were gone." He shrugged. "I figured you left with someone."

"No." I pinched the joint out and put the roach in an ashtray. Time for a change of subject. I hated not remembering. "What are you doing today?" I didn't even remember the guy with the goatee groping me. Definitely not cool. I decided then and there to stop drinking tequila under any circumstances. Never again, no way, no how. Not being able to remember things was totally un-cool, and besides, if I was so drunk I couldn't remember being groped by a hot guy, there's no telling what else I did that was completely lost to me forever. The thought was definitely sobering.

"I'm doing my laundry now. Just hang out, play on-line for a while, I guess. Ted's coming by at two, and Rhonda is supposed to be here around then to pick us up."

"Pick us up?" Rhonda is the name my sister chose for herself in high school when she decided Rain was far too weird for her and she wanted to be more "normal."

"Don't tell me you've forgotten about that skating thing tonight?"

I had, completely. Ted and David had been friends forever. David's first teaching job was at the school in Mississippi where Ted was head of the English department. Ted was in his late fifties, shaved his head, and had the most expressive blue eyes I'd ever seen. He usually drove over from Mississippi on Sundays for tea dance, but he was a figure skating fan. Tonight, for the first time ever, New Orleans was hosting Skate America. As Ted had explained to us, Skate America "was the first of the 'International Grand Prix of Figure Skating' events every year. It kicks off the season, and you get to see the new programs of all the skaters, the ones they'll be using at the Worlds at the end of the season."

Rain also loves figure skating. She and Ted had bonded over figure skating one night at a party for David's birthday. She grew up worshipping Dorothy Hamill, Katarina Witt and Jill Trenary. She'd had a crush on Brian Boitano for years.

I know that being a fan of figure skating is one of those gay things, like Judy or Barbra or Liza. Supposedly, the only sports that gay men will watch are figure skating, gymnastics, and div-ing/swimming. I'm not a big fan of skating. I mean, I really do enjoy it when I watch. (It's hard not to when Ted is giving you a running commentary on the skater, their outfit, and the music. I've often thought they should hire Ted to be a commentator on television—but then, he doesn't have to be nice in the privacy of someone's living room.) But I don't get out the *TV Guide* every week and highlight the skating programs. Ted and Rain both do. I don't tape skating events when I have to miss them. Ted not only does that, he tapes them while he's watching them, so he can watch them again later. He'd tape Skate America when it aired, even though we were there when it happened. He looks up the results of events as they happen, so he knows who wins when they air. He has a framed, signed poster of Michelle Kwan in his living room. Once, when a hurricane was threatening to hit New Orleans and the city was under a mandatory evacuation order, David and I evacuated to Ted's. We watched old figure skating tapes the entire three days we were there. It was fun, but after awhile the skaters all began to blend together. Ted and Rain together is something to see.

Although I will say this for them: male figure skaters have very impressive butts.

"That's only like two hours from now," I said.

"Yeah. You wanna go out after?"

I crumpled up the burger wrapper and put it in the bag it came in. "Yeah. What time will this be over?"

"Ted says about eleven." He sighed. "I don't want to go."

I didn't either, but Rain had bought tickets for all of us. Her husband didn't exactly share her passion for skating, and when she had offered, it sounded like a good idea. Well, at the time it did, but I didn't have a hangover then.

"Well, we have to." We really did. Ted's feelings would be hurt if we canceled at the last minute, and he can be real bitchy when he's hurt. And Rain is a pretty good sister to me. She rarely asks much from me, so it's really hard to say no to her. I don't see her as often as I should, partly because she lives all the way uptown on Octavia Street.

"Yeah." He got up and moved to the door. "See ya in a bit." The door shut behind him.

I got up and turned on my computer. Might as well check my e-mail before getting ready. I ran my hand over my cheeks to check for stubble. Yeah, I'd have to shave, which meant another shower. Shit. The pot was making me a little light-headed, but the dull throbbing was going away. I was actually starting to feel like a human being again. Thank you, Goddess. I signed on-line and waited for the welcome page to load. One of those pop-up instant messages dinged just as the computer said atonally "You've got mail!"

BTTM4U: Hey Scotty how you?

BTTM4U was actually named Mark and lived in Chalmette, just over the parish line in St. Bernard. He was only about five five, but really cute, with a tight hard body. He had dark black hair and always had a great tan. I'd seen him in the bars before, but had never actually met him. He was one of those people who doesn't seem to own any shirts when the weather is nice. His left nipple was pierced, as was his navel. He had a tattoo of a fleur-de-lis just above where his buttocks started to curve out from his back. I'd always thought he was a hottie, but had never talked to him. It was just one of those things. In New Orleans, you can see people for years in the bars and never talk to them. They're doing their thing, you're doing yours, you know? One night I was playing on-line when he struck up a conversation. He was funny, so we just progressed from there. He sent me a picture of his bare torso, and I immediately recognized him. I sent him a picture of me in a speedo lying out in the sun. That got him pretty excited, so he sent me a picture of his bare ass. And a quite nice one it was. One thing led to another, and he finally invited me over. When I went to his house, the front door was unlocked, and when I walked in he was lying on a blanket naked, his round hard ass turned up to the air. Condoms and lube were on the floor next to a lit candle.

How do you pass that up?

You can't, so I didn't.

A little hung over but fine, I typed in, then clicked on the mail-box icon. I scrolled through all the new mail. Junk, all of it. No, I don't need Viagra without a prescription. I don't care that Trixie's father has left her alone in the house with a webcam. I don't care that there is a secret camera in a fraternity shower. No, I don't need to add inches to my penis, thank you very much. I don't need any golf balls. I don't need to refinance my home. On and on and on. I deleted all the junk, with a sigh. I'd almost rather get telemarketing phone calls than deal with all of this bullshit. Isn't there a way the Internet access companies can block this shit from being sent? I swear to God, I spend half of my time on-line delet-ing this crap. There's this one guy I met on-line once who sends me pictures of naked men he finds all over the web. At any time of any day I can sign on and there will be about thirty e-mails of naked men sent to me. I have always wondered what he does for a living. I look at them, but I don't save them. If there's one I think David will like I forward it on to him. But as far as spam goes, at least that's a pleasant diversion, as opposed to all the other crap that gets sent.

The computer dinged again.

BTTM4U: I'm horny.

Big surprise, I thought, typing instead *I have to be somewhere in two hours.*

BTTM4U: Plenty of time for a quickie.

I laughed. I'm not really into quickies. I like to take my time, you know? Why do something half-assed, after all, and I really enjoy sex. *You know better than that—I'd end up having so much fun I'd want to stay longer.*

BTTM4U: And that's a bad thing?

Well, I didn't say it would be a bad thing, but if I'm late I'll be in trouble.

BTTM4U: I thought you liked getting in trouble. ☺

Hmmm . . . I'm not usually opposed to that, but this time it would be a bad thing.

BTTM4U: Do you want me to beg? I will.

Ah, the power of being irresistible. Time to change the subject, I suppose. *What did you do last night? Didn't see you out.*

BTTM4U: LOL. I saw you last night, remember?

Damn it! *No, I don't . . .*

BTTM4U: You were pretty drunk . . . you left with that hot little boy.

Did everyone in town know? I stared at the computer screen for a moment, shaking my head. Never again, I vowed, would I ever drink tequila.

BTTM4U: Too bad . . . maybe tomorrow bud? Or will you be out tonight?

It's possible, I typed. *I will probably be out tonight.*

BTTM4U: I'll look for you then. I really love your cock, man, and want it inside me again. ☺

And I love your ass.

The computer told me I had mail again, so I re-opened the mail-box. One piece of new mail—from Frank. The message line read "I miss you."

Uh oh. I clicked it open.

Dear Scotty:
I woke up this morning missing you. This past week was so in-credible, waking up with you in my arms every morning. Not having you here makes me realize how empty and lonely my life was before I met you. The bed seems so big and empty. I loved sleeping with your warm body cuddled up to mine. I loved mak-ing coffee for us every morning and bringing you a cup in bed. I loved taking you around and showing you the city, the sights. I can't wait to see you again. I can't wait for the day when every day starts with us waking up in each other's arms and making love. I miss kissing you. I miss feeling your muscles and touching you and holding you and smelling you and showering with you. Maybe I can make it down there before Mardi Gras . . . I have a lot more vacation time left, so maybe I can come down there for Thanksgiving or something? Would your family mind if I came down? I would like to get to know them better. I'd like to get to know you even better than I already do. I am looking forward to spending the rest of my life with you.

Talk soon,
I love you,
Hot Daddy

My stomach churned again. I clicked on reply, and typed *Dear Frank* . . . then stopped and just stared at the computer screen and the blinking cursor. What do I say to him? I couldn't tell him how I was feeling this way. It would be too cold, cruel. And I wasn't really sure what I was thinking anyway. I started to type, changed my mind, deleted what I'd written, and started again.

Dear Frank:
    Thanks for the email. I really enjoyed seeing you too, and I had a really great time. I'll talk to my parents about Thanksgiving, but are you sure you want to come spend it with my family instead of yours—

I stopped typing. It dawned on me that I didn't know the slightest thing about Frank's family. He never talked about them. In fact, Frank never said anything about his life. One of the things I'd been thinking about since getting back was how weird it was that he didn't seem to have any friends. But how even weirder was it that he never talked about his family? His past? Where he was from? Why did he become a Fed in the first place? I stared there at the cursor. I didn't know Frank at all. We always talked about me, my family, my friends, my life—and our future together. Granted, my family alone is fascinating enough to outsiders, but still, it was odd.

I deleted the response completely.

I'll think about this later, I thought. There's no law that says I have to answer him right away.

And why didn't he just message me?

Weird.

I sighed and signed off.

I walked back into the living room and turned on my stereo. Stevie Nicks's latest CD, *Trouble in Shangri-La,* was in there, and soon Stevie's voice was filling the room. I lit some white candles for purity and sat down at the coffee table, crossing my legs underneath me. I got my cards out and shuffled, trying to focus. I cut the cards, held them in both hands with my eyes closed, and focused on the question.

Will things work out with Frank?

I took a cleansing breath and laid the cards out.

Please, Goddess, help me out here, I prayed, and opened my eyes.

The reading was inconclusive.

Fuck.

It had been stupid to get so drunk. It didn't solve the problem with Frank. Maybe I was overreacting, but still. The poor man had no life outside of his job. Of course, that didn't mean he'd smother me when he moved here. Maybe I was just reacting to the whole concept of having a boyfriend. Was I capable of committing to someone for the rest of my life? I was pretty certain I couldn't be monogamous, and isn't that what relationships are all about? Total commitment to the other person, emotionally, spiritually, sexually?

Do I have that in me? Or was I simply destined to be a complete and total bar slut for the rest of my life? Do I love Frank enough to change my entire life, my entire lifestyle, to commit myself to him.

I reshuffled the cards, figuring I could just ask again. I focused, prayed to the Goddess to please help me out here. It's not like I was asking for much, I figured. I laid the cards out again and looked them over.

Nothing. It meant nothing to me.

I swept them back up and wrapped them back in their blue silk. I put the candles out. The headache was almost gone, and my stomach seemed to be doing better. Now I just had that drank-too-much-last-night-tired-and-dragged-out feeling. Maybe, I thought, another shower, long and hot, would do the trick.

I went to the bathroom to shave.

CHAPTER THREE

Nine of Pentacles

solitary enjoyment of the
good things of life

New Orleans Arena is tucked behind the Superdome snugly, like a little brother. When it was being built and was as yet unnamed, a lot of the radio stations in town had contests to come up with a name for it. My favorite was the Babydome, but they went with New Orleans Arena, which I thought showed a singular lack of creativity. It is a beautiful structure of steel, steely blue glass, and concrete. Its modernistic structure wouldn't have fit into many other parts of the city, but it seemed to work well in the Central Business District. Shortly after it was built, we got a new NBA team, the Hornets. I have yet to go to a Hornets game, but then I've lived in New Orleans my whole life and have never made it to a Saints game. Both Storm and Rain had season tickets for both teams, and offer them to me from time to time, but I don't see the point. Any event at either place is a traffic nightmare. Despite the best efforts of the police department, Poydras Street and the other streets in the area simply weren't equipped to really handle lots of cars. When there's something going on at either place it can take as long as twenty minutes to move one block up Poydras Street. David and I went to the Dome to see one of Cher's farewell tours, and the traffic totally killed our buzz. By the time we finally managed to get the car parked, we were both tense, cranky, and bitchy.

Never again.

Fortunately, Rain was driving us in her sleek, bullet gray Lexus SUV. Why a woman whose idea of roughing it is staying at a Holiday Inn would want a sport utility vehicle is beyond me, but I think it was part of her "keeping up with other Uptown ladies" thing. My sister is pretty. She's only about four eleven on a good day, with light brown hair she's worn in a long pageboy since her freshman year in high school. Her lack of height made her look even sillier behind the wheel of the tanklike SUV. Rain was the total antithesis of our parents. Storm might be a lawyer, which is only one step higher on the evolutionary scale than a politician to Mom and Dad, but Rain was everything they'd rebelled against their entire lives. My Diderot grandparents had done everything they could to turn my mother into a proper Uptown debutante. Rain was the daughter they had so longed for. Rain did everything right—went to McGehee, went to the University of Alabama and pledged Kappa, got a degree and married her high school sweetheart just as he was finishing up med school. She worked through his internship, but once he opened his own practice she switched careers to Uptown Doctor's Wife. Now, she lives in a big palace of a house on Octavia Street just off St. Charles Avenue, drives the SUV, does charity work, and throws parties. Her life is a complete mystery to Mom and Dad, who just can't understand her. Mom keeps hoping that one day Rain will wake up, call herself Rain again, and become an uber-feminist. I don't think it's ever occurred to Mom that her parents hold out the hope that one day she'll become like Rain.

Our family is so twisted sometimes.

Rain is an excellent driver, so David and I could completely relax and enjoy our stoner haze. Ted sat in the front. He didn't approve of pot smoking, and would occasionally lecture David on the evils of buying and using illicit drugs. (He always spared me the lectures.) I had often told David the way to cure Ted of this annoying habit once and for all was to have him come to dinner and meet my parents. All it would take was one remark, and my mom would be off and running, debunking the antimarijuana arguments one by one.

It's a lot of fun having radical parents.

The traffic was even worse than I thought it would be, and I thanked the Goddess again for Rain offering to drive us all. The New Orleans Tourist Council had poured a lot of money into promoting the event. It was a pretty big deal. We'd never had a major figure skating event in New Orleans before. The skating tours had been here before, but never something like this. We've had more Super Bowls than any other city. We have the Sugar Bowl every year. We always seem to have a stage of the NCAA basketball tournament here. But this was a first foray into international competitive skating, and the *Times-Picayune* had run several stories about how the NOTC was going to use this to test the waters. If Skate America went well, we would be bidding for not only the National Championships but also the Worlds. Since our economy is almost entirely based on tourism, bringing in new events is almost always a big deal, with lots of worries about whether it will be a success and so on. They almost always are (who doesn't want to come to New Orleans? It's Disneyland for adults, after all), but the mayor is always giving press conferences telling the locals to do everything we can to make the people coming in for the event feel welcome. Maybe I'm cynical, but after a couple of flammable drinks everyone feels welcome here.

Rain had managed to get us front-row seats for the men's and women's event finals.

Ted was almost beside himself with excitement. He hadn't been to a live skating event in years. He and his partner at the time had made the trek to Minneapolis in 1991 to see the Nationals. He was recounting it all to Rain as she maneuvered her SUV into the New Orleans Arena parking garage. I was tuning him out, for the most part. I'd heard the story a million times already. "And then Tonya Harding landed her triple axel right in front of us!" She did. I've seen the tape of it, which Ted always freezes so we can see him sitting in the front row as she landed.

"Wow," Rain replied, finally finding a spot large enough for her oversized vehicle. "I remember watching that on television. I always liked poor Tonya."

"Poor dumb Tonya," Ted agreed. "What a waste."

We got out of the SUV. I was pretty pleasantly stoned. David had brought his little sneak-a-toke, and we each took a hit in the parking lot and then hurried to catch up with Ted and Rain. They were still talking about Tonya Harding. There were people everywhere. Being stoned in a crowd is not always a fun thing, but David and I were busy pointing out good-looking guys to each other, which made it bearable. We finally made it through the lines, handed over our tickets, and then David and I made a beeline for the first concession stand we saw. Everything was overpriced, as usual, but I got a huge bucket of popcorn and a gigantic Coke. The arena was packed, which was obviously good news for the Tourist Council. Banners were up everywhere, cheering on certain skaters. There was an amazing energy in the building, and I felt goosebumps come up on my arms. We made our way to our seats, and almost immediately started shivering.

"I told you to bring a coat," Rain said.

A Zamboni machine was resurfacing the ice. I looked around. The place was definitely filling up. I nudged Rain and pointed. "Look, there's Dick Button and Peggy Fleming!"

"Where?" Rain followed my finger and almost swooned. She loves Dick and Peggy. In her words, they are the only commentators worth listening to.

The Zamboni pulled off the ice, and then about eight men came skating out through a gate at the other end of the ice. They zipped around the rink, some of them launching into spins or warm-up jumps. Both Ted and Rain made ecstatic noises. David and I looked at each other and rolled our eyes. Our seats were in a back corner, right behind the boards, and to our immediate left was the camera pit, with photographers and men working big bulky cameras with the ESPN logo on them.

"Here comes one." David nudged me.

I looked back at the ice. A speeding blur wearing tight, shiny black pants and a shimmery white top was coming right at us. He turned so that his back was to us, and then stepped right up in a triple axel. It spun beautifully, high above the ice, and then he descended to land on one foot, the other leg swinging back around and up as he glided back toward where we were sitting. The crowd around us burst into applause, and right before he reached the boards he turned on his blades to acknowledge the crowd. He stopped right in front of us.

I gasped.

It was Bryce.

Our eyes locked, and he smiled slightly before skating off.

"Who—who was that?" I asked.

Ted looked at me pityingly, giving out a long-suffering sigh. "You know, pot really *does* kill brain cells and affect memory." He folded his arms. "That's Bryce Bell. He's our best shot at the gold medal at the next Olympics. He's only nineteen, and he came out of nowhere last year to win the silver medal at Nationals and the bronze at Worlds—and most people think he should have won Worlds. He was the first person to land a quad loop, and rumor has it he is landing a quad axel in practices. If he can land the quad axel in competition, no one will be able to beat him." Ted was off and running now. "The judges really held him back last year on his artistry marks, which was bullshit. He is just as artistic as anyone else skating these days, but the judges always hold people down in their first year. . . ." He continued to drone on in this vein, about the unfairness of the judging, bringing up again the Salt Lake scandal, and on and on and on. I tuned him out, watching the kid zip around the ice.

David nudged me. "Isn't that the kid from last night?" he whispered.

I nodded, unable to speak.

I watched him skating around the ice. Ted was right. He was

beautiful to watch. Even when all he was doing was propelling himself forward, there was a fluidity to the movement that none of the other skaters on the ice seemed to have. He came back around to our end of the ice, and I got a really good look at his butt in those shiny black pants. Wow. It was perfection. It belonged on underwear boxes. It belonged on posters, magazine covers, billboards. It was the most perfectly round, solid butt I have ever seen, and believe me, I've seen plenty of perfect butts in my life. I've been told that mine is perfect—but mine was not even close to his.

Bryce was in a league of his own.

The skaters left the ice, and the announcer introduced the first skater, some guy from Germany. I didn't pay any attention to him. He was skating to a Rachmaninoff piece, but he fell on his first jump, which seemed to take the life out of him. He continued to skate around, but his movements seemed tired, tentative. He fell on another jump, and the crowd murmured in sympathy. You could tell he just wanted the whole thing to be over. I still couldn't believe that I had slept with one of the top skaters in the world—and couldn't remember a thing about it!

The next skater was announced.

Rain jabbed me with an elbow. "Nikolai Borzhov was world champion last year."

Nikolai Borzhov skated around the rink a few times. I took a close look at him as he passed us. He was pretty. His skin was very pale, like he never went out into the sun, and he was wearing a very dramatic-looking red and white top with flowing sleeves, over black pants. He seemed taller than Bryce, with long, dark hair and bright blue eyes. The announcer introduced him to thunderous applause, and he skated out to the middle of the ice and posed. The music started.

"Isn't this Pink Floyd?" I whispered.

"Yup." David nodded.

"You think he's a stoner?"

"Shhhh." Rain elbowed me in the side.

He started skating, doing some fancy arm movements and skating in sync to the music. He headed back toward our corner, picking up speed to the point that he was almost a blur. Right in front of us, he drove one of his skates into the ice, sending up splinters, and launched up into the air. He spun around four times, landed on one foot, stuck the other foot back into the ice and went back up into the air, rotating three times and landing on one foot. As he glided away on one foot, he pumped both of his fists in triumph.

"Quad toe-triple toe," Rain said as the crowd burst into riotous applause.

I decided I hated him.

Sure, he was pretty. Sure, he was a really good skater.

But I hadn't slept with him.

I wanted Bryce to beat him.

The crowd obviously liked Nikolai. They gave him riotous applause every time he landed a jump, every time he did one of his spins, pretty much every time he did anything more than just skate around. To give him his due, he was doing an excellent interpretation of Pink Floyd's music, and I do like Pink Floyd. But every time he started to launch into a jump, I clenched my hands and repeated, over and over, in my head, Fall! Fall! Fall! Probably not good karma, but I didn't care.

He didn't. As the music came to a close, he started spinning until he was just a blur of red, white, and black on the ice, faster and faster until I started to feel a little nauseous just watching him. Then he stopped, pushed off into another gliding pose, and as the last chord crashed he struck another pose.

The arena exploded with applause as everyone jumped to their feet screaming. Flowers and stuffed animals rained down on the ice. Nikolai, with a huge grin on his face, began bowing to every side, blowing kisses and waving at the crowd.

"If he wasn't skating so early he'd get 6.0s," Ted said, still applauding as Nikolai skated off the ice. "They always have to save marks for the later skaters."

The crowd sat back down, and as with the poor German guy, everyone looked up at the scoreboard, waiting for the marks. A group of little girls were skating around picking up the flowers and other debris that had been tossed onto the ice.

"The marks for technical merit for Nikolai Borzhov," the announcer said, as the board lit up with the scores and the crowd roared again, "5.8, 5.8, 5.9, 5.8, 5.9, 5.8, 5.8."

"Good marks," Rain said.

"And for artistic impression"—the crowd screamed again, everyone up on their feet—"5.9, 5.9, 5.9, 5.9, 5.9, 5.9, 5.9." Then the leader board changed to show N. Borzhov RUS in first place.

"That's going to be hard to beat," Ted said.

"Bryce can do it," I replied. I knew he could do it.

We had to watch some other skaters. They were all terrible. A Chinese skater; a couple of French guys; a Canadian. They all managed to fall at least once, and one poor guy from the Czech Republic managed to fall on every single jump he tried, even losing his balance on a spin and sprawling on the ice. He got polite, sympathetic applause when his music ended. He looked like he was about to cry.

"Poor thing," I said. All that training, all that practice, all for nothing. I sent him some positive energy with my mind.

Then Bryce skated out onto the ice to thunderous applause. He moved around the ice, crossing in front of us, but he didn't look at me. His face was deadly serious, completely focused. He skated out to the center of the ice. He was the last skater. He had to be perfect to win.

"This competition is so important," Rain whispered. "If he can beat Nikki here, it'll set the tone for the whole year."

I closed my eyes and sent a quick prayer to the Goddess.

Bryce posed.

The music started, and I recognized it. It was the *Titanic* soundtrack. He started swaying on the ice, his arms going up above his head, making fluttering movements, and then he pushed off and started to skate. He skated around the ice, posing as he flowed, every movement of his arms, hands, and head synchronized with the movements of his legs and the notes of the music. He began to build up speed.

"If he's going to try the quad axel, it'll be here," Ted whispered, his voice shaking with excitement. Both he and Rain were clutching their armrests, knuckles white.

All the hair on my arms stood up. *You can do it, Bryce! You can do it!*

He headed for us, then turned so his back was to us, and then turned again and propelled himself into the air, rotating.

One, two, three, four!

He came down, landing on one foot, and then reached back with his free foot and drove it into the ice, going back up into the air, one, two, three, and then gently landed on one foot.

The arena exploded. Everyone was on their feet, screaming and applauding madly as he headed back down to the other corner of the ice. He had a huge smile on his face, pumped his fist a bit, then got back into the character of the music again.

"I can't believe it!" Ted screamed, hopping up and down. "A quad axel *in combination*! OH MY GOD! Nobody has *ever* done that before!"

Tears were streaming down Rain's face.

I turned my eyes back to the ice.

Go, Bryce, go! I was hugging myself, and shaking a little bit.

I held my breath as Bryce launched into the air again. One, two, three, four.

He pumped his fists as he slid backwards on one foot.

Again, the arena exploded with cheers and applause.

I felt my own eyes filling with tears as he moved around the ice. He was really selling the program now and the audience was completely with him. Every movement was followed by screams and applause—but everyone was also holding their breath, their eyes following each movement, afraid to breathe in case he stumbled or fell. The movements were so beautiful, so breathtaking. And then finally, it was over.

He glided on both feet, bent over, his hands clamped over his face. His entire torso was shaking. He was sobbing.

So was I. So was Ted. So was Rain. Even David was jumping up and down and screaming.

So many flowers were falling on the ice that the surface would be covered, hidden. Huge stuffed animals were flying through the air, bouncing on the ice.

The crowd was screaming. My hands hurt as I slammed them together again and again.

He took his bows, tears streaming down his face, and as he left the ice, the announcer began giving his scores.

"For technical merit, 6.0, 6.0, 6.0, 6.0, 6.0, 6.0, 5.9."

The crowd cheered each mark, but the 5.9 was also greeted with some boos and catcalls.

"For artistic impression, 6.0, 6.0, 6.0, 6.0, 6.0, 6.0, 6.0."

Even though he looked tiny at the opposite end of the arena, everyone could see Bryce was jumping up and down, hugging people, waving, and saluting. The crowd had not sat down since his program ended. My throat was starting to hurt from screaming.

The next skater came out onto the ice, listening to the roar. He seemed a little dejected. It would, I thought, suck to have to skate after that. I sent him some positive energy.

"History, boys!" Ted grinned. "We've just witnessed history."

We all sat down again. I wiped at my eyes.

"Excuse me, sir?"

I turned to face one of the ushers. "I was asked to give you this," he said, handing me an envelope.

Rain, Ted, and David all stared at me as I opened it. There

was a sheet of folded paper as well as what looked like a hotel key card.

I unfolded the paper.

Will you meet me at my room tonight around midnight? It's number 315 at the Royal Aquitaine.—B

I grinned as I stuffed the envelope into my jeans pocket.

Wow. In the middle of all this, he could even think about me?

This time I wouldn't forget, and I'd give him the most memorable night of his career.

I was going to go for the gold.

CHAPTER FOUR

Three of Swords, Reversed

confusion, loss, disorder

The women's event final was highly entertaining, but after watching Bryce Bell make history, it did seem kind of anticlimactic. It was like just going through the motions. Applaud when they do something nice. Say "Oh!" when they make a mistake. Clap when they finish. Cheer when their marks go up. The key card in my pocket felt almost hot through the fabric. Every once in a while I would slip my hand inside to make sure it was still there. What can I say? I was completely starstruck. I've slept with lots of guys in my lifetime—even a couple of porn stars when I danced with them during my days as a go-go boy—but never anyone remotely like Bryce Bell. He was famous all over the world, and now he was going to be even more famous. He might win the Olympics. He might even wind up on a Wheaties box.

Never in my wildest dreams did I think I'd ever get naked with someone like that.

Every time I put my hand into my pocket David would just glare at me. Even Rain couldn't keep her mouth shut—although to give her credit, she waited until we were back in the car, trying to get out of the garage.

"Scotty, I cannot believe you." She shook her head.

"What?" I looked over at David, who was glaring at me.

"I can't believe you picked up one of the greatest figure skaters of all time in a bar last night." She looked at me in the rear view mirror. "And he spent the night? And then was able to pull off a skate like that?"

"I didn't know who he was." I shrugged. "You know crazy stuff happens to me all of the time."

Rain looked over at David. "David, if you want to smoke pot in here all you have to do is crack the window."

David pulled his sneak-a-toke out and took a hit, blowing the smoke out of the window. I looked at him. He gave me a withering look. "I don't know if you deserve any."

"Oh for Goddess's sake." I was starting to get a little pissed. "Why are all of you treating me like I'm some kind of criminal? I didn't know who he was, and besides, it's not like it hurt him or anything. He made history! It's not like he fell on his ass the whole time." I crossed my arms. "Maybe being with me last night gave him the inspiration to skate so well."

Both Rain and Ted snorted, and then started laughing.

David grinned and passed the sneak-a-toke to me. "I'm just fucking with you, man. I think it's cool."

"I'm not mad, I'm jealous," Ted said from the front seat.

Rain laughed. "Honey, I'm not mad either. I just can't believe all the stuff that happens to my baby brother." She is, like I said, pretty cool for an uptight Uptown Doctor's Wife.

"How do you think I feel?" I took a hit. "I have to live this life, after all."

"Better you than me." She shrugged. "I don't know if I could handle it."

It was about ten thirty when Rain dropped us off at the corner of Bourbon and St. Ann—the heart of the gay section of the Quarter. There were knots of people in front of Oz on one side of the street and the Pub on the other. Both balconies were starting to fill up. It was Saturday night in the Quarter, after all, and a lot of gay men had come into town for Skate America. I could almost see the drool filling up David's mouth as we climbed out of the SUV. I leaned in the driver's window and kissed Rain on the cheek.

"Call me tomorrow," she said. "Why don't you come over for dinner one night this week?"

Her dinner invitations always used to be some kind of setup. Rain is big on closure, and she felt it was her mission in life to find me a boyfriend. Since I'd met Frank, though, her dinner invitations had ceased to have ulterior motives, so I found myself going more often than I used to. I liked her husband, Peter, even if he was a little on the stuffy side, and Rain was a pretty good cook. "Okay," I said.

"What about Frank?" she asked.

I was confused. "Frank? He's in DC."

She rolled her eyes. "Does this mean you aren't with Frank anymore?"

Uh oh. Better head this one off at the pass. "Frank and I aren't exclusive, Rain."

"Oh." I could see she was trying to wrap her mind around that one. Finally, she just shook her head. "Well, call me." She rolled up the window. I stepped back and she drove off.

I sighed. How was I going to explain everything to her? She wouldn't understand, cool as she was. Her life was so completely ordered, meticulously planned out to the last little detail. Hell, I didn't even understand what I was feeling with Frank, myself.

David, Ted, and I walked into the Pub and paid our cover. I was going to stick with drinking beer tonight. No way was I going to get fucked up again and not remember the night. I even turned down David's offer to smoke a joint, much to his annoyance. I was going to remember everything that happened this time if it killed me.

The bars were crowded. It was a typical Saturday night in the Quarter. With the Lazarus Ball coming up the next weekend, a lot of the locals who'd been avoiding the bars since the excesses of

Decadence were out again. There were also a lot of new faces, undoubtedly the tourists in town for Skate America. Within five minutes of arriving at the Pub and getting our drinks, Ted saw a big burly daddy type and went off in chase of him. David and I just hung out in our usual corner by the video poker machine, watching the crowd, exchanging glances and smiles with cute guys. I kept glancing at my watch.

Finally, at about quarter till midnight I told David I was leaving to go meet Bryce. He walked me outside. "Have fun, and tell me all about it in the morning," he said.

"What are you going to do?"

He shrugged. "If I haven't found someone by two I'll probably head to the bathhouse for a while and see what's up there."

I walked down St. Ann to Royal Street. I always try to avoid Bourbon on the other side of St. Ann at night. Too many drunk, straight, macho men down there for my taste. You never know when all that alcohol and testosterone is going to ignite. Royal Street was fairly quiet, and I walked around a ghost tour that had stopped in the middle of the sidewalk. The tour guide was explaining that *Interview with the Vampire* had been filmed in the house they were staring at. My heart was pounding. What if he wasn't interested in having sex again? I'd gotten a sense from him that he was in some kind of trouble, and then there was that card reading. What I should have done, I told myself as I reached Royal Street, was gone home and read the cards again. But then again, my gift is not an exact science. Never has been and probably never will be. Maybe the sense of trouble I'd gotten wasn't trouble per se, but the tension he'd been feeling about having to skate against the world champion, about trying to make skating history. It couldn't be easy being America's top Olympic hopeful. That was a lot of pressure.

The Royal Aquitaine is one of those grand old New Orleans hotels whose reputation isn't really deserved. Maybe at one time it had been one of the great hotels of the world, but times have changed. I've tricked there before, and never could understand why people were willing to pay its exorbitant rates. Don't get me wrong, it's a nice place, but it's not even one of the better hotels in the Quarter. It's probably the location. One block off the heart of Bourbon Street, it's close enough to all the action but just far enough so the noise doesn't bother the guests. It does have a really good reputation, and maybe since I've never been an official paying guest there I'm not the best judge, but the rooms I've been in have always seemed a little on the small side. About ten years ago, one of the big hotel chains bought it and gave it a facelift, but it still seemed to be a little on the run-down side to me. It's a huge building made out of stone, with the obligatory wrought iron lace balconies lining the upper floors. Gaslights are set between the windows on the first floor to give it that nineteenth-century air. It's five stories tall, although the top floor seems more like an attic, with the windows set in eaves. On the Toulouse Street side, cabs were lined up outside the front door. The Aquitaine Room, their first-floor restaurant, has decent food but is really overpriced as well. I guess the guests pay for the convenience of not leaving the hotel to eat, even though there are better and less expensive restaurants within a few blocks in every direction. I stepped around a couple who had stopped to stare into the restaurant window at an overdressed couple eating steaks, and went around the corner to the front doors. The doorman smiled at me as he opened the door for me. Poor guy—they made the staff dress in eighteenth-century costume, from the buckled shoes all the way up to the powdered wigs.

The lobby is done up in an overly lavish style true to the hotel's history. It was built in the 1890s, when velvet and marble and gilt were in style for fashionable hotels. Huge chandeliers hung from the ceilings. The chairs and sofas scattered about on top of Persian rugs were done in an eighteenth-century style in keeping with the French theme. The restaurant hostess, standing at her podium just inside the door, was dressed like Marie Antoi-

nette in a heavy brocade dress, with white curls piled in a towering mass on top of her head. Even the waiters were dressed like
courtiers from Versailles, with hose and knee breeches and high-
heeled shoes. Taking orders, standing around, and serving food in
those outfits had to be a pain in the ass. I hoped the guests recognized that and tipped them well. One good thing about it, I guess,
was they never had to worry about costumes for balls. All they
had to do was wear their work clothes.

I looked at my watch. Ten minutes till midnight. The lobby
was pretty busy, with people sweeping out into the street, clus-
tered around having cigarettes and talking while drinking out of
plastic go-cups. I looked around to see if I recognized anyone—
after all, if Bryce was staying here it was highly likely that most of
the other skaters were too—but didn't see anyone who looked
even remotely familiar. I turned back to climb the marble steps to
the elevator bank and drew in a sharp breath.

It couldn't be.

Heading for the elevators was a short man in tight jeans and a
loose-fitting gray sweater. He had short blue-black hair and a great
body. He looked just like—

No, it couldn't be him. Absolutely not, no way.

I'd gotten a postcard a few weeks earlier from him, postmarked
Puerto Vallarta.

We'd met over Southern Decadence. His name, or so he told
me at the time, was Colin. We were working the same shift, dancing on the bar at the Pub. We'd hit it off that first night and gone
back to my place together. We had the most amazing chemistry.
I'd really liked him, and he'd really liked me, or so he said. Then,
in all the ensuing drama of that weekend, he had taken off and
didn't even have the decency to say good-bye. He claimed he was
a cat burglar—which I wasn't 100 percent sure I believed—and
with all the attention I was getting that weekend, not only from
the police but from the FBI, it was just too risky for him to stick
around. Understandable if he was wanted by the cops, I suppose,

but still. He could have at least said good-bye, rather than sending me a postcard from Mexico a few weeks later.

Then again, he didn't have to send the postcard either.

Why does *everything* have to be complicated?

I started up the steps. I wasn't really sure what to do. If he really was a cat burglar like he claimed, I could hardly just shout his name out in the crowded lobby of a hotel, could I?

He wouldn't have come back to town without telling me, would he?

It probably wasn't him. What were the odds, anyway?

No, I should just get up there and take a good look at him.

But by the time I had reached the top of the stairs, he had disappeared inside an elevator and the doors were just shutting.

Damn!

It was probably just a coincidence, someone who looked like him from behind. My imagination working overtime again, as it tended to do. I stood there waiting for the next elevator to come.

When the doors opened, I got in and pressed three.

The elevator moved up slowly.

Yeah, it had to be a coincidence.

It couldn't possibly be him.

And if it was him, I didn't want to see him. He could have called me, let me know he was in town. No, I was probably never going to see him ever again.

Which was probably a good thing.

The elevator dinged and the door opened on three. I wasn't paying attention, I admit that. It happens all the time—I get lost in thought and don't watch where I'm going. I'm also pretty clumsy. I trip over things all the time, walk into walls and doors, that kind of stuff. I started to step out and promptly collided with someone. I lost my balance and fell right on my ass back into the elevator with a spine-jarring thud.

"Oof!"

I shook my head. A woman was down on her knees, half in and half out of the elevator. A small black clutch purse had hit the ground and opened. She was scrabbling to pick up coins, make-up, and various other things.

"I'm so sorry!" she said without looking at me.

"It's okay—I wasn't looking," I said. I reached over and picked up a lipstick that had rolled over by me, and handed it to her. I climbed to my feet as she shoved things back into her purse and snapped it closed. She finally looked at me. She was pretty, maybe in her midforties, with curly brown hair pulled back into a pony-tail. She was not very tall, maybe about five one or two. Her fig-ure was slim beneath a shapeless black sweatshirt. She was wearing black jeans over sneakers that looked like they had seen better days. Her gray eyes were large and round, a little on the blood-shot side, and there were dark circles of worry underneath them. Her nails were bitten down to the quick and not polished. She wasn't wearing much makeup, and she smelled—

Of fear.

She was frightened.

Something bad had happened to her—

—and then the sense was gone as suddenly as it had come.

I shook my head again. No, she smelled like Elizabeth Tay-lor's White Diamonds, my mom's favorite perfume. Definitely not fear.

"So sorry about that." She stepped past me into the elevator and pressed the lobby button. I stepped out just as the doors started to close. Then I noticed a folded piece of paper lying just outside the elevator. "Hey, you dropped—"

The doors shut as she gave me a tired smile.

I knelt down and picked up the paper. It was newspaper, yel-lowed with age, and folded tightly. I tucked it into my pocket and stopped to take a look at myself in the mirror on the wall next to the elevator. Not bad, not bad at all. My shirt was nice and snug over my chest and shoulders, and the way I'd rolled the sleeves made my biceps look huge. I ran a quick hand through my un-ruly curls and took a deep breath, then started laughing at myself.

"I'm acting like a high school girl on her way to her first date,"

I said aloud, winking at myself. "He's just a guy, even if he's famous, and the guy hasn't been born that I can't handle." I took another deep breath, and followed the arrows posted on the wall for rooms 301–310.

Room 310 was on the Royal Street side, one of the rooms with a balcony. It was at the end of the corridor, right in the corner where the hallway made a ninety-degree turn to run down Toulouse Street. The wallpaper was some kind of a pale green, with velvet fleur-de-lis in a darker shade in a weird kind of pattern. The carpet looked worn, and I stepped around trays of plates from room service. I stopped in front of Bryce's door. I pulled the key card out and hesitated. I was nervous about letting myself in. He'd sent me the key card, so it was stupid to be so nervous. *He's just another guy,* I thought to myself, *so it was stupid to be so nervous. You hadn't been nervous last night when you didn't know a thing about him, so get over yourself,* I told myself.

Still, I couldn't bring myself to slip the key into the slot.

Should I knock first? Would I like it if someone just let themselves into my house? What if he was in the bathroom or not dressed?

Well, if he wasn't dressed, big deal. I had already seen him naked.

The door was probably locked. Maybe he'd sent the card along just in case I got there first and he wanted me to wait for him. Was that proper etiquette? I stood there for a few seconds, debating. Finally, good manners won out and I knocked on the door.

It swung open.

Every hair on my neck stood up.

Trouble. Danger. Maybe—

Maybe he left it open for me, I reasoned. Then why go to the trouble of sending the key?

Then why did I have this sense that something was wrong?

I stood there, indecisive. I said a quick prayer of protection.

I took a step inside. "Hello?"

There was a short hallway leading into the room. The bathroom was to the right. The light was on and I could see a toothbrush, toothpaste, a razor, all of the usual stuff lined up neatly beside the sink basin. It was a little cold in there, and cold air was blowing into my face. The doors to the balcony were open, and the sheer curtains were blowing in the breeze. I could see across the street into the windows of the apartment directly opposite. A group of people were eating dinner, talking and laughing. "Bryce?" I called out. "It's Scotty—everything okay?"

No response. Okay, then he *had* sent me the key in case he got held up. The thing to do, obviously, was just walk in and have a seat and wait for him. Maybe even go out onto the balcony and watch the street.

Something just didn't seem right, though.

I walked to the end of the hallway and looked into the room. "Bryce?" I called out again.

I turned my head to the left and stiffened, all the air rushing out of me.

A man was lying face up on the bed staring at the ceiling.

A knife was sticking out of his chest.

"Not again," I groaned.

CHAPTER FIVE

The Chariot, Reversed

uncontrolled passion leading to downfall

Okay, I admit it. My initial reaction was pretty callous and I'm not proud of it. I mean, it wasn't the first time I've had the great fortune to come across a dead body. The one thing I've learned is it usually doesn't bode well for the immediate future. For one thing, any cop will tell you the person who discovers a body is usually the main suspect at first. And here I was, in a hotel room not my own, with no sign of the occupant, and a dead body just a few feet away. No, this didn't look good for me.

After a few seconds, the beer, popcorn and Coke mixed in my stomach began to churn. I took a couple of deep breaths. My face got hot and I started to sweat even though it was cold in there. The room was starting to spin. I stumbled over to a wingback chair, and crime scene be damned, I sat down with my head between my knees until my stomach settled and my head cleared.

I reached into my pocket for my cell phone. I hate cell phones. I've never really understood why people always have theirs with them and turned on so it will ring during movies or dinner. Must you be accessible all the time? Mine is always turned off. Nobody, absolutely *nobody,* needs to get a hold of me RIGHT NOW! I carry one for emergencies, so I can make calls, not so everyone in the world can call me. This certainly qualified as an emergency. I scrolled through my speed dial until I found Venus Casanova's number, and clicked on it.

It might seem strange to have a police detective's number on my speed dial, but that's just the kind of life I lead.

"Casanova," she answered.

"Hey Venus, this is Scotty Bradley. You remember me?"

She barked out a short laugh. "Like I could forget you. Don't tell me you've stumbled onto another body?" Venus and I had met the last time I found a dead body. She's pretty cool, for a homicide detective.

"Um, actually, yeah."

Her voice got serious. "Where are you?"

"Room 315 of the Royal Aquitaine Hotel."

"Male or female?"

"Male."

"You're sure he's dead?"

"Well, I didn't think I should touch him, but there's a knife stuck in his chest, and he hasn't moved since I found him or made any noise, so yeah, I'm pretty sure." I walked over to the balcony doors. Someone was shouting, down in the street. I stood there, taking deep breaths, then went back to the chair and sat down again.

"You didn't touch anything?"

"I sat down in a chair because I was about to throw up, but other than that, no."

"All right." She put the phone down for a minute, and then she came back to it. "Go out in the hall. I've got a couple of beat cops on their way, and CSU should be right behind them. Wait outside for them, and don't touch anything!" She disconnected the call.

I folded up my phone and slid it back into my pocket.

I looked at the body. Okay, Scotty, I said to myself, you've been to detective school. What do you see?

The sheer curtains danced in the wind in my peripheral vision. The balcony doors were open. The bed was made, and the body was lying on top of the covers. The knife handle was standing at a ninety-degree angle out of his chest. He was wearing a gray pin-striped blazer and matching pants. It might have been a nice suit at some point, but it had seen better days. It looked worn at the knees and elbows. His shirt, which was open at the neck, had probably been white at one point, but now it was drenched in blood. There was blood spreading out from around him on the bedspread. The blood hadn't dried and started to get sticky, so his death was pretty recent. His eyes were open and staring at the ceiling, his mouth open, like he'd been caught completely by surprise. He had some gray and white stubble on his face. He obviously hadn't shaved in a couple of days. The hands were both lying palm down on the bed, and both hands were covered with wiry black hair. The nails were dirty and irregularly cut. The eyes were brown. His hair was graying and slicked down. He had a prominent nose with some stray hairs sticking out of the nostrils. Blech. There were acne scars scattered over his face. The body looked as though he'd been in shape at some point, but had allowed himself to go slack and soft as he'd gotten older. His shoes were black patent leather, scuffed and dirty.

I felt bile rising in my throat again and looked away.

Where was Bryce? I wondered. What the hell is this all about?

I was very careful not to disturb anything. I closed my eyes and prayed to the Goddess for guidance. Nothing came.

It's not exact, after all.

I moved over to the curtains, and looked carefully out on the balcony. Across the street, they were still eating, talking, laughing, unaware that just a few yards away violent death had come. From below came the normal sounds of Saturday night in the Quarter. There was a group singing "Blue Moon" a cappella, and they sounded great, their voices mixing and blending and harmonizing together. Other music was coming from further down the street, along with talking, laughter, and the occasional cab going by below.

The balcony itself was fairly empty. It was separated from the balconies of the other rooms by a waist-high wrought iron fence that matched the railing and the support columns. There was a wrought iron table with two matching chairs out there, as well as a rather large potted palm. I took deep breaths of cool night air. I stuck my hand in my pocket and felt the folded old newspaper.

I pulled it out and opened it up.

Fireman Murdered Execution-Style
by Thomas Fielding, *TP staff*

Rodney Parrish, 26, a New Orleans fireman, was found murdered in his Algiers home late last evening.

His wife, Juliet Parrish, was returning home from dinner with her sister when she found her husband tied up and gagged in the living room of their home.

A neighbor heard her screams and called the police.

Investigating officer Lee Young confirmed that Parrish had been assaulted, bound and gagged, and killed by a single shot to the forehead. "It appears to have been a professional hit," Young said. "There were no signs of a break-in, so apparently we have to surmise that Parrish either knew his killer, or at the very least allowed him entry into the house."

Parrish was born and raised in Algiers, joining the New Orleans Fire Department at age nineteen, assigned to the Vieux Carre district. He married Juliet Pryor several years later, and the couple have a five-year-old son.

"At this time we have no leads," Young said. A quick survey of the neighborhood determined that no one had heard the shot. "It appears as though a silencer was used, which also ties in with the professional aspect of the murder."

Long-time neighbor Victoria Blumberg, who called the police, stated that she has known the Parrishes since they moved in next door to her in the early 1980s. "Such a nice couple. It's a tragedy, it certainly is."

Anyone with information regarding the killing is asked to contact Sergeant Young.

58   *Greg Herren*

I folded the clipping and put it in my wallet. Weird that a woman was carrying around a clipping about an old murder on the same floor that another murder—

Maybe it was just a coincidence.

Yeah, right. Her fear had been so tangible I had practically smelled it over her perfume. She was frightened, nervous, terrified. I closed my eyes and tried to remember. Had she been standing there calmly waiting for the elevator? I'd been distracted in my excitement about seeing Bryce again. I couldn't remember. I wasn't paying attention when I'd stepped out of the elevator. But then, if she'd been standing there waiting for it, she would have seen me—I would have seen her and we wouldn't have run into each other. She'd knocked me hard enough to fall on my ass, and she'd been a pretty small woman. I'm not a big guy by any means, but I'm five eight and weigh one-sixty. There's no way she would have been able to knock me down if all she'd done was taken a step into the elevator. No, she'd had a head of steam up, and had barreled into me.

She'd been running away. Probably from this very room.

Who the hell was she?

I walked back into the room, careful not to look at the body again. I closed my eyes, trying to pick up vibrations from the room. Granted, this kind of stuff never happens when I want it to, but I figured the least I could do was try.

Nothing at all.

The door burst open and a couple of boys in blue came in, their guns drawn. "Put your hands in the air and don't make any sudden moves!" one of them said, his gun pointing right at me. I raised my hands up over my head while the other ran over to the bed to make sure the guy was dead.

The cop holding a gun on me said, "Toss me your wallet."

I slid it out of my pocket and tossed it on the floor in front of him. He flipped it open and removed my driver's license. He tried not to grin. "Milton Bradley?"

"Go ahead and laugh." I sighed. After almost thirty years I was used to it. "But you can call me Scotty."

"You didn't touch anything, did you?" He put his gun back into his holster. "Detective Casanova said you'd be waiting for us in the hall." He pulled out a notebook and a pen. He was kind of cute, with blond hair and blue eyes. He didn't look old enough to be a cop, and his uniform fit him pretty well. He kind of looked like those guys who'd been jocks in high school, but since graduation don't get as much exercise. He was carrying maybe an extra ten pounds, but he was still at the point where he could pull it off. Probably another couple of years of beer and fried food would add another ten pounds, and then he'd look fleshy. By thirty, if he wasn't careful, he'd be fat and balding.

"Well, yeah, but you got here pretty fast." I shrugged. "Can I put my hands down now?"

He gave me a cocky grin. "I put my gun away, didn't I?" I lowered my hands. "Now, what all have you touched in here?"

"All I did was phone it in and sit in this chair. Everything is exactly as it was when I got here."

"What about the door?"

"It opened when I knocked."

"What are you doing here?"

"I was meeting Bryce Bell, the guy staying here." I reached into my pocket and pulled out the key card. "He gave me this." He took it from me and looked it over, then pulled an evidence bag out of his pocket.

He tossed my wallet back to me. "CSU and Detective Casanova will be here soon. Come on, let's go talk in the hall."

I followed him out into the hallway. He had a really nice ass. I know, I shouldn't have been checking him out, but what the hell. I sat down in a chair and crossed my legs.

CSU was the next to arrive, and I just sat there while they went inside to do their jobs. The other cop came out and started going up and down the hall, knocking on doors. The cute cop knelt down beside me. "Okay, Mr. Bradley, explain to me how you came to be in the room."

I sighed. "Nothing personal, but can I just wait for Detective Casanova? That way I don't have to tell it twice."

He stopped smiling. "Suit yourself, buddy." He flipped his notebook closed. Uh oh. It's rarely smart to make a cop mad at you. My brother Storm, who's a lawyer, always says cooperate, or at the very least *appear* to cooperate, as long as you can with the cops. Mom and Dad, on the other hand, who see every authority figure as a fascist and a tool of a repressive imperialist government determined to take away all of our personal freedoms and liberties, think you should *never* cooperate. They also, though, get arrested a lot more than your average citizen. "Go ahead, Officer," I said. "Ask away."

"I'm Officer Cooper, by the way." He didn't smile again, but opened his notebook. "Now, what are you doing here?"

"It's a really long story."

"Take your time."

I had just gotten to the part where the woman in the hallway had knocked me on my ass when Venus Casanova came around the corner with what was undoubtedly a member of hotel management. He was sweating profusely, wearing a jacket and tie, and kept swallowing air. His face was flushed, and he was running a slightly shaking hand through his thinning brown hair. He was talking in a very low voice, the words seeming to run together into almost gibberish.

Venus held up a hand to stop him from talking, and glared at me.

Venus Casanova is an impressive sight. Over six feet tall, she always wears heels to add a few inches to her height. Her prominent cheekbones speak of Native American blood in her gene pool at some point. She wears her hair trimmed close to her scalp, and she has a great shape to her head. Her lips are full, and her skin is dark and smooth. Two large gold downward-pointing triangles now hung from her ears. Her white silk blouse hung loosely from her shoulders, but you could see the outline of her bra through it. She was wearing blue slacks with a matching blue blazer. Her body strong and powerful, but not overly developed, she obviously is no stranger to the weight room. She has a quiet air of competence, professionalism, intelligence, and strength—the kind of person you really don't want to fuck with.

She also has no patience for bullshit.

She dismissed the manager. "My team will be out of here as quickly as possible, and we'll try not to disturb any more of your guests than necessary. But I do need the list of everyone with a room on this floor about five minutes ago." She fixed her eyes on him with an expressionless stare.

He got the point. He nodded and vanished around the corner, pulling out a handkerchief and mopping his hairline.

"We meet again, Scotty." She sighed. "No offense, but I was kind of hoping I'd seen the last of you."

"None taken. This isn't exactly the highlight of my evening either." I shrugged.

"I've begun questioning him, Detective." Officer Cooper was an inch or two shorter than she was. "Would you like me to finish?"

"No, Coop." She shook her head. "I'll take over. Just include your conversation in your report. Now, start canvassing the people on this floor."

"Yes, ma'am." He moved off in the same direction the hotel manager had gone.

She pulled her notepad out of her blazer pocket. "So, tell me, how did you happen to find another body?"

I took a deep breath and told her. I didn't tell her why I'd gone out to get drunk on Friday—it wasn't pertinent, and I doubted that she cared. I started with meeting Bryce at the Brass Rail and bringing him home with me, and then seeing him again at New Orleans Arena, the note with the keycard, and so on. When I finished, she whistled.

"Bryce Bell, huh?"

"You've heard of him?" She didn't strike me as the figure skating type.

"My daughters are big fans of skating. I watched during the Nancy-Tonya thing, but then lost interest." She shrugged. "But I've heard of this kid. The room is registered in his name. You haven't seen him since you got here?"

"No."

"You wouldn't lie to ol' Venus, now, would you?"

"Of course not! I learned my lesson."

She rolled her eyes and then grinned. "Keep this up, Scotty, and you're gonna get a reputation—the fuck of death."

"Yeah, well. I didn't sleep with the guy in there, so it's not my fault."

"And you've never seen this dead guy before? You're sure?"

"Positive."

"And this woman in the hall? What about her?"

"The same. I'm pretty sure I'd never seen her before, either."

"Hand over that clipping." I pulled it out and handed it over to her. She unfolded it carefully, then read it. Her eyebrows went up. "I'm going to need you to talk to a sketch artist about the woman, you know."

"Okay." Like I had a choice.

One of the CSU guys came out. He kind of looked like a rat, with beady little reddish eyes, a long pointed nose, and a mustache that covered his entire upper lip. He was shorter than me, and looked rumpled. Everything about him was disheveled and wrinkled. There was a general air of sloppiness about him. His shirt was untucked in the back, and he had missed a loop while putting on his belt. He was wearing plastic gloves. He held a wallet out to her. "Took this off the guy. The driver's license photo looks like him."

She slipped on gloves of her own, then she flipped it open. "Ace Martinelli, of Telluride, Colorado." She raised an eyebrow.

"Credit cards are all there, and about a hundred dollars in cash, give or take."

She looked through it. "Well, we don't know all the cards are here—the killer might have only taken one, and I don't see an ATM/debit card." She handed it back to him.

He flushed. "Yes, Detective." I felt sorry for him. She was tough. I wouldn't have thought of that. Guess that's why she was the detective.

He went back inside, and the officer who'd originally held his gun on me came back down the hallway. "Nobody on this floor heard or saw anything, but a lot of the guests are out for the evening."

She nodded. "Cooper, I need you to take Scotty here down to the station and get his statement down, and get him with a sketch artist." She looked at me. "Any objections?"

I sighed. "Nah, I know the drill."

Cooper turned out to be pretty cool, for a cop. "So, how do you know Detective Casanova?"

"You really don't want to know." We walked out of the front doors of the hotel. The station house was only a couple of blocks up Royal Street, so we walked. I got some funny looks from people. You can expect that when you walk down the street in the company of a cop in uniform.

"Try me."

"I found a dead body once before."

"Wow." He looked at me. "That doesn't happen to too many people more than once, if at all."

"Tell me about it. That's the story of my life." I shrugged. "I'm one of those lucky people things happen to."

Once we got to the station and sat down at his desk, he got me some coffee (it was pretty good), took down my statement, had it typed up for my signature, and I was back out on the street by three in the morning. The sketch artist thing didn't take even half an hour. He was certainly efficient.

Officer Cooper even offered me a ride home. If it wasn't for the prominently displayed wedding photo of him and his blushing bride—a cherub-cheeked, cute little blond woman—I might have thought there was more to it than politeness. But I decided to walk.

Maybe I'd stop in at the Pub for a drink. Goddess knows I needed one.

Hell, tequila was even sounding good again.

CHAPTER SIX

Ten of Wands

one who is carrying an oppressive load

I changed my mind about having that drink by the time I got to the corner of Bourbon and St. Ann.

It's not that I didn't need one. The thought of numbing my mind a bit from the night's events was actually kind of appealing. So was the thought of losing myself in the crush of a crowd of gay men. By the time I actually got there and was standing on the corner, looking in through the doors of the Pub, I wasn't so sure anymore. Hearing an awesome upbeat dance mix of Pink, looking at the strippers shaking their groove things, and seeing all the happy people having a great time, it didn't seem like the thing to do. I didn't really feel like being around people. Besides, it would just be a moment or two after getting my drink that someone would hit on me, and I just wasn't in a pick-up-a-stranger-for-a-good-time place. I also didn't want to have to explain to anyone why I wasn't interested. It just seemed like a lot more effort than it was worth. There were a couple of bottles of Dixie beer in my fridge. That would do me just fine.

So, I started walking up the street again. The corner of Bourbon and Dumaine presented another choice: Lafitte's, my parents', or home. Lafitte's was quickly ruled out for the same reason I'd ruled out the Pub, but Mom and Dad's had a kind of pull on me. I looked at my watch. Almost four-thirty. I decided against Mom and Dad's. They'd be pretty stoned by now, and undoubtedly hard at work on some political cause, getting themselves worked up, and they'd have some radical friends over. They were going to find out about all of this soon enough, and I figured later was better than sooner. They might be radicals, but they were also parents. They'd be worried, they'd want to call Storm (appalled as they are at having a lawyer for a son, he comes in handy for them—frequently) and I definitely didn't want to get into it with *him*. So, the obvious choice was home, a bottle of Dixie, and solitude. Maybe I'd even take a soothing, long hot bath, light some candles, and play some nice jazz.

The Nelly Deli at the corner of Ursulines was almost completely deserted, except for the cashier and a guy sitting at the deli's lone table, smoking a cigarette. I was thirsty, so I went in and got a Coke. The guy waiting for his food order kept trying to make eye contact with me, but I was in no mood. I took my Coke and kept trudging home. I wasn't physically tired, but I was feeling pretty drained emotionally. I'd almost completely succeeded in keeping Frank out of my head since getting back from DC, but as I walked I wished he was waiting for me back at my place.

What the hell was I going to do about Frank?

The whole concept of having a boyfriend had always escaped me. Maybe that was why I'd never had one. I'd never met anyone before that was interesting enough for me to want to stick around. I'd accepted the fact that I'd never have one, and was fine with it. I liked being single. I liked not having to answer to anyone. I liked being able to sleep with whichever hot boy popped up at any given time. Frank wasn't asking me for monogamy. At least, not for now. But if he did retire from the FBI and move to New Orleans, wouldn't monogamy be in the offing? I liked Frank a lot—even loved him a little, but I've always been a cheap slut and rather proud of it. Could I do a 180-degree turn and settle down with one guy? One guy who doesn't seem to have any friends or life outside of his job?

Of course, that nagging little voice in my head said, *if you and Frank were monogamous you wouldn't be mixed up in this mess, now would you?*

"Fuck off," I said to the little voice as I crossed Esplanade, just missing being turned into roadkill by a speeding cab. I flipped the cab driver off and kept walking, drinking my Coke.

The Marigny was silent—no cars, no people about anywhere, no sound or noise except way off in the distance. Just silence. I turned down Kerlerac, and smiled in relief. I hadn't wanted to hope David would be home, but sure enough, his front lights were on. He'd given up on the bars and come home to play on-line. Perfect. I'd hang out with him while I drank my beer, smoke a little pot, and get myself into a better space.

I opened the gate in front of his half of the house and stepped inside. I almost jumped out of my skin when someone said my name.

I turned to see Bryce emerging from the shadows on my side of the house. My heart was racing and I tried to control my breathing. "What the hell are you doing here?"

He flinched and took a step backward. "I wanted to see you again."

I sat down on the steps on my side of the house. "Then where were you tonight? I went to your hotel."

He moved into the light, looking confused. "How did you know where I was staying?" He scratched his head. He was wearing those baggy jeans that hang off your hips by a thread, and a baggy sweatshirt with ASPEN on it.

"You sent me a note. With your room key." I stared at him. "At New Orleans Arena? An usher brought it to me?"

"I didn't send you a note." He sat down on the step below me and leaned back into my legs. "I just thought I'd come by here and wait for you."

"Well, someone did. And I went to your room. Just in time to find a dead body in your bed."

He pulled away from me. "A what?"

"A dead body." My head was spinning. "Come on, let's get inside." I stood up and pulled out my keys. I opened the front door and turned on the lights. He walked in ahead of me, and I locked the deadbolt. "Sit." I pointed at my couch, and went into the kitchen and got myself a beer, and a Coke for him. The message light on my phone was blinking. *I'll deal with that later,* I decided.

"Can't I have a beer?" he asked as I handed him the can.

"You're only nineteen," I replied. I opened mine and took a long drink. It tasted like shit. I should have had a Coke. I put the can down on the coffee table. "So, why was there a dead body in your bed?"

"I have no idea."

"His name was Ace Martinelli."

His face paled beneath his freckles and he choked on his soda. "Oh, good God."

"You know him?"

He looked away from me. "He was a reporter. For the *National Inquisitor.*"

The *National Inquisitor* was one of those grocery store checkout-stand papers. The ones that always have a cover story about some movie star's rehab, or a politician's messy divorce, or how the face of Satan was seen in a tornado cloud. You know the type—BRITNEY SPEARS PREGNANT WITH BIGFOOT'S BABY. They're an interesting hybrid of journalism and fiction. I never buy them, but how can you not pick it up and look at an article with the headline WHO'S GAY IN HOLLYWOOD? I *always* have to read those while I'm waiting in line. "And how did you know him?"

"He was threatening to out me."

Ah, outing. When outing first began in the late 1980s and early 1990s, it was a political act with a political purpose. Gay activists started outing closeted gays who were, either by their public action or inaction, hurting AIDS research and other gay political causes célèbres. An ugly act with a noble cause—a perfect example of the end justifying the means. Whatever opponents of outing could say, some of the very public outings actually did do some good. Mom and Dad supported it wholeheartedly until the inevitable day came when the tabloids realized that outing celebrities was an excellent way to sell papers. Suddenly, the veil that always seemed to protect closeted gay and lesbian celebrities was ripped away. Needless to say, this scared the hell out of a lot of people, and my parents became anti-outing. "It's an invasion of privacy," Dad would say, "no different from McCarthyism." Chastity Bono was one of the tabloids' victims, although in the long run, her public experience in the tabloids seemed to have worked out just fine for her.

So maybe it's not that bad a thing. I don't know.

"You're a figure skater. Doesn't everyone automatically think you're gay?" I blurted out.

He gave me a dirty look. "You know, not all figure skaters are gay. Just because we perform to music and have to wear makeup and showy costumes—that's such a goddamned stereotype! I'd like to see one of those beer-guzzling assholes who call us faggots slide around at eighty miles per hour on two tiny blades!"

"Um, but you are gay, Bryce."

"And isn't that *my* business, and no one else's?" He sighed and took a drink from his Coke. "It's because of that stereotype that I can't be out, can't be honest with anyone about who I am. Nobody in the business wants a figure skater to come out, because people already think figure skating isn't masculine. So why is a gay man not masculine anyway? Who says?"

"Well, there is this stupid idea people have that gay men are all effeminate." I shrugged. "Plenty of gay men are butch."

"Yeah, well, sequins and makeup aren't masculine, and since there are straight ones, none of us can be gay. The powers that be don't want parents to be scared off from getting their little boys into skating because it's filled with faggots."

I stared at him. "But aren't there skaters that are out?"

He nodded. "Rudy Galindo and Brian Orser are out."

"Has that hurt their careers?"

"Not as pros. I'm an amateur. And my career is totally dependent on a panel of judges who are sick to death of hearing that skating isn't masculine, and they aren't going to reward a skater who is openly gay." He sighed. "I mean, after I go pro, I can do whatever I want—within reason. We are talking about millions of dollars in endorsements, Scotty. Millions. I can't risk being publicly outed until after the Olympics." He scratched his head. "I hate this, Scotty. I hate not being able to tell people who I am. I hate having to hide everything from everyone. But the Olympics have always been my dream . . . and I can't let all the time and work and money invested in me just go down the drain so I can be on the cover of *The Advocate.*" He looked at me. *"After* the Olympics, Scotty. It's only two more years, and then I'll go pro and it won't matter anymore."

"So, this Martinelli guy wanted money?"

"Yeah." He exhaled. "That's not all he wanted, though."

"What else?"

"He wanted me to sleep with him."

"What?" I stared at him. That was truly contemptible. I have always been an advocate for sex—I'm in total favor of it, and the more the better. I think prostitution should be legal. I think anyone should be able to have sex whenever they want it, and if they have to pay for it, let them. Imagine what legalizing and taxing prostitution would do for our national debt! But unconsensual sex is disgusting, evil. Rape is a horrible crime. The very thought of child molestation turns my stomach. And blackmailing someone into bed is just the lowest of the low. What a sleazebag this Martinelli had been! He's the kind who makes all gay men look bad. Yeah, Bryce was a cute, hot, little boy. But why would anyone want to have sex with someone who didn't want them? I mean, there are plenty of people out there who want to have sex, and you should be able to find someone without having to force someone. It was disgusting, absolutely disgusting.

"I train in Colorado Springs." He got up and started to pace. "When I went on the Champions tour this last summer, one of the other guys on the tour helped me get a fake ID so I could go out dancing. In Chicago, I got my nerve up and went to a gay bar." He hugged himself. "I mean, my whole life has been training and school. I don't really have any friends outside of the rink. I knew I was attracted to men, but it was always pictures of guys I saw in magazines. I never was with anyone"—he blushed— "until I went to that bar in Chicago." His eyes shone. "It was so much fun! Nobody around to tell me I couldn't have this, or I couldn't do that, or whatever, you know? I was there all by myself, doing exactly what I wanted to. And the men were all so nice and good looking! I met a really nice, sexy guy and went back to his place with him. About a week later, I got some pictures in the mail. Me on the dance floor with my shirt off, kissing this guy. Me leaving the bar with him, holding hands. Me going into his house with his hand on my ass. Me leaving his house in the morning." He sat back down and buried his face in his hands. "There wasn't a note or anything. Just the pictures. I destroyed them. But the person had sent copies to my coach. That was a lot of fun, believe you me. My coach, my manager, my agent—they dragged me in and screamed at me. They sat me down and told me how stupid I'd been, that this could affect my chances at the Olympics, I couldn't do things like that anymore."

He looked at me, tears starting. "I didn't know what to do. And then this guy showed up at the rink one day. He had a press pass from the USFSA. He wanted an interview, so I said okay. We went to a restaurant. Once we'd ordered, he asked me how I'd liked the pictures? I wanted to punch him, but then he went on to say that he had copies of them, lots of copies, and the contacts to get them in print. And he was going to do that too—unless I slept with him."

"What did you do?"

"What could I do? I slept with him. I felt disgusting." He shivered. "Like a whore. When I got home I had to take a long hot shower because I felt so dirty and nasty. But he swore it would be just that once, and then I'd be safe."

"My God." I tried to put myself in his place. I couldn't. I've had a lot of sex, but it was always my choice. Okay, there had been times when alcohol had lowered my standards quite a bit, but still. Not once had I ever slept with anyone I didn't want to. Not once.

"Then he showed up this week, here, at one of my practices. He wanted me to meet him again at his hotel room after the short programs on Thursday night. I told him I couldn't, but I'd meet him on Friday. He told me to meet him at the Brass Rail."

"So that's why you were there."

"He was supposed to be there at two. He never showed up." He shrugged. "I figured he'd changed his mind. I started drinking because I was nervous. I didn't know what I was going to do when he got there—but I knew I wasn't going back to his hotel with him. Not again. Never again. Then you came in"—he gave me a half smile—"and I thought, why not? Why not have sex with someone who was cute and sexy?"

I walked over and sat down beside him. I put my arm around him and kissed his cheek. "You're going to have to talk to the police."

He sagged in my arms. "Do I have to?"

"The guy's body was found in your room. You're going to have to at some point. And it's going to come out at some point that you know him—and if he has those pictures, and the cops find them, it's going to look pretty damned bad for you. But I'll tell you what—my older brother is a lawyer. I'll give him a call and have him go with you. It can't hurt to have a lawyer with you." I picked up the phone and dialed Storm's number.

"Why are you calling me at four in the morning, my queen?" Storm didn't sound like he'd just been woken out of a deep sleep by the phone. One of his most annoying habits is to wake up immediately. No grogginess, no sleepy voice, nothing. He wakes up on the first ring of the alarm, too. I hate that about him.

I looked over at Bryce and smiled. "I know someone who needs a good lawyer, but a lousy shyster will have to do."

"Name calling ain't gonna get me out of bed at five in the morning on a Sunday, my queen." I could hear him rustling around and grinned. He was getting dressed.

"Storm, I found another body tonight." Bryce's jaw dropped. He was staring at me, his eyes round. I covered the mouthpiece of the phone and whispered, "It's a long story—don't worry about it." I winked at him and said into the phone, "I met this guy last night, and well—make a long story short, I went to meet him at his hotel tonight and found a body."

"And the body belongs to?"

"Someone my friend would have good reason to want dead." Bryce's face was getting paler by the minute. I walked over and patted him on the shoulder, and gave him what I hoped he recognized as a reassuring smile. "And the police are already looking for him." Bryce moaned. "But I think he should talk to you, miserable shyster that you are, before he goes in and talks to them."

"Finally—he's almost thirty and he's getting smart at long last!"

I resisted the urge to tell him off. He loves to tease. "I might be in a little trouble, myself. Venus let me go, but I don't think it looks good." I explained about how the key card had been sent to me. "Bryce says he didn't send it to me."

"That is bad, my queen." Storm sighed into the phone. "Sounds like someone wanted you to find the body—or worse. All right, I'm on my way. Don't answer the phone or the door until I get there, okay? And turn off all the lights . . . don't want anyone to know you're at home or awake, okay?"

"Okay." I hung up. I turned off the lights in the kitchen, got us both another can of Coke, turning out the lights in the bed-room as I walked through, and then shut off the lights in the liv-ing room after handing Bryce his drink.

"Why are we sitting here in the dark?" Bryce asked.

I sat down next to him and put my arm around his shoulders, pulling him in close to me. He was trembling slightly. "The cops might start watching my house. They're looking for you, Bryce, and they know that you know me. They might think you're going to turn up here, so it's better they think I'm asleep. As soon as Storm gets here, we're fine—then you'll have your attorney with you. They can only separate you from him if they book you, but they can't talk to you about anything to do with the case without him present."

"I'm in big trouble, huh?"

I closed my eyes and leaned my head into his. No, I didn't get a sense from him that he was anything but a truly frightened young man. "You might be, Bryce. You didn't kill him, did you?"

"No." He shuddered a bit, and I realized he was crying. Poor thing. Seven hours ago he made figure skating history, and now he was sitting on my couch, waiting for a lawyer to show up. I closed my eyes and said a silent prayer to the Goddess to watch over him. "I didn't think you did."

He sniffled a bit. "Thanks, Scotty. I appreciate it."

He's hiding something from you.

I opened my eyes.

What? What is he hiding?

There is more, and it could be dangerous.

And then there was nothing.

I sighed. I leaned my head back and closed my eyes again.

We sat there in silence until I heard Storm bounding up my front steps.

CHAPTER SEVEN

Queen of Wands, Reversed

*a woman who is strict, domineering,
and not to be trusted*

I finally got to bed when the sun was coming up.

I was pretty tired, so falling asleep wasn't a problem. Storm had arrived around six. I left him and Bryce alone so they could talk privately. Bryce hadn't wanted me to leave them alone, but Storm convinced him. My presence would apparently negate the attorney-client privilege, and I could be called to testify about anything they talked about. Even so, Storm had to do some heavy convincing. Hey, he isn't a damned good lawyer for nothing. Mom swears Storm could out-argue Satan. When he was ten years old, he'd presented an excellent case for why me, Rain, and Storm should all be allowed to have wine with dinner. "I knew then," Mom says with a sigh, "that he was going to grow up and be a lawyer. I of course hoped he'd work for the ACLU, but no such luck."

I'd gone back into my room and slid the parlor doors shut. I heard them talking as I undressed and got into bed. I fell asleep the minute I closed my eyes. Storm woke me up a little while later to tell me they were heading to the police station, and he'd come by later to talk to me. At that point I'd have sold my soul to be allowed to go back to sleep. I did hear the front door shut, and Storm locking it.

My little psychic gift is not an exact science. It never has been. I sometimes get a sense from people—little things like feelings about trust and honesty; sometimes it's a sense the person is in some kind of danger or in emotional pain. Sometimes messages come to me in dreams. One of the main reasons I use the tarot cards is because it helps me with the messages that come to me— but again, even that doesn't work sometimes. I'll spread the cards out, focus, and do a reading that isn't clear at the time. Later, it will all make sense to me, but at the time it means nothing. But there are other times when the meaning is unmistakably clear.

It can be very frustrating, and is also the main reason I keep it to myself.

That morning, I had a dream.

As the dream swirled around and struggled to take form, I became aware of the smell of smoke. I was in a room that looked kind of like an attic; there were boxes, and furniture covered in sheets, and dust everywhere. But the most powerful impression I was getting was one of smoke. Something, somewhere, was burning.

I could feel the heat from the fire.

The room was stuffy, it was hard to breathe because the air was so hot.

As the room became clearer, I heard lots of noise in the background. People shouting. Sirens. The sound of fire turning wood into ash, crackling and snapping. Somewhere nearby, some building was on fire. Whistles blowing. I became more aware of smoke. The room, which should have been bright with sunlight, was hazy with smoke, but the room itself wasn't hot enough—it definitely wasn't this building. The fire was nearby, close enough to hear the flames devouring another building, but at the same time I felt safe where I was. For now, this building was safe.

For now.

Then I began to experience some anxiety. It gripped my stomach, and my hands were shaking.

It has to be hidden, I thought. *Hidden where no one will stumble across it, where no one looking for it would think to look. It can't be found, but it has to be somewhere I can get to it when I need it—where can I put it? There has to be some place in here, some snug little place where no one will think to look, won't look for anything; I've got to hurry, no one can come up here and catch me, there isn't much time, hurry, fool, just pick a place and hide it, for Christ's sake everything depends on this, everything—*

The sound of pounding woke me up.

I sat up in the bed, the smell of smoke fading away. *What the hell was that about?* I wondered as I looked at my alarm clock. Ten-thirty A.M. Pretty fucking early.

Someone was pounding on my front door hard enough to shake the entire house.

That was another thing I missed about living at Millie and Velma's. No one had access to my front door from the street. There I was on the third floor, and people had to ring the buzzer, and I didn't have to answer it if I didn't want to. But then again, this was Storm, and he knew how deeply I slept.

I climbed out of bed and slid on my sweatpants. I glanced at the mirror over my dresser. My hair was damp and matted and standing up every which way. Great, he was going to give me shit about my hair. He really is an unbearable tease. I shook my head and walked into the living room. "All right already!" I shouted. "I'm coming!"

I unlocked the door and opened it a bit. It wasn't Storm. Instead, a short, round little woman was standing there glaring at me. I sighed and opened the door a little further. "Yes?"

"Where is he?" She began tapping her foot. "I know he was here last night. Where is he?"

"Who?"

She shoved the door with more force than necessary. I certainly wasn't expecting it. It smacked me right in the chest and I lost my balance, stumbling back a few steps while trying to regain my equilibrium, without any luck. I fell flat on my ass with a heavy thud and slid a few feet back. A jolt of pain shot up from my tailbone, and stars swam in front of my watering eyes. I shook my head, waiting for the pain to go away. I heard the door bang into the opposing wall and the whole house shook again. Vaguely I became aware that she had come inside and shut the door. She started walking past me. I reached out and grabbed her leg, tripping her. She went sprawling with another thud that shook the house. I heard something fall off David's wall next door and the sound of glass shattering. Great. He was going to be pissed.

"Ouch!"

I got to my feet, seriously pissed off. "Give me one good reason not to call the cops, bitch." I picked up my phone, finger poised to start dialing.

She got to her feet, rubbing her left hip. She was only about five feet tall, give or take an inch. She was wearing a pair of jeans a size or two too small for her stocky frame, a gray sweatshirt with blotchy stains, and a pair of dirty white tennis shoes on feet that were way too small for the rest of her body. The only way to describe her figure was round. Everything was round and exaggerated. Massive breasts, wide and full hips, and a bit of a round belly in between. A gold cross hung on the tented cotton cloth over her breasts. Her hair was a tangle of graying brown curls that looked like a perm gone bad. Her face was also round, with small gray eyes above full cheeks, and a pointy little chin that her neck seemed to grow out of. Her lips were a tight compressed line. She was wearing massive fake eyelashes, blue eye shadow, and her eyes were heavily outlined with thick black lines in a failed attempt to make them look bigger. Way too much makeup. In some places the makeup had caked into the lines on her face. She was seriously in need of a makeover. She'd make some department store counter beauty technician a fortune.

To my horror, she started to cry, watery tears stained black by the eyeliner. "I know he's here! How could he do this to me? Two nights in a row I've stayed up all night worried to death about him and he can't even give me a call to let me know he's alive? This is the thanks I get for all the sacrifices I've made for him?" The tears left trails of black on her cheeks.

Aw, hell. I handed her a box of tissues. "Who are you looking for?"

She blotted her face with a tissue and then blew her nose. "You know damned well who I'm looking for, you degenerate! Bryce Bell. I'm his mother." She was making an even bigger mess of her face with the tissues.

His mother? I thought. Poor Bryce. "Have a seat." I gestured to the sofa and she plopped down onto it, still blubbering and wiping at her face. "Bryce isn't here, Mrs. Bell."

"Then where is he?" She glared at me. "Isn't it bad enough that he stays out all night two nights in a row? No, that's not enough for him. Do you know what it's like to get woken up by the police at two o'clock in the morning? And they were looking for *him*! My son! A murder suspect! It's all too much, too much to be borne!"

"Why did you come looking for him here?" I watched as she pulled a compact out of her purse. She started wailing again when she got a good look at her face. I winced. Thank the Goddess she hadn't shown up yesterday when I was hungover. Then I would have had to kill her. After a few seconds she got herself under control again.

"Two nights in a row he's come here," she sneered. She started looking around the room. "And don't think I don't know what he's been up to with you, either." She looked up at the ceiling. "Why me, Lord? What did I ever do to deserve this?"

"How do you know he's been here?"

"I've been having him followed, if you must know, degenerate." She smiled at me. It wasn't a pleasant expression. I think I liked her better when she was crying. "I know he's been keeping things from me—his own mother! After all the sacrifices I've made for him! This is the thanks I get!" She pounded her ample bosom, a soggy blackened tissue in her hand. "All the years I've done without to pay for his training, to make sure he had the best, so he could be the best—and he wants to throw it all away so he can be a cocksucker?" She glared at me. "I won't have it. If I have to send him to one of those ex-gay places, I will. I will not have this, I tell you, I won't. He could be an Olympic champion. He could be a world champion. But they won't give it to him if they even *suspect* he's a faggot. I've spent hundreds of thousands of dollars on him, his training, moved all over the country to make sure he has the best coaches and choreographers, so he could be the best there ever was, a legend, and this is what I get in return! Disobedience! Sleeping with other men! And now a murder suspect! Do you have any idea what this scandal will do to his career? And as if that's not enough he's avoiding me! His own mother!"

I think I would have run away to the farthest corner of the globe, skating be damned, if I was Bryce. She was making my skin crawl. Again, I sent a prayer of thanks to the Goddess for blessing me with my parents. Yeah, sure, they named me Milton Bradley, but you couldn't ask for better parents. I didn't even begin to know what to say to this woman. What I really wanted to do was grab her by the shoulders and start shaking some sense into her. As satisfying as that would be for me, though, it probably wouldn't make a bit of difference to this homophobic bitch. I certainly wasn't going to tell her a damned thing.

"I knew no good would come from his looking for his birth mother," she went on. "I told him and I told him, she didn't want you, why do you think she gave you up? She was probably a prostitute or some drug addict, but would he listen to me? Oh, no, not Bryce! He wants to find his birth mother, he's going to find her and everyone else can go to hell! I mean, his coach thought it might make a nice little human-interest story, but he's my son, she gave him up, didn't she? I'm the one who's fed him and clothed him and paid for his training and sacrificed everything so he could be a champion—"

"Bryce was adopted?" Well, that explained it a little bit. I couldn't imagine this woman actually giving birth.

"And what a sweet little boy he was too." She closed her eyes and sighed. "The cutest little five-year-old you ever saw! Back then, he was so eager to please, he would do anything I asked, and always so polite. What did I ever do that was so wrong, so awful? What did I ever do to deserve such treatment? All I'm guilty of is loving him!" She started wailing again.

I could think of many things, but kept my mouth shut. The most important thing was to get this crazy bitch out of my house as quickly as possible. "He isn't here, Mrs. Bell."

"You're lying to me!" she screeched. "You don't care about him, he's just another innocent young man you're trying to convert, and I won't have it!"

I fought to control my temper, sending a prayer to the Goddess to give me the strength. "Look, if it'll get you out of here, you can look through the whole house."

She glared at me. "Oh, you've distracted me long enough for him to get out the back, haven't you? That was your plan all along, you degenerate."

That was it. "Okay, you miserable bitch, you've insulted me in my house for the last time. Get your fat ass out of here or I'm calling the police." I picked up the phone.

"All right, I'm going." She stood up. "You tell him to call his mother when he comes back." She sneered. "If you haven't corrupted him already." She stormed over to the front door. "And you stay away from my son!"

She slammed the door behind her.

What a monster, I thought as I walked into the kitchen and made coffee. Poor Bryce. I decided the next time I saw my mother, she was getting a big hug and a kiss.

I was sixteen when I told my parents I was gay. Storm was already in law school and Rain was off at college. I wasn't nervous about it; I was pretty sure Mom and Dad would be really cool. We'd been to dinner at the Diderots. My Papa Diderot kept pestering and teasing me about girlfriends all through dinner as he swilled down Wild Turkey and speared deep fried shrimp with a fork. He wouldn't let up, even though I squirmed and blushed and begged him to stop. As usual, Maman Diderot just sat there and smiled tolerantly as she drank glass after glass of red wine. Finally, Mom had yelled at him to leave me alone. He reddened and downed another glass of liquor.

The rest of the meal had been eaten in silence. As soon as the dessert plates were cleared, Dad excused us and we escaped out to the car.

Mom lit a joint as they backed out of the driveway. "Scotty, I'm sorry about that. He's never known when to quit."

"Your social life is no one's business." Dad said.

"I don't know why, just because you're a teenager, he thinks you aren't entitled to your privacy."

"I don't have any girlfriends," I said, steeling my nerve.

"That's fine, Scotty. You don't have to date until you're ready," Dad said.

"When I do date, it won't be girls," I said very quietly.

"What did you say?" Mom turned in the seat and looked back at me.

"Nothing." I looked out the window. I was already sorry I'd said anything. Now I'd just pretend I hadn't said anything.

"He said when he started dating it wouldn't be girls," Dad said.

"Are you gay, Scotty?" Mom asked.

"Yes."

Mom climbed over the seat, right there on St. Charles Avenue, and gave me a huge hug. "Scotty, oh, Scotty, I'm so proud of you!"

"You are?"

"Me too, son." Dad smiled at me in the rearview mirror. "The way our horrible society is set up, completely dominated by the white patriarchy which tries to convince everyone who doesn't fit into the little molds they try to force everyone into, being different isn't easy."

"Exactly." Mom puffed madly on the joint. "You've been socialized to feel being gay is bad. It's not bad, Scotty, it's who you are."

"I don't think I'm bad," I said.

"You aren't bad, Scotty." She hugged me again. "You're good, wonderful in fact, and your father and I both love you and are proud of you." She handed the joint back over the seat to Dad. "Now, are you having sex yet?"

"MOM!!!"

"Sex is nothing to be ashamed of, Scotty. I've always taught you that," Mom said. "But these are dangerous times. . . ." and she went on to explain to me the benefits of safe sex the rest of the way home. Once we got home, she called every single member of our family and told them I was gay, and if they had a problem with it, they'd have to answer to her. The very next day she and Dad joined P-FLAG and became AIDS activists. The day after that, when I got home from school there was a rainbow flag hanging in front of the Devil's Weed.

The memory made my eyes fill with tears. The Goddess had blessed me as surely as she had cursed poor Bryce with that monstrous woman.

Yeah, Mom was definitely getting a big hug and kiss when I saw her next.

That horrible woman actually called Bryce a *cocksucker!* What kind of mother could say such a thing about their child, adopted or not?

And she wondered what she was doing wrong?

No wonder Bryce was looking for his birth mother. If that witch had adopted me, I'd be looking for my birth family too, and running away would have definitely been taken under consideration. I wondered if he'd had any luck finding his mother.

I poured myself a cup of coffee and ignored the blinking light on the phone. The messages could wait. I wasn't expecting any calls anyway. It was weird that he'd been adopted at five, though. I always thought kids were only adopted as babies. Everyone I know who was adopted was a baby when it happened. The rule was prospective adoptive parents rarely, if ever, want the older kids. I couldn't imagine any adoption agency letting that woman have a child. Poor Bryce. Had he been orphaned and had no relatives who could have taken him fourteen years ago?

Fourteen years ago.

Rob Parrish had been murdered fourteen years ago.

Survived by a wife and a five-year-old son.

Nah, it couldn't be.

Could it?

CHAPTER EIGHT

Seven of Pentacles

growth through effort and hard work

I turned on my computer, and while I waited for the Internet connection to dial up, there was another knock on my front door. *What had the monster mother from hell forgotten?* I thought as I pushed my chair back. I'd been pretty polite, considering the fact she'd pushed her way into my apartment and then proceeded to act like gays were the result of some freakish, Nazi-planned genetic experiment. Maybe I was being a little oversensitive, but I don't appreciate it when people come into my house and insult me. I stormed over to the door, saying "What do you want now, *bitch*?" as I swung it open to look into David's smiling face.

He held up a plate almost completely covered with a piece of steaming gooey lasagna. It looked really good. "Um, I wondered if you wanted some lasagna? I just made it." He put his free hand on his hip and wiggled his head from side to side. "Bitch."

I took the plate from him. "Sorry about that. I thought you were someone else."

"Well, I would certainly hope so." He followed me into the kitchen. "What was all that thumping going on earlier? I thought the house was gonna fall apart. I almost lost one of my prints. Were you having some rough sex or something?"

"No." I shook my head. "I wish it had been that. Which print?"

"Well, Trent."

"Oh, no!" Trent was a weekend bartender who sold real estate during the week. He was also gorgeous, with bright blue eyes and curly blond hair and a body that belonged in a Greek temple with incense burning in front of it. He'd posed for a Mardi Gras poster several years ago wearing nothing but beads and a smile. David had managed to get hold of one of the prints, and had it framed and mounted. It was the centerpiece of his living room. "Was it ruined?"

"The glass shattered and scratched it up." He shrugged. "I might be able to get it fixed."

"Sorry about that, too." I got a glass of milk out of the refrigerator and handed him a Pepsi. He was always up for a Pepsi. "You wouldn't believe the night I had."

"I have a feeling." He winked at me. "Let me guess—it has something to do with the murder at the Royal Aquitaine last night." He popped open the can and took a big drink. "When I saw that in the paper this morning, I thought to myself—Scotty went there last night, someone was killed there last night. Now, if it were anyone else—anyone, say, who lives a *normal* life—I would never, ever, think to connect the two. But when it's you . . ." he toasted me with his can before taking another drink.

"Yeah, well." I cut off a piece of lasagna with my fork and popped it into my mouth, and moaned with pleasure. David will be the first to tell you he's not a great cook. But what he does know how to make he does very well. "When I got to Bryce's room last night there was no one in it but a guy with a knife in his chest."

He opened his eyes wide, slapped his open hand over his face so that his splayed fingers spread over his wide open mouth. "*Gasp.*" He dropped his hand and returned his eyes to normal. "I swear, Scotty, sometimes I think I shouldn't hang around with you. You're like the angel of death or something. You know, like how if Jessica Fletcher was a relative I would never let her come visit because it meant I was going to get killed or be a murder suspect, and who needs that kind of drama?"

I just glared at him. "I should be so lucky."

He laughed. "Okay, okay, I'm sorry, but Jesus, Scotty—your life is so fucking intense." He took a joint out of his shirt pocket and lit it. Taking a deep breath, he held the smoke in till his eyes began to water and he exhaled a huge graceful plume of smoke. "Whoa. Man. That sucks, Scotty. So what was up?"

I filled him in on as much as I thought I could. I mean, it was an open police investigation, so maybe I shouldn't have told him anything. Then again, his testimony would be stricken as hearsay, right? I'm not a lawyer's brother for nothing, after all. I left out the newspaper clipping, and Bryce's relationship with Ace Martinelli. David could be trusted not to tell anyone, but it's always better to be safe than sorry.

"You aren't telling me everything." He took another hit. "Because some of it doesn't make sense."

"Yeah, well." I shrugged. "Some of it doesn't make sense to me either. I can't picture Bryce killing anyone."

"I can't imagine ever having to tell someone that the guy I slept with two nights ago couldn't have killed someone. God, your life." He started laughing. "Well, at least Bryce is in Storm's hands now. You're pretty much out of it." He looked at me. "You are, aren't you?"

"I don't know." I mopped up the remaining sauce with a piece of bread. "I mean, I *am* almost a licensed private eye now. Don't I have some kind of moral obligation to keep looking into it? Isn't there some kind of code or something?"

"Did you have to take some kind of detective oath?" He kept grinning. *"I shall not rest till every criminal is behind bars,* or something like that?"

"It does sound stupid when you say it like that." I shrugged. "Yeah, I guess Storm and the police can handle it from now on."

I washed out the plate, dried it, and handed it back to him. He stubbed the joint out. "Want me to leave this for you for later?"

I shook my head. "I'm supposed to have dinner at Mom and Dad's tonight. They'll get me stoned."

"Well, I've got some stuff to do." He stood up and stretched. "You need anything from Home Depot?"

I laughed. "Yeah, right."

After he left, I sat down at the computer and checked my e-mail. Another one from Frank. No, not in the mood to deal with that, I decided, and didn't read it. I then did a search on the Internet for Rod Parrish.

I got several hits. I started clicking on links that looked like they could be the same guy as in the newspaper clipping. The first was the clipping I'd given to Venus, the initial report of his murder. The next was a follow-up story to the first.

Still No Clues in Fireman's Murder

Police still have no leads in the recent murder of Rod Parrish, an Orleans Parish firefighter whose body was found several days ago. Parrish's body was found in his home, tied up and shot, execution- style, in the head.

"We've found no indications that this crime was Mob-related," said investigating officer Sergeant Lee Young. "Parrish apparently had no ties to organized crime. Burglary was apparently the motivation behind the crime. We think Parrish came home unexpectedly and caught the burglar, or burglars, in his home."

Parrish was born and raised in Algiers. He went to work for the Orleans Parish Fire Department at age nineteen, and shortly thereafter married his high school sweetheart, Juliet Pryor.

"Rod Parrish was a fine fireman, and a great friend," according to coworker and friend John Quinn. "This is truly a tragedy and a great loss, not only for those who knew him, but for the fire department as well."

Police ask that anyone with any information contact
Sergeant Young.

A memorial service will be held at Holy Trinity Church in
Algiers at 1 P.M. on Saturday, May 22. In lieu of flowers, the
family asks that donations be made to the Firemen's Survivors
Scholarship Fund.

The next link led to a wedding notice.

There was a photo with the notice but it was so small I could
only identify who was whom by the clothes. I downloaded it and
then tried to enlarge it, so I could get a look at the faces. Unfortunately, the resolution was so poor that increasing the size made it
harder to recognize anything except large white, black, and gray
dots. With a sigh, I returned it to normal size. It was still too hard
to tell what Rod Parrish and his young bride, Juliet Pryor, looked
like clearly. I read the text.

Pryor-Parrish

Mr. and Mrs. William Pryor of Algiers are pleased to an-
nounce the wedding of their daughter, Juliet Marie Pryor, 18,
to Rodney Alan Parrish, 19, also of Algiers. The ceremony took
place at Holy Trinity Church on April 10.

The groom is the son of John and Harriet Parrish, and is
currently going through training to be an Orleans Parish firefighter. He is a graduate of St. Thomas More High School. The
bride is a recent graduate of Holy Trinity.

The maid of honor was the bride's sister, Gwendolyn
Anne Pryor, and the best man was John Quinn, also of Algiers.

The couple will honeymoon in Fort Walton Beach,
Florida.

I printed the piece out. John Quinn was the best man and a coworker. Hmmm.

The other links that came up for Rod Parrish were definitely not my guy. One was a soccer coach in southern California, the other a chef in Albuquerque who apparently wrote a cooking column.

I then went to a private search engine for investigators, and looked up Juliet Pryor Parrish, going back fifteen years. All I found was a last known address in Algiers.

Strange.

I leaned back in my chair. Still not much. So, why was that woman carrying around that clipping? Just on the off chance something might happen, I closed my eyes and focused on her. Nothing came through. Ah, well. It almost never works. It did once, and so I still give it a try every now and then. I sighed and went back into the living room, sat down on the floor, and shuffled the cards. I set them down and lit both white candles. I shuffled the cards one more time, sent a message to the Goddess mentally, and began to lay them out.

Things are not as they appear.
A deceitful young man, be careful what you believe.
An older woman who is fearful of the future.
Destruction of property, lives left in ruins.

Yeah, that was helpful. I swept the cards up again and put them aside, licking my fingers to extinguish the candles. I plopped down on the couch. *A deceitful young man?* Bryce?

Be careful what I believe.

There was another knock on the door.

"Hell's bells," I muttered to myself. I could go days without having a single knock on my door, but apparently today I was living in Grand Central Station. I looked through the blinds to see my brother Storm grinning back at me. I opened the door. "How'd things go?"

Storm is a big guy. He's five years older than me, with the same curly blondish hair, but he's also about five inches taller than me as well. He'd been a jock in high school, lettering in football and baseball, but once he got to college that was it for exercise. He enjoys his food, so his belly has been steadily growing, just as his hairline has been gradually receding. "Pretty good, considering." He walked in and plopped down into my reclining chair. "It doesn't hurt that he's a celebrity. It was his room, so it's easy enough to explain his fingerprints being all over the room. There weren't any fingerprints on the knife—which, incidentally, came from the hotel restaurant—but any idiot nowadays knows to wipe the handle clean. He had no idea how or why Ace Martinelli was in his room, or how you got his room key. The police still haven't found the usher who brought it to you." He frowned. "The main problem with his story is that he has no real alibi—he claims he went back to his room after the medal ceremony and changed, then went for a walk, looking for you, so from about eleven o'clock to three in the morning is unaccounted for."

"He probably was in a bar."

"Well, he wouldn't tell me any specifics either." Storm rubbed his eyes. "I figured he was out barhopping, but doesn't want to admit it since he's not of legal age. Do you know if he'd been drinking?"

"Not that I could tell." I leaned back on the couch, thinking. If he'd been looking for me, I hadn't been that hard to find. I'd been at the Pub. But he'd met me at the Brass Rail—maybe he'd gone back there hoping I'd show up there? If I'd been looking for someone in the bars, I'd have gone around to all of them. But then he wasn't from here, and I shouldn't take it for granted that he knew where all the bars were. "So they didn't arrest him?"

"No, they let him go, but he's been advised not to leave town. I took him back to the hotel to pack up his stuff and took him home with me. I personally guaranteed he wouldn't leave town."

"How does Marguerite feel about that?" Marguerite was his wife. I like her. She has a rather droll sense of humor. She needs it to survive in our family.

"Are you kidding?" He rolled his eyes. "She's thrilled to death to have him staying there—a real celebrity! She wants to throw some dinner parties to show him off." Marguerite, like my sister Rain, is the perfect Uptown wife. Something unexpected drops into her lap, and she has one tried and true response: throw a dinner party! Catered, preferably, with waitstaff and an excellent wine list. Maybe even valet parking. And an Olympic hopeful was definitely status-raising material. Not quite on the same level as a movie star, but pretty up there. "And Rain was on her way over to have him sign her program from last night."

"Um, does Rain know about this—why he's staying there?"

"And your involvement in it all?" He grinned at me. " 'Fraid so, my queen."

"Have you met his mother yet?" I briefly explained my experience with the delightful Mrs. Bell.

Storm frowned. "No. That's odd. He didn't say a word to me about her."

"That's very odd." I shrugged. "But if I were him, she'd be the last thing on my mind too. All she'd do was make a bad situation worse. What a monster." I shuddered.

"We're pretty lucky with our mom, huh?" Storm grinned at me. "So, you wanna work on this case?"

"Well . . ." My status as a private eye was still fairly shaky. Sure, I'd passed my course, but I still didn't have a sponsor. According to the state, I couldn't accept work as an investigator. The last thing I needed was to have the state pull my license before I even became official.

"I'll just pay you as a research assistant, how about that?" He winked.

I grinned. "Cool. Now that I'm on the payroll, am I covered by attorney-client privilege?"

"Yes."

I walked over to my desk and got the printouts about Rod Parrish. "Last night when I was on my way to Bryce's room, getting out of the elevator I bumped into a woman who was in rather a hurry. She dropped her purse, and I helped her pick every-thing up—but she forgot this." I indicated the first article about the murder. "She'd clipped it out of the paper when it originally ran. Venus has the original."

Storm read the clipping. "Interesting." He narrowed his eyes. "And the police know about this?"

"Yes."

His face lit up. "Great! Excellent! We have a mysterious woman on the floor right around the time the murder took place." I could practically see the legal gears in his mind shifting. "What's this other stuff?"

"More about this Rod Parrish guy. I thought it might be a good idea to see if I could find out more about him."

"Good thinking, my queen."

I shrugged. "I just thought it was weird she was carrying a clipping about an old unsolved murder in a hotel where someone had just been killed."

"Do you think they could be related?" He grinned. "And I mean something concrete—not something you've sensed, my queen."

I resisted the urge to punch him. "Well, Mrs. Bell let it drop this morning that Bryce was adopted. And when I searched the Internet for info on this Rod Parrish and his family—get this: his wife and son completely disappeared after the murder. No trace of them anywhere. I mean, I was able to get her social security number, but there is no sign of anyone using that number any-where since then. And Bryce is nineteen—he would have been five when Rod Parrish was murdered. Rod Parrish had a five-year-old son." I closed my eyes. What were her exact words? Oh, yeah. "And Mrs. Bell said, 'I knew no good would come of his looking for his birth mother.'" I crossed my arms.

"More here than meets the eye, eh, my queen?" Storm grinned. "Okay, keep looking for these missing Parrishes. But most impor-tantly, I want you to dig up everything you possibly can on Ace

Martinelli. Let me know as soon as you find out anything." He stood up. "I don't think Bryce is being completely honest—with me or the police, and that worries me." The front door shut behind him.

I walked back over to the computer just as my phone rang. I looked at the caller ID and answered it. "Hey Mom. What's up?"

"Honey, would you mind coming by a little earlier than we'd planned for dinner?" Her voice sounded odd.

"Well, no, of course not. Is everything okay?"

"I've got a surprise for you. When can you be here?"

"Just need to shower—probably about half hour, forty-five minutes."

"Great. See ya then." She hung up the phone.

Now what was that all about? I wondered as I walked to the bathroom.

With my parents, it could be anything.

CHAPTER NINE

Five of Cups, Reversed

return of an old acquaintance

The only constant with New Orleans weather is change.

By the time I got out of the shower, the sun had disappeared. A strong wind was blowing, rattling the house and sneaking in through cracks in the walls. The temperature felt like it'd dropped about fifteen degrees. The hardwood floors were cold to the bottoms of my feet before I could jump on my bathroom rug. I shivered as I toweled myself dry before dashing into the bedroom to get dressed. I put on a pair of jeans and an old sweatshirt and grabbed my umbrella.

It was just starting to rain when I walked out the front door. The sky was gray and filled with dark clouds. The wind was getting colder and seemed to go right through my clothes to the skin. I shivered and briefly debated going back inside for my jacket, but figured I wouldn't be out in it long enough for it to matter. Mom and Dad live about six blocks away so I could probably tough it out. I did open my umbrella—no sense in getting soaked if it turned into a downpour. A couple of fat drops of rain splatted on the umbrella as I stepped off the porch and walked through the gate.

I was crossing Esplanade Avenue into the Quarter when lightning flashed close enough by to make all the hair on my body stand up. It was followed immediately by a clap of thunder so loud every car alarm in the immediate area began wailing and shrieking. I stood there on the neutral ground, waiting for a few cars to go by before making the dash across. I'd just reached the sidewalk on the Quarter side when the deluge began.

One of the sad facts about New Orleans rain is umbrellas are almost completely useless against it. The most you can really hope for is to keep your hair and head dry. I clung to mine anyway as the wind tried to rip it out of my hands. Water was pouring off every side of it, soaking my legs. The slanted roofs were creating a waterfall effect, with the rain cascading in sheets off onto the sidewalk. The street gutters were filling with water, abandoned go-cups and cigarette butts and beer cans swirling and drifting. New Orleans is below sea level, which is problematic when we get a lot of rain really fast. The sewers fill very fast, and the water has nowhere to go. Low-lying areas turn into lakes, the streets look more like shallow rivers, and the gutters overflow onto the sidewalk. We have an excellent pumping system, but it takes a while for it to really kick into high gear. Cars drove by down Bourbon Street with their lights on to fight the sudden gloom. The balconies that hang over the sidewalks offer a brief, welcome shelter from the onslaught of water, but the shelter is deceptive. Many of the balconies leak, and the water draining off their roofs create an almost solid wall of water to pass through. Few umbrellas are up for the challenge, and mine apparently has several leaks. I tried to dash from balcony to balcony as I made my way through the Quarter. Crossing the streets resulted in splashing water up and soaking my socks, shoes, and pant legs. The wind succeeded in blowing the falling raindrops under my umbrella into my face. I was completely soaked and shivering by the time I made it to Dumaine Street.

Mom and Dad own a combination tobacco/coffee shop on the corner of Royal and Dumaine Streets, the Devil's Weed. Mom inherited the property from her maternal grandmother, who apparently was a lot like her. Family legend held that Victoire Sonnier Diderot had been a bohemian in every sense—an opium-smoking, gin-guzzling, world-traveling patroness of the arts before she settled down and married. The stories told about her reminded me of *Auntie Mame,* and I always regretted not knowing her. She died before I was born. We had all grown up living above the shop, sometimes helping out behind the counter when we weren't in school. As a result, I know a lot more about fine cigars and pipe tobacco than anyone needs to.

The bars on Bourbon Street were already starting to fill for Sunday afternoon's trash-disco tea dances. After having dinner, I'd probably stop in and look for David. We both love Sunday tea dance. It's fun listening to old music, and some of the music they play encourages audience participation. For example, they always show a video set to Abba's "Mamma Mia" that is all clips from *Mommie Dearest,* with the music occasionally stopping for classic scenes from the movie. Sure, it's probably in poor taste, but it's kind of fun watching Faye Dunaway as Joan Crawford slugging little Christina over and over again, or saying "I will always beat you, beat you, beat you, beat you." All the boys in the bars say the lines along with the video. David and I know the movie by heart. When they play "Love Is In The Air," the bartenders and staff pass out handfuls of napkins, and every time the line "love is in the air" is sung, everyone tosses their napkins into the air.

So much for the rain forest.

I used my key to unlock the big wooden gate behind the Devil's Weed and climbed the slanted stone stairs to the back door to Mom and Dad's apartment, which opens into the kitchen. The stairs are covered, but they were still wet and slippery. I could smell something strange cooking. Mom and Dad are strict vegetarians who don't eat anything that has a face. I understand the mentality—growing up I'd been shown more videos of the inhumane conditions food animals are raised under than I could remember—but with all due respect, I am a carnivore. There's nothing like a burger every once in a while—especially after you've had your fill of tofu lasagna, tofu casserole, or any of the million and one ways Mom knows how to make tofu. I could hear voices coming from the living room, and the ever-present odor of marijuana in the air. Mom and Dad are lifelong hemp activists, and always have bags of the best stuff available lying around.

"Mom? Dad?" I called as I shut my umbrella and put it in the basket next to the door.

"We're in the living room, dear."

I walked through the kitchen and stopped dead in my tracks.

"Hey, Scotty." Colin stood up with a shy smile on his face.

So, it *had* been him at the Royal Aquitaine last night, I thought to myself, standing there unable to move.

He just stood there staring at me.

I'd forgotten, really, how beautiful he was.

Colin is about an inch or so shorter than me, but outweighs me by about thirty pounds of solid, hard muscle. He has short black hair, darkly tanned olive skin, green eyes, and the fullest, thickest red lips you can imagine. He was wearing a tight black short-sleeved shirt that hugged his muscles like—well, like I wanted to, and a pair of tight black jeans that clung to the muscles in his thick, powerful legs like sausage skin. He just stood there, shifting his weight from foot to foot, licking his lips, waiting for me to do or say something.

"Scotty?" my mother said. Mom is in her early fifties, and looks great for someone who spends most of her waking time smoking pot. She wears her dark hair long and pulled back into a ponytail. The dark hair is now streaked with gray, which she refuses to do anything about. Don't get her started on society's ageist, sexist attitudes toward women getting older. She swears smoking pot keeps her face wrinkle-free. I look a lot like her, everyone thinks so, and I hope I still look as good at her age as she does. She is slight of build, about three inches shorter than me. She always wears worn-out jeans, and today she had her I'm Proud of

My Gay Son T-shirt on. She never wears a bra, which she claims is a torture device made by men to force women to conform to a certain standard of beauty. "Aren't you going to say something?" Her tone clearly said, *I raised you better than this.*

"I—" I turned back to Colin, and allowed my face to break into a smile. "It's just such a big surprise, I don't know what to say."

Colin walked over to me and threw his arms around me in a backbreaking hug, lifting me off the floor and kissing my neck. He felt warm, solid, good. After a few seconds I returned the hug and kissed him back. "Sorry I'm wet," I said.

"I don't care," he whispered into my ear, giving it a nuzzle.

"Let me get you a towel, and you should change out of those wet clothes," Mom said. "I think you still have some clothes in your room." She walked out and came back with a fluffy white towel. I can never get my towels to smell as good as Mom's do. I don't know how she does it.

I started rubbing it over my head, still not saying anything.

"Honey, can you help me in the kitchen?" Mom said.

"Sure, dear." Dad got up off the couch and followed her out of the room.

I was vaguely aware of them leaving the room, and then Colin hugged me again. "Are you really glad to see me?" he whispered, his big green eyes round.

"You know I am." I shook my head. "I just never thought I'd see you again."

"I said in my letter that I'd come back someday." He lifted one of my hands and kissed it.

"Yeah, well, like I believed that." I shrugged. "I don't even know what to call you. Colin? Or was it Bill? I don't remember."

He smiled at me and pulled me over to the couch. I sat down next to him. "I like Colin, actually. I prefer that."

He leaned over and kissed me on the lips. I allowed myself to kiss him back, my arms going around his neck as he gently pushed me down onto my back. "Um, my parents are in the next room."

He grinned down at me. "Well, you want to go back to your place?"

"Are you staying at the Royal Aquitaine?"

His eyebrows knit together. "Well, no, I'm actually staying at a B and B on Esplanade Avenue—the Esplanade Arms. Why?"

"Were you in the Royal Aquitaine last night?"

"What's this about?" He sat up and crossed his arms. "Aren't you glad to see me?" His lower lip jutted out into a pout. It looked sexy. I wanted to bite it, suck on it, make him quiver.

"Well, yeah, but—"

"Then why all these questions? What's going on?"

I was starting to get mad. "Well, what did *you* think? That all you had to do was suddenly show up and I'd drop my pants?"

"I was kinda hoping."

I shook my head. "C'mon, Colin. You breezed into my life for a couple of days, took off without even saying good-bye, sent me a letter—which was nice, but not enough, and now you show up out of the blue. How easy do you think I am?" Ordinarily, that's not a question I like to throw out there. Okay, I admit it—I *am* pretty easy. But he doesn't know that, and I kind of resented the assumption.

"Look, Scotty, I'm sorry." His face flushed. "I explained in the letter why I had to get away the way I did. Meeting you has made me think about the life I've been leading—and I'm tired of it. I want to give it up. I want to settle down someplace, and why not New Orleans? I thought maybe we could give it a shot." He shrugged. "I guess I was wrong."

My jaw dropped. First Frank, now Colin. I've never doubted that I was easy on the eyes; being a go-go boy, dancing on bars and getting fondled and groped for tips kind of makes that obvious. And I've always known that I am fairly irresistible. I don't think it's because I'm pretty or because I have this great body or anything. I think I just have this undefinable aura or something that draws men to me—which is great. I rarely, if ever, have a problem getting laid. But this boyfriend thing was getting totally out of hand. It was bad enough that I have this thing going on with Frank, whatever the hell it was, but now to have Colin wanting to move to New Orleans and "settle down?" It wasn't just raining men, it was pouring. Undoubtedly, somewhere an old man was snoring. "I don't know what to say."

"Can we please go back to your place?" Colin asked, rubbing my inner thigh.

It was all I could do not to purr. Damn, I *am* way too easy for my own good. "Yeah, might as well. We can't really talk in front of my parents anyway."

"Or anything else." He leaned over and nibbled on my earlobe.

Damn, he was good.

We said goodbye to my parents (Mom and Dad both winked at me) and headed back out into the rain. I opened my umbrella, and Colin crammed in with me under it as we started making our way back up Royal Street. He slipped an arm around my waist. "I've really missed you."

I couldn't lie. "I've thought about you. A lot."

He smiled at me. Goddess, but he was handsome. He squeezed me. "Do you want to stop for a drink somewhere? Maybe talk a bit?"

"Nah." As much as I love the bars, it sucks when it's raining. Everyone has to squeeze inside rather than spilling out onto the sidewalk. I don't usually mind crowds, but for some reason I get claustrophobic when you don't have the option of stepping outside. All the bar balconies seem to leak as well. Besides, you don't go to bars to talk. The music is way too loud to allow any kind of conversation to take place. "My place is just a few more blocks. I live in the Marigny now."

He nodded. "I hope you don't mind me showing up at your parents'. I just didn't have any idea of where else to find you."

Well, maybe if you'd stayed in touch you would, I thought to myself, trying to work myself up into some righteous anger. He squeezed me again. How could I stay mad at him? Much as I wanted to, I couldn't.

"No, that's okay." We crossed Esplanade into the Marigny and walked the two blocks to my house. We were both soaked to the skin.

"This is nice," he said after I unlocked the door and we stepped in.

"Thanks." I walked over to the thermostat and turned on the heat. We were both shivering.

We stood there for a moment in silence, looking at each other.

"You never answered my question," I said finally. "Were you in the Royal Aquitaine Hotel last night?"

"Why do you ask?"

"Why won't you answer?"

He sighed. "Yes, I was in the Royal Aquitaine last night." He sat down on the couch. "Okay? I met a guy at the Pub who was staying there. I went back with him. I just didn't want to tell you."

I started laughing. "Did you think I was going to be upset?" It was pretty funny. "I never thought I'd see you again! Why would I think you'd be celibate?"

He shrugged. "Well, I didn't know how you were going to react. Who knows? You might get pissed because I was in New Orleans and tricked before looking you up."

I sat down on the couch next to him. He draped a leg over mine. When he put it that way, I was kind of annoyed. "Why didn't you look me up right away?"

He sighed. "See? I was right—you are pissed." He took my right hand in his left. "Look, Scotty, I do want to give up the life I'm leading. I want to settle somewhere, make a home, not be such a vagabond travelling all over the place working. I'm here on a job, okay? And I've decided it's my last one. Once I finish this, it's all over."

"You're here to steal something?" I pulled my hand away. "And you want to settle here? Are you crazy? I mean, what if you get caught?"

"I'm very good at what I do." He grabbed my hand again. "I've never been caught—and I won't get caught this time, either."

"There's always a first time—and besides, the Feds and the police know about you anyway. Remember? During Decadence? Frank recognized you."

"Frank?" He frowned. "That FBI agent we dealt with? You're on a first name basis with him?"

"I've sort of been seeing him."

He started laughing. "Christ, Scotty. You're sleeping with that Fed? How on earth"—he shook his head—"never mind, I don't think I want to know."

"I'm pretty irresistible, remember?" I grinned at him. "It just happened—that same weekend after you vanished."

"He was pretty hot," he mused. "If you like that type."

"Who doesn't like that type?" I squeezed his hand. "It's good to see you again."

"Is it?" He looked deep into my eyes. Damn, he was hot.

"Of course." He put his arm around my shoulders and pulled me into him. I looked into his eyes, and we kissed. Nothing major, just a gentle little application of lips on lips. It was sweet and tender, not passionate. I pulled back. "So, this guy you were with at the Royal Aquitaine last night—what floor was he on?"

"You aren't jealous, are you?" He looked at me, his thick eyebrows knit together into a single line across his forehead. "I didn't think you were the jealous type."

"I'm not." I shook my head. "Colin, a man was murdered in the Royal Aquitaine last night."

His jaw dropped. "Oh, man—not again!"

"I know." I sighed. "It's a long story, but I wound up finding the body—right after I saw you getting into an elevator."

"You don't think I had something to do with it, do you?" He stared at me. "You do, don't you? Oh, Scotty."

"Have to ask." I shrugged. "I mean, you are a criminal, after all."

"I have never killed anyone." He made a face at me. "The guy's name was Mitchell Voight. He's from Nashville. Room number 234. On the second floor. You want any more details?" He wiggled his eyebrows at me.

"No thanks. Does the name Ace Martinelli mean anything to you?"

"No."

He was lying.

I could sense it. Obviously, Colin was an accomplished liar—one does not have a long, lucrative, successful career as an international cat burglar without being able to lie convincingly under pressure. There was no physical change in him at all—but I could sense a subtle change in his aura. He wasn't being honest. He was looking me right in the eyes, a serious expression on his face, and the words just popped into my head. *He's lying.* The name meant something to him. I wasn't sure exactly what his connection to Ace Martinelli was—the gift is never that exact—but there was definitely something going on there.

But there was also no sense that he killed him, thank the Goddess.

I don't think I could handle having a killer in my living room.

Not again, at any rate.

Especially one who was running his hand up and down my thigh.

I looked down at his hand, then back at his face. He smiled.

Ah, what the hell, I thought. I stood up, took him by the hand, and led him back to the bedroom. "We should probably get out of these wet clothes before we catch cold."

He grinned back at me as he started to unbutton his shirt. "Exactly what I was thinking."

CHAPTER TEN

The Hermit, Reversed

refusal to learn and experience new things

I woke up alone around seven in the morning.

He was gone.

Again.

Big surprise, right?

We'd fallen asleep in each other's arms, which felt incredibly comfortable. There really is something to the whole cuddling thing—feeling the warmth of the other person's body against yours, limbs entwined, the steady rhythm of their heartbeat and breathing lulling you into a deep, warm sleep. I sleep pretty deeply, but I still wake up when the person sharing the bed space with me gets up. Of course, as opposed to the law-abiding gay men who usually share my bed, Colin was a cat burglar. He has lots of experience getting in and out of places without disturbing anyone. Not a particularly cheery thought to wake up to, but true nevertheless.

I got out of the bed and walked naked into the kitchen to start my morning coffee ritual. There was a note on the coffee-maker.

Scotty—

Sorry I had to run, but I didn't want to wake you. It was nice to watch you sleeping.

I was serious about everything I said last night. I really want to see if we could make it work.

I'll give you a call later today—maybe we could have dinner tonight?

Love,
Colin

I turned the coffeemaker on. Goddess. What was with the boyfriends these days? They were coming out of the woodwork. That's why tricking is so much easier—no later complications to worry about. Yeah, sure, every once in a while you hook up with a guy who decides he's "in love" with you, but that's easy enough to handle. The phone calls and messages last for a week or so, until he goes out again and hooks up with someone else, and that's that. And if someone has hard feelings, well, eventually they get over it.

Goddess, it's just *sex* after all.

I turned on my computer while the coffee brewed and logged on to the Internet. I checked my e-mail. Nestled in amongst the offers to take over my debt, cheap Viagra, and sorority shower webcams, was yet another e-mail from Frank.

Terrific. In my mind I heard the words, *I will not be ignored, Scotty.*

With a sigh I clicked on it, and it opened.

My sweet love:

I'm starting to get a little concerned. I've called a couple of times and only get your voicemail, and this is the third email I've sent since you left Friday afternoon, and you have yet to answer any of them. What's going on?

I realize I may be overreacting—I don't have a lot of experience with this relationship business—but I had such a great time with you here last week. It broke my heart to take you to the airport Friday—I wanted you to stay so badly. I love you, Scotty, and having you here with me only convinced me how right we are for each other.

That's why I am so nervous about not hearing from you . . . did I do or say something wrong? Did I piss you off in some way? Please know that if I did, it was certainly not my intent, and please accept my apology. I love you so very much— I can't imagine life without you now, Scotty. Please let me know everything is okay.

Please.

With all my love,
Frank

Great. Just fucking great.

I was going to have to answer him sometime. But how?

I pushed back from the computer and walked into the kitchen. I poured myself a cup of coffee. I went into the bathroom and turned the shower on while I brushed my teeth. I stared at myself in the mirror. "You're an asshole," I said to the mirror.

I climbed into the shower. The water was scalding hot. I ducked my head under the showerhead. I've always, for some reason, found showers to be extremely therapeutic. I always feel better after a shower. There's something, I'm not quite sure what, about being scrubbed clean that just makes everything seem better. I stood there, letting the water wash over me.

Question: Why have you never had a serious boyfriend before?

Because I don't want to hurt anyone.

The words popped into my head out of nowhere. The Goddess again, perhaps, sending me a flash of self-awareness? She can be a bit of a bitch sometimes. Okay, process that, Scotty. You pride yourself on being enormously self-aware, so go with this thought. How could I hurt anyone? I'm a nice person. I always try to be nice. I do anything for my family and friends. All they have to do is ask.

Your family has always wanted you to find someone nice and settle down. Storm and Rain are always on the lookout for prospective boyfriends for you. Both Storm and Rain are happily married; so are your parents. So, why are you always so opposed to having a relationship? You have plenty of examples of happy couplehood to draw from.

I soaped up my torso. Interesting, I thought. I never thought I was *opposed* to having a boyfriend. I just never thought I would find one, let alone two.

I've met lots of nice guys throughout my life. I've slept with most of them, but rarely, if ever, did anyone warrant a second go-round—and those that did, called me. I never called anyone. I collected phone numbers from tricks by rote, always intending to call, but never calling. This is a pattern, easily identified. A fear of intimacy, perhaps? No, that couldn't be it. Go back to the fear of hurting someone.

Coach Phelps.

I was so startled by the thought I almost slipped in the shower as I reached for the shampoo. I hadn't thought about Coach Phelps in years.

"*I love you, Scotty,*" I could hear him saying again. It was almost like he was here in the shower with me. I could see the pain in his eyes.

Oh, sweet Goddess.

Coach Phelps had been my wrestling coach in high school. I'd always known I liked boys the way I was supposed to like girls, and I'd been small when I was a kid. Well, not that I'm a big guy now, but I was skinny and short, destined to be a ninety-eight-pound weakling getting sand kicked in my face at the beach. In junior high, when the boys really started noticing the girls and sprouting body hair and getting pimples, I was busy noticing the boys, stealing glances surreptitiously in the showers and the locker room after PE. I fantasized kissing those boys at night, alone in my bed with my underwear down around my knees while I played with myself. Some of the bigger, more macho boys somehow sensed I was different, and unerringly picked out the reason: *Scotty Bradley's a queer, a homo, a fag.* I didn't even know what "fag" meant the first time someone called me that. I just knew, from the way it was said, it wasn't something nice. They started picking on me, calling me names, knocking my books out of my hands in the halls between classes. It was horrible. The teachers had to be aware of it—how could they miss the laughs and nasty comments in class? They just pretended it didn't exist, it wasn't going on. I didn't want to tell Mom and Dad. I wanted to die. Every morning before school I got this horrible knot in my stomach. Every day I prayed to the Goddess to destroy the school, to do something, to somehow make it all stop. But my prayers went unanswered. I had to do something myself. No help was going to come from the teachers, from the Goddess, from anyone.

Storm came to my rescue, like he always seemed to when I was a kid. One day he picked me up at school. As I was getting into the car, one of the Neanderthals, a boy named Phil Connors, yelled "FAG!"

I wanted to die.

Storm didn't say anything until we were driving away. "Do you know what that means?"

"No." I was trying not to start crying. "It's something bad, though."

"A fag is a boy who likes other boys the way he's supposed to like girls," Storm said, lighting a cigarette. "It's nothing bad, Scotty. The correct term for boys like that is gay. Some boys like other boys. Some girls like other girls. It's nothing to be ashamed of, if that's the way you are."

"But I'm not!" And I did start crying. I couldn't admit it to anyone then. Not even to Storm. "Why won't they just leave me alone?"

"Because they're assholes." Storm shrugged. "Are they picking on you?"

"Uh huh."

"Then we need to teach you how to defend yourself." He grinned at me. "Sometimes, Scotty, you have to kick some ass."

"But Mom and Dad—"

"Mom and Dad say they're nonviolent, I know." Storm shrugged. "And that's a nice way to be. But I've seen Mom attack police officers at protests—haven't you?"

"Uh huh." I grinned through my tears. Mom can be a tiger when properly roused. "But that's because they were fascists interfering with the free exercise of expression guaranteed by the Constitution."

"Well, you have a constitutional right to go to school every day and not be harassed." He flicked his cigarette out the window and sprayed air freshener to cover the smell as he eased the car into a parking space. "And sometimes you have to kick some ass in order to keep your rights from being infringed."

So, I went out for the junior-high wrestling team. Storm figured wrestling was a great way for me to learn how to defend myself, since it required speed and agility rather than brute force. The bullies, he figured, would only know how to punch and street fight, but if I knew how to wrestle, I could dodge their blows and take them down. And once I had them down, I could immobilize them and cause a little pain.

I *liked* that idea.

I was timid about it at first. Mom and Dad's reaction was a surprise. They actually *liked* the idea of me getting into a sport. Dad said, "Wrestling is one of the oldest forms of sport known to man."

"And better that," Mom added, "than some stupid team sport like football, where you could get seriously hurt and are taught to be a lemming rather than an individual."

It was also a socially acceptable way to have body contact with other boys which no one could question.

I became dedicated. I checked out books from the library on wrestling techniques and moves. I threw myself into the sport. At every practice, if the coach needed someone to demonstrate on, I volunteered. I wrestled nonstop. I started lifting weights. I went on a body-building regimen, making sure I got lots of protein. Mom even relented and allowed me to start eating meat—although she still refused to cook it. I became pretty good. I lost my first few matches, but wound up going unbeaten for the rest of the season. I was named both Most Valuable and Most Improved on the team.

Chris Moore was the worst of the bullies. In eighth grade, he was already almost six feet tall and about 160 pounds. He was the big stud on campus—all the girls wanted to go steady with him and he was the star of the junior-high football team. Arrogant and cocky, he seemed to feel like junior high was his personal kingdom and everyone had to bow down to him and kiss his ass. I hated him. He always called me "Fagley." One day, after wrestling season ended, he called me that in the hall in front of a bunch of his zit-faced asshole friends and they all started laughing.

Enough, I thought.

He never knew what hit him. Before he even knew what was going on, I had him face down on the floor with his arm cranked up to his shoulder blades. "I can break it." I whispered into his ear. "Give me a reason why I shouldn't."

"Get off me!" He struggled underneath me, not sure how he'd ended up down there. After all, he was the one who always did the ass-kicking, right?

"Fuck you, Moore," I hissed. "Big tough Chris Moore getting his ass kicked by Scotty Fagley. What does that make you?"

"Fuck you, faggot!"

I cranked his arm again and he screamed. "I'll break it, asshole."

"Let me go!"

I glanced over at his buddies. They were staring, in shock. A crowd of other kids had gathered, and some were smiling. Obviously, I wasn't the only one who hated Chris Moore.

"Say, 'I'm a big pussy.' "

"NO!"

"Okay then." I shoved his arm up again.

"I'M A BIG PUSSY! I'M A BIG PUSSY!"

I let go and stood up. I looked at his friends. "Any of you wanna fuck with me some more? Huh?"

They shook their heads.

Chris Moore got up, rubbing his shoulder, glaring at me.

I made a feint towards him. He flinched and stepped back.

Someone in the crowd of kids started to laugh.

From the back a high-pitched falsetto called out, *"I'm a big pussy!"* and they all laughed.

His face red, he pushed his way through the crowd, his two dorky friends following behind, lesson learned.

Don't fuck with a wrestler.

After that, no one ever bothered me again. Yeah, I knew they still called me fag and other, worse, stuff behind my back. Every once in a while I would sit down in class and on the desk would be written *Scotty Bradley sucks cock.* But no one ever had the balls to say it to my face. Kicking Chris Moore's ass put a stop to all that.

Coach Phelps was my high school wrestling coach. He was only about five eight, weighed about 150 pounds, solid muscle, and was slightly bowlegged. He always wore a singlet to wrestling practice, which showed off the hair on his chest and arms. He'd wrestled in college, and was devoted to the sport. He was a great coach; in only a couple of years he'd turned our program from a loser to one of the strongest in the state. He was in his late twenties, had a wife and a baby daughter. He also taught Driver's Ed, Health, and PE—but wasn't one of those horrible gym teachers who picked on kids or made them feel awkward and uncoordinated. Like when we were playing basketball—some of the boys didn't know how to dribble and shoot. He set up the kids who knew how to play with a pickup game of shirts and skins, and took the other kids aside and taught them the fundamentals. That was his philosophy of teaching—kids can learn to do anything if someone will just show them how, and no teacher should ever make students feel bad about themselves.

Is it any wonder he'd been voted Favorite Teacher every year since he was hired?

He had a great sense of humor and loved being around kids. The first time I saw him on the mats in a singlet at practice I forgot about every boy I'd ever had a crush on. I stopped fantasizing about the Soloflex guy and Marky Mark. Coach Phelps liked me, too—he liked my work ethic, my willingness to give a hundred percent for the entire practice, how well I handled criticism and coaching, my total dedication to the sport, my ability to focus. Whenever he would praise me in front of the rest of the team, I felt bad—thinking, if he only knew how much I get off on wrestling with these boys, feeling their muscles and struggling against them, trying to come out on top. If he knew how sexual it all was for me, he would kick me off the team.

I dreamed about Coach Phelps at night.

It was the summer before my junior year when it happened. Coach Phelps asked me to help him at a wrestling clinic for kids out in Plaquemines Parish at a YMCA. It was the kind of thing Mom and Dad definitely approved of—helping out underprivileged kids, trying to keep them off drugs and out of gangs by focusing on a sport. It was a weekend thing, so we wound up staying at a Holiday Inn that Saturday night.

It all began innocently. I was wearing a pair of cut off sweatpants, sitting on my bed watching some really lame television show. Coach Phelps was lying on his bed in sweatpants. He wasn't wearing a shirt, and I kept stealing glances over at his bare chest, his thickly defined muscular arms and shoulders. I loved the way his chest and abs were covered with hair. I'd never really seen him shirtless before, so I was trying to take pictures with my mind camera for masturbatory purposes later. I was just wondering what he looked like in his underwear when he said, "You know, Scotty, I was thinking you haven't gotten that single leg ride down yet."

"Huh?" I didn't know what he was talking about. I was pretty good at single leg rides.

He stood up and walked over to my bed. "Here, let me show you how you're doing it."

Before I knew it he was on top of me, his legs wrapped around mine, but it was pretty easy for me to counter it. I wound up on top of him, controlling his legs with mine while I tried to get a grip on his arms. To my horror, I felt my dick getting hard. My crotch was up against his butt—which was round and hard as a rock—and I pulled back from him, letting go.

He rolled over onto his back and grinned at me. "See how easy it was for you to reverse me out of that?"

I put my hands down in front of my crotch so he couldn't see I was turned on.

I wanted to die, be anywhere else but there.

He winked at me. "It's okay, Scotty. Physical contact can lead to arousal. See?"

He pointed down at his crotch. He was aroused also.

"When I was your age, I always jacked off before practice and matches so it wouldn't happen." He went on as though he wasn't aware I was dying from embarrassment.

I couldn't take my eyes off of his tented sweatpants.

"Maybe we should just go ahead and take care of this"—he stroked himself—"so we can get to work."

It continued all through my junior year—every chance we had to be together, we were. Sometimes I would stay late after practice and we would go into his office and lock the door. Sometimes I would meet him at a motel out on Airline Drive in Kenner. I was horny constantly—what teenager isn't? Part of the appeal was the danger. I knew we would both be in trouble if anyone caught us. But I was all caught up in it. I knew he was married. I knew he had a kid. But at night, in my bed, I got swept away by fantasies of being with him, living with him, of going to sleep with his arms around me every night.

I loved Coach Phelps.

Funny, I thought as I put conditioner in my wet hair. I never called him by his first name. I always called him "coach."

And he loved me.

I won the State Championship my junior year. The tournament was held up in Baton Rouge, and after getting my trophy, Coach and I drove back to New Orleans. He took me out to dinner at Ruth's Chris Steakhouse, the one on Veterans Boulevard in Metairie. When we got back into the car, he said, "You mind stopping at my house? My wife is off at her parents' in Biloxi."

I never said no to a chance to be with Coach.

We were in bed, just lying there in the afterglow with our arms around each other, talking about what college scholarship offer I should take, when his wife walked in.

The rest of the night was a blur to me, as I scrambled to get my clothes on while they screamed at each other. I felt sick to my stomach, my wonderful steak dinner churning and turning to acid. I fled from the house, terrified, running down the street with my backpack slung over my shoulder, until I finally found a gas station with a pay phone so I could call a cab.

I never saw Coach again. He never returned to school; rumors swirled around campus. A substitute came in and finished teaching his classes for the rest of the semester. I tried calling his home a couple of times, only no one ever answered. About a week later I called and got that horrible message that the phone was no longer in service. Somehow, I knew his life had been destroyed, ruined, wrecked forever by what we had done together.

All for love.

I never wrestled again.

I turned the shower off.

I dried myself off with shaking hands. I got dressed and got another cup of coffee.

I went into the living room and lit the candles.

I knelt in front of the altar.

For the first time, I asked Coach Phelps to forgive me.

I asked the Goddess for strength, and purpose, and the clarity to do what was right.

I prayed for serenity.

When my emotions had stilled, I went back to the computer to answer Frank's e-mail.

CHAPTER ELEVEN

Six of Cups

living in the past

There are three fire stations in close proximity to the French Quarter. We take fires seriously in New Orleans. Chicago may have had one great fire, but we've had several, and any time there's a fire in the Quarter we all hold our breath. The houses are all made of old wood, some of it rotted, some of it termite damaged, and it wouldn't take much for a fire to get out of control. There's one across Esplanade from the old Mint, and another on the other side of Rampart. The French Quarter's main fire department is located on Decatur Street just beyond the little triangular park saluting the men who discovered New Orleans, the Sieurs de Iberville and Bienville, and just a block before you get to the House of Blues on your way uptown. It seemed like a logical enough place to start to find out anything about Rod Parrish, since it was most likely where he'd been stationed.

I walked up to the building. It was made of brick and marble, with three big doors for the trucks. Two of the doors were closed. The flags of the United States, Louisiana, and the city were whipping about in the wind atop the building.

There was a guy wearing jeans and a navy blue T-shirt with NOFD on his left chest inspecting the tires on a fire truck parked right outside the garage doors. I stood and watched him for a while. He had a great body. The jeans were baggy and hung low off his hips. The T-shirt was tight, and the sleeves were rolled up over his biceps. There was a tattoo of a mermaid on the right one. He couldn't have been more than twenty-two years old—he still had some adolescent-looking acne on his cheek. His skin was still soft and smooth looking, like he didn't really need to shave every day just quite yet. He had jet black hair cut close to his scalp. "Excuse me?" I said.

He looked up and smiled at me. His teeth were slightly crooked, but the smile could have lit every light in Harrah's. "What can I do for ya?" He had a very thick parish accent. Probably from out near Arabi, best as I could judge. He straightened up to his full height of about six three or four. Some curly black hairs were sticking out from the neck of his T-shirt. Definitely a candidate for a fireman's calendar.

"Yeah, I was, um, wondering if there was anyone around who worked here about fourteen years ago?"

The smile faded and the thick black eyebrows came together. "Why?"

I gave him my most winning smile—the one always good for a tip when I was dancing. "I'm a reporter trying to track down some information about a fireman who used to be stationed here fourteen years ago." Just a little lie wouldn't hurt, I figured.

"Oh." He thought about it for a minute, cocking his head to the side. "You'd want Buzz, then." He laughed, and angels sang. "He's been here since the Louisiana Purchase." He wiped his hands on his jeans. "Stay right here, and I'll get him for ya."

I stood there, waiting, watching cars, cabs, and the occasional mule-drawn carriage go by on the street. It was a pretty day, probably in the low seventies, without any humidity—one of those beautiful days that show New Orleans off at its best. The sky was intensely blue, with the occasional wispy white cloud drifting by. Maybe about ten minutes passed before an older man came walking out of the station. I judged him to be in his midforties. "You the reporter?"

"Yes." I held out my hand. "Scott Bradley."

"Buzz Quinn." He shook my hand. His hands were calloused and rough, but his grip was strong, tight, and firm. Like the younger guy, his hair was cut really short, but his was starting to gray at the temples. His face was tanned and deeply creased. The laugh lines around his mouth and eyes were pronounced. He was wearing a T-shirt and jeans, like the kid, but to better effect. His muscles were thicker and suggestive of coiled strength and power. His arms were free of tattoos, but there were pronounced blue veins bulging beneath the skin. "How can I help you, Scott?"

The name Quinn set off an alarm in my head. *Rod Parrish's best man's name had been John Quinn,* a voice said in my head. Coincidence?

"I'm doing research for a story." I pulled a notebook out of my gym bag.

"Ya wanna come in and have some coffee?"

"Sure."

Some other firemen were milling about inside the station as I followed him in. He started up a staircase in the back as I looked around for the pole. I didn't see it, but I did catch the eyes of a guy I'd seen in the bars before. He winked at me, and I grinned back at him so long I had to almost run to catch up to Buzz on the stairs, wondering the whole time why I'd never hooked up with the guy before.

I followed Buzz into a room where tables were set up in the center. One side of the room was lined with gray lockers. There was an oven, a refrigerator, and a microwave on a formica counter with a sink. He grabbed two navy blue mugs with NOFD on the sides and filled them with coffee. "The pot's fresh," he said. "I just made it. How do you take yours?"

"Milk and sugar."

He made my coffee and held it out to me, then poured himself a cup.

I took a drink and opened the notebook. "Buzz, how long have you been at this station?"

He sat down next to me at the table. "Nigh twenty years, give or take." He shrugged.

Cool, I thought. "Did you know a fireman named Rod Parrish?"

He drew back from me slightly, his eyes narrowing a bit. "Yes." He drew the word out into two syllables. "Why do you want to know?"

I looked at him. *Yes, it's him,* a voice whispered inside my head. *The best man. Rod Parrish's best friend.* "The story I am doing is on unsolved murders in New Orleans." I looked at him. "Is your first name John, by any chance?"

He nodded. "Nobody but my mama calls me that. I've been Buzz since school." He smiled slightly. "Rod was the one who started calling me that, actually." He stirred his coffee, looking down into the cup. "We grew up together. He lived down the street from me."

"I've actually been trying to track down his wife and son."

"Oh, Lord, I haven't seen Juliet or little Robby since just after the funeral." He scratched his head. "One day, they were just gone without a word to me, or anyone. Nobody knew where they went to. I called the house and the phone was disconnected. I went out there and the house was for sale. Juliet's parents were dead, and she just had her sister Gwen. Gwen always swore she never knew where they went, but I don't know that I ever believed her." He gave a half laugh. "That girl was a good liar, that I knew for a fact."

I looked up from my scribbling. "Really? How?"

"I dated her for three years. Biggest mistake of my life." He laughed again, shaking his head. "Rod and Juliet wanted us to be a couple so damned bad—you know, the best friend and the sister? That way we could all go do couple things together, and all that mess. It was more Juliet than Rod, but Rod always went along with anything she wanted. Lord, he loved that woman." He smiled a bit, remembering. "Me and Gwen, though, we wanted different things out of life, you know? She didn't want to just be some fireman's wife. She wanted to be Queen of Comus with a big house and a Mercedes and a housekeeper. She knew she wouldn't get that with me. She kept me around until something better came along. She wound up marrying a lawyer." He winked at me. "I don't hold her no grudges though. She was a good old girl, really. And she was a tiger in the sack, if you know what I mean."

I let that go. "Did you notice any change in Rod before the murder? Did he seem worried or upset about anything?"

"No, he was actually happier than I'd ever seen him." He cocked his head to one side. "You don't know about the boy, do you?"

"His son?" I shrugged. "I really don't know much about anything. I'm just starting to look into this."

"Little Robby was almost two months premature. Juliet almost died having him—and they told her she couldn't have another one, it would kill her. So they gave her that operation so she couldn't. That about broke her heart—her and Rod had always wanted to have a house full of kids. And then afterwards, she was in the hospital for months." He shook his head. "If that wasn't enough for them to bear, Robby was born with a hole in his heart. He was in and out of surgery for two years." He sighed. "It was all so sad. You know, the insurance would only cover so much, and they just seemed to keep going further and further into debt. They barely kept their heads above water—hell, half the time I had to loan him a twenty here or there to get him through to payday."

"Wow."

"Yeah. It seemed like that poor little boy was always sick—always at the doctor, always going into the hospital. And they sure loved that little boy." He rubbed his eyes. "He was a sweet little kid."

"How awful for them."

"There's no greater pain or worry for a parent than a sick

child." He leaned back in his chair. "Me and the wife have been pretty lucky with ours. Never anything more serious than a broke arm or the chicken pox—you know, the usual kind of stuff that happens to all kids. I don't know if I could have done what Rod and Juliet went through with that little boy. It was hard to watch. There wasn't nothing I could do, you know? I just watched Rod and Juliet get broken down every day, bit by bit, by this crushing debt they had. It was bad enough to worry every day whether the kid was gonna get sick or something without having them asshole bill collectors hounding ya." He shrugged. "I always kind of figured that was why she ran off. To get out from under."

"But you said Rod seemed happier before he was killed?"

He was lost in his memories. "Yeah. He had this spring to his step, you know? I hadn't seen him like that since little Robby was born. Don't get me wrong—he loved that kid. I remember he paid me back some money he owed me—and it wasn't even payday yet! I asked him where he'd got the money, but he wouldn't tell me—just said he came into a little windfall, and things were gonna be different from then on out." He got up and refilled his cup, and gestured to me with the pot. I shook my head. "He even gave notice. Was talking about going back to school, getting a degree, going into a different line of work."

"You have no idea where the money came from?"

He shook his head. "No, he wouldn't tell me. Just would say he came into an unexpected windfall. I figured maybe he had some rich relative who kicked off or something, though most of his family wasn't much better off than him. Maybe he won some money in the lottery. Hell, I don't know. If he wanted me to know he would've told me."

"And how long after this was he killed?"

"His last day with the department was May tenth, 1988."

I looked up. "You remember the exact date?"

He laughed. "You're old enough to remember that date too, though it seems nobody really remembers it anymore." When I didn't say anything, he sighed. "Rod's last day was the day of the Cabildo fire. What a way to go out, huh?"

The Cabildo fire. A flood of memories rushed over me. I'd been fifteen, a sophomore in high school. I'd just gotten home from school and was getting ready to go to the gym and work out when I heard the sirens. Whenever you hear sirens in the French Quarter, your heart sinks and you get a knot in your stomach; there's a short burst of adrenaline as every muscle in your body tightens. Will this be the time the whole Quarter burns down, you wonder to yourself, and pray that the sirens are just passing through on their way to another neighborhood, or at least far enough away so you don't have to worry. These sirens were close, damned close, so I'd run back downstairs. Everyone in the Devil's Weed was already outside. It was a warm spring day, not many clouds in the sky. I remember people were wearing shorts and T-shirts. My mom was wearing her traditional T-shirt, jeans, and ponytail. My mom grabbed my hand. All you had to do was look up to see the clouds of black smoke rising very close. We ran down Royal Street until we were at the courtyard behind St. Louis Cathedral, and looked up. The cupola of the Cabildo was engulfed in flames, the black smoke swirling in the wind as it rose upward.

"Oh, no, not the Cabildo!" I remember my mother saying, her voice shaking. She squeezed my hand so tightly it hurt.

St. Louis Cathedral might be the most famous landmark of the Quarter, but to New Orleanians, the two buildings that flank it are just as important—the Cabildo on the uptown side and the Presbytere on the downtown. The Cabildo dated back to 1795, and was the seat of the government when the Spanish ruled Louisiana. Don Andres Almonester had financed its building as a gift to the city. It was now a part of the Louisiana State Museum Complex. It was where the French and American emissaries met to sign the Louisiana Purchase treaty, making the city and almost the entire continent American. Priceless artifacts of New Orleans and Louisiana history were housed there—everything from furniture from Zachary Taylor's Baton Rouge plantation house to the death mask of Napoleon to original Audubon prints. "Did you fight the Cabildo fire?"

He nodded. "The Cabildo fire was the proudest moment in the history of the New Orleans Fire Department, and I was there."

Mom and I had walked down to St. Peter, but access was blocked off by the police. We headed up another block to Toulouse and walked up to Chartres, where the police had blocked off the street again. We got up as close to the police barricade as we could. "Why aren't they trying to put it out?" Mom said. Her voice was trembling. She had tears in her eyes. She wasn't the only one in the crowd, either. All around us were people just staring, mesmerized.

"I remember," I said. "I was there."

"Were you?" He patted my hand. "I can remember how none of us thought Chief McCrossen knew what he was doing at first, because we weren't turning the water on. He kept telling us to wait, to wait until he gave the signal. Some of the other firemen were bringing stuff out, paintings and stuff."

"Yeah, I remember." The firemen were bringing stuff out of the building rather than fighting the fire. They were stacking rare prints and paintings against the Jackson Square fence. Onlookers, some of them crying, all of them white-faced in horror, were muttering. The temper and mood was getting ugly. Mom put her arm around my shoulders and pulled me in tight. Somewhere in the crowd someone shouted, "PUT THE DAMNED FIRE OUT." This was greeted by some cheers and applause. "Chief McCrossen was trying to save everything inside," I said.

"Damnedest thing." Buzz folded his arms across his chest. "He knew when we turned the hoses on the entire building was going to be drenched in water and all that history was going to be destroyed. So he tried to save it. He asked for volunteers, and then sent in seven of 'em to salvage things, cover stuff that couldn't be moved with tarps, to protect them from the water, bring everything not bolted down outside. Rod was one of those seven men. And when the job inside was done, when they had everything out, Chief McCrossen gave the order to turn the hoses on." He grinned. "He was a smart man and damned good at his job. We saved almost everything, you know."

A huge cheer had gone up from the crowd when the hoses went on. The news crews from all the local television stations had been there, and later that night, on the news, when what Chief McCrossen had done was made public knowledge—well, he became the city's biggest hero since Andrew Jackson. Editorials in both the *Times-Picayune* and *Gambit Weekly* sang his praises. He could have been elected governor that week. The firefighters had also managed to limit the fire to the third floor of the building—the only damage to the structure below that was water damage, and even that was minimal. The cupola had actually acted as a vent, sucking all the heat, fire, and smoke up and out, keeping it from moving down. The fire didn't jump to any other buildings either—the firemen had soaked St. Louis Cathedral and the buildings behind to keep them from spontaneously igniting from the heat.

"And a week later, Rod was killed." His voice broke. "I'm sorry." He wiped at his eyes. "Even after all this time, it's hard for me."

"I understand." I thought about patting his hand, but he was a straight guy, and they don't do that, do they?

"He was a damned good man, and the best friend any man could ever want," he said, shaking his finger at me. "You make sure you say that in your story, okay? Why anyone would want to kill a good man like that, make that poor sick little boy an orphan, is beyond me. I just hope whoever did it is roasting in hell."

"At the time, the police thought it looked like a professional job, is that correct?"

His eyes flashed, his skin reddening underneath his tan. "That was a load of bullshit. Rod was a good man. He went to mass and confession every week. When we were kids, he never did anything wrong. He didn't lie unless he had to. He never broke the speed limit when driving his own car. He didn't even get drunk! Why would any mobster want to kill him? The police were just grabbing at straws, I'm telling you. They didn't have no idea then who did it, and they don't know now—if they even care." He made a spitting noise.

"Well, just from reviewing the press clippings, it seemed like a reach to me," I said.

"That detective in charge of the case didn't know his ass from a hole in the ground." He finished his second cup of coffee and slammed it down on the table. "Incompetent bastard. He didn't give a shit about Rod."

I closed my notebook and nodded. "I think I have everything I need for now. Would it be a huge imposition to ask for your home phone number? In case I have any other questions?" I wrote it down when he recited it. "And do you know how I can get ahold of Gwen Pryor?"

"It's Gwen Victor now." He shrugged. "We still send each other Christmas cards, but I haven't actually talked to her in years. She lives on the West Bank in Algiers Point. Listed in the phone book under her husband. Beau Victor."

"Beau Victor? Not the personal injury lawyer?" I stifled an involuntary laugh. Storm hated Beau Victor and all lawyers like him. Beau Victor ran commercials hawking his capabilities as a trial attorney ad nauseum all day. *Have you been injured in a car accident? Don't sign anything with their insurance company until you've talked to Beau Victor! Get what you deserve!* This would be followed by glowing testimonials from people who looked like they belonged in trailer parks and never progressed beyond the tenth grade proudly stating how Beau Victor got them cash money for their pain and suffering. And then it would cut back to the man himself, with his cheap suit and televangelist hair, grinning and pointing at the camera, saying again, "Get what you deserve!"

I always figured they got exactly what they deserved.

He grinned. "The one and only."

CHAPTER TWELVE

Two of Swords

possible trouble ahead

I don't own a car.

This strikes a lot of people as odd. There are a number of explanations I usually offer. First and foremost is the fact that I've lived in the Quarter or nearby for almost my entire life, and I never needed one. Another good reason is the Quarter's serious shortage of free parking. But the main reason is I hate to drive. I'm always amazed by how blithely most people take driving. Don't they understand that a car is a killing machine? Every time you step into one you're taking your life into your hands. You can be the best driver in the world—cautious, obeying all the traffic laws—and it doesn't matter. All it takes is one incredibly stupid driver not paying attention and *BLAM!* Instant death!

I did own a car once. My paternal grandparents bought me a car for graduating from high school, a really nice blue state-of-the-art Toyota Corolla, complete with CD player and every possible goofy gadget imaginable. It was a nice car (a convertible would have been nicer, but hey, it was a gift), but I drove it as little as possible. When I dropped out of college and moved back to New Orleans, I sold it. Insurance, maintenance—who needs all that extra expense anyway? Usually, if I ever need to get somewhere that requires the operation of a motor vehicle, I can get someone to take me. David, for example, is really good about driving me anywhere I want to go. Usually, if he can't take me, he'll let me take his car, which is the court of last resort for me.

Which is why I found myself driving his silver Honda Accord over to the West Bank with a dance-mix CD blaring.

The West Bank isn't really west of New Orleans; on the map it is due south of the city. Compass directions mean nothing in New Orleans. The West Bank is called that because it lies theoretically on the west side of the Mississippi River. But the river doesn't run in a straight line north and south. It twists and turns on its way through the city, which throws everything off. If you take I-10 west out of New Orleans, you don't cross the river; you actually drive due north to Baton Rouge, where the highway turns west toward Texas. That's where you cross the river. This is very confusing to tourists who make the colossal mistake of renting a car, or worse yet, driving their own cars here. Probably the most confusing thing about I-10 is just past the Superdome, where the highway branches off into two different directions: I-10 West to the right to Baton Rouge, or Highway 90 West to the left, which will take you across the river. Got it?

Traffic was as heavy as it got on I-10 at the Basin Street on-ramp. I don't know how people can stand to drive every day. On those rare occasions when I find myself behind the wheel of a car, my palms get sweaty and I get very agitated. I can never forget that I am in control of a weapon of potential mass destruction and death. And the way people drive! It's like they all have a death wish.

This time was no exception. Just on the short trip from David's driveway to the on-ramp, I'd been cut off by a cab on Esplanade and had to slam on the brakes. Someone else made a left-hand turn off Claiborne from the far right lane, cutting right in front of me without even signaling. My hands were shaking by the time I got to the light where I could turn onto the ramp.

As I drove around the circular on-ramp, I noticed a dark

green sedan behind me. Cars have never interested me much, so I don't pay attention to makes and models. This could have been anything from a Cadillac to an Oldsmobile. All I could say for sure was that it was big, ugly, and American made. David, on the other hand, can identify the make and model of every car he sees. But the only thing about this car I noticed was that it was big, a truly hideous shade of green, and the windows were tinted so you couldn't see inside. I wondered idly why people do that to their windows as we wound our way up to the highway and the speeding cars.

Keep an eye on that car.

My gift, such as it is, can be so annoyingly vague sometimes. I checked to make sure there was a spot for me to zip into as I headed into the highway access lane, and sure enough there was a spot coming along. All I had to do was wait for an eighteen-wheeler coming up behind me at warp speed to pass by. I slowed a bit and the truck whipped past, rocking the little Accord in the wind wake. I turned on my signal and cut over. Now, I only had to get across two more lanes in less than a mile to make the left-hand exit for Highway 90.

The Goddess was obviously watching out for me. I was able to accomplish this without a whole hell of a lot of maneuvering. *Yes!* I gave myself a mental fist pump. It should be relatively easy from here on out. I'm one of those drivers who gets into the lane he needs long before he needs to, and then just stays there. I can think of nothing worse than needing to get over, not being able to, and getting stuck.

I looked into my rearview mirror.

The green car was right behind me again.

Okay, so it wasn't that big of a deal, right? So the gift told me to keep an eye on the car. That didn't mean it was following me or anything. Lots of people were going to the West Bank. In fact, there was a line of cars heading over the ramp to 90. Maybe it just meant the driver was dangerous, might do something stupid that could cause an accident. All I have to do then is keep an eye on it and stop being so paranoid, I told myself as the line of cars progressed onto 90 at about thirty miles per hour. I managed to get onto 90, accelerating as cars and eighteen-wheelers zoomed by at a gazillion miles an hour heading for the river bridge.

I started singing along with a really hot remix of Cher's "All or Nothing" as I crossed the river. According to the directions I got from a web site, I had to exit onto Charles de Gaulle Boulevard, which comes up almost immediately after crossing the bridge. I had to maneuver a bit, but again, the Goddess had her hand on my shoulder. Or my gearshift. Whatever. I glanced back and the green car followed me.

Hmmm.

Gwen Victor lived in Algiers Point. Algiers Point is to the West Bank what Uptown is to New Orleans—expensive homes, wide tree-lined streets, and some snob appeal. It's right on the river. I found the directions to be pretty exact, and within ten minutes I was parking on the street in front of the Victor house.

The green car didn't turn when I did onto the street where she lived, and I felt a knot in my stomach relax as it kept driving.

The house was faux Tudor, with lots of glass and a big, green well-kept lawn, with a circular driveway. It didn't look very old, maybe had been built within the last ten years. The entire neighborhood had an air of newness to it. The subdivision planner had been very careful to give each of the houses enough distinctive touches, either on the building or the landscaping, to eliminate the sameness most subdivisions have, but it was still there subliminally. The lawns were all well maintained. Some had rock gardens with splashing fountains. The houses themselves were well maintained, but the whole area had an air of sterility you don't find on the other side of the river. There wasn't any character to the neighborhood. It just looked new and expensive. The driveways were empty for the most part, and there weren't any signs of life anywhere. No one clipping flowers or mowing their lawn. There was also an almost otherworldly silence. Ah, suburbia.

There was a black Lexus in the driveway. Hopefully, the car meant someone was home. I probably should have called first and set an appointment, but I hoped surprising Mrs. Victor at home was the right way to go. Storm always says the element of surprise is crucial in getting information out of witnesses. I guess I'd see if he was right.

I got out of the car and walked up the driveway. I pushed the doorbell. On either side of the door was that wavy glass that distorts everything, but I could see someone coming to the door. A set of glass wind chimes tinkled in the breeze. A woman wearing a green Tulane sweatshirt and tight blue jeans opened the door. "Can I help you?"

She had dark red hair that hung to her shoulders, and pale white skin. Her face was heart shaped, coming to a point at her chin. The skin around her eyes looked too tight, as though she had her eyes done more than once. You know how the eyes start to look a little sunken after several of those procedures? She certainly had that my-skin-has-been-pulled-a-few-too-many-times look to her that some celebrities start to get. It made her gray eyes look almost freakish; one seemed to have a sideways tilt to it the other didn't. She was wearing way too much makeup and her hair was sprayed to immovability. It would probably survive hurricane-force winds. She was pretty, even though her hips were starting to spread a bit and her breasts under the sweatshirt looked heavy as well. She was fighting the aging process with every means at her disposal. Her feet were bare, her toenails painted a bright metallic blue.

"My name is Scott Bradley, and I'm a reporter," I replied. I figured it was smart to use the same story on her I'd used on Buzz Quinn, in case he'd called her. Detective School Lesson Twelve: always use the same cover story when on a case. "I'm doing a story on unsolved murders in New Orleans."

"Rod," she said. She smelled faintly of liquor. "You're here about Rod."

"I really need to speak to your sister."

She didn't blink. "I haven't seen my sister in over fifteen years."

"May I come inside?" I gave her the big-tipper smile.

She shrugged and stood aside to let me in. The house was decorated in what my sister Rain would disdainfully call "modern whorehouse." Everything looked new, and the fabrics Mrs. Victor (or her decorator) seemed to favor were velvets and satins. In bright blues, greens, and yellows. The artwork hanging on the walls all seemed to be reproductions of famous religious paintings—da Vinci's "Last Supper," several representations of the martyrdom of St. Sebastian, the Madonna and child, that sort of thing. There was a massive silver crucifix hanging over the fireplace, with a tortured and bloody Christ hanging from it. Statues of various saints were lined up on the mantelpiece.

With a slight shiver, I sat down on a black leather overstuffed sofa. I could hear the central air pumping cold air through the vents, and it was maybe fifty degrees inside the house. The room smelled of potpourri burning. I flipped open my notebook and took out a pen.

"Would you like something to drink?" she asked.

"Anything soft and nondiet would be great."

She frowned. "I may have some iced tea." She shrugged. "I only have diet soda." She walked through a door, and I heard her rummaging for glasses.

She set a glass of tea down on a coaster in front of me, and sat down in a reclining chair holding a can of Diet Coke. She crossed her legs and looked at me. I took a drink of the tea. It was awful—too much lemon, too much artificial sweetener, but still bland, as though made from powdered mix rather than bags. I refrained from spitting it back out, and managed to choke it down, setting it back down on the coaster. "Thanks."

"As I said, I haven't seen or heard from my sister in over fifteen years." She started fidgeting with a locket hanging on a gold chain around her neck. "We used to be very close, and then she just disappeared one day. Without a word to me. Without a word to anyone." She looked out the window. "Like she disappeared off the face of the planet."

"Was her marriage a happy one?"

"Yes." She smiled, and I got an idea of what she'd looked like when she was younger, before the surgeons got at her face. It was a shame she'd bought into the youth cult. She'd be a handsome woman if she hadn't worried so much about a few damned wrinkles. "Rod and Juliet were really in love. They met in high school—although we went to different schools. I don't really remember how they met, to tell you the truth—it just seemed liked they were always together, you know how that is? And then they got married. . . ."

"And the baby wasn't healthy?"

"That was so awful." She sighed. "It seemed like that poor child was always in and out of the hospital. It didn't make any sense, you know? Rod and Juliet were both so healthy—Juliet had never been sick, except for chicken pox when she was little, and Rod was the same way. And good as Rod's insurance was, it didn't cover everything, and those bills just kept piling up. I had to loan them money now and again to help them get through some rough patches, and it seemed like our parents were always buying their groceries. . . . They were always struggling. And then for Rod to die in such an awful way." She hugged herself and shivered.

"Why did Rod quit his job?"

She stared at me. "What are you talking about? Rod didn't quit his job."

"Mrs. Victor, Rod put in his notice and was no longer with the fire department at the time he was murdered."

"That doesn't make any sense. Juliet would have told me about that. . . ." She sighed. "But then again, maybe she wouldn't have. I didn't know she was going to disappear, either." Her voice was bitter. "It broke Mom and Dad's heart, I can tell you that.

They were never the same after she ran off. Their only grandchild, too." She sighed. "I can't have children, so"—she glanced over at the saints on the mantel—"so little Robby was it. You know, having him almost killed her. And she couldn't have more." She clutched the locket again. "It was God's will, and we aren't supposed to question God, but I never did understand it all. . . ." Her voice trailed off.

"How did your sister seem? After Rod was killed?"

"Upset, of course. Who wouldn't be?" She closed her eyes. The hand holding the Diet Coke can was trembling. "That was a horrible time. I had just started dating Beau— my husband. Juliet didn't seem to want anyone to comfort her—well, she'd always been that way—and wouldn't cry or break down in front of anyone. She'd always been like that, even as a little girl. Didn't want to let the baby out of her sight, either. She wouldn't stay in the house—who could blame her, of course, considering—but she wouldn't stay with me or our parents, either. She checked into a hotel. A hotel. Can you believe that? She didn't want any of us. And then, after the funeral—gone. Without a word. And we never heard from her again."

"Did you ever try to find her?"

"Mom and Dad hired a private eye for a couple of weeks, but he didn't seem to be making any progress, and they couldn't afford to keep looking. The police were looking for her too—but she just vanished." She finished the Diet Coke and crumpled the can in her hand. "I always figured whoever killed Rod had gotten her and the baby, too—but Mom and Dad always insisted she was still alive. They always thought she would come home someday"—she laughed harshly—"but between you and me, I think it's more likely that a fisherman or a hunter will stumble across some old bones one day out in a swamp, and that'll be her."

"Do you have a picture of her?"

She looked at me strangely, then got up and walked out of the room. After a few moments, she walked back in and handed me a

tarnished silver frame. It was Rod and Juliet's wedding picture—
the one that had been in the paper, that I hadn't been able to
make out on-line.

It was her, all right. Much younger and much happier, but it
was definitely the woman from the elevator at the Royal Aquitaine. She was alive.

I touched the glass. They seemed so young, so happy—and
that radiated from the picture. I could sense it. They had been
young, beautiful, madly in love, and excited about their future together that day. There had been no forebodings of the tragedy to
come. "Do you mind if I take this and have it copied?"

She shrugged. "Just make sure I get it back. It's all"—she
swallowed—"all I really have left."

"I will." I pulled out one of Storm's business cards and wrote
my number on the back along with my name. "If you think of
anything that might help us out, you can reach me through this
number."

For the first time since I arrived, she smiled as she looked at
the card. "Storm Bradley. Are you his brother?"

I nodded. "Yes, ma'am."

"Well, you make sure and tell him and Marguerite I send my
love. We go way back."

I thanked her again as she showed me out. I got into the car
and looked at the picture again. I closed my eyes and touched the
glass. Nothing came. With a sigh I started the car and headed
back for the highway. I was pulling onto the on-ramp when I just
happened to glance in the rearview mirror and saw the green
sedan again.

My heart skipped a beat.

This couldn't be a coincidence. That was the same damned
car.

I was being followed.

Okay, Scotty, calm down. I took some deep breaths as I
merged onto the highway. Think. All right, they didn't know I'd

spotted them before, they don't know I've spotted them this time. So, that's a plus for me. Maybe I can lose them at the tollbooth.

There is no toll on 90 to cross the river out of New Orleans to the West Bank, but it costs a dollar to go the other way. New Orleanians smugly say "Nobody would pay a dollar to go to the West Bank."

We really are horrible snobs.

The traffic going back across the river was heavy, and all the tollbooths were open. Unless they got right behind me, I could probably get away from them. There was no way of judging how fast a toll line would go, and even if they were right behind me, I could probably floor it and lose myself in the traffic merging back into three lanes to cross the bridge. I kept glancing back at them as I maneuvered into a toll lane.

The sedan pulled into the next lane, which was about the same length as mine.

I tried to glance over as we slowly inched forward to the booths. I couldn't see through the damned tinted glass. Wasn't that illegal anyway?

I grabbed a dollar in quarters out of David's ashtray, my palms sweating.

We both kept moving forward, slowly.

An idea came to me.

We both reached our booths at the same time. I smiled at the young black woman at mine. "Hey." I reached out to hand her the quarters, and missed her hand. The quarters fell to the pavement. "*Shit!*" I grabbed for my wallet. "That's okay, darlin', forget it, I'll just give you a dollar."

She climbed down out of her booth. "That's okay, sir—I don't mind."

The green car pulled out from its booth slowly.

I put my car in park and climbed out to help her look.

The car behind the green one began to honk at it.

I read the license plate, repeating it in my head over and over.

It sat there for a moment, and then drove off.

The last quarter was under the car, and I reached for it and handed it over. "I am so sorry!"

She shrugged as she went back into the booth. "Happens all the time."

The light flashed green. I put the car in gear and headed for the bridge.

The green car was gone.

I grabbed a pen and scribbled the license number down.

Got you, you bastards!

CHAPTER THIRTEEN

The Wheel of Fortune, Reversed

there will be setbacks

I kept an eye out for the green car all the way home, but it never showed itself again. I was pretty proud of myself for being so clever until it dawned on me, as I parked in the driveway on David's side of the house, I'd initially spotted the car following me on the way to Gwen Victor's. Obviously, they already knew where I lived, so losing them wasn't that big of a deal. They could find me any time they wanted to—although they might not know it was David's car, not mine. So, by using his car, I may have put David into danger.

Nice job, Sherlock, I swore at myself. But then again, who knew if they were dangerous? All they'd done was follow me, after all. It wasn't like they'd tried to run me off the road or shot at me or something like that. But why were they following me anyway? What did they think I could lead them to?

I knew organized crime had once had a firm footing in New Orleans, but surely they didn't anymore. It was the twenty-first century. Crime families were a thing of the past. The police had seemed pretty certain that Rod Parrish's murder had been a mob hit, a professional job. But even that didn't make much sense. Why would a hit have been put out on a fireman with a sick child? What could he have done to piss off a crime organization?

The key to it all was the money he'd come into before he died.

Surely it wasn't a coincidence his last day on the job was the day of the Cabildo fire.

I let myself into the house, turning on some lights. My stomach growled as I went over to the computer and turned it on. While I waited for the computer to boot up, I went into the kitchen to make myself a tuna salad sandwich. I poured myself a glass of nonfat milk and sat down at the table. As I chewed, I thought some more about what Gwen Victor had said. If they'd been so broke, how had Juliet gotten the money to disappear so completely? Unless she'd started living on the streets, it was almost impossible to disappear. You need identification. You need a social security number to get a job. Fake papers aren't cheap, nor are they that easy for a suburban housewife to locate.

I finished my sandwich and called Storm on his cell phone. "Hello there, my queen, how are things going?"

"Well, I talked to the best man at the Parrish wedding, and he said that Rod seemed to have come into some money right before he died." I sighed. "He also connected me with Juliet Parrish's sister, and get this: she's married to Beau Victor."

"Gwen?" Storm whistled. "Gwen Victor is Juliet Parrish's sister? Talk about small town. We just had dinner with them last week."

"I thought you couldn't stand Beau Victor."

"No, I actually like him. I just don't like lawyers who advertise."

I raised my eyebrows. I've heard Storm go off on one of his tirades about lawyers who advertise plenty of times, and he always used Beau Victor as his example of everything that is wrong with today's legal system. Whatever. Storm's inconsistencies are legion. "Well, Gwen didn't seem to know anything. She claims she hasn't seen Juliet since she disappeared."

Storm whistled. "And you think Bryce is really the Parrish baby?"

"I don't have any proof, of course, but don't you think it's weird that Juliet Parrish just happened to be in the Royal Aquitaine, on Bryce's floor? And that Bryce was looking for his birth mother?" I finished my milk and rinsed the glass out. "And Juliet just disappeared after the murder. I can't find any trace of her anywhere after that."

"It would sure be a weird coincidence, and I don't like coincidences in my cases." Storm was quiet for a moment. "I guess I might as well tell you. Bryce is missing."

"*What?* How did that happen?"

"I had to go to the office and Marguerite had to take the kids to the dentist. It's not like he was under house arrest," he added defensively. "It's not like we locked him up. He was free to come and go as he pleased, you know. When she got back, he was gone. He left a note, saying he had some things to do and would be back later, so maybe he'll show up. Marguerite called me when she got home, which was about three hours ago. I just don't like it."

I got a sick feeling in my stomach. "Stormy, someone followed me over to Gwen Victor's. A green sedan, I think some kind of Oldsmobile, you know, one of those big gas-eating tanks? I managed to lose them on the way back, but—"

"Did you get the license plate?"

"Yes, you want it?" I started digging through my bag. "I was going to see if I could trace it on-line."

"Give it to me. I can trace it through the DMV."

I didn't ask how he could do that. Sometimes, it's better not to know. "You think whoever was following me has grabbed him?"

"It's possible."

I rubbed my eyes. "So, what do we do now, oh wise lawyer man?"

"I'm going to give him a few more hours—if he's not back by five I'm going to have to call Venus." He sighed. "It doesn't look good, him disappearing like this. The police aren't going to like this one bit. But we can't risk not telling them—if something has happened to him, we'll need their help finding him. I don't like this at all."

Man, this sucked big time. "Storm, I really think this is all connected somehow—Rod Parrish's murder, Ace Martinelli—all of it. And I would be willing to bet anything it has something to do with the Cabildo fire."

"The Cabildo fire?" He took a deep breath. "Is this your amazing psycho powers at work again?"

He really can be annoying when he wants to be. I could just picture the smug smirk on his face. "No, just plain deduction this time, ass-wipe. Call me and let me know if Bryce turns up, okay?" I hung up. I opened my Internet-access program and clicked to start the dial-up process.

Annoying as he was, it *wasn't* a bad idea to try to read the cards again. I walked into the living room after starting the log-on process to my Internet server. I lit the white candles, sat down at my altar, and whispered a short prayer for clarity. I cleared my mind of everything, trying to make my mind at one with the universe. Deep, cleansing breaths. I turned back to the coffee table and picked up the deck. I started shuffling the cards, focusing on the question *Are the two murders connected?* I prayed to the Goddess for enlightenment, and started spreading the cards out, my eyes closed.

Evil from the past affecting the present.
A young man in grave danger.
An unhappy mother.
The need to be cautious.

Thank you, Goddess, I thought as I swept the cards up. That was all I needed to know. It wouldn't hold up in a court of law, but I knew I was on the right track. I carefully shuffled the cards and wrapped them back in their blue silk. As I set them back in the cigar box I kept them in, the room began to spin out of focus.

Smoke. I smelled smoke.

And the heat from the fire was intense. The air was thick and I was choking.

Have to find a place to hide it, have to hurry, I thought. Have to be fast before they notice I'm missing, got to get back, where can I hide this thing?

Sirens. Crowd noise. Shouting. I was in an enclosed space. The fire was nearby, but in a different building. I saw boxes, covered in dust. There was sunlight coming in through some windows. Dust motes danced in the beams of light.

There had to be a place to hide it here.

There was a knot in my stomach. Anxiety. Pressure. Stress. I had to hurry, had to get back, it wouldn't do for anyone to notice I was missing. . . .

I heard the computer say in that toneless voice, "You've got mail." The vision faded away and I was back in my living room. What the hell was that all about? I wondered. The fire . . . I'd sensed the fire. It had to be the Cabildo burning. I didn't recognize the room, though. What was it I'd needed to hide? I walked back into the bedroom and sat down at the desk. I stared at the computer screen for a moment before clicking on the mailbox icon.

My on-line profile specifically states, without question, that I'm gay—so Amber, Vixen, Tiffani and others of your ilk, please take note that I'm definitely not interested in watching you shower or get it on with your sorority sisters or farm animals, thank you very much. Delete, delete, delete. How much time do I waste every day deleting this crap?

Well, I figured, at least spam had decreased the amount of junk mail sent through the postal service. This way the rain forest didn't have to be destroyed to sell products I wasn't interested in. So, maybe this is a good thing.

My heart sank when I saw the last e-mail. It was from Frank. With a sigh, I clicked it open.

Hey babe:

Is everything ok? You haven't answered any of my e-mails, or returned my calls. I'm starting to worry . . . my apartment, hell, my life seems so empty with you back at home . . . I love you so much, Scotty, and am so grateful that we got to meet…your visit here meant so much to me…you've become such an important part of my life in such a short period of time. Your e-mails always make my day, and I haven't heard from you since you went home. You aren't answering your phone either. Is everything okay, my love? I'm really getting worried . . . please let me know everything's okay . . . I haven't done anything to make you angry have I? If I have, please, answer this or call me and let me know so we can work it out, okay? I love you so very much and so look forward to the day when we can finally be together . . .

Love,
Frank

I closed the e-mail.

I was being a real shit by not answering him. It was wrong of me to make him worry, and he's a great guy, right? I was being an ass, I know, but it just didn't seem right to send him an e-mail and tell him that I was having doubts and second thoughts—an e-mail would seem so cold and cruel. Not that telling him on the phone would be much better. I liked Frank, I liked him a lot. He deserved better than that. He deserved better than me. He deserved some guy who wouldn't look at other guys, wouldn't jump in the sack with the next hottie who came along and made eye contact. He deserved better than a piece of New Orleans bar trash. He deserved someone who would love him, and cherish him, and appreciate him. All he would get from me would be heartache and pain. And if I were a good person, I would tell him that, make a clean break so he could stop thinking we had a future together and find someone who would have the ability to really make him happy.

Sigh.

I didn't want to let him go, either.

I really suck at this boyfriend thing.

And it was especially unfair not to tell him Colin was in town—even though telling him would probably make him nuts. Sure, the whole time I was in DC the specter of monogamy had never come up, but it was also possible he was assuming we were in a monogamous relationship. I didn't want to hurt him. And I couldn't ignore the fact Colin was a *wanted* criminal. Criminal or no, I liked him too. And it really wasn't fair to not tell Frank Colin wanted to move here and try to have a life with me.

Yeah, that would make Frank's day.

Hell, he might even tip off his local FBI buds to pick Colin up.

If that happened, I wouldn't be able to live with myself.

Goddess, what a mess. What was I going to do? Why does everything have to be so fucking complicated?

This, I told myself, is why I never wanted a boyfriend. My life is complicated enough without having to deal with this kind of crap. The smart thing to do was tell Frank and Colin both I didn't want a relationship and go back to how I was before I met them— bar and bathhouse trash, meaningless sex with people I never planned to see again.

Is that what you really want? a voice said in my head.

Shut up, Goddess, I don't need to hear this now.

Just answer his damned e-mail.

I clicked on the "answer" icon, and a blank page opened up before me. *Dear Frank*, I typed, *I'm sorry for not answering you sooner, but I've been really busy. A case has sort of dropped into my lap and I*

No, that wasn't fair or right. I couldn't blame it on the case. I deleted what I'd already written and started over.

Dear Frank,
I'm really sorry for not answering you sooner. I did have a really good time up there, and I miss you a lot too. But I am starting to wonder if things are going to work out for us. . . .

No, that was a bullshit, cowardly thing to do. Start over.
Dear Frank,
The cursor kept blinking, as though daring me to continue.
Asshole, asshole, asshole, it seemed to say to me. *You're an asshole.*

I signed off and shut the computer down. I'll think about it tomorrow, I decided. Scarlett O'Hara was not a dumb woman, and it seemed like a good policy. Right now I had things to worry about and focus on other than this mess with Frank. Okay, so ignoring the problem wasn't going to make it go away, but another day wasn't going to hurt anything, was it? Sure, it was shitty to leave him hanging and worried, but I couldn't answer him right now. I couldn't answer him until I knew what I was going to do, what I wanted.

Long-distance relationships are for the birds.

I got out the phone book and looked up the Cabildo's number. I dialed the administration office, and asked for the museum director.

"He's in a meeting right now, would you like his voice mail or Alice, his assistant?" a cheerful voice told me.

"Let me talk to Alice."

"Just a moment."

There was about a two minute pause, and then another cheerful female voice came on the line. "Alice Wolek, can I help you?"

"Hi, Ms. Wolek, my name is Scott Bradley and I'm doing

some research into the Cabildo fire, and I was wondering if you could answer a few questions?"

She laughed. "I can't help you there, sorry. I didn't work here then—neither did our current director. The person who would be the best for you to talk to is Kenneth Marsten—he was the museum director at the time of the fire. He retired last year. But I have to warn you—the fire is his shtick. Once you get him started you won't be able to shut him up."

"Do you have a number for him?"

"Sure, hang on for a second." I heard her digging through some things, then she came back on the line. "Here you go."

I repeated the number back to her after I wrote it down. "Thanks, Ms. Wolek."

"Anything else I can help you with?"

"Not that I can think of. Have a great day!"

She hung up. I looked at the number, and was about to dial it when someone knocked on the door. Cautiously I walked over and peered through the blinds. It was David, so I opened the door. He was still dressed from work, in blue slacks and a pale blue button-down shirt with a gray tie. He'd loosened the knot a bit and undone the neck button. He was taking a hit off a lit joint. He blew out the smoke. "Want some?" He held the joint out.

"No thanks." I let him in.

He plopped down on the couch. "Any trouble with the car?"

"No." I went and got the keys and tossed them to him. No sense telling him I was followed. Nothing happened, after all. "I might need you to take me somewhere this afternoon, though."

"Sure. What time?"

"Let me make a phone call." I picked up the phone and walked into the other room. I sat down on the bed and dialed.

Someone answered on the second ring. "Hello?"

"Yes, I'm calling for Mr. Marsten."

"You've got him." The voice was low and scratchy, like he'd been drinking a lot of whiskey and chain-smoking cigarettes.

"My name is Scotty Bradley, and I'm a reporter." Might as well stick to the same lie. "I'm doing some research for a story on the Cabildo fire, and you were the museum director at the time."

"You bet I was." He coughed. Maybe I was right about the smoking. "I know everything there is to know about that fire."

"Great." I got out my notebook. "Would you mind if I came to your home and talked to you in person?"

"Not at all, son. I hate talking on the telephone myself. When would you like?"

"Are you free in a couple of hours?"

"Since I retired, all I am is free." He sighed. "I dreamed about retiring, and now I'm just bored out of my mind all the time. Let me give you directions."

I wrote the directions down. He lived in the Elmwood area of the city. It was a relatively easy drive, mostly on I-10 out to Clearview Parkway. "Okay, thanks, Mr. Marsten. I'll be there in a few hours, is that okay?"

He snorted. "Call me Kenneth, son. And get here whenever you feel like it." I heard a cigarette lighter flick on. "All I'm doing is sitting around the house drinking beers and watching television. What kind of life is that?"

"Thanks." I hung up.

"You ready to go now?" I walked back into the living room.

"Sure." David pinched the joint out. "Where we heading?"

"Out in Elmwood by the Palace Theater."

"Cool. Let me get a soda and change out of teacher drag. Meet me out front."

I locked the door and sat down on the front steps just as Colin came walking up, wearing a snug pair of khaki pants and a skintight polo shirt. "Hey, babe." He sat down next to me and gave me a kiss. "What's up?"

"David and I are about to go run an errand."

"Can I tag along?" He grinned and put his hand on my leg. "And maybe later we can . . ." His voice trailed off, but his meaning was clear.

I looked at him. Damn, but he was pretty. "Probably not a good idea—it's something to do with the case I'm working on."

"Oh. Okay." He looked down. "Well, can we get together for dinner later?"

I looked at my watch. Four o'clock. Besides, I had to eat, and I was going to be strong and not succumb to temptation yet again. At least not until I'd definitely talked to Frank about everything. "Yeah, sure, meet me at the Louisiana Pizza Kitchen at seven."

He stood up. "You're not avoiding me, are you?" One of his eyebrows went up.

"No," I lied. I was going to have to straighten out this mess, and I'd do it over dinner, I decided. Colin was a nice guy for a criminal. He deserved better than this.

David came out in a pair of jeans and a sleeveless T-shirt. "You ready?"

"Yeah." I stood up and Colin hugged me, kissing me on the neck. "Seven o'clock. I'll be there."

I watched him walk away.

What in the name of the Goddess am I doing?

CHAPTER FOURTEEN

Nine of Swords

illness or injury to a loved one

"Okay, what's going on?" David asked as he backed out of the driveway. Colin waved, a sad smile on his face. His shoulders were a bit slumped. I waved back, and gave him what I hoped was a reassuring smile. "Who is that one, and where did he come from?"

"It's a long story," I sighed, watching Colin in the side mirror. He started walking slowly down Kerlerec towards Frenchmen. The spring I was used to seeing in his step was absent. I felt like a Grade A bastard. I had to stop leading him on. Him and Frank both.

But I didn't want to lose either one of them.

"Isn't it always with you?" David gave me a quick grin as he stopped at the light at Royal and Esplanade. "There's no such thing as a short Scotty story. At least I've never heard one."

I punched him in the arm. "Don't be a bitch. That's Colin. I told you about him—we met at Decadence?"

"That's the cat burglar guy? "David whistled as he shifted into gear and headed down Esplanade. "I hate you."

David always says that when he meets someone I've slept with he thinks is hot. Always. The way he says it, one would think the boys he gets are dogs, if he gets anyone at all. Don't believe it for a minute. David does very well for himself. Granted, in my opinion his standards slip a bit from time to time, but then again I've been guilty of seeing guys through liquor-colored glasses on occasion. I call it the "three A.M. pretty syndrome"—everyone's prettier after a couple of drinks. Especially when it's getting late. He has his fair share of scalps from pretty boys on his mantle. "He says he wants to give up his life of crime and move here. To be with me. What am I gonna do?"

"I should have your problems." He swerved to go around an SUV turning illegally onto Rampart. "Asshole!" he shouted at it, giving the driver the finger. "You got Hot Daddy up in DC and now the cat burglar all lined up for you. I really do hate you sometimes." What David wants more than anything is to have a boyfriend. Someone to make dinner with, watch television with, wake up with in the morning. He's totally bought into the "Someday My Prince Will Come" brainwashing of American pop culture. With forty approaching, he's starting to think it may never happen, but he doesn't get depressed about it. One night, when we were stoned out of our minds, he asked me what we would do for sex when we got too old to attract guys anymore. Without missing a beat, I replied "Pay for it."

"Yeah, whatever. You can have 'em." I reached for the ashtray. David always keeps roaches in there, and I really felt the need to take the edge off a little bit. Okay, so smoking a little pot probably wasn't the most professional thing to do on my way to get information from someone, but hey, I didn't have my license yet and who was going to rat me out to the licensing board? David? Yeah, right. I found a nice thick one and was about to light it when David hit one of the legion of potholes in the street and it flew out of my hand into the backseat. "Aw, fuck."

"That wasn't lit was it?" David glanced at me out of the corner of his eye.

"No, but still." I took off my seat belt and turned to reach into the backseat. David's car always looks like someone lives in it. Empty coffee cups, fast-food bags (no matter how many times

I lecture him on nutrition he still hits the McDonald's drive through at least once a week), sheet music, and various papers from his teaching job were scattered everywhere. Empty soda cans were rolling around on the floor. Finding that roach wasn't going to be easy, I thought. I rummaged around as he turned onto Claiborne, heading for the Quarter on-ramp. I finally found it on top of a framed picture of his junior high school band kids in uniform. "A-ha! There you are, you pesky roach," I said, grabbing it and sliding back into my seat. As I did, I looked out the back window.

The green sedan was behind us.

"Um, David, has that green car been behind us long?"

He looked into the rearview mirror as he started up the on-ramp. "I hadn't really noticed. Why?"

I put the roach back into the ashtray and shut it. "That same car followed me across the river this morning and back again."

"Are you sure it's the same car?"

"Pretty sure." Fuck, fuck, fuck. Granted, all it had done was follow me, but there was no telling what whoever was in it was up to. And now I had David with me. Damn it all to hell—I should have just borrowed the car again. "What kind of car is that?"

David looked in the mirror again. "It looks like an Olds-mobile—Delta Royale 88, I think. My mom has one of those."

"Do you think you could lose them?"

"I can try." He frowned in the mirror again. "Traffic's pretty heavy, though."

It was getting close to five o'clock. I-10, never the easiest way to get around, is a quagmire of traffic during rush hour. All the commuters rushing back home to the burbs, all the people who live in the city but work in the burbs coming back, not to men-tion all the through traffic heading east or west—it's always best to avoid I-10 from four to seven. There's also construction to deal with when heading west. The state has been working on the damned highway for years, trying to widen it to alleviate the traf-

fic problem. Which, of course, only makes it worse in the mean-
time.

David floored it and swung the car into an opening in the
next lane. I turned and looked back to see the Oldsmobile creep-
ing up on our right side. David cut off an old, rusted pickup
truck, which had to slam on its brakes in the left lane, and then
maneuvered back into our original lane. A white Lexus honked
its horn at us. "Fuck you!" David shouted at it.

I had this horrible feeling in the pit of my stomach as we
went around the curve heading out toward the airport. David is a
good driver, much better than me, but still. Maybe we shouldn't
try to lose the Olds.

Traffic was still moving, but I had been out this way enough
to know that just past the City Park exit, where 610 and I-10
merge, traffic always backs up, slowing down to a crawl until you
get past the exit for the Lake Pontchartrain Causeway. I looked
back. The Olds was keeping up with us, only a few cars back.
"Come on, David!" I half shouted.

"What do you want me to do?" he screamed back at me. He
was clutching the steering wheel so hard his knuckles were turning white.

"Take the Carrollton exit!" Stop overreacting, I told myself. It
might be nothing.

You need to lose that car.

Great, now the Goddess was kibbitzing.

You are both in grave danger.

"I get it, I get it," I said under my breath.

The Carrollton exit was coming up on our right. I could see
the tail lights of the cars already slowing for the traffic jam just
around the curve directly ahead of us. The Carrollton exit was a
nightmare to try to get to. The highway spread out to two extra
lanes on the right, and at the end of those lanes was the exit.

Unfortunately, the psychopath who designed I-10's route
through New Orleans had created those two lanes as an on-ramp

as well. There was a crowd of cars already there, practically bumper
to bumper, trying to merge onto the highway in the knot of cars
already there. To get to the exit, you had to avoid all these cars trying to move over to their left, none of them going as fast as the
cars already clogging the highway lanes. It was a massive traffic
accident just waiting to happen.

And we had to cross two crowded lanes to even get that far.

I closed my eyes for a moment and prayed.

I looked back and the Olds was directly behind us, coming
on very fast.

"Slow down there," I thought to myself. Then it dawned on
me. "David, speed up!"

DANGER DANGER DANGER

"I can't!"

WHAM!

The Olds slammed into the back of our car.

"FUUUUUUUUUUUUUUUUUUUUUCK!" David screamed
as the car started to swerve back and forth. We scraped up against
a blue Chevrolet in the left lane. The Chevrolet wobbled and
spun and then went off the highway into the median with a
screeching of brakes. David swung the wheel to the left and we
moved into that lane. I heard the screech of brakes and the un-
mistakable gut-churning sound of a collision behind us. I closed
my eyes and prayed to the Goddess.

*Please Goddess, keep us safe, please Goddess guide David and get
us out of this, oh please, Goddess . . .*

I opened my eyes to see the Olds right next to us.

David hit the brake and the car slowed. More brakes screeched
behind us and someone laid on their horn. He swung over behind the Olds and then cut right across two lanes of traffic. More
brakes, more horns. Sweat rolled down into my eyes. The Carrollton sign passed overhead. "Should I go left or right? *LEFT* OR
RIGHT, DAMMIT?" He avoided a pickup truck and swung into
the far exit lane.

"Right!" I shouted back at him. Taking the left exit lane would take us deep into the city, where we would eventually wind up in Riverbend, the furthest reach of Uptown. The traffic would be heavy there, lots of lights, and not many ways to lose them. If we went to the right we'd head into the Mid-City area, near City Park. For some reason it seemed smarter to go that way. There were lots of side streets, and we could always swing through City Park and get on 610 and head back home.

Or we could cut over to Leon C. Simon and head for Elysian Fields, which would also take us home.

Goddess please watch out for us and guide David safely please Goddess . . .

DANGER DANGER DANGER

My fingernails were digging into my palms. I forced myself to unclench my hands. Deep breaths, Scotty, stay calm, deep breaths, relax, it'll be okay.

We flew down the off-ramp.

I looked back.

The green Olds was coming after us, and gaining again.

. . . DANGER . . .

"Hurry, David!"

WHAM!

The Olds slammed into us again as we went around the curve heading toward Carrollton Avenue. My seat belt stopped my forehead about three inches from the dashboard. There was a stop sign coming up and traffic was zooming down the street. I gritted my teeth. David ran the stop sign and flew out into the traffic. I closed my eyes. I heard horns blare and brakes. We shot out onto Carrollton just as the light at Canal Street turned yellow. The Olds was behind us. David floored it. We made it into the intersection just as the light turned red. Cars started honking. He swerved to avoid a battered-looking Ford starting into the intersection. I looked back to see the Olds had ignored the light as well. David was weaving in and out of cars, the speedometer fixed at sixty.

Where, I thought, are the fucking cops?

The light at City Park Avenue turned green just as we reached it—and there was no one in the left turn lane.

David cut across another lane, forcing an SUV to slam on its brakes. As we went into the left turn, the car went up on two wheels.

The wheels on my side of the car.

I realized with a start that David had been screaming since we left the highway. Sweat was pouring in rivers down his face, which had turned red. He was grabbing the steering wheel so hard his hands had turned white.

I looked out the window and saw the pavement awfully damned close to my face.

I screamed.

The car came back down on all four tires with a jolt, and bounced.

My head hit the roof. I saw stars.

Please Goddess protect us and help us, please, please, please . . .

The next light was red, and there was a line of cars waiting for it to change.

WHAM!

The Olds slammed into us from behind again.

Without hesitation, David turned the wheel hard to the right and jumped the curb.

A woman walking her St. Bernard on the sidewalk jumped out of our way, and as we went past I saw her and the dog fall into the lagoon that ran alongside the sidewalk. David turned the wheel back to the left and the tail of the car swung around and then back. David fought the wheel, trying to straighten it out. The ground was muddy from yesterday's rain, and the tires spun, clods of grass and dirt flying.

I looked back and saw the Olds jump the curb as well.

Please Goddess, please, please, please . . .

The wheels finally grabbed hold of something solid and the car shot forward. We were driving on the sidewalk. A jogger jumped out of the way, a look of absolute terror on her face.

WHAM!

The car swung to the right, the reeds bordering the lagoon right outside my window. The car was tilting. We were about to go into the water—

"Oh my God, David!"

David fought the wheel, cranking it to the left. The back end of the car brushed the reeds as it swung back towards the sidewalk.

The Olds slammed into the driver's side of the trunk.

The car went into a 360-degree turn.

I screamed.

The wheels grabbed hold and somehow David managed to get us going again in the right direction.

A guy on a bike yanked his handlebars violently to the left, and we went right past him. His eyes and mouth were wide open as we just missed grazing him, his face white.

"OH MY GODDESS!" I screamed again.

Protect us, oh Great Goddess, Mother of us all!

The entry drive to City Park was coming up fast.

Way too fast.

On either side of the drive were brick columns, with iron scrollwork arched overhead reading Welcome to City Park.

We were going too fast to make the hard right turn we would have to make. The road was packed with stopped cars. We couldn't go back to the left. We had no choice. We were going to have to turn into the park. "Please, please, please," I whispered.

We were going to hit one of the brick columns.

At seventy miles an hour.

Oh Goddess save us, please, SAVE US!

The Olds was right behind us again.

my head fell back and bounced off the asphalt. Stars swam in front of my eyes.

Oh save me, Goddess, Kali give me the strength . . .

I was yanked to my feet.

"David!" I screamed. I couldn't see him anymore. Steam and black smoke were rising from the engine. The fucking car was on fire! My heart was pounding. Was he okay? I had to get him out of there! When the fire reached the gas tank—but I couldn't think about that, I had to get him out. . . . "David!"

Two men grabbed me and pinned my arms behind my back. I kicked out with my legs behind. I stomped down on someone's foot. The pressure on my arms lightened for a bit, and then a hand went around my throat and started squeezing.

"Shut the fuck up." Someone slid a blindfold over my eyes. They were lifting me now, carrying me. A gag was shoved into my mouth. I heard a car door open, and I was thrown into it, hitting my head on the opposing side door. Pain exploded in my head. They were tying my hands and feet. I heard doors slam, and a gruff voice—the same one that told me to shut up—say, "Get out of here, man! The cops must be on their way by now!"

The siren was getting closer.

Please, Goddess, lend speed to the police, don't let them get away with me, please, Kali, give me the strength and the courage to get out of this, Persephone see to David, make sure he's okay, please.

The car started up, and began to move.

My ribs hurt, and I had a headache.

Where the hell were the cops?

I was dizzy.

I smelled smoke again.

Anxiety.

The need to hurry.

I've got to hurry, I've got to hide this damned thing before anyone notices I'm gone.

I looked out of a window and saw the smoke billowing from the roof of the Cabildo.

I can't get caught, they can't notice I'm gone, hurry, there's got to be a place in here somewhere. . . .

And then everything faded to black.

CHAPTER FIFTEEN

Eight of Swords

those around him hold him too tightly

Strangely enough, this wasn't the first time I've been kidnapped.

Oh, I wasn't an abducted child or the Lindbergh baby or any-thing like that. My face had never been on the side of a milk car-ton. During Southern Decadence I was kidnapped by a group of crazy right-wing skinheads, but that was kind of different than this. (It's a long story, trust me.) Sure, that situation had been pretty damned scary, and I'd been pretty sure those nutcases were planning on killing me. But this—this was a *different* kind of scary. I had no idea who these people were, why they were taking me, or what they wanted me for. It also didn't make a whole hell of a lot of sense either. Why grab me now? Why the insanity on a crowded highway? If they wanted to grab me, they could have grabbed me a whole lot easier when I was leaving Gwen Victor's house by myself. It had been a pretty secluded street, no one was around to see anything, it would have been so fucking easy. They didn't need to go through all that chase bullshit, and David would be perfectly fine right now—sitting in his apartment, smoking pot and cruising for sex on-line. Instead of lying in his car . . .

Don't go there, Scotty.

I sent another prayer to the Goddess for David.

She didn't answer me.

She really can be a bit of a bitch at times.

I started taking deep breaths, which wasn't easy since I had to do it through my nose. My mouth was getting really dry—whatever they had shoved in my mouth was absorbing all of my saliva. Good thing I hadn't smoked that roach; I would have serious cottonmouth. After a few seconds the adrenaline rush went away and my heart started beating a little more slowly. I began reciting a calming mantra in my head. I needed to stay calm and cool, if I was going to get out of this alive.

"Are you having trouble breathing?" the man sitting next to me asked.

Well, I wasn't expecting that. A sympathetic kidnapper? Who am I to question anthing, right? Hey, whatever works. I nodded. A jolt of pain went through my head.

He pulled the gag out.

"Do you have anything to drink?" My voice sounded cracked and raspy.

"Yeah." He put up a cold can to my lips and tilted some into my mouth.

Blech. Diet soda. Beggars can't be choosers, though. It wet my mouth and got the saliva going again, which was all I needed anyway. I swished it around a bit before gagging it down. I really hate diet soda. "Thanks," I said after I swallowed it.

"You're welcome. I'll leave the gag out."

"Yeah, nobody would hear him if he screamed anyway," a voice said from the front seat.

Texas, I thought to myself, they have Texas accents. I've met enough guys from the Lone Star State to recognize that particular accent. We get a lot of Texans in New Orleans.

They grow some mighty sexy men in Texas.

Okay, so what do Texans have to do with all of this? I wondered. Nothing I'd turned up so far showed a connection to Texas. "Why did you take me?" I asked.

"Somebody wants to talk to you," the guy in the backseat replied.

"Well, you could have just asked me nice."

Someone up front laughed, one of those obnoxious nasal braying things. "Ya might have said no, and that wasn't an option."

"Obviously." My head was still hurting, and my ribs were a little achy. I didn't think there was much point, but I asked anyway. "What is all this about?"

"Don't play dumb, little boy. You already know." The guy next to me grabbed my arm, squeezing the biceps until it hurt. I tried to pull away, but with my arms tied behind my back there wasn't a lot I could do.

"I don't know anything that warrants almost being killed on the highway and then kidnapped!" I snapped. "Let go of my arm, already. That hurts, okay?"

The pressure on my arm let up, but he didn't let go. If I didn't know better, I'd think he was copping a feel. "You were never in any danger." He squeezed my arm again. "Hutch is a trained stunt driver."

I didn't respond to that. The stupidity of it was so unbelievable to me that at first it didn't compute. Hutch could be a trained stunt driver, maybe even the best in the world, but he couldn't control what the other drivers were going to do during that stupid Indianapolis 500 nightmare we'd just been through. Typical straight macho-man driver bullshit. That's how people get killed.

Like David. I swallowed as tears welled up in my eyes.

Please, Goddess, make sure he's okay, I'll never take him for granted again.

I didn't say anything else. No point in pissing them off. We rode on in silence. I didn't see any point in asking any more questions. They either didn't know the answers or didn't want to answer them. They were just flunkies. Apparently they were taking me to the brains of this operation, whatever the hell it was.

Maybe now I could find out what was really going on—what Rod Parrish's murder was all about, and what that had to do with Ace Martinelli's murder.

Then all I had to do was live long enough to somehow get away and tell someone. Piece of cake. Yeah, right. If David was dead, no one would know where I was. No one would know I'd been with him in the car, unless someone saw me being dragged off.

Colin, I thought. Colin knew I'd been in the car with David.

But how would Colin know what happened to David and me? When I didn't show up for our dinner date, would he think something was wrong, or would he just figure I was an asshole who'd stood him up? I hadn't exactly been thrilled to see him. He knew about Frank. Maybe he'd think I stood him up as a way of saying good-bye, and he'd just go about his business, do whatever the job was he'd come to town to do, and then leave without giving me another thought.

Telepathy has never been a part of my gift, but I had nothing to lose by trying.

At least it was something to do.

Colin, I've been kidnapped, please somehow let the police know, make sure that David's okay, if you don't want to go to the police at least give Storm a call, he'll know what to do, please Colin, realize I'm not the kind of person who'd stand you up, I wouldn't ever do that to you, I care too much about you to just not show and dump you that way, please know me well enough to realize that, please Goddess, let him know that, Aphrodite, carry my words to him, open his heart, if he loves me give him the understanding to realize something must be wrong—

The car stopped, and I heard a mechanized door open. Then the car moved forward again. I could hear the door sliding down behind us. A garage, then, either private or public.

Big help. We could be anywhere.

It sucked not being able to see.

The car turned sharply to the right at a ninety-degree angle, and came to a stop. The engine was shut off. I heard car doors opening, the sound of people getting out, the chassis rising from the weight being removed. The door next to me opened. Someone grabbed me and pulled me out. I stumbled, but was grabbed before I could fall. Someone got on each side of me, grabbed an arm, and started dragging me along with them. It was hard to keep up at first without running (they obviously were taller) until I finally said, "Slow down! I can't keep up and you don't want to drag me!" I let my entire body go limp, dead weight, to illustrate my point.

They slowed down.

We stopped walking, and I heard an elevator ding. We got in, I heard another ding, and the doors closed. We started going up, but the ride was too smooth and quick for me to count floors. The elevator stopped, the doors opened, and we started walking again.

"Ah, good. You got 'im."

The speaker had one of the thickest Texas accents I've ever heard—thicker than even the phony ones they used on *Dallas*. I was pushed down into a chair, and the blindfold was taken off.

I blinked at first, until my eyes adjusted to the light. A man was standing in front of me in a pair of tight jeans; the largest belt buckle I had ever seen started to swim into focus. He was wearing a rhinestone-studded black cowboy shirt with mother-of-pearl buttons. He was very narrow at the hips, and his belly ballooned over the tight waist of his jeans. His skin was deeply tanned and wrinkled, and white hair stood out underneath his black Stetson. His face seemed bloated, and the narrow bluish eyes were blood-shot. Tiny little red veins stood out on his nose. There was a thick white mustache hiding his upper lip. "How ya doin', Scotty?"

"All things considered, fine."

He walked over to me, his gray eelskin boots squeaking on the floor. He was holding a drink in one hand, and as he got closer I could smell it. Whiskey. Expensive Scotch, most likely. "Ya scared?"

"A little bit."

He threw back his head and laughed. The others, whom I couldn't see, laughed with him. Everyone was having a jolly old time, except me. He finally stopped laughing, wiping at his eyes with his free hand. "Son, ain't a damn thing to be scared of." His face came closer to mine. The whiskey on his breath was as thick as his accent. " 'S long as you're willin' to play ball with ole Rev here."

People who refer to themselves in the third person always make me nervous. It generally doesn't denote a healthy mindset. "I'd be glad to, Rev. Anything you want from me, just ask." I gave him a big smile.

"All I wanna know is where the mask is—that's all. The Parrish woman has it, don't she?"

Huh? "I don't know what you mean."

"The goddamned death mask!" he screamed at me, spittle flying into my face and hair. The sour fumes of the Scotch on his breath made my eyes water. His teeth were yellowed, and I could see gold fillings in the back of his mouth. His eyes had widened, and I could see some pesky hairs hanging down from his nose. "Don't fuck with me, boy—she has it, don't she?"

"I don't know what you're talking about."

He looked at me sadly. "Ya don't wanna play ball, do ya, son?" He stepped back. "That's not what I was hopin' to hear from ya."

"Seriously, Rev. I don't know what you're talking about, okay?" My mind was racing. Death mask? What the hell was he talking about? The only death mask I knew about was Napoleon's, and that was in the Cabildo.

The Cabildo.

The fire.

It started to click.

Rev stepped further away from me, and someone else came

into focus. "Here." He held a glass up to my lips. Whatever was in it smelled oily and rank. I tried to keep my mouth closed, but someone else pinched my nose. I held out as long as I could. Finally I had to open my mouth to breathe, and he poured the liquid straight in. I tried to spit it out, but he kept pouring. It was cold and oily tasting, and I couldn't help myself. I swallowed, and he kept pouring. It burned my tongue and my throat. Finally, he pulled the empty glass away from me.

I sputtered.

Rev stood there, watching.

"What-what was that?"

No one answered.

Rev's face began to blur a little. What the hell? I darted my eyes around the room. Everything was starting to become more vivid, more alive. A gilt-framed mirror on the wall caught my attention, and I couldn't tear my eyes away from it. Wow, the colors in it were so bright and alive and swimming . . . wait a minute. I shook my head and looked away. Everything was starting to swim around, the colors running and blending together and the furniture all seemed to be shimmering and made out of wavy lines like cheap animated cartoons and it was weird but it was kind of cool at the same time, and I kept blinking my eyes, shaking my head a bit trying to make sense of it all, my senses were on overload, and I looked up at Rev and his face was swimming in and out of focus, and I could see his breath, colored amber from the scotch, wow that's really kind of cool, and I could see patterns in the air, the air was getting colored, and everything was kind of blurring together, and it was really cool.

A feeling of calm came over me.

I giggled.

Wow. What was in that glass?

What was I just thinking about? Something had just made a lot of sense to me, what was it, come on Scotty think, think about it, don't be such a dope, you know what you were thinking about, it was important, oh yeah, the Cabildo, the fire, Napoleon's death mask, for a second there it kind of all made sense, I wonder why that painting is so vibrant, keep your head Scotty, look at the pretty lights on the river bridge outside the window, wow, I've never noticed how intense that looks at night before, I wonder why, and my skin is tingling, my scalp, I can feel all the individual hairs on my head, and the ones on the back of my neck, I didn't know I had hair back there, my skin feels so sensitive, I can feel the air, I can actually feel the air and I can smell it, what's that, Rev? no, I don't know anything about that, I really don't, I don't really, I'd tell you if I knew, you're a really nice man, aren't you, you're not going to hurt me, I don't know why I thought that, wow, did you see that helicopter go by, that was really amazing, no, I don't know where she's staying, I can't even keep track of Bryce—you know Bryce, the little figure skater boy, I think he's really her son, you know, Rod and Juliet's baby, he was adopted and he's about the right age, and I did see her in his hotel, wow, the air really feels nice on my skin, it's turning me on a little bit and hey now I'm looking at the floor, that's a really pretty floor, what kind of carpet is that, oh right, plush, that's what they call it, that's really funny, man my head feels really heavy, wow, I don't know if I can hold it up all by itself anymore, wow, I really like those boots Rev, they're really cool, even though it must be weird to have boots made out of real eel and how do you get the eels to stand still without wiggling aren't they kind of slimy and slippery, oh of course the eels aren't alive that's right you couldn't wear eels on your feet, that was pretty stupid I'm not really stupid Rev, I'm actually pretty smart but my eyes feel really heavy and my stomach isn't feeling right either, I feel like a sack of potatoes, oh, that's really funny, I can't seem to stop laughing and oh, look, there's the ceiling and the room is kind of spinning and everything is just—

Blackness.

Smoke.

Fire.

I've got to hide this thing, I've got to hurry there isn't much time, what the hell—

I opened my eyes and sat up. My head was groggy, my mouth dry. I tried to shake my head but it was too heavy, I couldn't move it.

What the hell happened here?

Light was coming in through a sliding glass door. I could see the sky, the stars, and looked down, to look for buildings, and all I saw were tiny little lights in the distance. Where the hell am I? I swung my legs over the side of the bed and tried to stand up.

My head spun. I took some deep breaths.

What the fuck had they given me?

I managed to get to my feet, holding on to the wall for support. There was a pitcher of water and a glass on the nightstand. I poured myself a glass, my hands shaking. As the glass came up to my lips it occurred to me it might be drugged, but hell, how much worse off could I be, right? So I drank. It tasted okay, even though my mouth kind of felt fuzzy and nasty.

Something clattered out on the balcony.

I turned and looked.

It looked like a metal spike.

It slid back and caught on the railing.

There was a rope hanging down from it that suddenly went taut.

What the hell had they given me? Acid?

I was having some kind of flashback, obviously.

I sat back down on the bed again, staring at the metal spike. Man, oh man, whatever it was sure had given me a hell of a trip. The room started to spin around again, slow at first, then faster and faster until everything was a blur. Goddess, what the fuck? My stomach lurched again. I reached for the water pitcher again. My hands were shaking and I spilled some on the carpet. The wet spot spread, darkening the fabric, and it kept spreading, further than possible, I didn't spill that much water did I? It didn't make any sense so I kept staring at it, it didn't make sense unless the carpet was made out of paper towels, was that possible but that made sense didn't it, why not make carpets absorbent? The colors on the walls started running again, mixing in with the carpet, making a hell of a mess, what was it called again? Oh yeah, *plush*. *PLUSH* carpet. I took a drink of water and spilled half of it down my shirt. It was cold, but it also felt good because my skin was hot, why had I not noticed that before? I held the glass up to my face and it felt nice and cold, I was sweating a lot, my whole shirt was wet, no that's from the water I spilled, man oh man oh man, what had they done to me? I started to giggle again. The bed-spread felt so good on my skin. I started rubbing my arms on it. Goose bumps. Wow. Get a grip, dude! I fell back onto the bed, taking deep breaths. I slid up to the headboard and bent my knees. I held on to them, trying to even my breathing. I felt for my carotid artery. My heart was beating too fast. Whatever it was had speed in it, obviously.

I sat there and watched as the rope pulled tighter and tighter.

Heaven help me, I had to be hallucinating.

A black-gloved hand grabbed the railing.

"Whoa," I said. My voice echoed in my head. It was a cool effect, so I said it again and started giggling.

Another hand grabbed the railing.

I closed my eyes and shook my head. What the fuck had they given me?

I opened my eyes just in time to see someone wearing a black mask climb over the railing. The figure was completely dressed in black, what looked look like a ninja outfit. Yeah, right, there's a ninja on the balcony.

Then again, things couldn't get a hell of a lot weirder than they already were, right? Why not a building-climbing ninja?

"Whatever they gave me, Mom and Dad have got to try this," I croaked out, and this struck me as funny, so I started laughing again.

The balcony door slid open. The black masked figure walked over to me. "Jesus, Scotty," a voice said. "What the hell? Are you on something?"

I knew that voice, even in my drugged state.

"Colin?" I asked unsteadily.

He peeled the black mask off, and grinned at me. "Hey babe, you know you stood me up." He sat down on the bed. "And I don't take kindly to that."

"I'm sorry." I stared into his face. For a second, it looked like it had been colored outside the lines, and then it went back to normal. I reached out and touched it. So soft. I slowly stroked it. It felt like silk, like velvet. I wanted to touch his whole body. I felt myself getting aroused. I love him, I really do, I thought. How could I not, look at that face, look at that body. What's not to love? I started laughing again, staring up into his beautiful face. "You're so pretty," I said. "I love you, Colin."

CHAPTER SIXTEEN

Temperance

working in harmony with others

"Man, you are wasted." Colin grinned at me.

"My hero," I said, starting to giggle again, but stopped when my head started aching. "Oh." My neck and ribs were starting to hurt a bit too.

"Are you okay?"

"Except for this headache. And my neck. And my ribs." I looked at him. He wasn't blurry anymore. He was definitely here and not a figment of my imagination. My stomach lurched. I swallowed. "I don't feel so hot." I didn't. I felt like I'd been ridden hard and put away wet.

Colin pushed a button and a watch face lit up. It was quarter to twelve.

I'd lost almost seven hours.

"We've got to get you out of here. Can you walk?"

"I can try." I tried standing up, and managed it without falling. I took a couple of steps. I was a little wobbly, but okay. "But I don't know how to get out of here. There's an elevator somewhere, though. That's how they brought me in."

He grinned at me. "We're going out the way I came in."

"Oh, uh uh." Some people are afraid of spiders, others snakes. My phobia is heights. I hate heights. I can't even look directly over the side when I'm on a second-floor balcony. I get nauseous and dizzy. Ferris wheels scare me to death. "There's no way I'm climbing down the side of a building. I'll just stay here. They can do their worst."

"It's a piece of cake. Besides, you're still too wobbly to climb for yourself."

"Then how—"

Colin kissed my cheek. "Come on." He walked back out onto the balcony. He waved at me. "Come on!"

I took a few steps. My legs weren't as wobbly as they had been. Encouraged, I walked faster. I stepped out onto the balcony. The fresh air felt good—my skin was still a little tingly. I could see the river spread out below me. There was a barge going downstream toward the Gulf, all lit up. I stared at the lights for a second before tearing myself away. I looked to the left and saw Café du Monde a long way down there. Canal Place was to the right. We were in one of the penthouse balconies on top of JAX Brewery. Pretty high up. Tentatively, I stepped to the railing and looked down.

Everything spun. My stomach did its best to climb out of my mouth. I stepped back.

The ground was a long way down.

"I can't." I was shivering. "I can't."

Colin was peeling a backpack off. He dropped it to the floor and zipped it open. "I was afraid of this, so I came prepared." He winked at me. "Just can't shake my Boy Scout past, you know." He held up a weird-looking harness made of what looked like black lawn chair material, with some metal links and hooks. "Put this on."

"I'm not going over the side."

"You don't have a choice." He put a hand on his hip. "It's either that or stay here. And if you stay here, there's no telling what might happen to you. They could kill you, Scotty. They mean business."

Like David. I swallowed and blinked back tears.

He held the harness out to me. "Put it on, Scotty. I won't let anything happen to you. Trust me."

Yeah, right. I don't even know what your real name is, and you want me to climb down the side of a building.

I slid my legs and arms through it, and he tightened it up on me. Then he turned his back to me and tied the straps somehow through the harness he was wearing. "Climb on my back and hold on."

I stood there.

"Come on, Scotty! We don't have a lot of time."

I put my arms around his neck and hopped up on his back. He didn't even stagger a bit. Damn, he's strong, I thought.

"Now put your arms around me and squeeze." I did. "Now do the same with your legs."

I did as I was told. I squeezed as hard as I could. I was never going to let go. I clenched my teeth and prayed.

He walked over to the balcony railing and climbed up on it. For one second that seemed like an eternity, all the lights in my line of sight blurred and spun. My stomach clenched again and I squeezed him. Then I was looking straight down for a minute and then back up at the sky. The contents of my stomach slid upwards into my throat, and I swallowed it back down. He checked the tautness of the line, and then without any warning, he stepped back off the building.

I screamed in my head.

I closed my eyes and clenched my teeth, holding on for dear life, as we fell through the air for what seemed like hours. The wind seemed to catch us and hold us suspended for a moment, and then gravity took over and we swung back towards the building. I opened my eyes as it zoomed towards us, Colin's legs braced out in front of him, and we hit the side.

"That wasn't so bad, now, was it?" he shouted.

"Oh, no, piece of cake." I closed my eyes. He pushed off, and we flew back out into the air again.

Oh holy Goddess protect us both—

And we were headed back towards the building again.

It was kind of like being in a swing, I thought as we rested for a moment against the side of the building. You swing out, and then back in again, yeah, keep saying that, you're in a playground, just playing on a swing, find a happy place—

And we launched back out into the air again, falling.

Oh Goddess protect and save us as we try to escape those men who took me—

Bounce and then back to a rest against the building.

—and watch over Colin and me as we try to make it down safely—

Launch out into the air again. My teeth were chattering. I could feel sweat trickling down my back.

—please save me and keep us both safe, oh Holy Goddess—

Bounce, then come to a stop.

"We're almost there, Scotty. Keep holding on!"

I prayed like I'd never prayed before, and then we were against the building again. "There," Colin said. "That was the hard part. We're almost down, Scotty. Just hold on—the rest will be easy."

We started going down more slowly, hugging the side of the building. My inner thighs ached from holding on so tight. I opened my eyes. Colin was walking down the side of the building.

He really *was* a cat burglar.

"Just a few more feet," Colin grunted. "And there—you can let go now."

I opened my eyes first. The breeze was blowing in my face from the river. I could hear the traffic on Decatur Street. I put my feet down. Solid ground.

My legs gave out, and since I was still attached to Colin we both fell, him landing on top of me. "Jeez, Scotty, can't you wait till we get back to your place?" He laughed.

My whole body started trembling. "Are you okay?" He could feel me shaking. He quickly undid the straps and rolled off me. "Scotty?"

I looked up at the side of the brewery, and saw how far we had come.

Oh my sweet Goddess.

What can I say? I threw up.

Colin had the decency to turn his back and not say anything until I was finished. "You okay?"

"I guess." My head felt like it was going to explode, and I had that wretched sour taste in my mouth, but other than that, just fine, thanks for asking. I stayed there on my hands and knees and resisted the urge to kiss the ground. Sweet, blessed, solid ground.

"Come on, then. My car's parked over here." He pulled me up to my feet. "Can you walk? We've got to get out of here."

Car? "Yeah. I think I can make it." I took a few wobbly steps. So far, so good. "Yeah, I'm fine."

He grabbed my hand and we hurried into the parking lot behind the brewery. The car was a sleek black Porsche. He unlocked it with a remote and the car chirped. I stared at the car for a minute, taking some more deep breaths. He opened my door for me and climbed in on his side. "Hurry, Scotty." I got into the passenger seat and he started her up. He revved the engine a couple of times, then headed for the exit. We roared out of the lot and onto Decatur Street. Once we had gone past Café du Monde, I asked, "How did you know I was there?"

"Well, I've been watching those guys, and I saw them come in with the car looking a little banged up. I heard on the radio about your little adventure on the highway, and it didn't take long for me to figure out they had you." He shrugged. "They followed you this afternoon across the river, so I figured they went after you again. They're going to have to ditch that car now. Every cop in town is looking for it."

Wait a minute. "You heard on the radio about me on the highway?" How was that possible?

"Well, I heard about the crazy car chase on the highway that caused a massive traffic pileup, and how one of the cars that caused the mess was a green Oldsmobile. I knew they'd been following you in one of those—"

"How do you know they followed me?"

"I told you I'd been watching them. I was following them." He turned up Dumaine. "But I decided to keep an eye on the boss tonight."

"But how did you know what room I was in?"

The light at Dumaine was red, so he stopped and grinned at me. "Let's get you home first, and then explanations, that okay?"

"Fine." Well, it wasn't, but a wave of fatigue swept over me, and I closed my eyes. All I really wanted to do was go to sleep and pretend this day never happened.

He pulled into David's driveway. I started to say something, but then I realized David's car was totaled—

And David had been, too.

A lump formed in my throat. I got out of the car. I had to hold the railing to help me up the stairs, and then I couldn't get my key into the door. Colin took the keys from me and unlocked the door, holding it open for me. I walked in.

David was sitting on my couch.

Okay, he was pretty unrecognizable. His entire face was swathed in bandages, and there were metal rods protruding from under the bandages by his nose. Under his eyes were dark purple bruises, but it was David all right. Just the way he had his head tilted to the side gave him away. My legs gave out again and Colin caught me as I started to fall. Tears filled my eyes. "Oh sweet Goddess."

David grinned at me. "Surprised?"

Colin helped me onto the couch. "Mom! Dad! We're back!"

Mom? Dad? I looked at him, but he just kept grinning at me. It is, I have to admit, a really nice grin. Dimples deepen in his cheeks, and his teeth are big and straight and white. His eyebrows move up just a little bit, bringing out some creases in his forehead. There are these spotlights behind his eyes that only get turned on when he smiles. I looked over at David. "What's with the headgear?"

"Broke my nose on the steering wheel. Stupid damned airbags."

"And the car—"

"It's at a garage. I'm sure it's totaled." He shrugged. "It sucks, but what can I do? I'll have to get a new one. At least it was insured. But I don't think I'll be offering to give you any rides anymore."

I do love David. I started to cry. I couldn't help it. I was just so glad he was okay—and with his usual oh-well-whatever attitude completely intact.

"Oh, Scotty, thank the Goddess!" I looked up just in time to get a crushing hug and kiss from my mother. When she was done, it was Dad's turn. That just made me cry harder. So, it wasn't the most butch thing in the world. Sue me. Mom handed me a cup of herbal tea, and then sat on the floor at my feet.

"Okay, what's going on?" I took a sip of the tea. Herb tea was her cure for everything. She'd dosed it with honey, just the way I liked it.

I have the greatest mom in the world.

David shrugged. "When they took me to the hospital I called your folks to tell them what happened. Got to tell you, it totally freaked me out to come to in an ambulance and be told I'd been alone in the car when they got there. I knew something was wrong."

"And then we called Colin, who knew exactly where you'd been taken." My father smiled at him, and my mother gave him a big hug.

"How did you know where exactly I was?" I asked him again.

"Mom? Dad?" Colin said, looking at them.

Why was he calling them Mom and Dad?

Had whatever they given me not worn off yet?

"Call us in the morning," Mom said, giving me another hug and a kiss before she and Dad went out the door. She paused for a moment and turned back. "And if he gives you any trouble, Colin, honey, you just drag him home to me and I'll take care of it, okay?"

Colin, honey?

"I will, Mom."

She shut the door behind her. Colin locked it.

What the hell was going on around here? "Why," I asked, "are you calling my parents Mom and Dad?"

He grinned and shrugged. "They asked me to. I think they like me."

I sighed. Great. Yet another complication in my love life. Exactly what I need.

Colin looked at David. He folded his arms. "David?"

"Uh uh, I'm not going anywhere. I've got a broken nose and my car is totaled. I deserve to know what's going on." He reached up and touched his bandages. "Do you have any idea how hard it's going to be to get laid with this on my face?" I grinned at him. Leave it to David. "I don't want to find out all about it later, okay? If I can't get laid for a while I want to know why."

Colin shrugged. "I guess it's okay." He sat down in the wingback chair and crossed his legs. "This goes back about fifteen years."

"The Cabildo fire?" I asked.

"Very good, Scotty." He smiled at me. "Yes, the Cabildo fire.

The man who had you kidnapped is named Rev Harper. He's an oil millionaire from Houston, and he collects Napoleon artifacts."

"An oil millionaire?" David said. "Will he replace my car?"

Colin shrugged. "His various criminal acts aside, he's actually a pretty fair man. He just might."

"He collects Napoleon artifacts," I mused out loud. The death mask. "They're going to try to steal the Napoleon death mask, aren't they? That's why the Cabildo was set on fire in the first place, right? They were trying to steal the mask, is that it?"

"Almost right, Scotty. The death mask was stolen during the fire."

"That can't be true," David said. "It's there. I've seen it."

"What's on display in the Cabildo right now is a copy. The original death mask was stolen during the fire." Colin shrugged. "Four bronze death masks were made from the original mold when Napoleon died. One is in Paris, one is missing, one was in the Cabildo, and the other is in the private collection of Rev Harper, in his mansion in Houston. The best we can figure it, Rev Harper paid off Rod Parrish to help steal the mask. He had someone inside the museum as well—but we've never been able to find out who it was. He might not have needed someone inside—but I've never believed that he paid off Rod Parrish and the fire started spontaneously. They had to have an inside man."

"Wait a minute." Maybe my brain was still addled from the drugs. I shook my head. "How do you know all this?" When he didn't respond, I said, "This is your last job, isn't it? Getting the death mask for someone else, right?"

"One last job, Scotty." He looked at me. "I swear, and then I'm through with all this, okay?" His face softened. I'm not telepathic, but I know what he was thinking. *One last job and then I'm coming here to be with you.*

"So, if they stole it, why are they still after it?" David lit a joint. He looked at it for a minute. "I wonder if it's okay to smoke this while I'm on painkillers?" He paused for a moment, then took a hit. "Guess I'll find out."

"Rev Harper doesn't have it." Colin looked at him. "I think Rod Parrish double-crossed them, and that's why he was killed. But they made a big mistake. They killed him without finding out where he was keeping it. Maybe his wife knows, but she disappeared after the murder. I've often wondered if she sold it to someone else."

"So Harper wants to find her." The room was starting to get fuzzy again. I shook my head. "And Ace Martinelli? How was he involved in all of this?"

"I told you, I don't know anything about Ace Martinelli."

"It was her." I rubbed my temples. "The woman I saw in the hall at the Aquitaine. It was Juliet Parrish."

"*What?*" Colin stared at me. "She's back in New Orleans?"

I closed my eyes. "Didn't it strike you as odd that Harper's men were following me in the first place, Colin? Why do you think they were doing that? They think I know how to find her. They thought I knew where the mask was."

Colin bit his lip. "Actually, I thought they were following you to try to find me."

I opened my eyes. They felt really tired, the lids incredibly heavy. "Wait a minute. You knew they were following me and didn't say anything to me?" He didn't answer. I could feel my temper starting to rise through the strange fogginess. "Of course not. As long as they were following me, you knew where they were and could do your own thing." The throbbing in my head was getting worse. "Is that why you dropped back in on me, Colin? To throw those thugs off your trail? To use me and my family and friends as decoys? Dude, David and I could have been killed!"

Boyfriend, shmoyfriend. Wait'll Mom and Dad get a load of this!

But somehow, I wasn't getting as mad as I should. I didn't understand—

"That's really uncool, Colin," I heard David saying.

"It wasn't like that." Colin's voice sounded like it was in a cave, echoing and echoing deep inside my head.

—what was going on here with me? I couldn't seem to stay focused—

"Well, how was it then?" David's voice sounded deeper and slower than usual, like I was hearing it through water.

—the candles on the altar, the white was bleeding down onto the red velvet—

"I didn't think Scotty was in any danger, or you either, David, you have to believe me—"

—which was puddling on the shiny brown floor, shining like the surface of a pond—

"—maybe you should be the one buying me a new car—"

—spreading somehow, the white and the red were mixing and making pink—

"I think I need to go to bed." I tried to stand up, but slipped back down.

"Scotty?" someone was saying my name somewhere, echoing and deep and booming like a baritone, the room was spinning around, and then I felt Colin touching me, and he was saying something but I couldn't understand it, but he took me by the arm and my skin was tingling where he was touching me, and it felt really really good, and then I was looking at my reflection in the floor, and his shoulder was digging into my stomach and it kind of tickled, and then everything blurred and I was lying on my bed, and then things kind of swam back into focus. I shook my head.

"You shouldn't be alone tonight," Colin said as he slipped my socks off and undid my pants. I lifted my hips so he could slide my jeans off, and then held up my arms while he removed my shirt.

"Are you going to take advantage of me?" I asked. His face was getting blurry again.

"I may be many things, Scott Bradley, but I'd never take advantage of someone who's drugged."

"Too bad," I said as I fell back onto the bed and fell asleep.

CHAPTER SEVENTEEN

Four of Cups

a time for reevaluation

Maybe there is something to this boyfriend thing, after all.

I woke up a little after eight in the morning with Colin's arms around me and his body cuddled up to mine. He was snoring a little, very softly, and he felt warm. I liked the way his skin felt against mine. We both had our underwear on, and he had a leg wrapped over mine. We fit together almost perfectly. I didn't want to move. It just felt nice there in his arms, with the bed so soft underneath me, and my wool blanket draped over the two of us. My face was a little cold, so I knew outside of the bed was going to be chilly. It was like being in a little nest, snug and safe. I stayed there for a little while, wondering what it would be like to wake up like this every morning, and decided that it would be kind of nice. Really nice, indeed. Frank and I—

Oh, Lord, Frank.

My entire body tensed. Colin moaned a little, and rolled over away from me. I moved into the spot where he had been laying. It was still warm from his body. It felt nice. He had his back turned to me now, and I reached out and stroked the line of it softly. He shifted a bit in his sleep. There's something sweet about guys when they sleep, something peaceful and sexy.

I was getting turned on.

Frank, Frank, Frank, I told myself.

I couldn't keep ignoring Frank's e-mails.

The spell definitely broken now, I got out of the bed and went to start coffee in the kitchen. The message light on my phone was blinking, so while the coffee brewed and I rummaged around in the refrigerator for something to eat, I listened to my messages. There were seven in all; the first from Frank, and then six hang-ups. The message from Frank was like his e-mail—concerned. I heard it in his voice. He sounded all butch and sexy, as always, but there was a slight, almost imperceptible quiver to his tone. Hearing his voice made me feel even worse. I checked the caller ID. All seven calls were from Frank.

Not good. Not only was it indicative of an obsessive personality—which I didn't know about him before—it also meant I was being a total asshole by not responding. I'd decided I'd think about it tomorrow, and it was tomorrow.

I do care for him, I thought as I got two mugs down from the cabinet. I might even love him a little. So what was I going to do?

I guess I'd have to be honest and not worry about hurting his feelings. Lying to him would be worse; leaving him hanging worse still.

Colin was still asleep when I went back into the bedroom. His head and shoulders stuck out from under the covers. I sat down on the edge of the bed and watched him sleeping. Sleeping, he looked innocent—like a little boy. Okay, a little boy with huge muscles, but still. His skin was completely smoothed out. His mouth was open just a little, those thick, soft, red lips parted so I could see his strong white teeth. I leaned down and kissed his cheek, gently brushing his face with my hand. He stirred a little, moaned again, and then his bright green eyes opened. He stretched a bit, muscles flexing. He smiled. "Morning, beautiful."

I set his coffee down on the nightstand. "I made you some coffee. Are you hungry?"

He yawned and nodded, sitting up. The blanket slipped

down, exposing his pecs. He has the sexiest nipples. I resisted the urge to pinch them. "Skipped dinner last night."

"You didn't take advantage of me last night, did you?" I crossed my arms.

He grinned. "No, although it was very very tempting." He picked up his coffee cup and took a drink. "There are rules, you know."

"I must be losing my touch, then." I grinned back at him. "You used to not be able to keep your hands to yourself."

"Hey, I don't take advantage of people when they're out of it." He pushed the blanket off and stood up, stretching. He was wearing a pair of tight white boxer briefs. My eyes lingered there for a moment. "Do you mind if I take a shower?"

"Nah. It'll give me a chance to make breakfast."

I turned on the radio while I rummaged in the refrigerator, coming up with eggs, butter, mushrooms, a bell pepper, and an onion. I melted the butter in a skillet while I chopped up the vegetables. After pouring the beaten eggs into the skillet and then dumping the sliced veggies in, I put some bread in the toaster. It was kind of nice, I thought as I hummed along with the latest hit from the newest teen Britney-wannabe. Maybe there is something to this domestic thing, cohabitation with another guy. It would be nice to wake up with someone every morning. It would be nice to cook and do those little couple things, like Mom and Dad, Storm and Marguerite, Rain and what's his name. Why was I always so reluctant to be in a relationship? I had all these great, successful marriages around me as role models. Granted, they were all straight people, but I wasn't like most people I knew, whose parents had been through enough divorces to make Liz Taylor and the Gabor sisters envious.

Maybe I needed some therapy. Surely the thing with Coach Phelps wasn't still weighting me down emotionally. That wasn't my fault. He was the adult. He should have known better than to get involved with a student. I was just a horny kid. If his life had been wrecked, it wasn't my fault, right?

Maybe that was the problem, I thought as I flipped the omelette. Maybe I always kept my distance from guys because I didn't want to hurt anyone else. The toast popped up and I buttered it. I didn't want to be responsible for hurting someone else.

I really needed to e-mail Frank.

The shower stopped while I was putting the plates on the table. Colin walked in with a towel around his waist and sat down. Beads of water spotted his big shoulders. He slid his arms around me and kissed me on the neck. Goddess, it felt good. I felt my body starting to respond. I put my hands on his chest and gave him a little push. "The food's gonna get cold."

He grinned. "When do I get my reward for taking care of you last night?"

"Eat." I pushed him back towards his chair.

We ate in silence for a while, and then I said, "Was it my imagination or were you calling my parents Mom and Dad last night?"

"Does it bother you?" he asked, putting his fork down, his eyebrows going up.

"No, not really. It just kind of threw me, and I was wondering how that happened."

"Well, when I went over there the other day looking for you, I had a long talk with your parents." He grinned. "They're really cool, you know?"

"Yeah, I know." Everyone always loves my parents.

"So anyway, while we were waiting for you to come over, we just talked and we really hit it off. Your mom asked about my parents and I told her that they stopped talking to me all those years ago when I came out to them, and how lucky you were, and your mom said, 'Well, from now on, just think of us as your parents,' and we kind of went from there. I gave them my cell phone number, so when David called them from the hospital last night, they called me. I kind of figured that Harper's people were behind it all, so I went over there to see if I could get you out."

"You never answered me when I asked you how you knew what room I was in."

"I've been up there before." He had the decency to blush. "You know, to scope things out. There are only two bedrooms up there, and one is definitely Rev Harper's, so I figured I'd take a chance on the second bedroom balcony. All the lights were off, so I assumed they'd gone to bed for the night. It was just blind luck, really."

"And if I wasn't there?"

"I'd have kept looking."

"I see."

We continued to eat in silence, and then Colin said, "Scotty, you know I have feelings for you."

"I know. I have feelings for you too. But I'm kind of seeing someone right now."

"Frank the Fed?" He made a face. "Your parents told me about that."

Mom and Dad have been counterculturists all their lives. They weren't thrilled with the idea of me dating an FBI agent, even one they liked. Frank knew how they felt about the government, and was confident that once he retired and moved to New Orleans, he could win them over. He probably could—he's a very charming man when he wants to be, which is why it didn't make any sense to me that he didn't have any friends up in DC. But then, from what I've seen of the people up there, maybe he didn't want to be friends with anyone up there. It was only natural that Mom and Dad would prefer the cat burglar to the Fed. They probably saw Colin as a hero, a modern-day Robin Hood, stealing from the decadent capitalist pigs and giving to the poor, when the truth was he was just a thief.

But a really good-looking one.

"I do love Frank," I said, getting up for more coffee. "He's a really great guy, and if you two weren't on opposite sides of the law, you'd like each other, too."

He came up behind me and put his arms around me while I poured the coffee, kissing the back of my neck. Obviously, he remembered how much that turns me on.

So much so that I spilled the coffee.

"Oh, damn!" I reached for the paper towels and pulled away from him.

He held up his hands and went back to his chair. "Sorry, man. I'll stay away from you if that's what you want."

What I want. I didn't know what the hell I wanted. "I just can't deal with it right now, Colin."

"Does Frank know you slept with Bryce Bell?" He had his hands on his hips.

I stopped mopping up the coffee. "That's really low, Colin. Even for a cat burglar."

"I take it you haven't told him."

"That's none of your business."

"And you haven't told him I'm in town either—or about the other night, have you?"

"Same answer."

"I might just be a cat burglar," he said, "but even I know the best way to ruin a relationship is to not be honest."

"I don't need any advice, thank you very much."

"Maybe I should just go." He stood up.

"Maybe you should."

He walked out of the room and the towel dropped off. He left it where it was, giving me a nice view of his should-be-an-underwear-model body on his way out of the room. Very cheap shot there, Mr. Cat Burglar.

Don't let him go like this—he doesn't deserve it.

All right, already!

I walked back into the bedroom. "Colin—"

He turned back to me as he buckled his pants. "Look, Scotty.

I know I'm being out of line here. I ran off and didn't even say good-bye to you. It's stupid of me to expect to be able to waltz back into your life and have you waiting for me. I just hoped—well, never mind."

I hugged him. "I don't know what I want, Colin. I have a lot to think about, okay? And with all of this other shit going down . . ."

He pulled his shirt on over his head. "You need some time and space. That's cool. I get it." He took a card out of his wallet and wrote a number down on it, then placed it on the nightstand. "That's my cell number. Call it anytime, okay?"

I walked him to the front door, where he gave me a big hug and a chaste little peck on the lips. "Be careful," we said at the same time, and then both laughed. I watched him walk out of the gate before I closed the door. Was I being stupid to let him go? Maybe I was just fooling myself. Maybe he was the right one for me, not Frank.

And that body! Goddess!

I took a shower and got dressed. The phone rang. "Hello?"

"You okay, my queen?" It was Storm, and he didn't sound normal.

"Is that concern I hear in your voice, brother o' mine?" I teased.

"Well, yeah." He sounded embarrassed. "Mom and Dad called and told me you were okay—that somehow this Colin guy had managed to get you away from the people that nabbed you." I could almost see the perplexed look on his face. "Who is this Colin guy?"

"The cat burglar from Decadence."

"Oh, him." I could practically hear the wheels turning in his head. "He's back in town?"

"Yeah."

"What about Frank?"

"Let's not go there."

"Okay." I could almost see his trademark shrug. "Anyway, Bryce never came back."

"Damn." I sat back down on the bed. "That's not good, Storm." I filled him in on what Colin had said about the Napoleon death mask.

He whistled. "But he doesn't think Ace Martinelli had anything to do with this?"

"He had to, Storm. Why else would those guys take me? That was all they were interested in—all they wanted to know." I sighed. "I'm trying to wrap my mind around all of this, but there's still too many pieces missing, you know?"

"It's possible that Ace's murder had nothing to do with this death mask stuff."

"Oh come on, Storm, you're the one who always says there are no coincidences.

"Yeah, but we can't rule out the possibilities." He sighed. "I had to call Venus about Bryce disappearing. I didn't want to, but he really didn't leave me much choice. All we needed was for her to come looking for him and me not able to produce him. He's lucky they haven't sworn out a warrant for him already. It really pisses me off when a client doesn't do what he's told by his lawyer, particularly when he has one as brilliant as yours truly. You haven't heard from him, have you?"

"No."

"Well, if you do, tell him to get his ass back over here." He hung up.

I walked back into the living room, and lit the candles on my altar. I knelt down in front of it, clearing my mind.

Oh, Goddess, hear my prayer. Thank you for sending Colin to save me last night, and for watching over us as we climbed down the side of that building. Please watch over Bryce as well. He is in danger, I know he is, and please guide him and grant him the wisdom to do the right thing. And watch over Colin as well; I know he is a lawbreaker, but he is a really good-hearted person who just took a wrong turn somewhere along the way, but I believe him when he says he is going to give that all up and stick to the straight and narrow from now on. And grant me the wisdom, the serenity, and the ability to treat Frank with the love and respect he deserves from me.

Okay. I felt a lot better. Praying to the Goddess always seems to have that effect on me. I walked back into the bedroom and turned the computer on. I got myself another cup of coffee while the dial-up connected. I checked my mail. Today it was all junk. I deleted it all and opened a new window.

Dear Frank:

First of all, I need to apologize for not answering your e-mails sooner and for not calling you. It was bad of me, and completely unfair to you. You deserve better than that.

I did enjoy seeing you up in DC. That was truly a wonderful experience. But at the same time, it worried me a little. You see, I'm really not used to the concept of having a boyfriend. I've never really had one before, and I'd be lying if I said it didn't scare me more than a little bit. But it's not out of a sense of YOU scaring me; I am scared for you. I'm not really a good person, you see. I'm selfish and I think only of myself. We've never discussed monogamy, and if that's something we are going to be committed to if this relationship continues. I'll be honest with you—I don't think that's something I am cut out for. I know it's a lot to ask from a boyfriend—and I certainly wouldn't expect you to be monogamous either.

I just don't know if I'm cut out for this. I don't want to ever hurt you or cause you any pain.

Maybe it would just be better if we stayed friends.

Love,
Scotty

I stared at the screen for a moment, then clicked Send.

The die was cast. I closed my eyes and sighed. *Please don't hate me, Frank,* I thought.

I signed off and turned the computer off. Yeah, staying single was probably the best choice for me. I make a lousy boyfriend, just like I always thought I would. I was better off picking up guys in bars or going to the bathhouse to take care of my sexual needs, and having my emotional needs satisfied by my family and my friends. That way no one would ever get hurt. And when I got too old to attract guys, like I'd told David, I'd just hire escorts and be done with it.

But if breaking up with Frank was the right thing to do, why did I feel so empty?

Might as well get some work done.

I picked up the phone and dialed Gwen Victor's number. She answered on the third ring. "Mrs. Victor? Scotty Bradley here."

"I told you yesterday, Mr. Bradley, I don't know where my sister is." Her words were a little slurred. I glanced at the clock. It was only nine-thirty. What time did she start drinking every day? Sweet Goddess!

"Mrs. Victor, I think you do." I closed my eyes and tried to get a read on her. I could sort of sense some agitation and nervousness coming through the phone line. Yeah, she was lying, and didn't feel comfortable with it. The liquor wasn't helping her, either. "I know for a fact your sister is in town—I saw her several days ago. She's in a lot of danger, and she won't be able to face it all alone. She needs help, and my brother and I can give it to her. The people who are after her killed her husband—and are willing to kill her for what she knows. Are you going to tell me where she is, or not?"

She didn't answer.

"Mrs. Victor?"

The only response was her labored breathing. I was glad I couldn't smell her breath. It was undoubtedly flammable.

"Well, it's on your conscience then." I hung up. Damn. That had gotten me nowhere.

All right, I thought to myself. If I was trying to hide in New Orleans, where would I go?

Other than canvassing every hotel and guesthouse in town, which would take weeks, I couldn't think of a thing to do. Although I was pretty confident I could rule out the major hotels. I doubted she was at the Ritz Carlton, the Fairmont, or hotels like that. Then again, for all I knew, she might be staying at her sister's. She could have been in a back room when I was there.

Bryce, on the other hand, might be easier to find, if he was just hiding and hadn't been grabbed by Harper's men. Maybe I should call that vile, wretched adoptive mother of his. He might have checked in with her, even though I would have avoided her like the plague. I grabbed the phone book and looked up the number for the Royal Aquitaine.

I jumped as the phone rang. I looked at the caller ID, and smiled to myself. Maybe I'm not so bad at this after all, I thought as I picked up the phone. "Hello?"

"Mr. Bradley, I just spoke to my sister, and she said it was okay to send you to see her." Her voice sounded very tired, but was somewhat clearer than before—more sober. "I personally think this is a mistake, but it's not my decision to make. She's staying at the Charlemagne House on Esplanade Avenue. She's registered under the name Felicia Tuttle."

"Thanks, Mrs. Victor," I said, but she'd already hung up.

Excellent!

CHAPTER EIGHTEEN

Queen of Swords

a woman of strong character who can bear her sorrow

The Charlemagne House is on Esplanade just past Bourbon Street, on the Marigny side. It was a French Colonial plantation house, with slender wooden columns supporting a wide front gallery on the second floor, and three dormer windows protruding through the attic roof. A wreck just a few years earlier, it had looked as though the next big wind would blow it over and that would be the end of it. It had been one of the tragedies of Esplanade Avenue, with broken windows and unpainted shutters hanging loosely off their hinges, uninhabited for years. People in the neighborhood would just shake their heads over it. Owned by an absentee landlord, the city had finally declared it blighted and seized it for resale. A gay couple from San Francisco, on the verge of retirement, bought it at a bargain-basement price and renovated the building from top to bottom, restoring it to its former glory. When they finished, they retired from their jobs and opened it as a guesthouse. It was now one of the showplaces of the avenue.

I walked up the wide cement stairs to the second floor gallery and opened the front doors, stepping into a hallway with a thick Oriental rug on the floor and a glittering chandelier hanging from the ceiling. Gilt-framed mirrors hung on opposing walls. To my immediate right was the breakfast room, decorated with what looked like old plantation antiques. Over the marble mantelpiece hung a painting of an eighteenth-century belle. A nineteenth-century desk was centered at the rear of the hall, with big potted ferns on either side.

"Hey, Scotty! What are you doing here?" The guy sitting at the desk stood up with a big grin.

"Westly!" I grinned. I'd known Westly Lattimore for years. We'd met at the bathhouse one night about seven years ago, and had a pretty good time together. He also worked out at my gym. He was about my height, with a strong, lean, muscular build. His head was now shaved completely bald, and it gleamed in the light from the chandelier. He had big gray eyes over high cheekbones and sunken cheeks, with a strong nose and a square jaw. He was wearing khaki shorts, and a white T-shirt that read CHARLEMAGNE HOUSE in big, red, old English lettering. He lived Uptown with his boyfriend. "I didn't know you worked here."

"Two years now." He grinned. He was a sculptor, I recalled, with a studio in a converted shed behind his house on Jena Street. We'd had sex there once, with him bent over his worktable. "It's a nice gig."

"Cool." I gave him a hug and a peck on the cheek. "How's"— I tried to remember the name of his boyfriend, but couldn't. I'd only met him once, and I'd been drunk at the time.

He grinned. "Taylor's just fine. You got your costume figured out for the Lazarus Ball this weekend?"

"Yeah, you?"

He sighed. "Well, I wanted to go as an Egyptian, but fucked around and never got it together, so I'm just gonna have to see what I have in the closet and throw something together. I'll probably just wind up wearing leather again." He looked good in leather.

"Cool." I shrugged. "Actually, I'm here to see one of the guests. Felicia Tuttle. Where is her room?"

He flipped open the guest book and ran a finger down a column. "Tuttle. She's in room eight, which is in the slave quarters." He jerked a thumb over his shoulder. "Just head out the back door and down the steps. It's on the first floor, the door on the left."

"Cool." I winked at him. "See ya."

I went out the back door and down the stairs into a courtyard that was more like a jungle than anything else. Two massive oaks, one on either side, shaded the entire area; a fountain with a statue of a Greek maiden pouring water out of a jug on her shoulder bubbled and splashed in the center. Wrought iron tables and chairs were placed at discreet distances from each other. The courtyard was flagstoned, and big planters with massive ferns were strategically placed to give the tables some privacy from the others. The slave quarter was burnt umber, made of what looked like cement plastered over the facade. There was a small gallery on the second floor with a flight of cement steps leading up to it. I turned to the left and knocked on the glass door.

The door swung open. Felicia Tuttle was the woman from the hallway. She looked a lot more haggard and worried than she had when we'd bumped into each other. Her face was devoid of makeup, making it look washed-out. She had a scarf tied around her hair; some stray hairs had escaped and were hanging into her eyes. She was wearing a gray sweatshirt with a coffee stain on it, and baggy jeans. Her feet were bare. She showed no sign of recognizing me. "Scott Bradley?" she asked. She sounded tired.

"Mrs. Tuttle?" I held out my hand.

She took it and limply shook it. "Come on in." She stood aside to let me pass.

There was a big front room with another opening off the back. It was very dark and gloomy. She had all the shutters closed and the curtains shut. She turned on a light. The room had hardwood floors polished to a dull gleam.

"Scotty!" Bryce squealed and almost knocked me down as he

threw his arms around me. "You found us!" He squeezed me, and then stepped back a bit. He had a big grin on his face.

I hugged him back, and then pushed him away from me. Damn, but he was a little cutie. "You're in big trouble, young man." I sounded like one of my grandparents—Mom and Dad never talked like that.

"You didn't tell anyone where you were going, did you?" Felicia shut the door and deadlocked it, then put the chain on as well.

"No." I sat down in a chair. "I don't think I was followed either, but I can't guarantee it." I'd kept an eye out for anyone who looked suspicious on the way over. I hadn't seen anyone, but it was still possible.

"Then we'll have to move again." She sank down on the bed, dropping her face into her hands. "I'm so tired of running."

"It's time to stop running," I said. "My brother can help you, Mrs. Tuttle."

She smiled tiredly, pushing stray hairs out of her eyes. "You can call me Juliet. There's no use pretending with you. You already know who I am."

Bryce sat down on the bed next to her and held her hand. "I told you, Mom, Storm is great. He can help us."

I tried not to smile. So I'd been right. Bryce was her son.

"I don't know." She smoothed his hair. "I've been running for so long . . . I don't even know what it's like to be normal anymore." She laughed, a dispirited sound. "Normal. Yeah, right. Like that's even possible for me anymore."

"Why did you run, Juliet?" I asked.

"They killed my husband!" Her eyes flashed, and then became sad again. "You'd think it would stop hurting at some point, wouldn't you? That's what they always say, right? Time heals all wounds. . . . I've missed Rod every day of my life." A tear rolled out of her left eye. "Even after all this time"—she paused to get control of herself again—"I still miss him. You have to understand, Scotty—this wasn't how it was supposed to be. We were supposed to raise our son together, grow old together." She swallowed. "He wasn't supposed to get killed."

"Do you know why he was killed?" I looked over at Bryce. His eyes were wet.

"I didn't know what was going on. I knew Rod was up to something, but he wouldn't tell me what he was doing. 'It's better if you don't know,' was all he would say." She touched Bryce's face with her fingertips, then let her hand fall away. "He was such a sickly little baby, and I couldn't have any others. It was so hard—I couldn't work because we couldn't afford someone to stay with him and care for him, and the insurance would only cover so much. The bills kept piling up—my parents tried to help, and so did Gwen, but they didn't have any money either. Then one day Rod came home from work and said he had the answer to all of our problems. I knew, deep down, that it meant even worse trouble—Rod was going to have to sell his soul or something—but I was just so tired of worrying and getting all those horrible phone calls from the collections people that I just didn't care anymore. I should have known better.

"It was so horrible." She stood up and walked over to the window. "It's so horrible to be poor. I remember going to the grocery store one day—we didn't have any money, and there wasn't any food in the house, and I needed milk for the baby, so I wrote a bad check for about five dollars, thinking maybe the bank would go ahead and honor it because it was for so little. They didn't. And then the store started calling, threatening to put me in jail. . . . I just wanted to die. So, maybe, when Rod said he had the answer, there was a part of me that knew it was wrong, that there was something criminal going on, but I just didn't care anymore. I didn't care what it took." She swallowed and a tear ran down her cheek. "If I'd known—oh, God, if I'd known. Maybe I should have put my foot down and told him to get out of whatever it was. But I was so beaten down, Scott. All I could think of was getting out from under. All I could think of was not worrying about answering the phone and getting screamed at by some ass-hole from a collection company, who didn't care I had a sick baby. Who wanted me to not pay the mortgage so I could pay them." She stood up, wringing her hands, and walked over to a mirror. She stared into it. "And then one day we had the money, and Rod wrote checks to pay off all the bills, and took us out for a nice dinner. It was so wonderful. It was like we'd escaped. . . . Things were going to be better. Rod told me so, and I believed him."

"You didn't know where the money came from?"

She shook her head. "He wouldn't tell me. Oh, I knew he was doing something illegal. Rod always told me everything, but he wouldn't tell me this. He said it was better that I not know. For my own good. And then the next day, I came home from my sister's and"—she choked up again—"and found Rod. I was in shock. I couldn't react. I just put Bryce in his room and shut the door. And the phone rang. I answered it. It was this horrible man—I'll never forget his voice—and he said that if I didn't tell them where Rod had hidden it, they'd kill my son next. That's when I started screaming, and the neighbors called the police. The next day I cleaned out our bank accounts and started getting ready to go. After the funeral, we got in the car and left." She wiped at her eyes.

I looked over at Bryce, who was crying silently. "Where did you go?"

"Mexico." She turned away from the window. "I figured I could lose myself more easily there than I could up here. But the baby got sick again, and then I met *her*."

"Her?"

"Lucinda Bell." She spat the words out. "We were in Mexico City, and she was so taken with little Bryce, and she knew he was sick . . . I was about out of money then, and she offered to—oh, I can't say it."

Bryce spoke up. His voice was bitter. "She offered to buy me."

I looked from him back to Juliet. "What?"

"It was the ultimate, unforgivable sin. I'll go to hell for it." Juliet covered her face in her hands. "I was out of money, my son was sick, my parents couldn't help me—it wasn't about the money. You have to believe me. *It wasn't about the money!* He was sick, she had money, she could take better care of him than I could . . . and I figured they would never find him if he was with her. They were looking for a woman and a child—if we were separated, they might not ever find him. He was the one they threatened, not me. Lucinda knew a lawyer, a crooked lawyer, there in Mexico City. He put the adoption through, and then they got on the next plane for the United States and they were gone. And I never saw him again until last week."

I couldn't speak.

"Please forgive me, Bryce, please." She started sobbing. "Every day I thought about you, and prayed for you, prayed you were okay, getting the medical attention you needed, and were safe. That was the most important thing. I didn't care if they found me, as long as they couldn't get their filthy hands on my baby!"

He got up off the bed and went to her, hugging her, kissing her cheek, stroking her hair. "Mom, you know I understand. I didn't at first, but I do now. And you'll never have to worry about money ever again, I promise."

She smiled at him. "Whatever else Lucinda may be, Bryce, she did take care of you, and look at you now! A champion skater!" She ran her hand through his unruly curls. "I'm so proud of you."

He smiled at her, then turned back to me. "I always knew Lucinda wasn't my mother, no matter how much she tried to make me forget my real mother. I remembered my real mom. I remembered my dad. She couldn't take my memories away, no matter how hard she tried. Do you know she had me go to a hypnotist to make me forget them?" His face twisted. "What kind of woman does that to a child? She kept telling me my real mom was dead, that she was my mother now, and to just forget all about it. But I always, always, knew my mom was alive, and one day I'd find her again."

"And what about Ace Martinelli?"

His face flushed. "Okay, I lied to you about him working for the *Inquisitor*. He was hired by Lucinda to follow me around. He was threatening to out me, though, if I didn't sleep with him. What a sleazoid! But then, Lucinda would only hire someone like that—she only understands sleaze. Lucinda found out I'd hired a private eye to find my real mother"—he smiled at Juliet—"and Martinelli was her strong arm, you know? She got him to do her dirty work for her."

"And do the police know this?" He really had a strong motive now, I thought to myself, my heart sinking.

"I told them everything Storm told me to." He shrugged. "But I didn't tell them about looking for my mom. He said not to, that it probably didn't have any bearing on the case and not to worry about it."

This didn't sound kosher to me, but then Storm is the lawyer, not me. He rarely loses a case, so he must know what he's doing. "And you weren't the one who sent me your room key?"

He held up his fingers in a parody of the Boy Scout salute. "Swear to God, Scotty." He grinned. "Not that I was opposed to seeing you again."

It really is a trial being irresistible sometimes.

I tried to get a sense of whether he was telling me the truth or not, but I got nothing. So much for Scotty Bradley, Psychic Detective. It never works when I need it to.

Juliet sat back down on the bed. "So, what do we do now?"

"Well, we need to make sure the two of you are safe. And if Bryce didn't kill Ace Martinelli . . ."

Juliet took a deep breath and fidgeted with the collar of her sweatshirt. "I might as well tell you. Martinelli was the one who found me."

Bryce and I both looked at her.

"I never came back to the States until now, you know. Not even when my parents got sick." Her face twisted again. "I didn't even go to the funerals." She struggled for a moment to regain control. "I've been working at a Hilton in Mexico City." She went on. "A few weeks ago, Ace Martinelli checked into my hotel, and he kept hanging around my desk. I'm a concierge. Finally, one day, he came up to me and handed me a picture of Bryce. I knew the minute I saw it that Bryce was my son. Oh, I'd tried to track Lucinda down—my sister Gwen even tried—but we couldn't find her without help, and we were afraid to ask anyone for help. She was afraid to even say anything to her husband. I didn't know if we were safe yet or not, you know? I started crying, and he was the one who told me that Bryce would be in New Orleans for Skate America, that he was a world champion–class figure skater. So, I called Gwen and came." She smiled at Bryce again. "I wasn't going to get in touch with him, you know. I just wanted to see him, to watch him skate. I had to." She took his hand. "And then, when I saw him skating at practice, I had to say something to him, and I'm not sorry. I'm not!"

"What about the investigator you hired, Bryce?" I asked.

He laughed, "That loser. He never found anything. All he was doing was taking my money and doing nothing. When Mom approached me the other day at practice; that same day I fired him."

"Did you tell him why?"

"Yes! The idiot! I told him my mom had found me and"—realization dawned on his face. "Oh, God, that's how they knew she was here. . . ."

I looked at Juliet. "The night Ace Martinelli was murdered, what were you doing at the Royal Aquitaine?"

"I was at the arena that night. I got a note from Bryce, asking me to meet him in his room there at eleven-thirty." She shrugged. "Of course I went. When I got there, the door was open. I walked in"—she shuddered—"and I saw that man's body on the bed. I knew I had to get out of there, so I did . . ." She looked at me for a moment. "You were the guy I ran into at the elevator, weren't you?"

"I didn't send her that note, Scotty," Bryce said. "I didn't send you my key and I didn't send Mom that note. I swear, I didn't."

"Someone was setting up both of us, Juliet." My mind was racing. At that point, my connection to Bryce was very tenuous. All I was then was last night's trick. So who had known about me and Bryce?

Besides Bryce?

"Martinelli was following you around," I said slowly. "Did he know you'd been to my place the night before?"

"I didn't tell him."

"Did you have any contact with him the day of the murder?"

"No. Cross my heart and hope to die."

He really is young, I thought, suppressing a smile. "Someone knew about me. Someone knew enough about me to send me your room key, Bryce." And you knew I was there, I added silently, remembering him warming up on the ice, our eyes meeting, the big smile he'd given me.

"You have to believe me. It wasn't me, Scotty. I didn't send you that key, and I didn't kill Martinelli."

"Something is very rotten here," I said, pulling out my cell phone. "You two need to stay put, do you understand?"

They both nodded.

"I'm going to call Storm and have him meet me at my place, okay? You two have to stay here. Don't answer the door. Don't answer the phone. Don't let anyone in except for me or Storm. Got it?"

"Where would we go?" Juliet laughed bitterly.

Bryce got up and gave me a big hug. "Be careful, Scotty."

I walked out into the courtyard. I heard the dead bolt slide closed behind me. I sat down at one of the tables and dialed Storm's number.

"Hello?" Storm answered on the second ring.

"Scotty here. I need you to be at my place like yesterday. And get Venus over there too." I sighed. "I've found Bryce and his mother. His *real* mother. And it doesn't look good, Stormy."

"I'm on my way."

I closed my phone and put it in my pocket. I looked at the door to their room.

Who had sent me that key?

And why?

CHAPTER NINETEEN

The Devil

wrong use of force, disregard for human dignity

I walked down the front steps of the Charlemagne House, my mind racing. Calm down, boy, I told myself. When I reached the bottom of the stairs, I looked up and down Esplanade. There was a guy in shorts and no shirt walking a rather large fluffy black poodle on the neutral ground. A pack of tourists were standing outside Port of Call across the street, waiting to be seated. There were cars parked up and down the street, but all of them appeared to be empty. Of course, they'd probably dumped the green Oldsmobile by now. Well, they'd probably lost all interest in me after drugging me and finding out I didn't know anything. That was a relief, at any rate.

Feeling kind of silly, I started walking home as quickly as I could without running. No sense drawing attention to myself. Every so often, I'd stop and check to make sure no one was following me or showing undue interest in where I was going. I was feeling pretty paranoid by the time I turned to walk into the Marigny.

The day had turned chilly while I was inside with Juliet and Bryce. The sun was gone, hidden by dark, ominous-looking clouds. The wind was cold, and I wished I'd worn a sweater, or at least long sleeves. It was going to rain again, and the way the wind was starting to blow it was going to be a major storm. In the distance, on the other side of the river, lightning flashed. A few seconds later came the crack of thunder. The clouds were moving pretty fast, too. There'd be tornado watches somewhere.

I managed to make it to my porch before the rain started to fall. I let myself in and headed for my room. I turned on the computer and checked the messages on my voicemail while I waited for it to come up. There was only one message.

"Mr. Bradley? This is Kenneth Marsten. We spoke yesterday about the Cabildo fire, and you'd made an appointment to come out and see me. I'm assuming something came up, but you could have called to say you weren't coming. I'm free all day today if you want to reschedule." He sounded annoyed. I couldn't blame him. I'd forgotten all about him. He went on to leave his number.

If you only knew, I thought as I hit the callback button.

"Hello?"

I took a deep breath. "Mr. Marsten, this is Scott Bradley. I'm sorry I didn't call to cancel, but I was in a car wreck yesterday on the way and—"

"You weren't involved in that mess on I-10 I saw on the news last night, were you?" He whistled. "That was quite a mess. I wondered if that was the problem when I saw it, you know. Are you okay?"

I was actually the cause of it, I thought, but said, "Yes, I'm okay, and yes, I was involved in that crash. As much as I would like to meet you, the car was totaled, and—"

"Give me your address, son, and I'll come to you. I have some things to do, but I can be there around five this afternoon. Will that work for you?"

"Sure. That would be great." I told him the address, and hung up just as there was a knock on the door. I peered through the blinds and saw a bedraggled Storm. I opened the door. "Hey, bro. You're looking a little worse for wear."

"Venus is on her way." He shook his head, drops of water flying. "Can I get a towel?" He was completely soaked. Water was running down his face. His white shirt was wet and clinging to his undershirt. Blotches of wet covered his pants.

I looked at him. "You want a pair of sweats to change into?" I grinned. "That's about all I have that'd fit your fat ass."

He glowered at me. "Yes, my queen, that'd be nice. Towel, please?" He was shivering.

I tossed him a towel and found some ratty old sweats for him to wear. I turned the heat on, and started a pot of coffee while he changed. It was getting very cold in the house. "I'm soaked through," he groused. "Hope Venus has an umbrella with her."

I handed him a blanket. I had no idea how long it would take for the heater to make the house warm. He wrapped himself up in it and gratefully took the cup of coffee I offered him. "Well, I don't know what all Bryce told you, or what you can legally tell me, so I'll just tell you what all I found out." I started talking, beginning with Rod and Juliet, and winding up with Ace Martinelli.

Storm whistled. "So what are you thinking, my queen?"

"I'm thinking that when Ace Martinelli started digging around in Bryce's past, he found out about Rod Parrish's murder and the whole stealing-the-death-mask nonsense." I shrugged. "I don't know if Rev Harper was the one who paid Rod to steal the death mask, but I think it's kind of interesting that now that Juliet and Bryce are back in New Orleans after fifteen years, he just happens to be on the scene. And Ace Martinelli winds up with a knife in his chest. It all has to be connected, Stormy. Someone was trying to set up both Juliet and me." I frowned. "I just don't know why. That part doesn't make any sense to me yet. I don't know why whoever it was picked on me." I gave a half laugh. "All I did was pick the kid up in a bar."

"The curse of being irresistible." Storm finished the coffee and set it down on my coffee table. "One of these days, you know, you're going to pick up a serial killer. And then what are you gonna do?"

"Ah." I waved my hand. "I'll cross that bridge when I come to it."

"And Colin is certain that the death mask was actually taken?"

"He seems to be." I frowned. "But who knows if he's telling the truth? I mean, he is a cat burglar, after all." I still couldn't forget he knew those thugs were following me and didn't warn me.

"Mom and Dad are quite taken with your cat burglar."

"I know." I shrugged. "Anyway, if the real death mask is still in the Cabildo, why are Harper and his men looking for it—and so desperate to find it they're willing to cause that mess on the highway yesterday just to get me, to find out what I know? And if Rod Parrish didn't steal it, why did they kill him and threaten Juliet?" I frowned. "I don't know if we'll ever be able to prove it, but I'm pretty sure Harper's behind all of this."

"I wouldn't be so sure, my queen, unless this is your psychic powers at work?" Storm rolled his eyes at me.

He can be so fucking annoying. "No, it's not," I snapped.

"It doesn't make sense, my queen. Why would they kidnap you when they were perfectly willing to kill Parrish and Martinelli? All they did was drug you." He sighed.

"Well, maybe they were planning on killing me and getting rid of the body later," I replied. "But Colin got me out before they could."

He whistled. "My queen, I want you to listen to me."

What now? "Okay."

"You may be in some danger."

I shook my head. "They think I don't know anything."

"You can ID them, Scotty. They kidnapped you. They caused a huge pileup on the highway yesterday. A lot of people were seriously injured, and you can ID them." He pounded his fist into his other hand. "And I know Mom and Dad really like him, but I'm not sure I completely buy Colin's story about how he knew where to find you."

"What do you mean?" My head was spinning. I don't really like being in danger, or even thinking about it.

"If Colin is a cat burglar, doesn't it make more sense that he's in on it with them? And cat burglar or no, why would anyone take that risk unless they were absolutely certain that was the room you were in? He could have just as easily walked—er, climbed—in on some of Harper's men."

"Maybe because he's madly in love with me and was willing to take that risk?" I was grasping at straws, and we both knew it.

"Baby brother, we both know you're irresistible"—he winked at me—"but Colin hasn't lasted as long as he has without getting caught by taking those kinds of chances. He's not stupid, and that was a really stupid risk. I'm afraid we have no choice but to keep him on our suspect list. And I think you need to disappear for a while—at least until we get to the bottom of all of this."

"Where would I go?" My heart sank. But surely, if Colin was really one of the bad guys, wouldn't I know? Wouldn't the Goddess tell me? "I suppose it only makes sense—they arranged the whole thing so I'd think I'd gotten away, and maybe lead them to Juliet and Bryce, and the mask." I swore to myself. Damn it all to hell. Colin could have been playing me all this time. I grabbed for my cell phone and the white pages. I quickly looked up the number for the Charlemagne House and dialed. "Room eight, please." There was a pause before Juliet answered. "Hello?"

"Juliet, this is Scotty. I'm here with Storm—you and Bryce are okay?"

"Yes, but—"

"You need to get out of there as fast as you can. Don't pack anything, don't check out, just get the hell out of there and go to another hotel! Here, take down my number." I gave it to her. "Now, hurry, and be careful—keep an eye out for anyone who's paying any attention to you, do you understand me?"

"Scotty, what's going on—"

"There isn't time to explain! Just go!" I didn't have the heart to tell her I might have led the bad guys directly to her door. *Goddess, how could I have been so stupid?*

"Okay, we'll get out of here, but—"

"*GO!*" I hung up the phone. "Oh, Christ, Storm, do you think we should get the police over there?"

Someone started pounding on my door, and I just about jumped out of my skin. I hurried over to the door and looked through the blinds. It was Venus.

I opened the door. "Oh, thank Goddess, it's you."

"What the hell is going on?" She stalked into the room, closing her umbrella and getting my floor wet. She was wearing a gray pantsuit and a maroon silk blouse. Somehow she'd managed to stay dry under her umbrella. Lightning flashed close by, followed by a crack of thunder so loud the entire house rattled. "Now, where the hell is Bryce Bell? What the hell is going on around here?"

"Coffee?" I asked.

She glared at me. "I don't want no goddamned coffee! I ought to run you both in for obstruction of justice! Where the hell is that kid?"

"Right at this very moment, I don't know." Storm winked at me. "Have a seat, Venus, and let Scotty get you some coffee. It's a long story."

The look she gave him was freezing, but she sat down in the wingback chair. "Cream and Sweet'n Low, if you have it," she said to me as she crossed her long legs. "And this had better be fucking good, you got it?"

"Scotty makes excellent coffee."

Is there no one he won't fuck with? I wondered as I fetched her coffee. She was still glaring at Storm as she took a dainty sip from it and set it down on an *Out* magazine. She looked at me in surprise. "That is good." She shook her jacket off her shoulders. "Now, what the hell is going on around here?"

"We've found out some rather interesting things, Venus,"

Storm said, giving me a look that plainly said *Leave the talking to me, my queen.* Whatever. As my mom always said, "Let the lawyer talk to the police—keep your own mouth shut."

My mind started to wander as Storm began filling Venus in on what we'd found out. Every once in a while, Venus would interrupt Storm and say, "And what does this have to do with Ace Martinelli's murder?" Then Storm would respond, "I'm getting to that." She kept sipping her coffee. When Storm finally finished, she looked at me. Her facial expression was blank. "So you went and got yourself kidnapped again? Any particular reason you didn't report this to the police? And how did you get away?"

"Uh, well, I didn't really see much point." I looked to Storm for help, but he just smiled at me. "I mean, I did get away, after all, and well—"

"Never mind. I have a feeling I'd rather not know the details." She shrugged. "Well, I read the report on your friend David's accident. Fortunately, a lot of people witnessed exactly what was going on during this I-10 incident, and we were able to confirm that he was being chased by another car—although it seemed like a case of road rage. Why didn't he report that you were in the car with him and taken?"

"I advised him not to," Storm replied. "Scotty's life was in danger, and we had someone working on finding him already—I didn't want to jeopardize that."

Venus rolled her eyes. "You Bradleys are a royal pain in my ass, you know that?" She turned back to Storm. "That's a pretty interesting yarn you spun, counselor, and it might even fly in court. But the facts remain the same—your client is still our leading suspect, and if he weren't a celebrity the circumstantial evidence against him would be more than enough for us to arrest him. And you haven't told me anything to make me think someone else killed Martinelli."

"Oh, come on, Venus," Storm protested. "Ace Martinelli was employed by Lucinda Bell to keep an eye on Bryce. . . . Has she told you that?"

"As a matter of fact, she did." Venus finished her coffee. She looked at me. "Mind if I smoke?"

"No." I handed her an ashtray. She lit a Virginia Slim and blew smoke up into the ceiling fan.

"So, what you're telling me is that Bryce Bell is the son of Rod Parrish, who was murdered fifteen years ago." Venus flicked ash. "His wife, Juliet, gave her son away and went on the run fearing for her life, because—you think—her husband was involved in a plot to steal Napoleon's death mask, which—according to you— he succeeded in doing, but then he somehow double-crossed his coconspirators and wound up dead. And now, fifteen years later, this all has something to do with why Ace Martinelli got killed in the Royal Aquitaine." She sighed. "I can tell you several different reasons why this whole story makes Bryce Bell look even guiltier." She ticked them off on her fingers. "Revenge for his father. Revenge for his mother. He knows where the death mask is and is trying to get it himself. Given time, I could probably come up with more." She sighed. "And we don't even know for sure that the death mask was stolen, do we? Has anyone tried to verify that with the Cabildo?"

"Not yet." Storm smiled at her. "We figured the police de- partment would be able to get that information a lot easier than we could."

"It doesn't fly, Storm. For one thing, there'd be an insurance claim—and they couldn't collect on it without a police report."

"What if the Cabildo people don't know it was stolen?" He looked at me and winked. "Suppose the real mask was stolen and a copy put in its place. They wouldn't know they had a fake, would they? And it's not like they'd ever try to verify the one they had was real, would they? They'd have no reason to."

She made a face at him. "Oh, don't worry—I'm going to check on all this. You can count on that."

"More coffee?"

"That would be nice, thank you." As I picked up her cup, she looked at me. "You do need to tell me where Bryce and his birth mother are holed up."

"They were at the Charlemagne House, but they were switching hotels." I swallowed. "I thought it was a good idea for them to move. I might have led the crooks to them when I went over there this morning."

She sighed. "You are both such a pain in my ass."

I picked up her cup and started to walk back to the kitchen when I heard something out front—someone was out there. Venus and Storm heard it, too. Venus was reaching for her gun. I turned just as the front door was kicked open.

I dropped the coffee cup.

The glass window in the door shattered as it slammed against the wall.

The wind came howling in, picking up loose papers and swirling them around.

Two men moved into the room. They were wearing all black.

I recognized them as two of the thugs who'd kidnapped me from David's car.

They were both holding guns.

Fuck, fuck, fuck.

"Get down!" Venus shouted.

I dived for the floor. Out of the corner of my eye I saw her pulling her gun.

I hit the floor just as the shooting started.

I crawled behind the couch and crouched there, covering my head with my hands. A fucking shoot-out in my living room.

Someone screamed.

One of my prints fell to the floor with a crash, glass shards flying.

There was a thud, followed by another.

It seemed like an eternity but it was only a couple of seconds, tops.

"Scotty, you can come out now," Venus said.

My ears were ringing.

The room reeked of gunpowder.

Someone was groaning.

I stood up.

One of the men was sprawled backward across the doorframe where he'd fallen. Blood was spreading underneath him, dripping from his blood-soaked shirt onto the floor. The other guy was lying up against the wall right next to the door, his eyes closed, blood seeping through his shirt, both blood-covered hands clutched to it.

I looked around for Storm. He was still sitting on the couch, his face white, his eyes about to pop out of the sockets. "Are you okay?" I asked him. He nodded.

Venus had her cell phone out. "I need a backup team, NOW! Shots fired, two men down, get an ambulance over here!" I stood there, staring at the two men.

"Scotty, get some towels." Venus walked over to the one at the doorframe. She knelt down and felt his pulse, then dropped his arm. She moved over to the other one. She looked back up at me. "I said, *get me some FUCKING TOWELS!*"

I ran to the bathroom.

Lightning flashed nearby, followed by another roar of thunder.

Thank the Goddess she was a good shot.

I grabbed some ratty old towels I didn't care about and brought them back to her. She had gotten the guy to drop his hands and she pressed one of the towels against his chest. It immediately turned bright red.

My body started to shake. I felt my breakfast coming back up. I went to the back of the house and opened the door. Rain immediately soaked me as I stood there shivering, and leaned over and threw up.

I walked back into the house. I could hear sirens approaching. I stopped at the sink and wiped my face and hair with paper towels.

Car doors slammed in front of the house.

Oh Goddess, I prayed, please watch out for Bryce and Juliet. Protect them and see them to safety.

Shaky, I went back into my living room. Paramedics were working on the wounded guy. Venus was wiping her bloody hands off on a towel. Storm, his face white and his eyes closed, hadn't moved off the couch. Someone was giving him oxygen. He was trembling.

I felt another wave of nausea sweep over me.

We could have been killed.

There was blood everywhere.

So much blood.

My teeth began to chatter.

I hoped Bryce and Juliet had gotten away.

Watch out for them, Goddess. Don't let anything like this happen to them.

Venus gestured to me. She got her notepad out of her pants pocket. "Do you recognize these guys?"

I nodded. "They're the ones who kidnapped me yesterday."

The paramedics strapped one to a gurney. I turned my head away.

Venus put an arm around me. "Why don't you go sit in your bedroom, and take Storm with you?"

"Okay." I swallowed. "Venus—"

She looked at me, her eyebrows up.

"Thanks."

She nodded. "Just doing my job."

CHAPTER TWENTY

The High Priestess

hidden influences

A very nice police detective with a thick St. Bernard Parrish accent took my statement in the kitchen. His name was John Lamothe. He had the typical olive skin, blue-black hair, and bright eyes of a Cajun. He took his jacket off and straddled one of my kitchen chairs while he asked me questions. Very butch. Masculinity and testosterone oozed out of every pore. His strong forearms were covered with thick, wiry black hair. There was a mermaid tattoo on his left forearm, a wedding ring on his left hand, and a huge high school class ring weighed down his right. He had a gold watch with a diamond inset on the face on his right wrist. He was the one who told me the thug sprawled over my doorjamb was dead. Venus had shot him twice in the chest. The other was unconscious but would live—she'd winged his shoulder. An ambulance siren started wailing right in front of the house, carting off the wounded thug while the city morgue took care of the other.

"So, Mr. Bradley, who fired first?" Detective Lamothe asked me, his eyebrows going up.

"I don't know," I replied, shivering, pulling my blanket tighter around me. "They kicked in the front door and had guns out. Venus shouted to get down, so I dived behind the couch when the guns started going off."

"I see." He chewed on the end of his pen for a moment. "You're absolutely certain you don't know who fired first?"

I closed my eyes and relived those moments again briefly. "No, I don't."

"Did you know these men? What did they want—do you have any ideas?"

"Well, sort of." I sighed. This was going to take a while, and all I really wanted was be done with it all. I explained how I'd recognized the guys as the ones who'd kidnapped me the day before. This, of course, led to the question of why they'd kidnapped me. I wasn't sure how much I could tell, but then Venus was most likely going to spill the beans about everything else anyway. So, I explained how I'd found Ace Martinelli's body, and that Storm was representing Bryce, and hired me to do some digging around. I left the death mask out of it. There was time for that later, after I'd talked to Storm.

"So, there's no question in your mind that Detective Casanova's actions were necessary."

"None."

Detective Lamothe closed his notebook and stood up, holding out his hand. I stood and shook it. "We'll need you to come down to the station and make a formal statement at your convenience, but sooner would be better than later."

"Venus isn't in trouble, is she?"

He smiled weakly. "Not from what you've told me. But that isn't for me to decide."

I stayed in the kitchen while they finished with the apartment. After Storm was finished with Detective Lamothe, he joined me in there. "Hell of a day, huh?" He grinned at me, but he was still shaky.

I just shrugged. "Venus isn't in trouble, is she?"

"Well, there's always an investigation when an officer kills someone." He ran a hand through his thinning hair. "But I'd be willing to swear she didn't use excessive force."

"Did she fire first?"

He didn't answer right away, then finally let out his breath in a big sigh. "I don't know. It all happened so fast. But when two thugs kick in the front door and have guns drawn—well, I'd say she was justified if she did fire first. I know I could make a convincing argument to a jury with about a ninety-percent chance of getting her off scot-free." He grinned at me. "Even a lousy lawyer would be able to. I just hope for her sake it doesn't come to that."

Shortly after that, Detective Lamothe gave Storm permission to go home, and after giving me a hug, he left through the back door. I wrapped myself up even tighter in my blanket. I just sat there and prayed to the Goddess.

"Mr. Bradley?"

I looked up. Detective Lamothe was framed in the door to the kitchen. "We're finished in here, so we'll be taking off." He was holding a cigarette. "You should get that door window boarded up if you're planning on staying here. And don't forget to come down to the station and make a formal statement." He pulled a business card out of his wallet and placed it on the table. "Give me a call when you're ready to come in, okay?"

I stared at the card. "Thanks, Detective."

"If you want to stay here tonight, you can go ahead and clean the front room up." He coughed. "It's a mess up there, I'm afraid, but we're finished with it. I'd recommend staying with a friend or your family tonight, though."

"Why?"

He knelt down beside me. "You've had a pretty traumatic experience, Mr. Bradley. Sometimes it's best to get away from it for a day or two."

"I'll be fine."

"Okay." He held up his hands in mock surrender. He stood up and walked out.

I stayed in the kitchen until I heard the front door shut once and for all. I took a deep breath and walked back into the living room. Lamothe hadn't been kidding about the mess. Broken glass was scattered all over the floor. It was ground into powder in some places, from being walked or stepped on. The finish of the floor had grooves in it from the glass. In one place it had been dug into so deeply I could see raw wood. Several holes gaped, bleeding crumbling plaster, from where they'd dug bullets out of the walls. There was a smear of drying blood on the wall where the one thug had fallen after being shot, running down to a dry-ing puddle on the floor. It had also soaked into the baseboard. There was another puddle of blood over by the front door. I felt a little sick to my stomach. I walked over to the door, stepping around the pool of blood, and opened it. It continued over the doorjamb onto the porch. Streams of it ran to the edge, where the falling rain washed it away.

David's lights were out. Thank the Goddess he wasn't home, I thought as I walked off the porch and got the hose from the side of the house. I stood there, shivering in the rain as I directed the stream of water onto the porch. I kept running the hose even after the streams of water running down the porch became clear instead of pinkish. I turned the hose off and just dropped it. David was really anal about rolling up the hose, but he could go fuck himself if he wanted to make a big deal out of it.

I walked to the back of the house and in the back door. On my service porch was where I kept all of my cleaning stuff. I got the bucket, some pine cleaner, a thick brush, plastic gloves, and some bleach, and walked through the house, dripping water. I filled the bucket in the bathroom and pulled the gloves on. I scrubbed the blood off the floor and wall of my living room. That black finger-print dust was everywhere. It looked like soot. I swept up the broken glass from my Greg Gorman print of a really pretty young dark-haired boy with a symmetrical haircut and a beautifully smooth body. I'd loved that print. It was a complete loss. When it fell off the wall, the glass had shattered and pierced the print in several places, scratching it in even more. I sighed and crumpled the print up.

It was around seven when I finished cleaning the room, and sat down in the wingback chair. The rain had finally stopped.

I immediately started trembling.

I grabbed hold of the arms of the chair. It was a delayed stress reaction to almost having been killed for the second time in two days. My breath was coming very fast, my heart was racing, and my entire body was shaking. Shock, I told myself, I am going into shock. I got up and somehow made my way back to my bedroom where I wrapped myself back into a blanket. I then went into the kitchen and started another pot of coffee, taking deep, measured breaths, trying to get control over my body again. I focused my attention on the stream of coffee dripping down into the Pyrex pot, and went into a nice, deep meditative trance.

The ringing of the doorbell brought me out of it.

I almost jumped out of my skin.

I stood up and dropped the blanket, stretching my muscles and taking deep breaths again. I walked back to the front of the house and opened the door.

"Scott Bradley?" The man standing on my porch appeared to be in his late sixties, or perhaps his early seventies. His white hair had thinned so his pinkish scalp was clearly visible. His blue eyes were bloodshot and watery, and he was about my height. He was wearing a sweater that stretched over his potbelly, and jeans over spindly legs that were about a foot apart at the knees. "My name is Kenneth Marsten—we spoke on the phone?"

"Oh yes." I'd completely forgotten about him. I shook his hand, which was warm and moist. "Do come in. Can I get you some coffee or . . . ?" Like a true Southerner, I left it dangling.

"Just ice water if you don't mind."

"Please. Have a seat. I'll be right back." I looked around the room. Other than the missing glass in the door, it looked about as good as it could. I'd managed to get rid of the fingerprint dust. It still looked like a war zone, but at least it was a neat and clean one.

When I returned with the ice water, he'd sat down on the sofa and was looking around with his hands clasped together on his chest. He looked as though he had melted into the sofa. He took the glass from me, took a sip, and set it down on the table. "What happened here?" He looked at the holes in the walls.

I waved a hand. "Long story." I was going to have to do something about the window, though. As long as it was open like that, I wasn't safe in the house. I felt pretty sure David had some wood back in the shed behind the house to board it up. I was always amazed at what David could pull out of the shed when we needed something. I'd often joked about it as his "utility belt"—anything we could ever possibly need was in there. Until the window was boarded up, anyone could just reach in and unlock the door. I shivered again.

"So you wanted some information on the Cabildo fire?" He crossed his legs and beamed at me.

"Yes," I replied. Focus, Scotty.

"What would you like to know?" Marsten crossed his spindly legs.

"Maybe you could start at the beginning."

"Okay." He took a deep breath. He smiled at me. "You have to understand—that day is pretty much burned into my memory. Let's see . . . I had a meeting with the Mayor's office that morning, about a special Mardi Gras exhibit we were bringing in, and we wanted the Mayor to be there when the exhibit opened. The meeting ran long so I missed lunch. About three, my assistant came in and wanted to know if I wanted to take a break and get some coffee? I said sure, so we walked over to, you know, where La Madeleine is now? And we sat at a window table." He leaned back on the couch, closing his eyes. "The Cabildo was being renovated then—we were having some work done on the rain gutters and some work done on the roof, so there was this big ply-wood fence all around the building."

"I remember that."

"Well, apparently—and this is what came out at the inquest later—one of the guys working up on the roof had been welding some steel plates together, and his foreman had told him that when he was finished with that, he could take a lunch break. So, when he was done, he leaned the plates against a wall up there in the attic and went to lunch. Well, the welded plates were still extremely hot, and they were leaning against some insulation material—felt, I think it was. After a little while, the insulation started to smolder, and then actually burst into flame."

"Wow," I said.

"I was just sitting there, enjoying my coffee, when I heard the fire engines." He smiled at the memory. "They just got louder and louder, and then I looked out the window and saw one coming up the St. Ann pedestrian mall right in front of me from Decatur. I remember thinking, Why is it heading the wrong way up St. Ann? Why didn't they go up Dumaine? And then it turned left. I got a chill. Keep going, I said to myself, just keep going. But it pulled to a stop in front of the cathedral." He laughed. "And God forgive me, I thought, please God let it be the cathedral, not the Cabildo. And then I saw a puff of white smoke rise up from the roof of the Cabildo, and my heart dropped into my shoes. I got up and ran out." He closed his eyes. "They moved quick. The police sealed off the entire mall. No one could get past either St. Ann or St. Peter. The only people allowed in were cops, firefighters, and museum staff. I don't know how many times I had to show my ID. Fortunately, I had some of my business cards with me, otherwise they wouldn't have let me in. I was, needless to say, going crazy. I couldn't understand why they weren't turning the hoses on. But Chief McCrossen was one hell of a smart man. He'd sent a salvage crew in through the St. Peter entrance—where we used to take deliveries; it's where the gift shop is now—

to cover things up and bring things out. They started pumping water into the alleyway between the Cabildo and the cathedral. I was beside myself. I couldn't believe they were letting the fire burn down the Cabildo. It seemed like all they wanted was to save the cathedral. But then I saw some of the stuff coming out from the front, and I knew what McCrossen was doing. He was a genius. He sent someone over to me to get my staff together to start taking the stuff over to the Presbytere for safekeeping." He opened his eyes. "When the last fireman came out the front door, they turned the hoses on the Cabildo. I'll never, as long as I live, forget the sound of the crowd cheering for the firefighters."

"I was there," I said.

"Were you?" He smiled. "It did seem like the entire city was there. The first call went in about three forty-one or three forty-two. A cop walking through Jackson Square saw, like I did later, some white smoke go up, and phoned it in." He folded his hands. "The fire never went below the third floor, you know. It spread from where it started, on the cathedral side, to the outer wall and then up the roof. The cupola acted as a chimney, sucking the smoke and the flame upward. That's why the heat didn't come down to the lower floors. The cupola was completely destroyed in the fire—the one up there now is an exact replica of the original. The irony of the whole thing is, this was the second Cabildo fire—almost two hundred years to the day after the first one." He laughed. "So, I hope two hundred years from now the museum director keeps a close eye on the building when the anniversary rolls around again."

His glass was empty. "More water?" I asked.

"I'm fine." He went on. "Forty percent of the fire department and police department were there that day. I didn't find out until later, but McCrossen had fireboats out on the river, and had even called the Coast Guard in. There were about six fireboats there, pulled as close to the levee as they could get, prepared to turn their hoses on the Pontalba buildings to keep the fire from spreading that way." He stared off into space. "And we did lose some things in the Cabildo—but it could have been much, much worse. When we finally got the all-clear signal, I walked into the building with fire gear on, to inspect the damage. The water was pouring down the staircases, ankle deep. When I reached the third floor, I could see sky." He looked at me. "And the most amazing thing was, on the second floor, directly under where the fire was burning, with all that smoke and heat, two firemen had taken the time to cover a display case—took the time to not only cover it, but to tuck the tarp in underneath it on every side. With the fire burning directly overhead.

"I still stay in touch with some of the firefighters." He shrugged. "I cannot even begin to stress to you how amazing what they did that day was."

"Mr. Marsten, I have to ask this." I took a deep breath. Might as well get to it. "After the fire, was the Napoleon death mask still there?"

He closed his eyes and didn't speak.

"Mr. Marsten?"

"How did you know that?" he finally said, his eyes still closed.

"I'm afraid I can't tell you—it's part of the case I'm working on now."

"Yes," he whispered. "The death mask was gone from its case, and we never found it."

"And you didn't report this to the police?"

"We had a copy." He sighed. "It was in storage over in the Presbytere. It was what we put on display when we loaned the real mask to other museums. I made a decision to simply put the copy back in the case, and not report it to the insurance company or the police. You have to understand, the death mask was worth millions, and the scandal—not to mention our insurance rates, which were already going to go through the roof because of the fire—well, we decided to keep it quiet. The museum board authorized hiring a private detective agency to try to locate it. Unfortunately, they never were able to."

"Was it possible that it was an inside job—someone who worked at the museum?"

"If so, they covered their tracks very thoroughly." He sighed. "No one left our employ after the fire. No one seemed to come into money."

"What do you think?"

"Rev Harper owned one of the original masks—the only one in a private collection. He's an oil millionaire from Houston. He had, several times, made offers to buy ours, which we naturally always turned down. I always thought he had something to do with it." He shrugged. "There's quite a market in Napoleonic artifacts, you know. A New York dealer once offered me the chance to buy Napoleon's genitals for the museum—why anyone would think a museum would be interested in that is beyond me, but the dealer did eventually sell them for several million dollars. . . . After Napoleon died, his body was mutilated by his attending doctor in St. Helena. Some scholars believe the doctor actually poisoned him. Napoleon's fingers and toes sometimes come up for sale by dealers. That was how we came to be in possession of the death mask—the doctor made four, and eventually he wound up living in New Orleans. He brought one of the masks with him, and he gave it to the Cabildo. It disappeared once before, during the Civil War. It was eventually found in a garbage dump."

"So, how much would you say the mask was worth?"

"Rev Harper's last offer to us was for three million dollars, and that was sixteen years ago." He shrugged again. "Adjust that for inflation—it would probably be worth about ten million today. I always thought the mask was taken by someone Rev Harper had hired. These Napoleonic artifact collectors—it's like an obsession with them."

"Wow."

He glanced at his watch. "I should probably be getting back home. Is there anything else I can help you with?"

"Who at the Cabildo today was working there at the time of the fire?"

He grinned. "That's easy. Only the curator, Marie Simenon." He stood up. "She's a very good woman, very hard working, diligent, devoted to Louisiana history. I can call her, if you like, and let her know you'll be getting in touch with her."

"That would be great." I walked him to the door.

He stopped at the top of the stairs and looked back at me. "The death mask . . . do you think it'll be recovered?"

"I don't know, Mr. Marsten." I gave him a half grin. "But we're going to do what we can."

CHAPTER TWENTY-ONE

Five of Pentacles

dark night of the soul

I was still standing on the porch when David came walking up. He looked pretty ridiculous with all the bandages around his face. He was wearing jeans and a sweatshirt from USM, where he'd gone to school. He didn't look like he was in a very good mood. He looked at me, at the door, then back to me. He put both hands on his hips. "All right, Missy Sue, what in the name of God happened here?" He only calls me *Missy Sue* when he is really annoyed.

"You really don't want to know." I hugged myself.

He walked past me and looked in the front door. "Oh, dear Lord." He turned back to me. "Please tell me those aren't bullet holes in the walls."

"Be glad I got the blood cleaned up already." I leaned against the wall. "Where have you been, anyway?"

"I had a date." He rolled his eyes inside the bandages. "As you can imagine, it didn't really go very well. Hot guy, too." He sat down on the couch, and traced one of the holes with his fingers. "Oh, these aren't so bad. I can just fill them with spackle and they'll be right as rain. We'll have to paint, though." He turned back to me. "Ah, well, he said he'd go out with me after the bandages come off. Can't really blame him for not wanting to get fucked by someone who looks like Hannibal the Cannibal. I probably wouldn't either." He laughed.

"Yeah, well." I sat down on the edge of the coffee table. I really wasn't in a good place yet.

"Are you okay?"

"As good as can be expected, considering there was a gunfight in my living room a couple of hours ago, and I spent about an hour mopping up some crook's blood off my walls and floor." I shivered again. The wind coming through the broken window was icy.

David stood up. "Come on. We've got to get that window boarded up." He shivered. "It's fucking cold in here."

I grinned. "I knew you'd have something for it."

He just looked at me like I was insane. "I have boards to go over every window in this house. I cut them special, in case of a hurricane. Everyone in New Orleans should have them. You never know when the big one's coming."

Always prepared for every eventuality, that David. I offered to order dinner for us both while he boarded up the front door. He just grunted, so I ordered us both cheeseburger po'boys from the Nelly Deli.

Once the board was in place, he just said, "You know, Scotty, this wasn't exactly what I had in mind when I let you move in."

"David, I'm really sorry."

"It's not your fault." He shrugged. "I'm just glad I wasn't here when all this was going on." He pulled on the board. It didn't move. "I'll go get a piece of glass tomorrow and replace this. You're paying for it, you know."

That wasn't a worry, actually. I'd bill Storm for it, and he'd charge it to Bryce's account.

The po'boys arrived by bicycle delivery, and we ate and smoked pot over at his place, and watched a DVD of *Serial Mom*. It's one of David's favorite movies, and he always watches it to make him feel better when he's having a shitty day. I did have to explain to him what happened while we ate. He didn't say anything, but he did stare at me for a while. I wondered if I was going to get evicted. Finally, he just said, "You know you aren't getting your security deposit back."

And that was the end of it.

After the movie, I was pleasantly stoned and he'd even rolled a joint for me to bring home. David is really a good person. I am truly blessed by the Goddess, I thought as I walked across the porch to my front door. Good friends, great family, so what if every once in a while my life goes crazy?

The apartment seemed alien to me when I walked in. There was seriously bad energy floating around. I couldn't go to sleep without cleansing the place. I turned up the heater. The place was freezing cold inside. I went into the bathroom and filled the tub with hot water, and then poured lavender into the water. I lit candles, turned off the lights, then stripped and slid into the water. I closed my eyes and put my head back on the edge, and cleared my mind of everything. I focused on sending out positive energy into the universe, and focused on receiving it back.

After I was sufficiently relaxed, I got out and dried myself off. Naked, I walked back into the living room. The candles on my altar were broken and strewn about. I hadn't messed with the altar when I'd been straightening up. I went to the closet and got new white candles. I placed them in the holders and lit them, kneeling before the altar.

Oh, Vesta, goddess of the hearth and the home, please cleanse my home of the negative energy and vibrations left from the senseless violence brought into it by those men. Help to cleanse the air and the energy. Help me to make this home a place of peace and tranquillity again. Bring back the positive energy, help it to flow through me and into the apartment again. Please watch out for the man who was injured, even though he is a violent and possibly evil man—help him to see the error of his ways, of his life, and bring him health, peace and prosperity. Watch out for me, and watch over my apartment.

I stood up. I put some incense in a burner, and carried it to every corner of the room and repeated the prayer.

I put the burner back on the altar and extinguished the candles with my fingers.

I stood in the center of the room and closed my eyes, stretching my arms out, sending psychic tendrils into every corner of the room, looking for any trace of negativity.

There weren't any.

I was very tired, and it was almost ten.

I went back to the bedroom and looked at the phone. The message light wasn't blinking. Why the hell hadn't Bryce called? I hadn't thought about him in hours. I picked up the phone and called Storm.

"Hello?" He seemed sort of subdued and un-Stormlike.

"Stormy, are you okay?"

"As good as can be expected. What's up, my queen?"

"You haven't heard from Bryce, have you?"

"No." He barked out a weird laugh. "To be honest, I'd forgotten all about him."

"Understandable." I frowned. "He said he'd call me when they got settled into a new place."

"He'll call when he's damned well ready to." Storm sighed. "And not a minute before."

"I'm worried."

"I'll call Venus and let her deal with it." He yawned into the phone. "I'm going to bed, my queen. I suggest you do the same." He hung up.

I said a quick prayer for Bryce and Juliet's safety, and then slid under the covers, which felt warm and soft against my clean skin.

I fell into a deep sleep.

Smoke.

Heat.

Fire.

I glanced around. No one was watching me. I could hear the fire

up above me. I looked at the case in front of me. Napoleon's bronze
face stared back at me. I raised my ax and slammed it into the glass,
which shattered. I looked around, my stomach knotting with anxiety.
No one was watching, no one was around, I was in the clear, no one
would suspect me, but I had to move fast, grab it and go, grab it and
get out. I reached in and picked the mask up off its shelf, and slid it
inside my rubber coat.

No more bill collectors calling in the middle of the night.
No more worries about the hospital bills.
Now, to get it out of here and get on with our new lives. . . .

I sat up in the bed. Light was streaming through my bedroom
window. I looked at the clock as the remnants of the dream faded.
Nine-fifteen. I'd slept almost ten full hours. I got out of the bed
and brushed my teeth. I felt practically normal. I stared at myself
in the mirror. There were bags forming under my eyes. Not good.
At this rate I was going to age ten years unless we got this case
wrapped up soon. I took a shower and got dressed. I made myself
some breakfast, and while I ate, I thought about the dreams.

The Goddess sometimes speaks to me in dreams. The dreams
usually don't make a lot of sense at the time—it's not until later
that I can look back and say, oh yeah, that's what that meant. But
these dreams were different, unlike any I'd had before. Usually,
when I get dreams like that, it's me in them, witnessing something
or being told something by the Goddess. This wasn't the same. It
was like being inside someone else's head, watching things happen
through someone else's eyes, hearing someone else's thoughts. What
the fuck did that mean? Was my gift changing? I'm not telepathic. I
can sense energy sometimes from other people but I can't read their
thoughts. This last dream had been about stealing the mask. I'd seen
the whole thing through the eyes of whoever had taken it. Was it
Rod Parrish? I tried to remember things from the dream, but had
waited too long. It had faded away.

I washed my dishes and headed down to the Cabildo to see
Marie Simenon.

It was muggy, but still a little on the cold side. There were still puddles here and there, and the sun was still hiding out behind clouds. Water still dripped from balconies from yesterday's storm. There was a feeling of cold dampness to the air, the kind of cold chill that goes right through you and makes your bones ache. If this weather was an indication of what was to come, we were going to have an unnaturally cold winter.

There weren't many people out and about. The streets were practically deserted. The tarot readers and artists weren't set up in the Square the way they usually were, probably because it looked like it might rain again. The Lucky Dog vendor was down at the corner by St. Peter, though. Rain or shine, the Lucky Dog folks were always out hawking their dogs. I stepped into La Madeleine for a cup of coffee to help warm me up.

The administrative offices for the Louisiana State Museum were in the Presbytere, the Cabildo's almost identical twin on the other side of the Cathedral. The only difference was that the Presbytere didn't have a cupola. The Cabildo had originally been built by Baron Almonaster as a government building; the Presbytere was to house priests. Now they were both museums of Louisiana and New Orleans history. I climbed the Presbytere steps and walked through the wrought iron fence. There were large papier-mâché dummies in Carnival garb lined up on either side of the entryway. According to a sign, there was a "History of Mardi Gras" special exhibit going on. I put my empty coffee cup into a trash can next to an old Spanish cannon and went inside.

I walked up to the ticket desk. "I'm here to see Marie Simenon," I said to the black woman in a gray security uniform. She was reading what looked to be a trashy romance. Beyond her, I could see a display case filled with the crowns of former Kings of Carnival. There was some traditional Mardi Gras music coming through the speaker system.

"You have to go through the door on St. Ann to get to the offices," she said, without looking up from the book she was reading.

"Okay." I walked back outside and around the corner of the building. I signed in at the security desk and was sent up in an elevator to the third floor.

I took a seat in the reception area.

"Mr. Bradley?"

Marie Simenon was in her early fifties, with gray streaks in her black hair, which she wore cropped close to her skull. She was taller than me and thick; she had to weigh about two hundred pounds—but she didn't appear to be fat, she looked solid. She had broad shoulders that tapered down to narrow hips and legs that seemed a little too short and out of proportion to her body. She wore cat's-eye glasses with a little rhinestone in each corner, which seemed to always be slipping down her long nose. She wore very little makeup: some lipstick, a bit of eye shadow, and not much else. Her skin was starting to sag just a little beneath her chin, and wrinkles sprouted out from both eyes. Her hands were long and veiny, ending with bitten-down nails painted red. "My office is this way."

I followed her down a hallway, and she opened a big oak door.

Her office was filled with dark, heavy, oak furniture, and the walls were covered with framed Mardi Gras and Jazz Fest posters going back quite a few years. She had a corner office, and light filtered in through massive windows spaced symmetrically along both walls. I glanced out one of the windows, and the vast panorama of Jackson Square spread out below me. Books and papers were spilling over on every available flat surface. I sat down in a very comfortable overstuffed leather chair opposite her desk. "Ken Marsten called and said I should be expecting you." She looked at me over the top of her glasses. "Can I offer you coffee or tea?"

"No, thanks, I'm fine."

"Ken also told me you know about the death mask. I don't want to know how you found out. " She took her glasses off and set them down on a pile of thickly stuffed file folders. She rubbed her eyes. "I just want you to know I was against keeping the theft a secret. But it wasn't my decision."

"I really don't understand why it was kept a secret." It didn't make any sense to me. "I mean, wouldn't the police and the FBI have been the best people to look for it?"

"I didn't say I didn't understand the decision, I said I didn't agree with it." Her tone reminded me of one of my high school teachers—Mrs. Levecque, English Lit. She always sounded like her students were the stupidest humans born since the invention of language, and every word out of her mouth was condescending. "After the fire, everyone was worried about their jobs. Even though the fire department did a great job saving the museum, and the majority of the exhibits, everyone in the city wanted answers." She frowned. "Half the time they can't even be bothered with anything to do with the museum—try to get them to donate money to keep this place going, and you'll see what I mean—but suddenly, after the fire, it was like everyone in New Orleans owned the place. And the knowledge that the crown-jewel exhibit was stolen—well, heads would have rolled." She smiled a little bit, one corner of her mouth rising just a little bit. "And for those of us in the museum business, well, it's not that easy to find a job to begin with. Getting fired from one museum pretty much guarantees you won't get hired by another. The museum world is very small. The board understood that it wasn't the fault of anyone on the staff, but the city would have wanted someone's head on a platter. That's why they made the decision not to file an insurance claim or a police report, and to hire a firm of private investigators." She smiled. "And they did hire one of the best—have you heard of the Blackledge Agency?"

"No."

"One of the best in the world, based in New York—and they

always, always, operate with the utmost discretion." She slid her glasses back on her nose, and they immediately slid down to the tip again. "And they weren't able to find out anything."

They couldn't be that good, I thought, if they didn't make the connection to Rod Parrish. Well, I had to be fair. I wouldn't have made the connection if I hadn't bumped into Juliet, and if she hadn't dropped that newspaper clipping. A lot of private eye work is just blind luck. "Are they still on the case?"

"No, the board discharged them after about a year when nothing had turned up. They are very expensive, and since the only conclusion they could come up with was that Rev Harper was somehow behind it all—which we all suspected anyway—we let it drop." She sighed. "I think it's wrong, and I've always thought it wrong, that we have that phony mask out there masquerading as the real thing."

"Why was everyone so sure Rev Harper was behind it?" I asked. "Surely there are other collectors out there—"

"On a scale like this?" She shook her head. "If anyone could mount an operation like this, it would have to be him. But I've always kind of thought someone just acted on their own, on an impulse. Nobody knew the fire was going to break out, you know. That was the flaw in the whole 'conspiracy' theory to me. If the fire had been set, not an accident, then I would be more apt to believe it." She scratched her head. "You see what I mean? I think someone just acted on impulse. Everyone here knew Rev Harper wanted the mask, to go with the one he already had. They took advantage of the confusion of the fire to steal it, and sold it to him. That's where I believe it is now—in his mansion in Houston." She made a face. "You know, it's really kind of odd, after all this time, that you come here asking about all of this."

"Really?"

"A couple of weeks ago, another private investigator came by asking about the mask, too." She opened a drawer and started rummaging around. "I, of course, didn't tell him that the mask was stolen—discretion above all else, you know—but since Ken said it was okay to talk to you about it . . . now, what did I do with that man's card?"

I made a note to have Storm get in touch with this Blackledge Agency to see if we could get ahold of their file on the mask.

"Ah, here it is." She passed the card across the desk to me.

It was a basic business card, of standard thickness.

AL WESTON INVESTIGATIONS
DENVER, COLORADO

There was a phone number and an e-mail address, as well.

Denver, Colorado.

"What did this man look like?" I asked, making a note of the address.

"You can keep the card." She waved a hand. "I'll never call him—let's see, what did he look like? He was big, about six three, looked like he'd played football, but kind of let his body go, you know what I mean? Handsome, but not like a movie star—in that rugged way, with a broken nose. Brown hair, starting to gray a bit, probably in his late forties. Beefy. Deep voice. Probably a lady-killer when he was younger—kind of arrogant, if you know what I mean. Charming, but in an unctuous way—not the kind of man I would be interested in." She sniffed.

He sounded like one of the men who'd broken into my apartment—the one Venus had wounded. "So, back to the theft of the mask. You think someone who worked at the museum stole it?"

"It's the only explanation to make any sort of sense." Her phone buzzed. She excused herself, spoke into it for a moment, and then said, "I'm afraid I have to take this call, Mr. Bradley."

I stood up. "Thank you for talking to me, Ms. Simenon."

"My pleasure." She rose and shook my hand. She had a good grip. "Are you looking for the mask, too?"

"I really can't tell you about my case, ma'am."

"I understand." She smiled. "If there's anything else I can help you with, please let me know."

I thanked her again and walked out. I sat down on the steps of the Cabildo and pulled out my cell phone and called Storm. I got his voice mail, so I filled him in on this Al Weston, and everything I'd found out so far about the mask.

Might as well head home, I thought, and see if Bryce has called.

CHAPTER TWENTY-TWO

Eight of Cups

disappointment in love

My stomach was growling when I left the Cabildo, so I stopped in at the Royal Street Deli and ordered a roast beef po'boy. I debated walking down another block to the Devil's Weed, but it was still too early for Mom and Dad to be up. Mom always says, "No one truly civilized is awake before noon. Or at least no one I want to talk to." I did wonder if Storm had told them about the shoot-out in my living room, but finally figured if he had, they'd know I was okay. I did buy a copy of the *Times-Picayune* to read while I waited for my po' boy, but there was nothing in the paper about it. At least the grandparents probably weren't going to find out. Not today, at any rate. Maybe never, if I was lucky—but knowing Storm as well as I do, it would probably come up over Thanksgiving dinner with the entire family gathered together.

After I finished my po'boy, I wandered down Royal on my way home. I got out Al Weston's card and looked at it as I walked. He was from Denver, Colorado. Bryce trained in Colorado Springs. If this Al Weston was indeed a private eye—well, he obviously had missed the lecture on ethics at Private Eye School. But the Colorado connection was worth looking into.

When I got home, my door was off its hinges. David was installing the new pane of glass and had the door leaning against the fence.

"Shouldn't you be at school?" I asked, swallowing the last bite of my sandwich.

He pointed at his face. "I'm taking a few days off. No sense scaring my students while I look like Hannibal Lecter, tempting as it is. Maybe they'd mind better if they thought I was going to eat their kidneys." He grinned. "You owe me one-fifty for the glass, by the way." He went back to work on the door.

"I'll get my checkbook." I threw the trash from my sandwich into a garbage can and walked up the stairs. I flipped open to the register and groaned when I saw the balance. Writing this check would leave me about sixty dollars—if I had remembered to record all of my ATM withdrawals. *Ah, well,* I thought as I wrote David's check, *maybe Storm will give me an advance on all this work I'm doing.*

I'd just torn it out when I heard someone walk into my apartment. Thinking it was David, I got up and walked back into the living room just in time to get my face slapped.

Really, really hard.

"You faggot!"

Stars swam in front of my face as my eyes watered. My ears were ringing, but I still recognized Lucinda Bell's voice. Her hand had gone back and she was getting ready to swing again. There was a nasty smirk on her face.

I grabbed her arm and twisted it. "No you don't, crazy lady." I turned it behind her and she squealed in pain. I got a grim satisfaction out of it. Okay, maybe I was a little rougher than I needed to be, but I really didn't like this woman. I shoved her down onto the couch and stepped back, picking up the telephone. "Give me one good reason why I shouldn't call the police and charge you with assault, and breaking and entering."

"I didn't break in." Her jaw set defiantly. Her piggish little eyes gleamed. "You don't have a front door." She folded her arms across her sagging bosom.

"You still entered my home without permission. You also hit

me and called me a derogatory name." I smiled at her. "I don't know how they do things in Colorado, bitch, but we have what's called a 'hate crime' ordinance here in Louisiana. The fact that you called me a name while hitting me makes the assault count as a 'hate crime,' which adds, oh, I don't know, a couple more years to your sentence, and changes it from a misdemeanor to a felony. I assume you know the difference?"

"Call the police, then." She managed to cross her chubby legs, encased in black stirrup pants, and smirked at me. "I do know Louisiana has a sodomy law, and you're a sodomite—you sodomized my son."

"Goddess above, are you really that ignorant?" I raised my eyebrows. "Go right ahead and charge me with sodomy, you moronic bitch! First of all, all I'd have to do is deny it all—you have to have proof. And I doubt Bryce is going to get up in court and testify against me, because he'd incriminate himself. And those companies who want him to endorse their products would really like that, wouldn't they?" I leaned back against the wall. "And my brother is one of the best lawyers in the state." I reached up and rubbed the spot where she'd slapped me. It was still tingling. She really could pack a wallop. I imagined Bryce had felt her heavy hands more than once while growing up. "I could also sue you for damages in civil court, tie you up in legal knots for years." I was enjoying this a little more than I should, and would have to atone to the Goddess for this negativity later. "Bring it on, bitch. Bring it on."

Her entire body sagged. "All right, then." She held up her hands in defeat. "You win." Her eyes glinted with malice. "Go ahead and call the police."

"I won't call the police if you answer some questions for me."

"I'll answer if you tell me where my son is."

"I don't know where he is." I shrugged. "And he isn't your son."

Her lower chins jutted out. "He *is* my son. I raised him, I paid for his training, I've provided for him and loved him—that woman sold him to me. SOLD him for money. I gave him a home, I took care of him, I gave him love. She didn't want him, she couldn't take care of him the way I have, and how does he repay me?" She spat the words out. "By sleeping with men and jeopardizing everything we've worked towards! Everything!"

"Did you hire Ace Martinelli to spy on him?"

"I was trying to protect him!" Her voice quivered. "To save him from himself!"

"And you didn't tell the police he was in your employ?"

She shrugged. "I didn't see what good that would do."

So she had lied to the police. Good to know—that could come in handy. "Ace Martinelli was the one who found Juliet Parrish—did you know that?"

Her face whitened under the heavy makeup. "What?"

"Ace Martinelli found her in Mexico City and told her where to find her son. That's why she came to New Orleans in the first place." Ah, the delicious irony. She'd hired Martinelli to spy on Bryce—and he was the one who'd brought her worst nightmare into reality.

"That's a lie! Bryce hired that horrible Al Weston to find her!"

Al Weston? The man who'd questioned Marie Simenon about the death mask? I stared at her.

"Snooping around, asking me all kinds of questions, digging into things that were better left buried." She raved on, working herself up. Her face was now flushing. "I told Bryce to forget about all that, to just let the past stay buried, but did he listen? Does he ever fucking listen to me? Of course not! I don't know what I'm talking about, of course, I'm just some stupid woman that doesn't know her ass from a hole in the ground! Well, he wouldn't be in this mess if he'd listened to me, now would he?"

She got to her feet and pointed a pudgy finger at me. "You tell Bryce he needs to come home, do you understand me?" She stalked to the front door. "I'm the only one who can get him out

of this mess he's created. Maybe *now* he'll listen to his mother."
She stormed out of the house.

I sat down on the couch. My head was spinning.

Al Weston was apparently the key to everything. I got his
business card out, and picked up the phone. I dialed the number
on the card. It rang three times, then a machine clicked on.

"You have reached the office of Weston-Martinelli Investigations. No one is available to take your call at this time, but if
you want to leave a message for Al Weston, press one. To leave a
message for Ace Martinelli, press two. Otherwise, just wait for the
beep."

I stared at the phone.

Martinelli and Weston were partners?

Martinelli had worked for Lucinda. Weston had worked for
Bryce.

Coincidence? I didn't think so.

Something was rotten in the state of Colorado.

I walked out on the porch. My door was still leaning against
the fence, but the glass panes were installed. There was no sign of
David anywhere, but his front door was open. I started to walk
over there as a car pulled up and Venus got out.

Great, I thought as she opened the gate and walked in. "Hey,
Venus. Everything okay?"

She looked like she'd aged ten years since last night. Usually,
she has the ramrod-straight posture of a model. Today, her entire
body seemed slumped. She hadn't taken the usual care with her
clothes I had grown used to. She'd missed a button when putting
on her blouse. Her slacks looked wrinkled. There was a coffee
stain on her beige silk blouse, close to the collar. She was wearing
flats rather than heels. "The guy I wounded is okay—just a shoulder wound."

I followed her into my apartment. "Well, isn't that good
news?"

Her eyes were bloodshot. "He's claiming I opened fire on him and his buddy unprovoked. I'm currently on paid leave until the IA investigation is completed." She sank down on my couch with a loud exhalation. "I spent the entire morning being grilled."

"But Storm and I were here—we saw everything! They had their guns out." My heart sank. This was a real mess. "I'm going to have to talk to them, aren't I?"

She nodded. "I'm afraid so, Scotty. And another detective has taken over the Martinelli murder case. I'm completely out of it now." She rubbed her eyes. "He's a good guy—new to the detective force, but a pretty good guy. Blaine Tujague. He'll probably want to talk to you as well."

The name sounded vaguely familiar to me. "Great."

"Have you heard from Bryce Bell since last night?"

I shook my head. "No, I haven't."

"The guy I wounded—he claims he was working for Bryce, trying to locate his birth mother." She sighed. "And he's clammed up—wants a lawyer." She buried her face in her hands. "We have to find Bryce—promise me you'll call me if he gets in touch with you. IA needs to talk to him, and Blaine wasn't too thrilled to find out I don't know where he is, either. If my lieutenant finds out I lost the kid . . ." Her voice trailed off.

I sat down next to her and put my arm around her. "Venus, this so sucks."

She looked at me. "Yeah, it really does."

"Word of honor." I held up my hands. "I swear to call you the minute I hear from Bryce."

She stood up. "Thanks, Scotty. I appreciate it."

"I do have some good news for you." I slid Al Weston's business card to her. "I met with the curator at the Cabildo this morning—Weston had questioned her about the Napoleon death mask. Isn't that interesting?"

She perked up visibly. "Yeah, that's very interesting."

I grinned. "I just called his office number before you got here, and guess what? He and Ace Martinelli were business partners."

"Which connects him to the murder!" She hugged me, her face lit up with a real smile. "Scotty, this is great news!"

"Do you think it's possible he might have killed Martinelli?"

"Martinelli and Weston were playing the mother against the son." She tapped her foot, her mind racing. She hugged me again. "I've got to get down to the station." She paused at the door. "Thanks, Scotty. Good work."

Maybe I was good at this kind of work, I thought as I watched her leave. I heard her car driving off as I checked my voice mail. No messages still. My heart began to race. Come on, Bryce, where the hell are you?

I walked back into the living room and sat down at the coffee table. I lit a couple of white candles and began shuffling the cards. I laid them out, closed my eyes and focused. Come on, Goddess, speak to me, I pleaded, then began turning the cards over.

Nothing. They told me nothing.

I tried again.

Again, nothing.

"Damn it!" I swept the cards up and was about to throw them against the wall when someone said my name.

My apartment was apparently turning into Grand Central Station—but I knew that voice.

It couldn't be.

I turned.

Frank was standing in the door, with a bag draped over his shoulder. He was wearing a tight gray sweater that outlined every muscle in his upper torso, and there were quite a few of them. It was tucked into a tight pair of jeans, which in turn were draped over a pair of black, steel-toed cowboy boots.

He looked fantastic, as always.

"Frank?" I still couldn't believe my eyes. "What are you doing here?"

His smile faded. He looked down at the floor. "I was kind of hoping you'd be glad to see me."

Oh, my poor baby! I thought as I flew across the room and threw my arms around him in a big hug. When his arms came around me and squeezed, I couldn't help it. I started to cry. Great big sobs that made my whole body shudder and shake.

He kissed my cheek. "There, there, honey, it's okay." He stroked the top of my head.

"I *am* glad to see you," I blubbered into his chest. "I miss you and I—" I do love him, I thought, my heart swelling with relief at seeing him. I love him I love him.

I started crying again.

I hate when that happens.

He swept me up into his big arms and carried me back into the bedroom, putting me down gently on the bed. I heard his bag hit the floor as he dropped it. He pulled my shirt over my head and started kissing my neck, lying down beside me, his big strong arms going around me again. "You weren't returning my calls or answering my e-mails." He kept kissing me. "And then you sent me that e-mail"—his own voice broke—"and I thought something must be wrong. I couldn't just answer the e-mail or call, I had to see you, so I grabbed the next plane and came down."

It was very tempting to just lay there and let him kiss me. He is so damned sexy. His hands had slid down and were cupping my butt, and my body was starting to respond to his. That wouldn't be cool, though—I had to tell him everything first. "Frank, you wouldn't believe what's been going on."

He smiled at me. He is so handsome when he smiles. He has this big nasty scar on the right side of his face which makes him look really mean when he isn't smiling, but when he does, his gray eyes light up and he looks like the sweetest, kindest, gentlest man ever to draw breath. I rubbed his bald head. "You forget how we met in the first place, Scotty. Nothing could happen to you I wouldn't believe." He pulled his sweater over his head. One of the things I love about Frank is that he doesn't shave his torso. There's hair all over his strong pecs, and covering his six-pack abs. It really feels nice pressed up against my skin. I wanted him to just keep kissing me and holding me, make me forget everything, forget the last few days, but I just couldn't. I had to tell him the truth.

I started laughing, and then started crying again. It was all such a mess.

He wiped my tears away and kissed me again. "Now, just start at the beginning, and tell your Hot Daddy all about it."

He really does love me, I thought. And I do love him. Please, Goddess, let him understand what I've been going through. I said, "I freaked, Frank. I just freaked. When I was up in DC, I got scared about everything. You know, me, you, us—I'm not used to having a boyfriend. I've never really had one. This is all new to me, okay? I don't know how to act, you know? And you know, when I was up there, your phone never rang once, and I didn't meet any of your friends, and I know you're not out because of your job and all that, but it just seemed like you don't really have a life outside of your job, and that freaked me out and I got scared, so when I got home I went out and got really really drunk."

He smiled at me, stroking my cheek. "You are so funny, my little love, you know that?" He pulled me into a tight hug.

Goddess, how could I have ever doubted my feelings? "I am?"

"I have friends, Scotty. Lots of friends. Both gay and straight. All over the country, not just in DC." He winked. "Granted, there's a lot you don't know about me, just as there's a lot I don't know about you. Everyone I know knew you were coming—it was all I talked about for weeks! You wouldn't believe all the teasing I had to put up with . . . and they all wanted to meet my pretty little go-go boy from New Orleans. Trust me, Scotty, everyone who knows me knows all about you. In fact, part of the reason they all want to meet you is because they don't believe anyone could be as perfect as I make you out to be—you are perfect, you know that, don't you? But I wanted you all to myself—I didn't want to share you with anyone." He kissed my cheek, running his hand gently down my arm. "We only had a week, and I wanted all of our time to be for us, you know? There's plenty of time later for that kind of stuff—friends and dinner parties and all that. You can understand that, can't you?"

I actually could. I felt really stupid. "Oh." How could I have been so stupid? He'd planned this wonderful, romantic week for us, and I'd reacted like a neurotic junior high school girl. That was beyond stupid.

"And when I move down here, my friends will all be coming to visit us. They all want to meet you, and the idea of New Orleans certainly appeals to everyone. And you know, every once in a while we'll go up to DC to visit them." He kissed me again. "Is that all?" He grabbed the fly of my jeans. "Can we get down to what I've been wanting to do ever since I got on the plane?"

If only that were all. Reluctantly, I pushed his hand away and sat up. "Well, I picked up this guy Friday night and brought him home with me, and that's when this other mess all got started."

His smile faded a little. "So, you spent a week with me and then came straight home and hooked up with someone?" He shook his head. "Wow."

"Frank—"

He got off the bed and picked up his sweater, slipping it over his head.

"Frank, don't do this. Listen to me." Damn it!

"What do you want me to say, Scotty?" He shook his head. "So, all this time I've been worried about you, you've been too busy whoring around to return my calls or answer my e-mails? Thanks a lot."

"That's not what I meant! Damn it, Frank, you have to listen to me!" I am really bad at this kind of thing. Obviously. I sounded like a hysterical soap-opera housewife.

He picked up his bag. "I probably should be going."

I got off the bed. "Let me finish, Frank! Come on, Frank, be fair."

"Fair?" He tucked his sweater back into his jeans. "Just how exactly do you define fair anyway, Scotty?" He folded his arms, the biceps bulging. "Fair is letting me get all worried and worked up about you while you're out boozing and whoring? That's really interesting."

And then I heard someone call my name from the front door. I groaned. As always, Colin's timing was impeccable.

CHAPTER TWENTY-THREE

Eight of Wands

approach to a goal

"Scotty?" Colin called again. "You home?"

Frank's face reddened, and he turned back to me. His jaw clenched. A vein popped out in his forehead. "Is that who I think it is?" he hissed.

Out of the frying pan, I thought as I stepped around Frank and through the door into the living room. "Um, Colin, this isn't really the best time."

"Is that Special Agent Sobieski?" Colin's face broke out into a large grin. "Hey, Frank!" He crossed the room and stuck out his right hand. "Good to see you again, guy!"

Frank looked at Colin, at me, then down at the outstretched hand. He didn't move.

Colin's smile faded a bit. His eyebrows came together, and then his grin spread across his face again. He started to laugh. "Don't tell me you've got the wrong idea?" He was laughing so hard he doubled over. "Oh, that's just too much! Scotty, haven't you told him what's going on?"

"I was trying to when you barged in here!" I threw my hands up in the air. Frank looked like he was going to strangle Colin with his bare hands. Exactly what I needed—another body in the living room.

"Give me one good reason why I shouldn't run you in right now," Frank said through clenched teeth. That vein in his forehead was throbbing. He was tapping his fists against his legs.

This just made Colin laugh even harder. "Because you'd be making the biggest mistake of your career, big guy—that's why."

"Colin, we're kind of in the middle of something here. . . ." I have never wished I was telepathic more than I did at that moment. "Please?"

Colin glanced over at me. His smile faded away. "And apparently it's not going very well." He held up his hands and stepped back a bit. Frank looked like the top of his head was going to blow off at any moment. I could practically see the smoke coming out of his ears. At the very least, he was on the verge of a stroke.

"I'm getting out of here," Frank snapped at me. He started toward the door.

Colin stepped right in front of him. "Uh uh, no way, Special Agent. You're not leaving on my account."

"Don't tell me what I can and can't do, buddy." Frank stepped right into Colin's personal space. Frank's taller, so Colin's eyes were at about chest level.

This was just going to get uglier.

Please Goddess, calm Frank down!

"Calm down, Special Agent, and take a load off." Colin winked at him. "Once you hear what's been going down around here, you're going to hate yourself for leaving."

"Get out of my way!" He bumped into Colin, who stumbled back a couple of steps.

"Frank, knock off the macho bullshit," I said. I was getting a headache.

"No harm, no foul." Colin held up both hands. "How would you like to be part of busting Rev Harper?"

Frank's hands unclenched. He looked at me, then back to Colin. "What?"

"Have a seat, Special Agent." Colin was practically hopping up and down in excitement.

Frank gave me a long, hard look, but he did sit down. A good sign, I thought. What the hell was Colin up to? I wondered, sitting down on the couch next to Frank. He moved away from me to the opposite end of the couch.

Fine. I glared at him. He had a nerve. Since when did we promise to be monogamous, anyway? Asshole.

I was beginning to remember why I'd never wanted a boyfriend in the first place. Being single was looking pretty damned good to me again.

Colin pulled a leather billfold out of his back pocket and handed it to Frank. "This might explain a few things."

Frank opened it, and there was a badge, along with a picture ID of Colin. The name read COLIN CIONI.

"I am an investigator for the Blackledge Detective Agency," Colin went on. He looked at me. "I'm sorry not to have been honest with you, Scotty, but I couldn't blow my cover."

I just stared at him. Goddess, how many lies had he told me?

"My agency was hired to find the death mask of Napoleon, which was stolen during the Cabildo fire fifteen years ago." Colin shifted his weight from one foot to the other. "We've been watching Rev Harper and his people for quite some time."

Okay, this was too much. "But you were stripping during Decadence," I said. "I mean, come on, Colin. You expect me to believe this?"

"I go undercover all the time. It's my specialty." Colin shrugged. "Even then, I was on the trail of the death mask. That's why I couldn't take a chance on talking to the cops or the Feds then—I couldn't blow my cover. Once they checked into my background, they would have found out who I was, and I couldn't let that happen just yet. We're very close to nailing Harper and the whole gang behind this, Scotty—I couldn't take the chance the police or the Feds would fuck it all up."

"But I thought the Cabildo had discontinued the investigation." That was what Marie Simenon had told me. "This doesn't make a lot of sense, Colin." Obviously, he was making this up on his feet. He was good at improvisation, I'd give him that, but this wouldn't hold water for long.

"STOP RIGHT THERE!" Frank roared, making us both jump. "WHAT THE HELL IS GOING ON AROUND HERE?"

"Oh, now you want to listen to me." I glared at Frank. "And let me ask you something, mister. When did we agree to be monogamous? What right have you got to march in here and pitch a hissy fit because I slept with someone else, anyway? Have you been celibate since you went back to DC last month? Have you?"

His face reddened. "That's not why I got mad, Scotty." He took several deep breaths. "You didn't return my calls or answer my e-mails—and I was worried, damn it! Then I get here and you start telling me how you slept with someone else—"

I took his hand. "Frank, calm down. That's how this whole mess started in the first place. It didn't mean anything to me, and it probably wouldn't have happened in the first place if I hadn't been drunk, okay? And then I wouldn't be involved in all of this." I took a deep breath. "I got drunk and picked up this guy, who turned out to be Bryce Bell—"

"The figure skater?"

Obviously, I didn't know Frank very well. I wouldn't have figured him for a skating fan. Maybe there is something to that gay gene. "Yes, the figure skater, only I didn't know it at the time." I filled him in on how I'd seen him again at Skate America, and how someone had sent me his room key, and how I'd stumbled onto Ace Martinelli's body. When I got to the part where I was kidnapped, Frank stopped me.

"You were kidnapped? Again?" He was inching closer to me on the couch.

"And Colin rescued me." I let Colin take over at this point.

At some point during the story, Frank took my hand and squeezed it. I smiled at him.

Maybe everything would be okay, after all.

"Okay," I said when Colin finished. "So you have been tracing the death mask for fifteen years—and you're certain Rev Harper was behind it?"

"The money that was paid to Rod Parrish was traced back to Harper," Colin went on. "Half a million dollars, to be exact. Oh, they were clever about it—the check was written on the account of a dummy corporation, and we had to do some digging, but we did finally trace it all back to Harper. Someone had to be the inside person at the Cabildo, though, and that's something we've never been able to figure out—who that was. We've gone through all the employees and volunteers' lives over and over again, with a fine-tooth comb. But we never found anything. That fire was set."

"But the inquiry found it was an accident." This wasn't making a lot of sense to me.

"The inquiry findings were what we wanted the public to know." Colin shook his head. "The fire was set—the welder up on the roof was set up. And Harper doesn't have the death mask—it's just disappeared. Rod Parrish, we believe, hid the mask and wanted more money for it. That's why he was killed, and why they were after his wife—they think she knows where he hid it. She, of course, disappeared—we were never able to find her after she went to Mexico." He frowned. "Of course, we were looking for a woman with a five-year-old son. We had no idea she'd given the boy away."

"And the boy is Bryce Bell?" Frank whistled. He squeezed my hand again. I smiled at him.

"What about Ace Martinelli?" I asked. "Bryce didn't kill him."

"Martinelli was hired by Lucinda Bell to follow her son for her own reasons. I don't know how he got involved—"

"He found Juliet in Mexico City," I interrupted. "He's the

one who got her to come back to New Orleans—he told her who her son was, and that he'd be here for Skate America." A light bulb should have appeared over my head. "Lucinda must have told him how to find her. But why would she do that? It doesn't make any sense. The last thing she wanted was for Bryce to find Juliet—unless Martinelli was playing her too."

"Lucinda Bell has been playing a very dangerous game." Colin scratched his head. "Do you think she knew about the death mask?"

"I don't see how she could have." I shrugged. "I'm sure Juliet didn't tell her when she turned Bryce over to her."

"Yeah." Colin sat down in the wingback chair. "I guess we'll have to ask Juliet, if we ever see her again."

"And Bryce hired Al Weston to find his mother, and get this—he's Martinelli's business partner. And he was one of the guys who kidnapped me." I filled them in on what happened last night.

"I was wondering what happened to your front door." Colin laughed. "I kind of wondered if the Special Agent here hadn't kicked it in or something."

Frank gave him a sour look. "I'm still not sure I believe you aren't a criminal, Cioni, or whatever your name is. I checked on you when I got back to DC in September. You're wanted for stealing a painting in France."

Colin shrugged. "Yes, I stole a painting in France—but I stole it to return it to the rightful owners, the grandchildren of a Jew who died at Auschwitz. The so-called upstanding French citizen who had it, the Marquis de Merteuil, was a real slimebag. He was supposedly this huge Resistance hero from the second World War, when he was actually an anti-Semitic Nazi sympathizer who turned hundreds of French Jews over to the Nazis. A lot of the art in the famed Merteuil collection was nothing more than Nazi plunder. The heirs of the original owner have tried everything to get that painting back, but had no recourse. No French court would believe their story—the marquis, like I said, was this big hero of the Resistance, but he was playing both ends against the middle. He turned in some of his Resistance compatriots as well."

"Nice." I felt sick to my stomach.

"And the French government wasn't exactly eager to have the truth about one of their so-called war heroes come to light." Colin shrugged. "The easiest way to recover the painting was to steal it and smuggle it out of France, so I did."

"Nice story." Frank looked at me, and then over at Colin again. "But they knew who stole it."

"I left a trail wide enough for a blind man to follow." Colin shrugged. "My orders were to recover the painting, and I did that. But my own inner sense of justice was outraged that this monster, responsible for the deaths of thousands of people, was getting away with it. I kind of wanted to get caught . . . I thought it would be justice for it all to come out at the trial." He grinned. "I'd be more than happy to return to France to stand trial—although that's the last thing the collaborator wants. He just filed a police report to collect on the insurance. He didn't have a provenance for the painting—and we have proof on file at the main office that it did, indeed, belong legally to our clients."

"I can check this out, you know." Frank's vein was throbbing again.

Colin shrugged. He pulled out his wallet and handed Frank a business card. "Give this guy a call."

I looked at the card as Frank stared at it. It was from the FBI, and had the name ANDREW MATTHEWS embossed on it. "Do you know this guy?" I asked.

Frank fingered the card. "Andrew Matthews is my boss."

"The Blackledge Agency has worked very closely with the FBI on many cases," Colin said. "I believe my boss, Angela Blackledge, actually went to college with Agent Matthews."

Frank pulled his cell phone out. He stood up and walked out onto the porch, dialing.

"Were you ever going to tell me you were a private eye?" I asked. My head was spinning.

"At some point." Colin winked at me. "You know, Scotty, I hated lying to you. But I couldn't compromise my investigation."

"You could have told me!"

"With your penchant for getting kidnapped and drugged so you'll talk?" Colin was trying very hard not to grin. "I know you'd never consciously blow my cover, but given what happened the other day, you have to admit I was right."

"So why tell me now?"

"My cover was about to be blown anyway." He shrugged. "If Special Agent Frank had tried to arrest me for stealing that painting, it would have all come out anyway—and I couldn't take that chance. I can't risk the loss of time. Every second counts now—we're so close to solving this I can practically taste it."

"Okay." I sighed. "Do you have any ideas where Parrish could have hidden the mask? Juliet claims she has no idea, and I believe her. She didn't know what he was up to. When I told her about the mask, either she didn't know or she's an undiscovered Meryl Streep."

"He couldn't have gotten far with it." Colin folded his arms. "The cops were watching everyone very closely the day of the fire. I've always believed the mask never actually left the Cabildo—he hid it somewhere inside."

"But were the police watching the firefighters?" I cast my mind back to that day. "I doubt it. They were watching the crowds, and the museum staff. They wouldn't have suspected a firefighter."

"That," Colin grinned, "is exactly why they needed to bribe a firefighter. But even if the police weren't watching them, any strange behavior would have been noticed. It's not like he could have walked down the street in his gear and no one would have noticed. People would have wondered why he was leaving the fire." He shook his head. "He had to have hid it in the Cabildo."

He was wrong. I knew it as sure as I knew my name was Milton Scott Bradley. The visions, the dreams . . . I was certain I was seeing that day through Rod Parrish's eyes.

And he was not in the Cabildo. He was somewhere else. It nagged at me.

I knew the place.

I'd been there before.

Frank walked in, putting his cell phone into his pocket. He looked sheepish. He walked over to Colin and held his hand out. "I guess I owe you an apology, detective."

Colin shook his hand and nodded. "No apology necessary, Special Agent."

"Call me Frank, okay?" Frank plopped down on the couch next to me. "And I owe you an apology, too, Scotty." He slipped an arm around me and squeezed me.

I cuddled in next to him. Oh, he felt so good. He smelled clean, slightly of deodorant and Calvin Klein's One. Underneath that was his own smell, which I actually preferred. He didn't need to cover that up. I made a mental note to tell him that sometime.

However, this was probably *not* the time to tell him I'd slept with Colin on Sunday night.

Colin was staring at us. He had a strange look on his face.

Okay, I was going to have to tell him. I couldn't do that to Colin, pretend it never happened.

Goddess, why does life always have to be so fucking complicated?

I pulled away from Frank. "Frank, there's something else I have to tell you."

He looked into my eyes. "You've been sleeping with Colin, haven't you?"

"Just once." I know the proper thing to do was to say it meant nothing—but I couldn't. I couldn't deny I had feelings for Colin.

He looked away from me, over at Colin. "Well, I'd have to be an idiot not to understand why. He's pretty good looking."

"Thanks." Colin grinned at him. "You're pretty hot yourself

there, Special Agent." For a brief moment, I pictured Frank and Colin in bed together, naked.

That's a porn movie I would buy and watch over and over again. I shook my head. Back to reality, Scotty. There's a lot that needs to be worked out here.

He nodded, and turned back to me. "Is it more than that for you, darlin'?"

"I don't know." I stood up. All these romantic entanglements were getting to be too much for me. I walked over to the door and looked out onto the street. I turned back to look at them both. "I have feelings for both of you. I like you both a lot. I don't get it—it's like some cosmic joke the Goddess is playing on me. All of my life I've never had a boyfriend. I've never wanted one. I always thought they were more trouble than they were worth."

No, that was wrong. Be honest.

"No, that's not right." I looked over at the altar. "I never wanted a boyfriend because I never wanted to hurt anyone. And I always thought I'd hurt anyone who got involved with me. I mean, I'm a slut. I can't say no to a hot guy who comes along and wants to have sex with me. I can't be faithful to a boyfriend. I can't be faithful to anyone. I'm a dog; a slut." I smiled at them both. "But I'm not ashamed of who I am. It is who I am—and I don't think there's anything wrong with me. I believe there are people who just can't fit into the molds society creates. I'm not a white picket fence, Irish setter in front of the fireplace, having friends over for dinner and good conversation kind of person. I like to smoke pot. I like to drink and go dancing. I like to have sex. And I don't like having to explain myself or justify who I am to anyone. This is me, this is Scotty." I shrugged. "I doubt that I'll ever change. Maybe someday, I don't know—maybe my grandparents are right and someday I'll grow up. But I don't want to grow up if it means becoming normal and boring."

"Somehow," Frank said, "I doubt you'll ever be normal and boring."

"Ain't that the truth," Colin said, and they looked at each other and laughed.

A good thing, I figured. They were bonding. So what if they were bonding at my expense? It was better than the way it had been, right?

My cell phone rang. "Hello?"

"Scotty, this is Bryce."

"It's about fucking time!" I half shouted into the phone. "We've all been worried sick—the police are looking for you! Have you talked to Storm?"

"Yes, and I already got the lecture from him." Bryce sounded very tired. "After we moved out of the Charlemagne, Mom and I were tired and we didn't want to deal with anything, okay? Sue me."

I would gladly strangle him, but the irritation was mixed in with relief they were both okay. "All right—I won't lecture you. Where are the two of you staying now? I'll be right over."

"The Royal Ursulines Guesthouse."

I knew exactly where that was. "What room?"

"Room eight. We registered under the name Mom used before—Felicia Tuttle."

"Okay, then. We'll be there in about ten minutes. Stay put." I closed the phone. "All right, guys. Let's go see if we can get some answers."

The other stuff could wait.

CHAPTER TWENTY-FOUR

Knight of Swords, Reversed

tyranny over the helpless

Ursulines is not one of the more famous streets of the French Quarter, mainly because there aren't any bars or restaurants on it, unless you count the Nelly Deli at the corner of Bourbon. It's in a primarily residential section, and is always very quiet, except for the occasional car driving by. Massive oak trees shade the sidewalk from behind the six- or seven-foot concrete walls hiding the houses and their lush courtyards from street view. You can hear fountains bubbling behind the courtyard walls, and occasionally quiet conversation and laughter. Tourists rarely find their way down to Ursulines. The ones who do generally just keep walking without turning, which is their mistake. Ursulines is one of the most beautiful streets downtown.

The Royal Ursulines was a Creole townhouse converted into a guesthouse, and unlike some of the other old buildings, actually fronted on the sidewalk. There were three sets of double French doors on the sidewalk level, with emerald green shutters latched open. Above the doors were half-moon–shaped windows with beautiful stained-glass designs. The second floor had a freestanding, uncovered balcony running the length of the front of the house, and wrought iron patio furniture was placed at privacy distances. The third floor was merely rooms with windows, with their shutters latched open as well. Two dormers jutted out of the slate roof.

The three of us walked in through the front door into a tastefully decorated lobby area. The floor was black-and-white–checked marble. A chandelier hung from the ceiling, sparkling in the afternoon sunlight. A baby grand piano polished to a mirrorlike shine was in a far corner. A young woman in a blue floral print desk was sitting at a gilt-edged desk. She looked up with a sad smile. "I'm sorry, gentlemen, but we're booked full right now."

"Actually, we're here to visit one of your guests. Room eight?" I asked.

She nodded. "Just follow the hallway on your left to the back courtyard. Take the staircase up to the second floor. Room eight is in the back opposite corner from the staircase."

"Thanks." We walked back through the hallway. The courtyard was shaded by three massive oaks. There were chairs and glass-top tables set out in the shade. A fountain bubbled in the center; the statue in the center was three mermaids. Both Frank and Colin inhaled sharply. "You guys okay?"

Frank just shrugged, but Colin said, "This city is so fucking amazing. Who knew something like this was back here?"

I shrugged. Having grown up here, I take the courtyards for granted.

We climbed up and made our way back to where Bryce's room was. When I knocked on the door, I heard Bryce's voice, lowered an octave or two, say "Who is it?"

"Scotty." I managed to say it without laughing. He kind of sounded ridiculous.

The big wooden door swung open, but the smile on Bryce's face faded when he saw I wasn't alone. His lips turned down, and his lower lip protruded a bit. I pushed past him into the room, Frank and Colin following behind me.

Juliet Parrish was sitting in a blue velvet-covered wingback chair staring at the television, the remote in her right hand. Her other hand was clutching at the neck of her faded blue sweatshirt. She looked up at me, her eyebrows going up. Her eyes were tired. Everything about her suggested a world-weariness, as though she were ready to just give everything up. I couldn't blame her. Fifteen years on the run was a long time.

"Who are these people, Scotty?" Bryce looked like he wanted to be tapping his right foot but was controlling the urge. He did have his hands on his hips, though.

"Bryce, Juliet, this is Special Agent Frank Sobieski, with the FBI." Frank nodded to both of them. "And this is Colin Cioni, a private eye who's . . ." my voice trailed away. How exactly did I explain him to her?

Colin leapt into the breach, smooth as silk. "I work with the Blackledge Investigation Agency. We were retained fifteen years ago to recover something that had been stolen from the Cabildo during the fire, and I'm afraid, Mrs. Parrish, that your husband was involved."

She gave a half laugh. "My husband was involved in something criminal?" She raised her eyebrows, but looked down at the floor. She shrugged. "I accepted that a long time ago, Mr. Cioni." She looked over at me, her eyes pleading. "But he only did it because of the hospital bills, you understand that, don't you? Rod was a good man!" Her voice rose a little.

My heart went out to her. Fifteen years later, and she still loved her husband, still needed to justify his behavior. What had those years been like, I wondered, in Mexico City, without her son, with her childhood love brutally murdered, wondering every morning, when she woke up if this was the day the past would finally catch up to her? I couldn't even begin to imagine it myself. There was a lot of inner strength in this woman. Most people would be in a sanitarium, babbling and playing with fingerpaints.

Her hands shook as she poured herself a glass of ice water. "I've gone over those last days in my head I can't begin to tell you how many times, everything he said to me, and I honestly don't know what he was up to—there was no hint of anything." She took a drink. "He wouldn't tell me what he was up to—I wish I could help you. Believe me, I wish I knew. I wish I knew what he'd done, I wish I knew where he hid whatever it was! I would have just given it to them all those years ago—and I would have been able to see my son grow up." She looked at Bryce, and her eyes softened.

"Let me ask you this," I said, looking into her eyes. "What were you doing in the Royal Aquitaine the night Ace Martinelli was murdered?"

"I didn't kill him, if that's what you want to know." She sat back down on the edge of the bed next to Bryce, who took her free hand and squeezed it. She smiled at him. "I was there to see Bryce. I went to his room and knocked on the door, and it opened. I walked in, and"—she shuddered and took a deep breath before continuing—"and I saw the body lying on the bed. I had to get out of there. I knew I didn't kill him"—she squeezed Bryce's hand again—"but I was afraid Bryce might have."

"I didn't do it, Mom."

"I know that now." She shuddered. "So much death . . . why can't it just end?" She smiled weakly, and looked back at me. "But I couldn't be found there, you can understand that, can't you? I had to get out of there. I couldn't let the police find me. I couldn't let whoever killed my husband find me. It was horrible, just like it was fifteen years ago. Sometimes I wonder if I'm cursed. Death seems to follow me around. . . ." She shook her head. "And than I bumped into you getting into the elevator."

I nodded. "When you spilled your purse you dropped a newspaper clipping about your husband's murder."

"Yes, I missed it later that night and wondered." She gave a bitter laugh. "Of all the things to lose, right? I wanted to get on the next plane back to Mexico. Why didn't I just leave my passport lying on the floor?"

"Mrs. Parrish, the thing your husband helped steal from the

Cabildo was the Napoleon death mask." Colin knelt on the floor in front of her. "I need you to think back to the day of the Cabildo fire. Did Rod have any places in your home where he hid things? Any secret hiding places?"

"Rod never hid anything from me." She shrugged. "That's why this whole thing was—*is*—so strange to me. Rod and I fell in love when we were in junior high school. We never hid anything from each other—our relationship was based in honesty. We told each other everything—until all this happened." She sighed. "Well, at least I always thought so, but apparently I was wrong. He was just trying to protect me, I know that if he'd had the slightest inkling how dangerous these people he was dealing with were, well, he wouldn't have gotten involved—the money be damned." She shrugged. "Besides, the house was sold years ago. My sister told me it was torn down. So, if this death mask thing was there, it would have been found when they leveled the house, don't you think?"

"Is there any place you can think of where he might have hidden something?" This came from Frank, who'd been quiet so far.

I didn't understand this. Why go over this all again? We knew Rod hadn't gotten the mask out of the Quarter. We were wasting time.

She shook her head. "No."

"Guys, can I talk to you in the hall?" I asked. Both Frank and Colin headed for the door. I turned back to Bryce and Juliet. "You need to talk to Venus—go ahead and call Storm and have him meet you here, and have him get in touch with her." I smacked my forehead. Venus was off the case.

Juliet winced. "Is it necessary?"

"Yes. If neither of you had anything to do with Ace Martinelli's murder, then you have nothing to worry about—Storm will take care of it for you." I pulled out my cell phone and hit Storm's number on speed dial. When he answered, I said, "Hey, Stormy. Guess where I am?"

"I'm hoping you're with my idiot client." He was pissed. "He hung up on me, the little shit! After everything he's put me through these last couple of days—he hangs up on me and doesn't even tell me where he is!"

"He'll tell you now. I'm handing you off to Juliet Parrish." I handed her the phone. She hesitated for a moment, then took it. "This is Juliet Parrish, Mr. Bradley."

That taken care of, I joined my partners out in the hall. They were glaring at each other in silence. Great. Hadn't we decided to put all this on hold for now? "All right, guys, why all the questions about secret hiding places? I thought we'd decided Rod hadn't gotten the mask out of the Quarter."

"He might have hidden it the day of the fire and gone back and retrieved it later," Colin said. "We have to cover all the bases, Scotty. A detective has to be thorough."

I rolled my eyes. "Whatever." Okay, maybe not the most mature reaction from me, but we were wasting time. I knew the mask was still in the Quarter, and standing around talking about it wasn't helping us find it any faster.

"Ace Martinelli was working both ends against the middle—he was taking Lucinda Bell's money and watching Bryce, all right, but somehow he found out about the death mask, and started playing his own endgame," Colin replied, scratching his head. "Maybe Rev Harper found out and ordered him killed."

"Stabbed in a hotel room?" Frank snorted. He rolled his eyes. "I hardly think so. If Rev Harper was behind Rod Parrish's murder fifteen years ago, then why wouldn't this have been handled in the same way?" He started pacing. "No, the Martinelli murder couldn't have been connected to the death mask. People who are knifed are generally killed in the heat of the moment—it's too hard to plan that kind of murder. For one thing, you have to be sure you can get close enough to the victim to stab him—were there any signs of a struggle in the room, Scotty?"

I thought back. After a few moments, I said, "No."

"So Martinelli had no idea he was about to get killed." Frank held up his hands. "And the only people who had a motive to kill him were those two. Unless we have proof of some connection between Harper and Martinelli, other than that his partner was working for Harper—which is a very tenuous connection, I might add; any competent defense attorney could poke major holes in it without further proof, and Harper can afford the best—then we've got nothing. I'm not ruling it out, but we need proof."

"If the murder wasn't connected to the death mask then our only suspects are these two, you mean. We can't rule Al Weston out, either." Colin turned to me. "What do you think, Scotty?"

"I don't think either one of them killed him," I said, rubbing my chin. "I don't get a sense from either one of them they could do it, you know what I mean?"

"You'd be surprised what people are capable of." Frank shrugged. "The one thing we know for sure is that the death mask is still missing, and we're no closer to finding it than we were before."

Colin raised his eyebrows. "We?"

Frank glared at him. "Whether you like it or not, buddy, we're all in this now."

Colin grinned at him. "The more the merrier, right? Besides, it's always nice to have a Fed on your side."

"I say we go have a look at the phony death mask." Frank folded his arms, the biceps bulging. "If the real one is hidden somewhere, we should get an idea of what size it is. At least then we can figure out where it couldn't be hidden, you know?"

Colin nodded agreement. "Good idea, Frank. Besides, it can't hurt."

I knocked on the door, and walked back into the room. "What did Storm say?"

Bryce was wiping tears off his cheeks. Uh oh, had Storm read him the riot act? "He's on his way over."

"Is everything okay?" He looked like a lost little boy.

Juliet looked up at me. Her voice quivered a bit. "Yes. I, uh, I just can't believe this is all going to finally be over. Fifteen years of running"—she started to sob again, and Bryce pulled her into a hug.

I walked over and patted each of them on a shoulder. "We're going to leave. We're going to follow up on a hunch. Just do whatever Storm tells you to, okay?"

They both nodded, and I walked out. At the door I paused and looked back at them. They were still holding each other.

They will be okay, a voice said in my head.

The three of us walked out of the Royal Ursulines Guesthouse and headed up Chartres Street in the direction of Jackson Square. It was one of those fall days that make you glad to be alive—bright and sunny and not humid at all. I resisted the urge to link arms with my two guys. I could hear music filtering down from the Square, which was alive and swarming with people. A fire-eater was performing right in front of the cathedral. There was a unicycle propped up against the wrought iron fence behind him. I've seen him perform before—anyone who can balance on a unicycle while eating fire is definitely worth a look-see, and more than worth the few dollars I'd dumped into his open guitar case. There was a crowd gathered, tourists snapping pictures of him. Just as we walked up, he blew a huge plume of flame from his mouth.

"Remind me not to eat where he had lunch," Colin said with a grin.

"This guy is really good," I replied.

"Much as I'd like to watch him, we need to be working," Frank said.

"Lighten up, Frank," Colin said.

I looked at him for a second, and then shrugged. Frank is a Fed, after all. Business is business.

As we reached the bottom of the steps to the museum, Frank

stopped us. He looked at me. "That's the kid you slept with, huh?"

Not this again. "Yes, Frank, and it didn't mean anything."

"I just don't get it, Scotty." He looked at Colin. "I mean, I can understand you sleeping with this one, but Bryce? He's just a little boy."

"I was drunk, okay?"

"I don't understand it either, Frank." Great. Now they were going to gang up on me. "Sure, he's a cute little boy, but he is a little boy."

"He's nineteen!" I grumbled. I didn't need this. "Come on, let's go inside."

Thank the Goddess, they both dropped it, although I was fairly sure I was going to hear about it again. Is there anything worse than having the two guys you're seeing bond? A few hours ago, I would have thought it would be great to see Frank and Colin getting along.

But did it have to be at *my* expense?

We stood in line for about twenty minutes to get into the Cabildo, behind a bunch of giggling and fidgeting Catholic junior high school girls in their white blouses and plaid, pleated skirts. A nun kept shushing them. Finally, we got to the ticket window, paid our three-dollar admission, and headed up to the second floor.

"The mask is over here." I led them to the glass case. I'd been to the Cabildo a million times as a schoolkid. What better field trip for a Louisiana history class than the Cabildo? Okay, I hadn't been the best student in the world, and for the most part had thought Louisiana history was boring, especially since I lived a few blocks away from the Cabildo, but field trips were a way to get out of all my classes.

We stood in front of the glass case. I stared at the round face of Napoleon, frozen at death in bronze. His pinched-looking little nose, his prominent chin, the wisps of hair on his forehead.

This is the man, I thought, who terrorized Europe for twenty years. He toppled thrones, conquered the entire continent, carved an empire out of centuries-old countries and tottering old empires; who made crowned heads tremble in their palaces throughout the continent with his armies, his unending ambition, and his lust for conquest. He changed the face of Europe forever. He changed the world forever. This is the man who sold Louisiana and almost the entire continent of North America west of the Mississippi to the United States for a couple of million dollars because he needed the money to finance an invasion of Great Britain. His ambitions, his grand design for remaking Europe, had indirectly resulted in the creation of the United States as it is today.

What had been on his mind when he was dying? The loss of his empire? Did he die thinking he was a failure, that his grand design for reshaping the world was misbegotten? Did he have any idea what he'd accomplished? Did he sense, as he died, that he had been instrumental in creating the mightiest nation in the history of the world, and it *wasn't* France?

And this face, shaped from bronze, was now worth about ten million dollars.

Almost two hundred years after his own death, he was still causing the deaths of innocent people.

Rod Parrish had died because of this thing. His wife had given their son away and had gone into hiding in a foreign country for fifteen years.

For what? A bronze casting taken from the face of a dead man? Such an incredible, incredible waste.

"Scotty?" It was either Frank or Colin, but the voice seemed to be coming from so far away I couldn't tell who it was.

I didn't reply.

I stared into that implacable bronze face.

Death. Destruction. Horror.

My vision was starting to cloud around the edges.

Touch the case, Scotty.

I started to reach out to it. There was heat emanating from it. Weird.

Touch the case, Scotty, just reach out and touch it. It won't hurt you.

"Are you okay?"

Death, destruction, horror.

The killing has to stop.

It was like I was developing tunnel vision. All I could see was that face in front of me.

"Honey, are you okay?"

"Just fine." My voice seemed to echo inside my head. It sounded hollow and far away, as if I were underwater or something.

I could hear some of the schoolgirls giggling, the nun shushing them again.

The mask seemed to glow, becoming more alive and real.

I stared at it. Was it trying to tell me something?

Touch the case, Scotty.

Death, destruction, horror.

I looked around, and there wasn't anyone in the near area.

I leaned forward and placed my hands on the case.

And everything swam out of focus.

CHAPTER TWENTY-FIVE

The Chariot

victory through hard work

I could smell smoke.

I could feel the heat.

I could hear sirens blaring.

I saw men dressed in the slick, yellow jackets and pants, their heads covered with matching fire hats, covering things with tarpaulins.

Others were removing paintings from the walls, and quickly hurrying back to the staircases with their precious cargo.

The death mask was in front of me, and I knew what I had to do.

It was the only way, even though it was wrong, a criminal act, and I had lived my entire life with a strong sense of right and wrong, with integrity, and what I was about to do was contrary to everything I believed in, a betrayal of my principles, my family, my church, everything.

But there was no other way.

The damned medical bills just kept piling up.

My son was sick. He might not ever be well. We could never pay the bills off.

This was our only chance for any kind of life, any kind of peace in this life.

We would leave New Orleans, I decided as I stared at the mask *before me. We would go somewhere else and make a fresh start. Part of the boy's problem is the air here—it's too thick, it affects his lungs, all the crap in the air. We could move to Arizona or New Mexico, to the desert, and start life over.*

This is our only chance.

My heart filled with love for my wife and my son.

It wasn't like I was doing this for myself, for personal gain.

No, I was doing it for them.

They deserved a better life than I could give them now.

They deserved to be happy.

I waited until the guys covering some of the other cases with tarps were done, and moved into the next room.

I checked around again to make sure I was alone.

I picked up my axe and smashed it into the case. Again. Again, until it finally shattered under the blows.

I reached in and pulled the mask off its shelf.

I slipped it inside my coat.

I covered the shattered case with the tarp.

There wasn't a lot of time, I had to hurry, I had to get the thing out of here and get back before anyone noticed I was gone.

It's not like I wasn't conspicuous in my gear.

I made my way to the back staircase, the one that opened out onto St. Peter Street.

I stood there in the sunlight, looking around for a brief second.

No one was watching me.

The cops were trying to hold back the crowd watching the fire.

I saw a beautiful woman, with no makeup on, her hair tied back into a long ponytail that went down her back. She was wearing a T-shirt that said LEGALIZE POT. *There was a handsome little boy of about ten or eleven holding her hand. He was staring at me. I tipped my hat to him, and he smiled at me.*

Please God, let my son grow up, let my son grow up and be like that boy.

I heard a siren from the river.

The boy looked away.
No one was watching me now.
And I knew where to go.

As everything began to swim back into focus, I heard Frank saying my name. I shook my head as the roaring in my ears went away; I came slowly back into the present as the heat of the fire and the smell of the smoke began to fade away.

"Honey, are you okay?" Frank asked again.

"Did you have another vision?" Colin asked.

"My Goddess." I shivered. "I saw him. I saw him!"

They both stared at me.

"The day of the fire," I explained. "I grew up a block away from here, you guys. You've both been to my parents' house! The day of the fire, my Mom and I came down here to watch them fight the fire. We were standing behind the police barricade, just over there." I pointed wildly in the general direction of St. Peter Street. "I remember it all now. I saw him come out of the building. Our eyes met. He tipped his hat to me." I was so cold, why was I feeling so cold? I shivered and wrapped my arms around myself. "Then, I got distracted and looked away. When I looked back, he was gone. I forgot all about it till now."

That was why I've been able to see into his head. Somehow, that day, we'd connected. His spirit was reaching across fifteen years to tell me what I needed to know.

I shivered again.

"Are you okay?" Frank asked, frowning.

"It's just so cold in here."

"Um, actually, it's kind of stuffy in here, really." Colin and Frank exchanged glances.

I looked at them both. "I think I know where the mask is." I shivered again.

Colin grinned. "The Goddess came through again, did she?"

"Are you okay?" Frank's voice seemed to echo in my head.

"I'm just cold." I rubbed my arms.

"Come on, I think we should get out of here."

I ignored them both and walked back to the stairs, down and out into the bright sunshine. I stood there in the sunlight. The sense of cold was beginning to fade away. I shook my head. I still felt kind of fuzzy. My vision began to swirl around at the edges. I walked over to a trash can, one of the ones made of wood balanced in a wrought iron frame, and leaned against it. I turned and looked at the corner where Chartres dead-ended at the mall and St. Peter.

I heard voices.

Many voices.

A crowd.

"Stay back, stay back!" a policeman was shouting.

I saw Mom and I standing there, holding hands again.

I saw myself, a young boy again, but I was looking up St. Peter Street.

I walked around the corner of the building. There were a lot of pedestrians out wandering around, carrying bags from shopping, and the occasional car or taxi making the turn from Chartres onto St. Peter. I walked back to where Rod Parrish had come out of the building. I stood in front of the door, and turned back to the street, and started looking around, just as he had fifteen years ago with the death mask under his coat.

And there we were again, Mom and I, standing there behind the police barricade.

Our eyes met again.

I reached up to tip my hat to the boy.

The siren wailed at the river.

The boy looked away.

And then it was gone.

I was freezing, shivering.

I stood there.

And just like Rod Parrish had, I saw the sign hanging on the building across the street on the corner.

Le Petite Theatre du Vieux Carre.

The Little Theater of the Old Square.

I wasn't aware of whether or not Frank and Colin were following me, or if they were even talking to me. I walked across the
street and followed the sidewalk to the front door of the theater. I
stood in front of the doors. In the glass-covered case to the right
was a poster for the current show, a production of *Cabaret*. I
opened the door and stepped inside. I stood there looking around
for a moment.

The lobby of the theater was deathly silent. I rubbed my arms
again. There was a woman behind the ticket window, reading a
magazine, flipping the pages, her head bobbing back and forth
like she was dancing to music only she could hear.

Where did you go next, Rod? I asked silently.

He didn't answer.

I heard the door open again behind me. I was vaguely aware
of Frank and Colin. I stepped into the next room. Black-and-
white photographs of past productions lined the walls. The obligatory chandelier swayed gently overhead.

I saw the French doors leading out into the courtyard. I
walked past the baby grand piano, polished to a dull gleam re-
flecting the chandelier overhead, and pushed my way out into the
courtyard. The late afternoon sun left the back of the courtyard
in shadow. A fountain adorned with cherubic angels bubbled
peacefully; brightly colored fish darted about in the leafy grasses
growing inside of it. There were two doors in the courtyard's right
rear corner, at the top of three brick steps. I walked over to them,
pulled them open and stepped into the darkness of the backstage
area.

There was a staircase to my left, and I climbed up. I could
hear Colin and Frank following me. They were silent, not speak-
ing, as though the strange silence inside the theater had cast a
spell on the two of them, stilling their tongues. When I reached
the top there were two doors on the landing—the one to the left

was open. I could hear voices in there; a woman was bitching about the director, who didn't know shit from shinola about acting or how to stage a production. A male voice, agreeing with her, but saying what can we do, we're stuck with him for this play, it's too bad, it could have been something really remarkable, one of those legendary productions people would talk about for years.

No, that wasn't the way. I pulled on the door in front of me and it swung open, revealing another flight of stairs.

Is this the right way, Rod?

Yes, this way. Hurry!

The sense of coldness increased as I started climbing the steep steps two at a time, feeling an urgency I couldn't quite understand. Images of Juliet and Bryce were flashing into my mind, a much younger Juliet, a childlike Bryce; the image of Juliet holding him in her lap, like a Renaissance Madonna, and a sense of deep and abiding love. I was cold, so unbelievably cold, it felt like I would never be warm again, and then I reached the top of the stairs, where there was another door. I turned the knob and it swung open.

I stepped through it into another time.

Smoke.

Heat.

I could hear the fire burning.

A sense of anxiety.

I have to hurry, they'll notice I'm gone, I've got to get rid of this thing quick and get back. . . .

And then it was gone.

I began to warm up, as though my blood was actually starting to flow again.

The attic was silent, dust glittering in the beams of light coming in through the eaves. It was as though the attic room existed outside of time, silent and peaceful for just that split second.

And then I heard a car horn down in the street, and the spell was broken.

I heard Colin and Frank come in behind me.

"It's here. In this room," I said, keeping my voice quiet.

"Are you sure?" Colin whispered.

"I know." And I did know. I just didn't know exactly where.

Rod was gone from me. It was up to me now, without any help from him. I murmured a quick prayer to the Goddess for his soul.

What he'd done was wrong, but he'd done it with a pure heart. Surely that atoned for his act.

Let him rest in peace now, Persephone.

Boxes and furniture were piled in no particular order, some of them covered in dust, with cobwebs dangling like Christmas tinsel around them. Some of the boxes had been labeled with markers; Shoes, Candlesticks, things like that. This was where the theater stored props. From the looks of things, stored and forgot them.

In the corner was a stack of boxes, the cardboard somewhat water-stained, covered in a thick layer of dust, like they'd been sitting there undisturbed since the Civil War. I walked over to them. I reached out and touched one of them.

And I smelled the smoke, heard the sirens and the sound of a crowd outside, a crowd that had dispersed fifteen years ago.

I reached behind the bottom box into the dust of what seemed like a thousand years.

And I felt something cool to the touch. Solid.

I grabbed it with my fingers and slid it out.

And looked down into Napoleon's face.

"So it was here, just across the street, all these years," Colin said quietly.

I kept staring down at it.

Rod Parrish had died because of this thing, Juliet had been forced to live in Mexico City under an assumed name, had given up her son, all because of this thing.

And how many others throughout history?

"This is the stuff that dreams are made of," I said. My voice sounded cracked and dry.

It felt cool to the touch, but it seemed to be getting warmer.

"Thank you," a voice said behind us. "I've been looking for that for a very long time."

I turned around.

Kenneth Marsten stood there.

He had a gun in his right hand, pointing at us.

He was smiling.

"You killed Rod Parrish," I said, and knew I was right. In that instant, I saw it, the sun shining through the kitchen window, Rod tied to the kitchen chair, pleading for his life, begging for it, the gun being placed against his temple. I flinched as I heard the sound of the shot again, echoing across fifteen years.

He shrugged. "He deserved killing." His gun hand moved from me to Frank to Colin. "He'd already been paid his share of the money."

"And he wanted more?" This from Frank. His voice was calm, low, and quiet.

There is something, I decided, to be said for FBI training.

Marsten laughed, spittle flying from his lips. "The idiot. He needed more, he said, because of his son's illness. Like I cared about his snot-nosed son and his slut of a wife! I wanted the damned mask. It was worth two million dollars to me."

"How much did Harper pay you up front?" Colin's voice was equally soothing. I glanced over at him. He was to my right, and his body looked tense despite the calmness of his voice.

"Half a million." Marsten's eyes darted over each of us. There were beads of sweat dotting his forehead. "The rest to be paid when I turned the mask over to him."

"Why did you do it?" To my left, Frank was shifting farther away. I immediately knew what he was doing. Colin was doing the same on the other side. Obviously, the idea was for the three of us to get far enough apart so he couldn't cover us as easily with the gun. I sent a quick prayer to the Goddess in her Kali incarnation. Kali the destroyer, the warrior. *Give us your strengh, Kali. Protect us from this evil man.*

He shrugged. "I had two million reasons." He gestured with the gun. "Now, turn it over and this can all be over."

"It is over," Colin said. He'd taken another step to the right while Marsten had been lookng at me. "You can't get away with this now. You'd have to kill all three of us."

"You think I won't?" Marsten replied. Just as he said this, Frank moved again to the left.

But Marsten saw him, and turned and fired.

My ears exploded. I screamed as I saw Frank go down. I screamed again, just as Colin jumped across to Marsten and tackled him. I heard the gun go off again. I stood there for just a moment, then put the mask down and went to Frank's side.

No, no, no, no . . .

My eyes filled with tears.

Frank was grimacing, and blood was spreading through his fingers as he held on to his right shoulder. Beads of sweat were running down his face. "Are you okay?" I asked, as I heard the scuffling continue behind me.

"Help Colin," Frank grunted. He looked up into my face. His face softened. "I'll be okay, darlin'."

I stood up and heard footsteps coming up the stairs. Colin had Marsten pinned down, and was trying to make him let go of the gun. I was there in three steps. With no small satisfaction, I stomped on Marsten's wrist. I felt bone crack and shatter under my foot. He screamed and dropped the gun. Colin quickly grabbed it and stood up, panting, backing away.

Marsten got to his knees, holding his shattered wrist.

The door swung open again.

Was there no end to this?

I recognized one of the two men from Harper's apartment. They were both holding guns.

I picked up the mask.

It felt warm to the touch.

Dollar signs danced in my head.

"It would easily be worth ten million today," I heard the museum director saying again in my head.

Death. Destruction. Horror.

The mask was an evil thing.

I shook my head.

"This is what you want, right?" Every instinct in my body fought me as I walked across the room and held it out to them. "Here. Just take it and leave."

"NNOOOOOOOOOOOOO!" Marsten screamed and leaped at me.

His body collided with mine at about waist level.

The mask flew out of my hands.

I fell down, my head banging on the floor.

My vision swam again as I struggled to a sitting position.

There was another gunshot, and Marsten crumpled to the floor.

I turned to Colin. The gun in his hand was smoking.

One of the two men walked over to where the mask had landed in the dust. "I'll just be taking this. Thank you, gentlemen."

"But—" I said.

"Let them go, Scotty," Colin said. "Just let them go."

One of them placed the mask inside of a duffel bag he was holding, and they turned and went back down the steps.

"Get help," Colin said. "I'm going after them."

I knelt down beside Frank. His face was gray, his eyes closed. His body was shivering. He was going into shock. I took out my phone and dialed 911. I managed, somehow, to stay calm—it was probably the prayer to Aphrodite I was reciting over and over again in my head—as I gave them the particulars. I closed my phone. "It'll be okay, Frank, help is on the way."

I knew it was just a shoulder wound, but what if it had hit a major artery?

Tears began streaming down my face.

I tore my shirt off and held it against his wound to staunch the flow of blood.

Please be okay, Frank, please Aphrodite, Kali, Persephone, anyone, please make sure he's okay.

He opened his eyes and looked at me. His eyes looked glassy. "I—I—I love you, Scotty."

I heard shooting from downstairs.

"I love you, Frank." I was sobbing now.

I found a dusty, dirty blanket. I wrapped it around Frank to keep him warm.

"You're going to be all right," I said, and felt the tears coming to my eyes.

I do love him, I realized. I do love him.

I heard more gunshots from downstairs.

Colin, I thought, my heart sinking. Oh dear Goddess. The tears starting flowing down my face.

I love him, too.

I heard a siren coming closer.

Several people were running up the steps.

A team of EMTs burst in, pushed me aside, and started working on Frank.

They strapped him into a gurney and started down the steps.

I followed them, my head reeling. I love them both.

What the hell am I going to do?

When we reached the courtyard, I saw Venus tapping her high-heeled foot. There was another man with her, a really good-looking one with a great body. Somehow I didn't care.

She smiled at me. "We got them—and the mask." She nodded at the good-looking guy. "This is Blaine Tujague, who took over the case for me."

He smiled at me. I'm sure angels usually sing when he smiles, but I didn't notice. He stuck his hand out. "Nice to meet you. Heard a lot of good things about you."

"Thanks."

He pulled out a notebook. "Can you tell me what happened up there in the attic?"

The EMTs came out with Frank strapped to a gurney, with an IV stuck in his arm and an oxygen mask strapped to his face.

His skin looked gray.

Detective Tujague followed my eyes, then closed his notebook. "How about if I meet you at the hospital?"

"He'll be okay, Scotty," Venus said from a million miles away.

I just nodded, following the EMTs out through the theater lobby and outside.

As they were lifting Frank into the ambulance, I felt someone tug my arm. I turned. It was Colin. "I'll meet you at the hospital."

I threw my arms around him and squeezed for dear life.

"He'll be okay," Colin said. His voice sounded small and sad.

Now wasn't the time.

I'd talk to him later.

I climbed into the back of the ambulance and it screamed off towards the hospital.

CHAPTER TWENTY-SIX

Justice

justice will be done

There is nothing worse than sitting in a waiting room in a hospital.

Well, waiting alone would be worse.

I wasn't alone. Colin arrived about five minutes after I did, and held me while I cried. Okay, so it wasn't the most butch possible reaction, but give me a break. I'd had a rough couple of days, okay?

"Hey, he'll be okay." Colin stroked my hair.

"I know."

"I do understand, you know." Colin sighed. "I'm not thrilled about you and Frank, but I do understand."

"I'm glad you do," I replied. "Because I don't."

"You love Frank—I could see it in your face." He shrugged his muscular shoulders. "I know when it's time to step aside and let nature take its course."

"Shut up." I turned to him. I had thought of nothing else in the ambulance, since they had wheeled Frank into the ER. "I love you, too, Colin, okay? I love you both." There. I'd said it. It was out there. Scotty Bradley, confirmed bachelor and lone wolf, always a single never a pair, had thrown it out there. I was in love with two men. It was like some big cosmic joke, right? The Goddess definitely has a weird sense of humor sometimes. I mean, you aren't supposed to be in love with two people at the same time. That's just wrong. And how the hell was I supposed to choose between them?

He squeezed my forearm just as the doctor came out. "Mr. Bradley? He'll be fine."

"Fine?" Relief coursed through me. I'd have fallen if Colin hadn't been there to hold me up.

"It was just a flesh wound, really, but it did nick an artery so there was some major blood loss. We've sewed him up, and he should be able to go home in the morning. They've taken him up to his room. You can see him if you like."

"Can we talk about this some other time?" I asked Colin. "Oh, you might want to call Juliet and Bryce and let them know everything is okay now."

"I'll call your family, too." He squeezed my hand. "Everything will be fine, Scotty."

How could I NOT love him?

I sat with Frank while he dozed. The painkillers they'd given him had knocked him out almost completely. I sat next to the bed and held his hand. It was cold and clammy, but every once in a while he squeezed my hand and moaned in his sleep. He slept through the night, while I dozed from time to time in an extremely uncomfortable chair.

You'd think hospitals would get comfy chairs. I mean, how many people have had to spend the night trying to sleep in one of those awful things?

Frank was released the next morning.

We took a cab back to my place. I called Colin on his cell phone and asked him to meet us there. He sounded kind of weird, but he said he'd be there. When we arrived, I was glad to see David had gotten the front door fixed, and the place looked almost good as new.

I was going to have to do another ritual cleansing to purify the place, I thought as Frank laid down on the couch.

There was a knock on the door. I checked through the blinds. Colin, Juliet, Bryce, Rod, Venus, and Storm. I opened the door and let them in. Each one of them gave me a big hug, and then went over to thank Frank.

"There will have to be an inquest, of course," Venus said, "but I'm reasonably confident the case will be closed. Marsten did shoot an FBI agent, after all, and we can finally close the case on Rod Parrish."

"What about you?" I asked. "Is everything okay with you?"

Venus flashed me her old smile. "Yeah. Al Weston couldn't make a deal fast enough, after what happened yesterday. He claimed his companion fired first, but I've been cleared."

"And Rev Harper?"

"There's always someone willing to take the fall for rich people," Storm said. "Weston and the thugs from yesterday all claim they were trying to find the mask to sell it to Harper—and Harper's story was he was interested in finding the mask to return it to the Cabildo."

"What about my kidnapping?"

"Weston claims you went along willingly."

I felt my face redden. "But that's a lie!"

Venus took my hand and patted it. "Honey, it's your word against theirs. And the only other person who can testify to you being drugged is Colin, and the district attorney really doesn't think a jury will buy the rescue story."

I thought about it for a second. Okay, I had to admit the district attorney had a point. Climbing down the side of a building? "It just sucks that Harper is going to get away with it all. Even if he didn't kill Rod Parrish, if it wasn't for him, none of this would have happened."

Storm coughed. "Well, Harper has agreed to buy David a brand new car." And he reached into his shirt and handed me a piece of folded paper.

I opened it. It was a check for fifty thousand dollars, on the account of Rev Harper, made out to me. "What is this?"

Storm grinned. "Harper claims that when the mask disappeared, he offered a fifty thousand dollar reward for it. You've earned it." He winked. "Of course, it's really just his way of atoning for what his people put you through."

Fifty grand. Wow. Okay, so it was hush money. Maybe I shouldn't accept it, maybe I shouldn't cash it and spend it. Maybe it was morally wrong—but you know how long it would take me to earn that kind of money a dollar at a time, dancing in a thong in a crowded bar?

"I can't believe it's all over." Juliet smiled. She looked as though a shadow had lifted from her face. Years had melted from her. She looked young, alive, and vital. She clutched Bryce's hand. "No more hiding."

"But why would Marsten kill Ace Martinelli?" I asked as someone started pounding on the front door. I walked over and peered through the blinds. I groaned. "It's Lucinda."

"Let her in." Bryce's voice was like ice water. "We have some things to discuss with her."

Reluctantly, I opened the door. She shoved me out of her way and waddled over to where Bryce was sitting, ignoring everyone else. "Darling! I've been so worried—" She tried to throw her arms around him but he blocked her. She stepped back, her eyes darting around the room. "What's wrong, honey?"

"This," he said, slowly and deliberately, "will be the last time you ever see me."

She stepped back. "What are you talking about, honey?"

"I'm over eighteen now, Lucinda." He folded his arms. "And I don't want to ever see you again."

"But Bryce, darling—"

"And I won't change my mind. Ever."

She stood there, her mouth open, her eyes darting around from face to face. Her face went white, and then flushed red. "So." She spat the words out. "This is the thanks I get for all the sacrifices I've made for you and your career." Her voice rose with each word. "I made you, you nasty little faggot! And this is what I get in return! That bitch sold you to me! *Sold you like a pair of shoes!* And I nurse you back to health, help you become one of the greatest figure skaters the world has ever seen—spend all of my money for your training, do without, work two jobs sometimes, you fucking little ingrate, and this is what I get! Oh, that's just perfect! After everything I've done for you—"

"Including murder?" Everyone turned to look at me.

Her eyes narrowed to slits. "I don't know what you're talking about."

"*You* hired Ace Martinelli to follow Bryce around, to find out what he was up to." I went on. "It wouldn't be hard for you to get the spare key to Bryce's hotel room, would it? You sent me that key."

"I—I—" her bloodshot eyes goggled at me. She looked like one of those black goldfish whose eyes jut out at the sides.

"Ace followed Bryce to my house last Friday night," I went on. It was all falling into place. "He told you about it Saturday morning, so you came over here yourself. You saw Bryce leave—and got a look at me. I don't know if you'd planned it already, but when you saw me at the competition that night, you sent me the spare key so I would come meet Bryce in his room."

"She picked a fight with me that night." Bryce stared at her. "Knowing I would get tired of it and leave."

"And she arranged for Martinelli to come to your room that night as well." I shrugged. "Were you planning on killing me, too?"

"Martinelli." She spat the word out. She began to shake. "That miserable son of a bitch! I hired him to follow my boy, to find out what he was up to. The miserable snake—he was taking my money and then trying to corrupt my boy!" She flung out a hand in Juliet's general direction. "And he digs up this bitch! And he wanted more money from me—or he was going to go to the papers." She brushed a hand through her hair. "All the hard work

I've put into Bryce's career—he was going to destroy it all. I couldn't let that happen. No, I wasn't planning on killing you—I just wanted to kill him." She shrugged. "You were both faggots—I was hoping maybe the police would figure it was some kind of sick, perverted passion killing. Yes, I sent the key to you. And I killed him." Her face twisted into a sneer. "But no, all of my careful plans—I had just stabbed him when someone knocked on the door. I slipped out onto the balcony . . . and who should walk in but her?" She turned and glared at Juliet. "I wanted to kill her too—but I couldn't take the chance. It was supposed to be you." She turned back to me. "You were going to get there at any minute. So I climbed over the balcony railing onto the balcony of my room and went inside." She shivered at the memory. "And I watched through the peephole. I saw her leave, and then a few minutes later you went by." She opened her purse.

For the second time in less than twenty-four hours I had a gun pointing at me.

I was getting a little tired of this.

"Don't be stupid, Lucinda," I said. I felt oddly calm in spite of everything. "You can't kill me in front of all of these witnesses, and you certainly won't be able to kill us all."

She gave a bitter half laugh. "Who said I wanted to kill you?"

And she turned the gun on herself.

The gun clicked.

"Did you forget to load it, Mommie dearest?" Bryce asked from the couch as Venus leaped to her feet and spun her around, cuffing her and going through her Miranda spiel. Lucinda didn't resist, didn't do anything.

All the life had gone out of her.

I almost felt sorry for her.

But not quite.

After Venus had taken her out on the porch and called for backup, Frank looked at me. "You know, Scotty, this is a hell of a life you lead."

"You're telling me, Special Agent?"

"If you're going to stick around, you'd better get used to it," Storm laughed. He stood up and yawned. "Well, I'm going to get going." He looked at Juliet and Bryce. "Can I give you all a lift anywhere?"

"Yeah." They both rose. They hugged Colin and Frank, and then gave me a big hug. I walked them both out to the porch just in time to see Venus putting Lucinda into a squad car. Lucinda looked like nothing so much as a zombie. "Storm, can you give me a minute with them?"

He nodded and walked down to his car.

"There's something I want you both to know." My eyes filled with tears, but I fought them down. "I haven't said anything about this to you before, because it's kind of weird, but I'm a little bit psychic."

They both looked at me like I was nuts.

"I wouldn't have told you anything about this at all, but I think you should know." I hugged myself. "Almost from the beginning of all this, I was getting flashes. I mean, I usually just read my tarot cards, and sometimes I get visions, but this time—well, it was different. It was like nothing I've ever experienced before. It was like I was inside someone else's head—very strange for me. It wasn't until yesterday that I realized what it was."

I took a deep breath. "The day of the Cabildo fire, fifteen years ago, my mom and I went down to Jackson Square to watch them fight the fire. I didn't really remember this, but while we were watching, I saw a firefighter come out of the St. Peter Street door. We made eye contact, and he smiled at me, and tipped his hat to me. I looked away—I heard a siren or something that distracted me, but when I looked back, he was gone. I know now that firefighter was Rod Parrish."

Juliet's face had gone white. "Oh my God."

"I don't know what you all believe—I know you went to Catholic school, Juliet—but I believe in fate and karma and kismet. And I think that the day of the fire, when he came out of that building, with the death mask stuffed inside his coat, somehow when our eyes met, we *connected* on a different plane."

I reached out and wiped the tears off Bryce's face. "And I think last Friday night, your father's soul led me to the Brass Rail. I never go to that bar, Bryce—and it's not even on my way home from Bourbon Street. I think your father guided me to you. Just like I think your father guided my sister to buy tickets for me to go to Skate America. The flashes I was getting, they were from your father. Whatever he did, he did it because he loved the two of you both very, very much. When I was in the Cabildo yesterday, it was like I was inside his head. And I had the most overpowering sense of love for the two of you."

Bryce and Juliet were holding each other.

"And I don't know—maybe you both think I'm crazy, I know sometimes I think I am. But I wanted you both to know how much he loved you—so much so that his soul couldn't rest until you were both safe."

Juliet reached up and kissed me on the cheek. "Thank you, Scotty."

Bryce gave me a big hug. I held on to him, and felt my own tears start.

Then they both walked down and got into Storm's car.

I waved as they drove off.

Thank you, Scotty, a voice whispered in my head.

You're very welcome, Rod. Now, finally, you can rest in peace.

I went back inside my apartment, wiping my eyes.

Frank and Colin were sitting together on the sofa. They looked up, guiltily.

"All right, what's going on here?"

Colin grinned. "Oh, Frank and I have been planning our lives out."

I sank down into the wingback chair. "Oh, boy. Let me have it."

"Well, you're not exactly a conventional person, you know," Frank said, and grinned at me. "So, both Colin and I have kind of come to the realization that neither one of us has much of a shot at a conventional relationship with you."

I didn't know if I liked the sound of this.

"So, Frank and I have come to a mutual decision." Colin went on. "You love both of us, right?"

"Uh huh." Uh oh.

"And we both love you." This from Frank. "So, therefore, if you love us both and we both love you, it only stands to reason that we'd like each other, right?"

It did make a kind of twisted sense. "Yes."

"So, this is what we've come up with." Colin started stroking Frank's leg. "Frank and I aren't exactly conventional people, either. So, we figured, we all need to get to know each other better to figure out if anything would work, right?"

"Uh huh."

"Well, there's no rule that says all three of us can't be in a relationship together." Frank grinned at me, and then at Colin. "I mean, the whole couple idea is a straight thing anyway, and we're not straight people."

Wait a minute. "Are you saying you want a three-way relationship? All three of us?"

"See, I told you he could grasp the concept." Colin grinned at Frank.

"He is pretty smart," Frank agreed.

"And who knows?" Colin said. "Maybe we'll find out the three of us together won't work out. Maybe it'll work out for two of us. Maybe it won't work out for any of us. But I think it's worth a shot. What do you think, Scotty?"

I stood up and walked over, sitting down between the two of them, putting a hand on the thighs flanking me. "I think—"

"Yes?" Colin and Frank said together.

"I think we should videotape the three of us in bed to-gether—we'd make a mint!"

"Always the romantic," Frank said, kissing my neck.

"Well, come on then, boys." Colin stood up, removing his shirt. "Let's start our first rehearsal."

Frank and I followed him into the bedroom.

Lucinda Bell pleaded not guilty by reason of mental defect.

I couldn't disagree with her on that—she was nuts. But eventually her lawyer worked it all out. She was sentenced to twenty years in a mental-health facility, until such time as she could be deemed no longer a danger to herself and others. It sounded like a life sentence to me. I was kind of worried she might try to destroy Bryce's career in the process, but she's a crafty one. She claimed Bryce's decision to look for his birth mother had unhinged her, since she'd spent her entire life devoted to him and his career; she'd hired Martinelli to find Juliet first, and pay her to vanish off the face of the earth. When Martinelli was unable to do it, she went nuts and stabbed him.

Bryce e-mails me from time to time, and says she writes him every day. He doesn't read the letters. Juliet travels with him everywhere now, and they are bonding like a mom and a son should. She has no problem with his sexuality, and in his last e-mail he said that his mom had started dating his coach. Good for her, I thought when I closed the e-mail. I don't think Rod would begrudge her one bit of happiness.

Ironically, Lucinda's murderous rage, rather than hurting Bryce's career, helped him. Every article, every sportscaster in the country, had nothing but sympathy for him. Stories about Lucinda's craziness began to surface, and Bryce became a national spokesperson for abused children. He went on to win the other Grand Prix events he'd entered—Trophee Lalique in Paris and Cup of Russia in St. Petersburg—and was a heavy favorite to win the world championships, which were going to be held in Prague. He promised to give me, Frank, and Colin an all-expense-paid trip to the world championships if he qualified for them.Considering the way he's been skating, I already have my bags packed. I can't wait to see him standing on the podium with a gold medal around his neck while our national anthem plays.

Being shot was a blessing in disguise for Frank. His early retirement was moved up, and right now he is packing up his apartment in DC, preparatory to moving to New Orleans.

The other good news is that Blackledge Investigations has decided to open a branch office in New Orleans, headed by Colin. So, now I actually have a job. And he has promised to hire Frank once he gets down here. Of course, Frank and I will have to be apprentices for a while first, which makes Colin our boss. That should be interesting.

In a way, we're going to be like Charlie's Angels, only hot gay boys. Colin says nobody has seen Angela Blackledge in years—she only talks to her employees on the phone. Supposedly, she lives on a private island somewhere in the Carribbean.

So, the three of us will be working together. It makes sense—we've worked together well before. And as Colin says, most of the work we'll be doing will be safe and boring—insurance investigations, cheating spouses, the occasional missing person.

But somehow, I just don't believe I am destined for a boring life. It certainly hasn't worked out that way so far, has it?

Oh, yeah, David did get his car from Rev Harper. A nice white Lexus, which he just loves.

I'm in the process of packing up my apartment. My old place is finally ready, and I'll be moving back to Decatur Street. As much as I've loved living next door to David, I've missed my old place. I've missed living upstairs from Millie and Velma. And they've rented the upstairs to Frank and Colin. It's a three-bedroom place, after all, pretty darned huge, and even though they've pretty much lived alone most of their lives, they're looking forward to living together, and just upstairs from me.

The three-way relationship thing is working pretty well. The sex is pretty incredible. We've never actually videotaped ourselves, but that's kind of become a running joke between us. David has signed up to get the first tape should we ever do it.

Oh, yeah, I forgot to mention the Lazarus Ball. Even though it was short notice, since he wasn't going to work, David was able to whip up hot costumes for Frank and Colin, too. We all went as harem boys, and I have to say I felt incredibly proud of my men when I walked into the Lazarus Ball on their arms.

I am one lucky guy.

AUTHOR'S NOTE

On May 11, 1988, the Cabildo, a part of the Louisiana State Museum Complex at Jackson Square, caught fire. It is true that the New Orleans Fire Department's methods of fighting the fire while at the same time preserving the historic contents of the building were unexpected, a complete innovation, and one of the most incredible achievements of any fire department in history. Watching videotapes of the fire department in action was a truly awe-inspiring experience for me, and opened my eyes to the major contributions the NOFD makes to our city's history and heritage every day.

The NOFD and their handling of the Cabildo fire obviously inspired the writing of this book. The purpose of this book was to preserve, in a fictional setting, their achievement, and pay tribute to them.

Please turn the page for an exciting sneak peek of
Greg Herren's next
Scotty Bradley mystery
MARDI GRAS MAMBO
coming in March 2006!

CHAPTER ONE

Three of Cups

merriment, pleasure, a time of enjoyment

New Orleans is not a city for the timid.

Timidity doesn't last long here. Maybe there's something in the air or water. Whatever it is, people behave here in ways they'd never dream of at home. Some think it's the ready availability of liquor—at gas stations, grocery stores, and bars that are open twenty-four hours. Where else would a repressed forty-year-old spinster librarian from a small town in Kansas get drunk and flash her boobs for beads? New Orleans is about excess—a local performer always says our city motto should be "Anything worth doing is worth doing to excess." For those of us who live here, it makes visiting other places in the country seem dull and tame. We don't understand the term "last call"—because it doesn't exist here. We take it for granted that New Orleans is normal and everywhere else is weird, repressed and uptight. Nowhere else in the country could Mardi Gras exist the way it does here—although places like Galveston and Mobile try. It's about sin, after all—farewell to the flesh, and nowhere else is sin taken as seriously as it is here. If you're going to do it, do it properly. It's all about more: more fun, more sex, more alcohol, more, more, more. It's a time when anything goes. No other state in the country has a statewide holiday specifically so everyone can get drunk. Business comes to a complete halt the weekend before Fat Tuesday—unless your business involves food, liquor or renting rooms. Since Lent begins at midnight on Fat Tuesday, the theory is to get it all out of your system before forty days of penance. Of course, it's not like the bars close until Easter—but you get the general idea. Nothing is like experiencing Mardi Gras firsthand—books, movies, and television shows can only capture a small facet of the ten-day celebration that climaxes on Fat Tuesday. What happens at Mardi Gras stays in New Orleans—mainly because you won't remember it.

And the most important thing—more important than any other part— is the throws.

That's right, *throws*, not beads. The parading krewes don't just throw strings of beads to the screaming crowds with outstretched hands. They throw plush toys, plastic spears, plastic go-cups, doubloons and various other things—if it's portable and can be thrown, it is. People will whore their babies and small children for throws. People line up along Canal Street for the Endymion parade days ahead of time. Women take their tops off, men flex their muscles, and I've seen people roll around in mud wrestling over plush toys. It's madness—a weird kind of fever that takes control of your mind. You *have* to get more—until you're so weighted down with beads that your neck and back are sore for weeks. No matter the weather, the streets are lined—no matter if it's raining, no matter if it's freezing. If the parade rolls, they will come.

The most treasured throw of all is the Zulu coconut—I've caught a few of those in my life. The hardest thing about getting the Zulu coconut is fighting off all the assholes that think they can take it from you. Throws are fair game after all—even after it's safely in your hands, there's always some drunk moron who'll try to take it away from you. Fights have broken out over the Zulu coconut—but the ever-present NOPD will intervene.

Throw fever at Mardi Gras is something to see, all right. One of the most fun things is watching people who've never been before catch the fever. Frank Sobieski, reserved, retired FBI special agent, was one of those. All the weeks leading up to Mardi Gras, he kept saying, "I just can't believe people will make fools of themselves for this stuff," as he looked at the big box of beads I keep in my bedroom closet. I don't keep all of my catches, of course—only the best ones, the ones that sparkle and shine in the light. I've got some pretty awesome ones.

Colin Cioni had never been to Mardi Gras either, and I just smiled to myself as I listened to them talking about how they would never scream for beads. *Just you boys wait*, I thought to myself with a smug grin.

There are certain rules about the beads people who aren't from New Orleans don't ever seem to understand. I call it "bead karma"—if you break the rules, you get bad bead karma and won't catch the best throws. First of all, you *never* buy beads. The rule is, you can only buy beads if you are going to give them away to a total stranger. The second rule is you *only* wear beads you were given or caught. And of course, the most important of all: you only wear beads during Carnival. Every little tourist shop in the Quarter sells beads, and it never ceases to amaze me when I see people walking around wearing beads when it isn't Carnival. Nothing screams *tourist* louder than out-of-season bead wearing.

The parades begin about ten days before Mardi Gras, and there's at least one a night leading up to Fat Tuesday. The closer it gets, the more parades there are. My personal favorite is the Mystic Krewe of Iris. There are several reasons for this. First, Iris is a women's krewe, which means the masked figures on the floats tossing things are not men. Men always look for women (the larger the breasts, the better) and children in the crowd to reward. They only throw to men by accident, or if someone yells particularly loud. This *sucks* if you like to catch throws. However, the ladies of Iris are just as sexist as the male krewe members. They throw to men and children. And since Iris rolls on the Saturday afternoon before Fat Tuesday, usually it's sunny and warm. Sunny and warm means I don't wear a shirt.

I get lots of throws at Iris every year.

The Saturday of Iris dawned warm and sunny. Up to that point, parade season had been a bit of a disappointment to me. Fat Tuesday, tied as it is to Easter, is never the same date every year. This year, it was early, with Fat Tuesday in the middle of February, which meant our weather hadn't turned yet. It was still what we consider "winter" down here at the bottom of the country—cold, drizzly, foggy, and just kind of nasty over all. (It beats snow, though.) The parades rolled anyway—it would take a monsoon to stop them—but it's not good weather for catching throws. When your hands are cold, the beads sting when you catch them, and it's never fun to wear a jacket anyway. Everyone was watching the weather—there's nothing worse than cold and rain on Fat Tuesday. Plus you can catch a cold—and is there anything worse than trying to party when you're sick? So, we'd pretty much stayed in and not gone to the parades, and it was driving me crazy. But I love the Iris parade, and unless the streets were flooded, we were going. Attending Iris is also a family obligation—my older sister Rain is in Iris. So, I woke the boys up early so we could go to the gym and pump up—the bigger the muscles, the more the ladies of Iris like it—and then catch a ride with my workout partner, David Uptown. We parked near the corner of Baronne and Polymnia, then walked down to St. Charles Avenue.

That's another important thing to remember about Mardi Gras. NEVER watch parades on Canal Street. That's where the mobs of tourists are. That's where women flash their boobs. It's much more fun to go Uptown and watch along the St. Charles route. That's where the locals go—the way Mardi Gras used to be before the hordes descended on the city and it became an internationally known drunkfest. That's where you see families out with their kids, portable barbecues set up on the streetcar tracks, and coolers everywhere. Sure, people are drinking, but New Orleanians know how to pace themselves—or we know how to handle our liquor. You don't see people puking or passing out on

St. Charles. You don't see men taking a piss in a corner. You don't see college girls from Iowa auditioning for *Girls Gone Wild* videotapes.

Many locals leave town during Carnival. They're sick of the hordes of tourists, the problems getting around the city—St. Charles and Canal close for the parades, and it's easy to get trapped within the parade route. Not me. I don't think I'll ever get sick of Carnival. I love everything about it. I love the green, purple and gold decorations everywhere. I love the tourists, even though they do stupid stuff. I love the parades, catching throws, the non-stop fun atmosphere. Not that New Orleans is ever boring, mind you—but Carnival is *different* somehow.

The first dull floats had already passed—the ones with the royalty of the krewe—the Queen, the Captain, the maids, princesses, whatever. These floats only have a couple of people on them and they can't throw as much stuff. The best ones are the later ones, which have as many as twenty people on them throwing stuff out by the handful. I could tell Frank and Colin were unimpressed so far. I'd caught a nice string of red beads from the Queen of Iris, and I had my shirt tucked into the back of my loose-fitting shorts, which just hung off my hips. I hadn't worn underwear, and the shorts had crept down almost to the top of my pubic hair. David had already taken his shirt off, and he'd caught some beads too. Frank and Colin, though, were just standing there with bemused expressions on their faces, their shirts still on, shaking their heads at us. We were standing on the neutral ground, David and I down on the curb—Frank and Colin standing further back on the slight upward slope on the other side of the streetcar tracks.

"Just wait," I nudged David, gesturing back at them, "till they catch their first beads."

David winked back at me. David is the best friend anyone could ever ask for. He's the kind of person you could call and say, "David, I just killed someone," and without missing a beat he'd reply, "Well, the first thing we have to do is get rid of the body."

He's in his early forties, but was blessed with one of those bodies that don't gain weight. We've been working out together for almost three years, and he'd managed to put on a lot of lean muscle without gaining a whole lot of weight. His entire body had changed. His reddish hair had gone almost completely white, and he buzzed it down to the scalp. He has that white skin that burns easily in the sun—he never turns brown, just varying shades of red. He has a massive tattoo of a dragon running down the left side of his body, from the shoulder down around the left pec.

He looks pretty good.

We moved back as the marching band from Warren Easton High School approached. The public school bands are amazing. You haven't lived until you've watched a New Orleans public school band—even the junior high ones are awesome. They are almost entirely black, and they put on a *show*. They dance and sway as they play their instruments, and get into it in a way no predominately white school band can. And because they don't subscribe to the image of bone-thin women being sexy, their cheerleaders, drill teams and majorettes are a mix of different sizes and looks. The girls all have taps on their boots, and they know how to dance in their skin-tight sequined body suits. And their hair! They have these incredibly elaborate hairdos (what we call "parade hair") towering masses of curls and curlicues and crimped hair, crowned with rhinestone tiaras. Interestingly enough, the bigger girls—the ones white schools would think too fat, and make fun of—are usually the better dancers.

They are *fabulous*.

The band stopped right in front of us and launched into a version of a current hit hip-hop song. The batons started twirling and the pompons shaking as the girls went into their dance as the crowds cheered. I looked back at Colin and Frank. They were staring, their mouths open. I walked back to them.

"Those kids are good," Frank said.

Colin pointed to a large majorette, stuffed into a tight form-fitting sequined bodysuit. "That girl can *move*."

"She'd be considered too fat to be a majorette in most schools," I said, feeling proud of my city. Our public school system might be one of the worst in the country, but we could produce some amazing marching bands—that has to count for something. "Isn't this fun?"

Frank and Colin exchanged that look I'd come to know fairly well since they'd moved here. It was the "Scotty-is-such-a-cute-little-whack-job" look. I just rolled my eyes. The band was moving along, and the first real float was coming. "Come on, guys, come get some beads," I pleaded. They gave each other that look again. I shrugged and moved back up next to David.

Okay, the most important thing about catching throws is to pay attention. You HAVE to pay attention. When the throws start flying, you've got to keep your head up and your eyes moving. If you don't, you're likely to get smacked in the face by some beads. Take my word for it—that can fucking *hurt*. (We have a city ordinance protecting the krewes from being sued for injuring people. The reason for this is that the riders are partying just as hard as the crowd, so some of the drunker krewe members will whip beads into the crowd like they're trying to win the World Series. I got a black eye once from a particular nice string of green, gold and purple beads. That's a strand I kept.) As the float got closer, David and I both put our arms up and started shouting. The beads started flying. I jumped up and grabbed a nice string of purple ones, then a couple more—red, green and a really nice set of blue ones with miniature dice interspersed within the beads. I made eye contact with a woman on the first level, and she tossed me a handful of real beauties, and then the float was gone . . . but another was coming up behind it.

I looked back at Frank and Colin. They had each caught some. Colin was putting his around his neck and had a huge grin on his face. But Frank was just holding his loosely in his hand, looking at them like they were radioactive or something. His arms were still crossed, his bare biceps bulging. *Loosen up, Special Agent*, I thought, shaking my head, and I turned back to start screaming at the next float.

I'd just caught a nice strand of special beads—red ones with little white masks mixed in, when I realized Colin was standing next to me, screaming, his shirt stuck into the back of his jeans. I glanced over at him. He was flexing his biceps as he screamed, trying to get the attention of a woman on the lower level, winking and flirting! He was justly rewarded for this gorgeous display of masculine musculature with a full bag of beads. I couldn't help myself. I started laughing. *I fucking love Mardi Gras!*

Bead fever . . . it's really hard to resist.

After the float moved on, and another marching band—this time the ROTC band from Dillard University—was on its way, Colin grinned at me. "Okay, this is fun."

I looked back at Frank, who was tucking his shirt through a belt loop. He gave me an embarrassed smile as he looped several strands of beads over his head and walked up to the curb.

"Having fun, Special Agent?" David asked.

He glared at us for a minute, then threw back his head and started laughing. "This is awesome!" he said, in a dead-on imitation of my voice.

And once again, I thanked the Goddess for the amazing life she was giving me. Is there anything better than having two men who love you, who have a sense of play, who can go to a Carnival parade and have a good time in the sunshine?

Ah, life is good.

And the sex is even better. Have I mentioned that?

My cell phone rang, so I pulled it out of my pocket and walked to the other side of the neutral ground so I could hear before answering it. "Hello?"

"Hey, Scotty," said a heavily accented voice. It was Misha, my

Ecstasy connection. He was from Russia originally, and I love his accent. "Just wanted to let you know your Avon products came in." Avon is our code for Ecstasy, because when you're on it, you feel beautiful. Hell, everything's beautiful when you're X-ing.

"Cool. I'll come by around eight, is that cool?"

"Perfect." He hung up.

I walked back over to the others. "That was Misha. Our beauty boosters are in."

"All right!" David grinned. Okay, one of the bad things I'd done in my life was to get him to try Ecstasy for the first time.

Frank's smile faded. He sighed. "I really don't think this is a good idea."

Here we go again, I thought, trying not to roll my eyes.

"Come on, Frank." Colin lightly punched him in the chest. "We've been through this already. It never hurts to try something."

"But it's *illegal*," he growled. "I hate the thought of Scotty taking the risk of getting arrested buying it."

"I've done it a million times." I shrugged. Okay, that was an exaggeration—at least I hoped it was. "And it's cool. I mean, every time we walk into Mom and Dad's we take that risk." Mom and Dad always have a big supply of marijuana on hand, and they get the best stuff. I don't know how or where they get it, but a police drug raid would probably put them behind bars for the rest of their lives.

He held up his hands. "Okay, okay, I said I'd try it."

I reached over and squeezed his rock hard ass. "Trust me, honey—you'll like it."

He gave me a guarded smile. "Okay." Another float was coming, and we all assumed our bead-whore positions.

By the time Rain's float, one of the last, arrived, we were completely buried in beads. Frank was practically hoarse from screaming, and when I recognized Rain behind her mask, she waved us forward and began raining beads down on us. Rain is cool. She prefers to be called Rhonda, and she's married to a successful Uptown doctor. She used to try to fix me up with every gay man she met. While she was a little confused by the Scotty-Frank-Colin arrangement, she treated my boys like members of the family. Her car had broken down once and Colin, being Colin, had gone over to her house and in an afternoon repaired the engine. She swore it ran better than it had when it was new. Now, she was always asking Colin to check out every sound her engine made. And Frank had taught her how his grandmother used to make brownies—and they were the best brownies ever. "Who knew," she once whispered to me as Frank whipped up another batch in her kitchen, "that a Fed would be such a good cook?"

And then the float was past, and there were only two more before the police cars and their flashing red lights signaled the end of Iris. We'd already decided not to stick around for Tucks, the parade behind Iris. Since we had a car, and the biggest parade of Carnival, Endymion, would roll later that night down Canal Street, we had to get David's car back to the Marigny before the cops closed down Canal. Driving through New Orleans is always like an obstacle course anyway, and during Carnival it was magnified a hundredfold. David always said he was going to design a videogame based on driving through the city. Besides, it was better to get home and rest up for the evening before putting on our costumes and heading out into the insanity.

Costuming in New Orleans is almost as important as eating. I'm not sure why we have such a tradition of costuming here—maybe it's Carnival, I don't know—but we all put on costumes any chance we get. And God forbid you wear the same costume twice! I am always on the lookout for something new and interesting to dress up as. That's another way you can tell the locals from the tourists during Carnival—the locals start wearing costumes when they go out at night. Frank and Colin had both been here for Halloween, and we'd all worn harem boy outfits, which looked really hot. We'd even got our picture in the *Times-Picayune*.

The boys still hadn't quite grasped the whole costuming concept, but they good-naturedly went along with me when I said we had to start dressing up on Saturday. Tonight's costumes were pretty simple—black tights and Zorro capes and black sequined masks with black feathers. The tights would show off our legs and asses, and just wearing a cape allowed us to show off our upper bodies. I'd planned our costumes so that each day they became more complicated—and more sexy. By Fat Tuesday, we would be running around practically naked. (Another reason to pray for warm weather.)

After David dropped us off, we all went up to my apartment and I got out a salad I'd made the night before. By the time I'd put servings in bowls and walked into the living room, Frank and Colin were already laying down on the couch, kissing.

"Hey!" I said. "Sheesh—can't you two wait for me?"

They broke apart and grinned at me.

Colin propped himself up on an elbow. "Well, what are you waiting for? A written invitation?"

"This," I said as I slid down in between them, surrounded by hard muscles, "is going to be the best fucking Mardi Gras *ever.*"

Boy, was I going to live to regret *those* words.

You'd think I'd know better by now.